BABY FOR THE BOSSHOLE

NADIA LEE

Baby for the Bosshole

Copyright © 2022 by Hyun J Kyung

All rights reserved.

To my family for their infinite understanding and love as I hide in my office, working.

1

AMY

I'll show him.

That's the motto that hauls me out of bed at the crack of dawn on a Friday so I can be at work before eight. It's also the motto that keeps me going when I've been sleeping four hours a night for close to three months now.

Some might say, "Why don't you say something to your boss?"

I'd rather jump off a plane.

I'm probably going to regret this...

Those muttered words came out of my boss's mouth before he said that I was hired. He most likely doesn't know I heard him. Or maybe he did and was hoping I'd turn down the offer and go elsewhere out of pride.

But I accepted the job. If he wanted me to turn it down, he shouldn't have offered such a high signing salary and bonus, both of which I desperately need to pay off my student loan.

But those words linger. Every time I feel like slowing down or taking a break, they float up like some kind of psychic cattle prod and I work even harder.

I'm not a quitter. Dad didn't raise some shrinking violet who wilts at every criticism or doubt. I fight for what I want, and I will leave my critics and doubters choking in my dust.

I *will* show my incomparable bosshole Emmett Lasker that hiring me was the best damn thing he's ever done before my two years at the firm are up. And he will beg me to stay when I turn in my resignation.

I might even consider staying—for a split second—if he offers to pay off my student loan. My college degree and MBA together cost me almost half a million dollars, and since my family isn't swimming in money, most of it was paid for with loans. Dad offered to take some out in his name, but I turned him down. He's done so much already.

Anyway, even if I get that kind of an offer from Emmett, I'm probably going to say no. He'll have to do better. Maybe promise to get me that lovely beachfront cottage in Florida where Dad wants to retire. I mean, I plan to buy my father his dream home. I ran the numbers and can afford it, if everything goes according to plan. But having Emmett buy it would be so much better.

What if he begs on his knees?

Now *that's* an image! In reality, that egomaniac wouldn't get on his knees for anyone. But the idea has a hot sexual undertone. All because the man is ridiculously good-looking. It's like God ran out of decent personality, felt bad about it, and overcompensated by giving him a gorgeous face.

But still. Face or no face, without some unimaginable offer, my answer will remain a big, fat no.

By seven forty-five a.m. I'm in the lobby, waiting for an elevator to take me to my office. The bosshole wants the finalized updates to the financial model that we need for Monday by two, and I have three hours of work left on Excel.

Assuming I can work through the fog in my head. The caffeine jolt from my morning coffee is dissipating like a thimble of salt in the Pacific. I already need another boost.

Once I turn in the model, I'm going to have an exciting—and *secret*—lunch meeting. Given that I've been prepping for it for five days, I'm hoping it will go well. I'm even wearing my power outfit, including some slinky new power underwear.

Once the model and interview are out of the way, I won't have anything urgent to do—a true miracle. And if the day continues in such miraculous fashion, I plan to go home by five and catch up on sleep. I would literally kill for a solid eight hours.

–Dad: Happy Friday, princess!

I smile at the cheery text. Dad sends me one three mornings a week. Sometimes more, if he feels like it.

A selfie pops up. He takes one every time he texts me because he hates using face emojis to show how we're doing.

"What do those yellow cartoon faces show? Nothing! They're impersonal and soulless. Phones come with front-facing cameras for a reason."

And he's right. I love getting his morning selfies. They let me know he's doing fine out in Vegas. I look at the screen again. No sign that his back is bugging him. No sign that the new apprentice he took in at the shop is driving him crazy. Just a wide grin and twinkling blue eyes that curve slightly every time he smiles. His face shows lots of laugh lines, evidence of a life well lived.

He could've become bitter and selfish after Mom dumped me in his lap and split after a hookup that resulted in an accidental baby. She said she couldn't deal with a baby that wouldn't quit crying and a man who couldn't do more to give her the "good" life she deserved. I don't know what more she expected of an infant barely two months old, or an enlisted marine in his late twenties who was doing his best to provide for an unplanned family.

But dump me and split she did. And he did everything he could to raise me—including giving up his career in the military—and show me how much he loves me.

Sending him morning selfies a few times a week? A small, small repayment for all that he's done and sacrificed for me.

–Me: Looking fantastic, Dad! Here's me this morning!

I take a quick shot, making sure to smile happily so he knows I'm doing well. Thankfully, the lighting's good and my makeup hides the dark circles from sleep deprivation. Concealing those circles was just about the first thing I mastered when I started working in finance.

As a bonus, the sleek GrantEm Capital logo is in the background. That should make Dad extra happy. He's proud of the fact that his little girl, without any tutoring or standardized test prep courses, got a perfect SAT score and became the first in the family to go to college. And not just any college, but Harvard.

My big mountain of a father, whom I never saw shed a tear until then, bawled over my acceptance letter and at my graduation. He threw a party when I started working at Goldman Sachs, then wept some more when I got an MBA from Wharton. And he bounced around with joy when I said I'd be working for Emmett Lasker at GrantEm Capital in Los Angeles. Not because he knows what a big deal Emmett Lasker is—he doesn't—but because he was thrilled I'd be closer to home.

I send the photo.

—Dad: Already at work? It's barely eight.

I'm here to prove Emmett Lasker wrong. Plus he's hell to work for. But I don't text that. Instead, I opt for a non-worrying response.

—Me: Got here early to beat the traffic. The L.A. morning rush is a killer.

—Dad: So does this mean you get to leave early too? To beat the rush hour?

Hahaha. He's so adorable for asking. Although he was happy when I started my career in finance at Goldman, he was upset when he realized how many hours I would be working. He thought I should quit and go someplace where people valued me more.

So I explained that if I left before hitting the two-year mark, I'd be labeled a quitter who didn't have what it takes to hack it. Which in turn would mean that I'd never get hired in finance again. It's just a thing in this business, and I can't afford to burn a bridge to an entire sector when I have no clue what the future holds. But the possibility of being labeled somebody who couldn't stay the course was enough to make my dad fume—"How dare they! You have more grit than any of those elitist East Coast punks!"—and stop complaining about my hours. Instead, he switched to "Nobody out there works as hard as you do" in that sweet, encouraging tone of his that never fails to make me want to do better.

Unfortunately, the damned two-year mark applies at GrantEm, too. Why?

The signing bonus.

GrantEm Capital offered me more than double the signing bonus of other firms. That kind of money comes with a catch: stay for two years or give it back, prorated.

What nobody told me was that that basically gave Emmett Lasker carte blanche to turn my life into hell for his sadistic pleasure. Nearly every Excel model and memo I turn in has to be redone. Almost every evening and weekend plan changed or canceled. And sleep? Ha ha. It is to laugh.

But I grit my teeth and grind along because I refuse to give a single red cent back. Not after all the abuse I've suffered.

Eight more weeks. Then I'll be free of Emmett Lasker and this indentured servitude.

–Me: I hope so.

I pray Emmett doesn't ask me to stay late and tinker with the Excel model that's due at two today. He has an uncanny talent for finding something for me to do when I'm getting ready to go home. Not only that, it seems like every task he assigns me that late always takes at least three hours.

Asshole.

The elevator pings; the doors slide apart.

–Me: Gotta go. Love you!

I add lots of kisses and hearts, then put my phone away as I walk into the waiting car. As it goes up, another text lands on my phone. I look down with a smile. *Probably Dad thinking of one last thing to say.*

My good mood vanishes.

–Emmett: Which is better? Diamonds or pearls?

He's attached two images. The first is of diamond chandelier earrings that sparkle like stars on a navy velvet background. The second shows pearl drop earrings made with four pearls each. The ones on the very bottom look to be as big as my thumbnails. Holy cow.

Elegant and expensive. His current girlfriend of the month would like both. I've seen her photo, not because I was looking for it, but because Dad sent it to me a couple of weeks ago, texting, *Is this your boss?*

The picture showed Emmett smiling with a pretty redhead at some gala. Dad was impressed that Emmett was on the gossip sites because none of my bosses at Goldman Sachs ever made it to those sites. I didn't have the heart to tell him that Emmett Lasker is seen with different women on his arm all the time. No need to shatter Dad's illusions.

I try to bring up a more specific image of the woman, but I'm too sleep-deprived. Besides, why does it matter? Diamonds and pearls are both classic.

–Me: Either should work great.

–Emmett: That's not an answer. I asked which is better.

Yeah, and I told you neither because they're both equally fine. But he's not going to stop until I pick one. And if I pick the one he doesn't like, he's going to ask me to defend my selection.

Argh. Why doesn't he bug his assistant instead? Marjorie is one of the best-dressed women in the office, and not utilizing her for something like this is a huge waste of talent. She wouldn't be annoyed, either, because she loves shopping. According to her, humanity created civilization specifically for shopping.

When Emmett first started texting me for jewelry or fashion advice—within a month of my starting at GrantEm—I subtly asked Marjorie if he did the same with her. Maybe he was using me for a second opinion.

But nope. Marjorie has never been asked. Just me. Aren't I special, hahaha.

When I requested that he quit asking me, he said he couldn't. Apparently, I have excellent taste and he wants my input.

This is what happens when a man with terrible fashion judgment is the decider. I wear business casual I buy off clearance racks. My accessories are made with cubic zirconia or cheap semiprecious stones. The whole point of my wardrobe is to be functional and attractive on a budget.

So in the midst of working over a hundred hours a week, I also need to help Emmett pick out gifts.

The next two months can't go fast enough.

—Me: What's the occasion?

—Emmett: No occasion. Just something I'm thinking about.

I give my phone the side-eye. My boss isn't the type to do things *just because*. He believes in efficiency and proficiency. He probably just doesn't want to tell me what it's about. For all I know, it could be an I'm-sorry-I-messed-up grovel gift.

Or maybe he's doing this to annoy me enough to make me quit my job *now*, so he can claw back some of my signing bonus. Who knows what floats around in his diabolical mind?

—Me: Diamonds.

Three... Two... One...

—Emmett: Why?

Argh! The inevitable question! It's like death and taxes. Like Thanos.

I should've picked the damned pearls. But I can't take it back now. The one time I tried, he asked me so many questions I felt the need to create a PowerPoint presentation.

—Me: They look more expensive. They'll mean more.

The redhead seemed like a diamond kind of woman.

—Emmett: Seems like a thoughtless reason.

Shallow, too, I add silently.

—Me: Cheap things are cheap for a reason.

—Emmett: Pretend you're spending your own money.

Oh for God's sake. I wouldn't be spending my own hard-earned dollars on those things. I'd be making an extra payment on my student loan. Or saving it for a down payment on Dad's future house in Florida.

But I can't tell my boss I'd rather spend the money on unromantic practicality. Plus, his dates probably aren't mired in debt.

–Me: The diamonds. They sparkle more.

–Emmett: So sparkly wins?

–Me: Yes.

Can I go now? I add silently.

–Emmett: Thanks. :)

Jesus, look at that smiley face. It's more destructive than a hydrogen bomb.

Articles on bosses from hell always mention the ones who constantly berate you and never thank you. The authors of those articles clearly have never met Emmett Lasker. He flings his smiling "thanks" around like preemptive strike grenades. And it's diabolical. There's no way to complain about his behavior after a seemingly friendly "thanks."

He is a bosshole for the twenty-first century. None of that classic pathological shouting stuff. There are too many people with cell phones recording your every move, eager to post your bad behavior on social media for public shaming. A modern bosshole can fake being a decent human while making your life miserable at the same time.

And it's the *worst*. You can't file a complaint with HR for abusive behavior or language. If he tells you at four thirty p.m. you have to redo all your work because he isn't happy—never mind that his reason for dissatisfaction with your deliverable makes zero sense—then it's you who must've failed to measure up, not him. If he calls you at eight thirty in the evening while you're on a date, asking you to come in because he decided he doesn't like some variable you used in your latest financial projections, that, too, is a sign of your failing.

I drop my phone into my purse. The elevator stops on my

floor, and the doors open like the maw of a monster starved for innocent souls.

Taking a deep breath, I march forward to my desk. *First one in the office today.* As I boot up my laptop, my gaze falls on the standing desktop calendar. Five red circles around today's date. With a big star above, a reminder of my all-important lunch meeting with Marion Blaire from the Blaire Group.

My heart does a funky little dance as excitement shivers through me. The Blaire Group is a well-regarded private equity firm in Arlington, Virginia. A month ago, I gave my résumé to a few headhunters I know, asking them to be discreet—which they promised to do, since they know it wouldn't be good for me if my boss found out I was looking for a new position. Within a week, the Blaire Group contacted me for a Zoom interview. Afterward, they wanted to fly me out to Virginia for the in-person stuff.

I wish I could take the time off, but Emmett would never approve it, not on such short notice. I could always take a sick day, but last month a guy from another venture capital firm called in sick and got caught at the airport because somebody took a selfie and posted it on Instagram, and a coworker from his firm recognized him. He was summarily fired and became the topic of tittering gossip.

So, one of the Blaire Group's junior partners is going to interview me during his business trip to L.A. this week. He said he could swing a lunch interview after his final meeting.

I have high hopes. The hours are generally better in private equity, and I'm going to get a higher salary if I'm offered a position.

A step closer to paying off my student loan and buying Dad his dream home. *Sweet!*

Another text comes in. I check immediately; something from the Blaire Group about the interview? But it's Rick, who's up early this morning. Normally he sleeps in until nine.

–Rick: Hey, babe, you ready?

–Me: I just got to work. Ready for what?

–Rick: For our six-month anniversary trip!

A bomb seems to go off in my mind.

–Me: What are you talking about?

–Rick: I told you to mark your calendar! And put a heart over it.

I think back for a second, then realize he's right. He asked me to do it last month. So I put a circle around the date on the wall calendar in my apartment. No heart, though. That would've been sort of embarrassing and a little dishonest—I don't quite feel like Rick's worth a heart...yet.

But what does that have to do this outlandish trip thing?

–Me: You never said anything about a trip! You know I hate surprises.

I made that clear when we started dating. I was a week out of breaking up with my previous boyfriend, and told Rick specifically that I didn't like unpredictability or my plans getting derailed. It was something we both agreed on.

–Rick: I did tell you! I told you to look at my Pulse feed!

I start to get a sinking feeling. He did that, too...but never told me *why*. So I didn't bother, since I don't have time to look at funny videos or memes. I have so much crap on my plate right now.

–Me: You put our trip on social media and didn't tell me directly?

I just stare at my phone, speechless. Who shares plans like this? He *knows* I don't have time to check my Pulse account! I only opened it because he insisted that I join "civil society" and get connected to the "people of the world." He doesn't understand that unless being connected to all of humanity is going to get me an extra half an hour of sleep per night, I'm not interested.

–Rick: I wanted to do something creative. And I wanted everyone to know how special you are. My God, Amy, the post with the plan got over three thousand likes!

As if that matters!

Part of me wants to tell him there's no way I can go. I'm

annoyed he did it the way he did. But another part of me whispers at least he's trying to be the kind of boyfriend who remembers important dates. I just wish they didn't include a six-month anniversary. Who celebrates *half* a year?

–Rick: I guess people liked the idea of a fun weekend getaway in a cabin in Tahoe. I filled my tank and got everything we'll need for hiking and campfire cooking.

Hiking? Campfire cooking? Those sound like chores, especially when we'll have to spend over twenty hours driving back and forth between L.A. and Lake Tahoe. We talked about what we liked to do for relaxation once, and I told him anything that doesn't require me to be active. He should've known then that hiking is not my idea of fun.

If he'd asked about the trip before he booked it and announced it via Pulse, I would've suggested a weekend package at a hotel with a view of the ocean not too far from L.A. One that included couples massages and room service.

His poor planning and communication are irritating the crap out of me. Not even Emmett has pulled something like this.

–Rick: All you have to do is show up in front of your office building by six today.

–Me: What do you mean? I have nothing to wear for the next two days in the office. I have to pack first.

–Rick: Then just go home and grab a few things. I can pick you up at your place. No biggie.

I prop my elbow on the desk and rest my forehead in my palm. Why hasn't it penetrated his skull that he can't just drop something like this on me without notice? Although I was hopeful Emmett might let me go home at a somewhat decent hour, now I'm pessimistic. He has a finely tuned radar that just *knows* when I have social plans. And his default response is to nuke my evening.

–Me: I'll do my best, but I can't promise anything. My boss can dump stuff on me at any time. You know how he is.

–Rick: It's Friday! And not just any Friday, but a special one. Our six-month anniversary means something.

Over a billion emojis follow. They don't add to his argument and make me want to fire back an equal number of angry ones.

–Me: Do people really celebrate six-month anniversaries?

–Rick: Hell yeah! It's the thing these days.

My gut says that's doubtful. But what do I know about stuff like that? I barely have the time to breathe, much less keep track of the latest dating trends.

–Me: Okay. I'm going to try, the operative word here being TRY, to do this trip. But no guarantees.

–Rick: Awesome! Everyone's gonna be soooo jealous when we post about the trip!

More annoyingly bouncy and happy emojis fill my screen. I shake my head at how ahead of himself he's getting. He's a premature emojinator. He seems to have a certain vision about our relationship and its milestones. I'm beginning to see more and more clearly that our visions don't align as well as he believes. Posting about what I'm up to and making everyone insanely jealous has never been on my priority list.

Still. I said I'd try, so that's what I'm going to do. One silver lining: I can probably sleep in the car while he drives to Tahoe.

To make sure I don't forget about this impromptu trip, I write *6MAT* next to the star on the calendar. Six-month anniversary trip.

Okay, work. I open the Excel file Emmett wants. I better make it good because I don't want to stay in the office late again. Or hear Rick's whining because he'll pout if I have to work late today. Right now, my tolerance for any kind of bullshit is so low that even the slightest provocation will push me over the edge.

Cracking my knuckles, I hunch over my laptop to slay another day.

2

AMY

"Working hard?"

I start, then look up from my laptop to see Emmett standing above me. I check the time on the monitor. Only ten minutes since I pulled up the file.

He's carrying a fresh mug of coffee and his sleeves are rolled up, which means I wasn't the first to get here. He always rolls them up when he arrives in the office, showing off lean, muscled forearms that never fail to make me salivate.

Then there are his gorgeous eyes. They always seem to burn with hunger when he looks at me. Any other man, and I'd say he was attracted. But with Emmett, I know better. What he's really hungering for is another opportunity to torment me.

Yet...

Despite the fact that we've been working together for a year and ten months, my heart still does those funny gymnastics—tumble, roll and twist. It never did that before I met him, and it's increased over the last twenty-two months because even my belly feels weird these days, all fluttery in response to what my heart is doing. Hot shivers run through me at the most inopportune times, like when I should be focusing in meetings or paying attention to what my boyfriend's saying during the few dates we can manage.

The only thing that makes my inopportune attraction to my boss bearable is that I also feel a furious need to slap him ninety percent of the time, especially when that murmured "I'm probably going to regret this..." pops into my head. Or when he wrecks another of my evenings or weekends with his casual sadism.

I actually thought I was at the wrong address when I came in for the final interview. It was like I'd walked into a modeling agency by accident and somehow come face to face with their top model.

At six-four, Emmett Lasker towers over most people, his shoulders impossibly wide, his hips narrow and tight. Dark, slanted eyebrows cut decisive lines above his deep-set eyes that are such a light blue they appear almost silver. His facial features are masculine and finely balanced, as though chiseled by a master sculptor. A straight blade of a nose, not too long, not too short, just perfect. High forehead and square jaw with a hint of dark stubble. The only thing soft on his face is his mouth, which is surprisingly full. One corner lifts up frequently, as though he's sardonically amused at the world.

And maybe he is. He's one of those rare prodigies of finance with the Midas touch. He sees things that most of us mortals can't.

Working at GrantEm is basically the absolute best ice-cream sundae available in the world of finance. Working directly with Emmett Lasker himself? The cherry on top.

It's too bad I'm not feeling any of the smugness or satisfaction that people must get when they work for a genius. The hot, uncomfortable knot in my belly? That's forty percent lust over his gorgeous self, forty percent dread over what he's going to do to ruin my day and twenty percent self-recrimination over the fact that I still think he's an exceptionally *fine* specimen of masculinity. If it weren't for the fact that he's my boss...if we'd met under *any* other circumstances...I might've gone for a one-night stand, something I'd normally never even consider. But when you run into a guy who heats your blood just by breathing, why the hell not?

However, he is my boss. And not just any boss, but a boss who's driven to make my life hell. Who's hired me against his better judgment (I'm *still* not sure why he did that), and who's apparently determined to show me that I don't belong, no matter how well I perform at the firm.

But how can he look so fresh and hot this early in the morning? He seems to glow from within. The man didn't leave the office until after I did last night. And he got here before I did this morning. How is it possible that he can look like a million bucks when I feel a need to IV three or four quarts of espresso?

He raises an eyebrow expectantly.

Does he want the Excel file now? He told me he needed it by two, and I'm not giving it to him until later. I'm entitled to the hours allotted for this task!

Then I remember he said, "Working hard?"

I give him my best professional smile. "Yes. You said you wanted it by two." I gesture at the Excel spreadsheet on my monitor.

"That I did." He glances at my calendar, and his mouth flattens a bit.

Shit. I don't want him to think the circles, star and 6MAT over today's date mean something personal. If he does, he'll find a way to ruin it. Maybe toss in an "extremely urgent" task I'll need to work through lunch to get done.

I'm not canceling my interview with the Blaire Group. "I even marked it on my calendar, so I wouldn't forget."

"Mmm." His eyes narrow slightly.

Crap. Does he know what the circles and star really mean? I don't think he'd fire me for interviewing, but I don't want to give him another reason to dedicate his life to making me miserable. I don't know how much more he can do at this point, but I'm sure he'll think of something. There's a reason he's the founding partner of a venture capital firm at his age. And it isn't his daddy's money.

"I'm wondering what that '6MAT' stands for." Emmett gives me a smile.

His casual tone doesn't fool me. I make sure to keep my face pleasant and innocent. "It's my personal code to indicate urgency, 6MAT being the most important. The work I'm doing for you is obviously my top priority."

"Yes, but what does it stand for?"

"Uh, you mean the letters? Themselves?"

"Yes."

"Oh, it's simple. Most Absolute Top. And I have six numerical levels of priority, six being the highest." I smile again.

He raises both eyebrows, then nods slowly. "I see. It *is* important to mark one's priorities."

"Exactly."

"Keep up the good work," he says, although his tone indicates he's going to pick apart my deliverable until he finds something to complain about. Then he goes into his office.

Once the door closes behind him, I let out a soft breath. Whew. Safe. And I think my laying it on so thick like that stroked his ego. *Damn, I'm good.* I don't care if he gives me crap about my Excel model, because Emmett wouldn't be Emmett if he didn't.

Of course, once I get a new position and move on after eight weeks, this kind of passive-aggressive abuse will be over. Ah, the sweet smell of freedom. It's *so* close!

As the morning matures, GrantEm starts to bustle with more people. A first-year associate, Webber, goes into Emmett's office with a folder. Twenty minutes later he comes out, his shoulders rounded and the skin around his eyes red. He's an impressive guy —two years at Morgan Stanley before getting his MBA from Stanford. But no match for the bosshole. Emmett must've eviscerated him in there, all without raising his voice. He knows exactly how to stick a knife in and twist, even as he smiles like some demon angel.

Another analyst goes into the Hell Cave and comes out looking like her high school crush told her she was ugly and her vagina smelled like dead fish.

Poor Diana.

The worst thing is about the office layout is that people might not hear what Emmett says, but they can see your humiliation. This is why, no matter what my boss says or does to me, I paste on a smile. I'll be damned if anybody's going to see how I really feel after an Emmett Lasker encounter.

By eleven fifteen, I've had three coffees, reviewed the Excel model one last time, making sure it looks perfect, and emailed it to Emmett. I don't know how long the lunch interview is going to take, but I don't want this deliverable hanging over my head the entire time I'm at the restaurant.

I check Emmett's office. The door's closed. And I didn't see him leave after he got his midmorning coffee, so it's probably safe to make a quick exit before he notices I'm not slaving away to make him money.

My purse slung over my arm, I trot to the elevator bank. I keep my eyes forward, not looking at anybody. The key is to look like I have an urgent business meeting to get to, not that I'm sneaking off to a secret job interview.

I hit the elevator button and wait for the car to arrive. It's coming all the way from the lobby. Still, I have time. I've built in a ten-minute cushion just to be safe.

I look over my shoulder at Emmett's office. The door's still closed; he has no idea.

If Emmett were even the slightest bit of a decent human being underneath that gorgeous package, I might feel a little bad. After all, hiring me despite his misgivings has made me a valuable commodity. But all I'm feeling is exhilaration. And a desperate hope that he won't notice anything until I have a firm offer.

After what seems like an eternity, the elevator pings and I make my escape.

I drive over to the Aylster Hotel, park and get to Nieve, a posh bistro decorated in snowy white, with exactly ten minutes to spare.

A maître d' in a crisp white jacket stands at the entrance to the restaurant. I give him my interviewer's name—Marion Blaire. He nods without checking the reservation log and takes me back to a private booth. It's set with a white tablecloth and a gorgeous centerpiece made with blue and lavender flowers I don't recognize.

Marion's already at the table, nursing a glass of champagne that's still fizzing. It's a little surprising that he's here so early.

"Amy! Hi, I'm Marion Blaire. Nice to finally meet you." He stands and extends a hand.

I pump it a couple of times. "Hi, Marion. Nice to meet you, too."

The camera on his computer must be subpar, because he looks much better in person. He's a prototypical American golden boy with sandy hair, cornflower-blue eyes and a wide, bleach-assisted grin. He wears a three-piece suit, too formal for SoCal, but he might be overdressed to compensate for his age. He's in his mid-thirties, too young to be a junior partner at a private equity firm. But that doesn't matter, since he's senior enough within the Blaire Group to make hiring decisions.

I plan to impress the hell out of him.

Our waiter takes our lunch order. I ask for lightly seared sliced sea bream in green sauce, since it's easy to eat and talk this way. Marion opts for steak with mashed potatoes.

We chitchat a bit, mainly personal stuff. I let Marion take the lead, since he's the interviewer. I tell him about my dad in Vegas, and he tells me about his father, who works at the top of the Blaire Group, then about his mother's trips.

"She absolutely *loves* to travel."

I merely smile and say, "Awesome," since I don't have a female parental figure to speak adoringly about.

Our food arrives, and he starts the actual interview. "Before we begin, I just want you to know the in-person interview is something we do just to make sure. So you don't have to be overly nervous or anything. We really liked your résumé and experience. And the Zoom talk was very productive."

"Thanks." I give him a smile. I know why we're here, but it's always nice to hear positive reinforcement.

"So. Why are you thinking about leaving Emmett Lasker?"

An odd way to phrase the question. Most people would name the firm, not my boss himself. And most wouldn't gaze at me like they're eager to hear what a horrible human being he is.

Well. Emmett Lasker is the biggest bosshole in this half of the galaxy, but I'm not going to trash-talk my boss to a potential employer.

I paste on a neutral smile. "I'm looking for new challenges and opportunities, and I think the Blaire Group can provide that."

"Uh-huh. I'm just surprised because most think of venture capital as an exit opportunity, not something you grind through looking for something better."

"Sure. But private equity is also a great exit opportunity." I expected a question like this. "I like the deals the Blaire Group has done, and I think that's where I can grow the most professionally."

"Won't you miss working for Emmett Lasker? He has a rep."

Again bringing up Emmett. Marion is the second son of the founder of the Blaire Group, and there was probably a bit of nepotism involved for him to make junior partner at his age. Emmett, on the other hand, founded his own firm with one of his brothers. So Marion might be feeling a little inferior by comparison.

But I'm not going to let him know I suspect any of that. "I've spent almost two years with him, so the reputation doesn't hold much attraction for me anymore."

A corner of his mouth quirks up. "Aces. The whole feet of clay thing, eh?" He smirks and takes a bite of his steak. "So tell me about your hobbies. Anything interesting?"

I can't tell him my main hobby is trying to get as much sleep as possible, so I lie. "Not really. But I enjoy reading." He doesn't need to know the last book I read was *The Mathematics of Financial Derivatives* for my MBA.

"So do I," he says with a smile.

Bet the last thing he read was somebody's PowerPoint presentation. I can relate. Most people like to claim they're readers because it makes them appear smart, even if the only thing they read is social media. Modern life keeps us too busy to sit around just reading.

We chat some more between bites. My fish is excellent, but I'd like it more if I didn't have to fake some of my answers to appear well rounded and normal. The last thing I want is for Marion to think I'm harried or suffering under Emmett Lasker's authoritarian dictatorship. The goal is look like I can effortlessly handle anything and everything thrown my way.

Marion gets our check, then smiles. "Here's my card. I really enjoyed talking with you, and I'll be in touch within a week with our decision."

I smile back, taking the card. "Thank you."

As I drive back to the office, I take deep breaths. I'm a little puzzled that Marion didn't seem that interested in my work experience. Although he was present during the Zoom interview and we spoke a lot about the deals and so on I've worked on, I expected him to have at least one or two additional questions. He spent most of our lunch discussing our personal interests—while making sure to throw in questions about Emmett.

On the other hand, interviewers all have their own style. He could be one of those people who only hire people they can be friends with.

"Think positive," I tell myself as I park and run back up to the office. If the Blaire Group wasn't pretty sure about hiring me, Marion wouldn't have wasted his time meeting for lunch. He could've flown back to Virginia after his morning meeting.

And there are other firms out there. I have eight weeks to make my escape.

3

EMMETT

Five twenty-nine p.m.

I look at the digital clock on my desk and watch the seconds tick by. Even through my office door, I can feel the palpable excitement of a few of the analysts and associates over their weekend plans.

I tap on the Pulse icon in my phone. As a rule, I don't do social media—it rots your brain and sucks up time and energy. But Pulse is something I own a thirty-six percent stake in. Most importantly, it's where an up-and-coming influencer wannabe named Rick does his Rick on Romance spiel. The account's content is geared toward single men trying to navigate the life complication called a relationship.

In my opinion, if you're over the age of eighteen, you should know how to wine and dine women properly. But according to the follower count for Rick on Romance, over five hundred thousand men out there are pathetically clueless and desperate.

Rick's latest video has just gone live. He's in his SUV, a pair of reflective sunglasses wrapped around a narrow-ish face that reminds me of a horse. Not a sexy stallion, but a boring workhorse. The kind that farmers used to tie to a wagon full of shit to fertilize their fields.

"So I'm taking my girl out for our six-month anniversary." His voice is full of faux excitement.

His girl? Ha! He hasn't done any of the things I'd expect a real boyfriend to do for his girlfriend. Like take her out to a decent restaurant. And not regard every date as an opportunity to grow his follower count.

He's treating Amy like a prop in his zeal to "guide" men who are even more hopeless than he is. That should be criminalized for the sake of all the poor women out there. Rick and his kind are why women are convinced that all the good men are either taken or gay.

"It's important to celebrate every milestone, you know," he continues.

Is it now?

"So I reserved a rustic cabin in Lake Tahoe."

But why? When I asked, "Cabin or all-inclusive resort?" Amy picked resort, no hesitation. He should know her preference if he's really her boyfriend. *I* know what she likes, and I'm just her boss!

"Only the very best for my girl." He grins, flashing large, square teeth. I guess he can say he's hung like a horse...from the gums. And what's up with that gap between the two front incisors?

What does Amy see in this guy?

She's a second-year associate at GrantEm Capital, the venture capital firm I founded with my brother Grant. She has a degree in economics from Harvard, a two-year stint as an analyst at Goldman Sachs and an MBA from Wharton. It's a damn impressive résumé. Too bad all those amazing qualifications and education didn't do a thing to improve her judgment in men.

When a woman is as hot and smart as Amy, she can do better than Rick. The guy's a six at best. And not a solid six. A sad, barely there, slippery-grip-on-a-six six.

Rick laughs. He sounds like a donkey.

Forget the six. He's a five.

"And we're going to go hiking because it's good to be active when you're having fun," he says.

What's he smoking? Amy likes getting massages when she wants to kick back and pamper herself. Hiking is her idea of torture. How can he not know this?

"I'm also packing *this* for our meals." He waves a roll of aluminum foil.

For a split second I wonder if he plans to feed her the foil. But no—he intends to wrap stuff in the foil and toss it into a fire to cook.

He can't take her to a nice restaurant? Given a choice, Amy prefers room service versus cooking it yourself. I know because I asked.

How self-centered do you have to be to date a woman for six months and not know anything about her? How narcissistic do you have to be to plan activities that only *you're* going to like?

What a garbage human being. He reminds me of my dad—without the money and drive.

"And when the time is right, I'm going to surprise her with something romantic I picked up from a cute booth at a fair. It's a bit nontraditional, but it has the coolest design. I'll share a picture of it once I give it her."

Uh, no. Amy likes diamonds, not some cheap costume jewelry you picked up from a fair.

Given how little he's spent on this so-called milestone celebration, I'm sure he waited until the last minute of the fair and bought whatever was half off in the seller's desperate attempt to offload unsold inventory.

"Share how *you're* romancing *your* girl with #rickonromance so I can be sure to check out how you're doing!" he says cheerily.

I close Pulse and check the time again. Five thirty-four. Amy's probably ready to head out. To Lake Fucking Tahoe. That bit about "6MAT" on her calendar didn't fool me for a second.

Five circles and a star. Pssh. Like an outing to Tahoe is some big deal.

I have no idea what bullshit Rick fed her to get her excited about the trip, but when a guy says "rustic cabin" with that insincere   aw-shucks-I'm-just-an-everyday-guy-romancing-a-cute-girl smile, he means a primitive shithole without electricity, running water or room service. A quarter step above a cave, possum-pelt rug upgrade optional.

If I were to take Amy on a six-month anniversary, I'd spring for an overwater bungalow in French Polynesia with a glass floor so we could see all the sea creatures swimming in the crystal-clear water underneath our feet. A place so exclusive and secluded we'd need to charter a yacht to get there and a full staff to cater to our every whim.

After all, Amy is a sparkly diamond kind of girl. She shouldn't have to settle.

Maybe she knows that deep inside, which is why she lied to me so shamefully about what the circles and star meant. I'm not sure about the 6MAT she added today, but it has nothing to do with making me her priority.

I look at the Excel projections on one of the new business ideas we're funding. Amy sent them this morning before heading out to a long lunch, undoubtedly to pick up last-minute stuff for her trip. She probably doesn't think I noticed, but I notice everything about her.

Her work is good. Only needs a few minor adjustments. But I'll be damned if she goes to some Tahoe cave this weekend.

Besides, it's good training for her to do some negative projections and rebuild the entire model. I've done that many times, just for fun.

Five thirty-seven.

I get up and head out. Some of the staff are ready to call it a day; some are still working away on their laptops. At GrantEm, Friday doesn't always mean you get the next two days off. But that's why we pay top dollar. You can't expect people to work the hours we demand and not compensate them properly.

Amy's desk isn't far from my office. From where I stand, I can see her well. Intelligent baby-blue eyes framed by thick, dark lashes. High cheekbones that would make most models shriek with envy. A slightly pointed, pixie-like chin. A wide and soft mouth that reminds me of Japanese camellia blossoms in full bloom. Her golden hair is pulled back into a loose ponytail, making her look like a kid fresh out of college. A pale cream top and charcoal-gray skirt fit her slim body well, showcasing the swell of her breasts and long, pretty legs. She's lost some weight since she joined GrantEm, which is a shame, because she didn't need to.

But I've seen what Rick's been feeding her on the few dates they were able to sneak in despite my best efforts to save her. I'd lose weight too if I had to eat what passes for food in Rick's world.

As I study her, need clutches my gut, hot and brutal. It's grown more intense over the past several months. But I shove it aside, put on my most charming boss smile and go over.

"Amy."

She looks up at me, all professional and pleasant. "Hi, Emmett. Heading out?"

Her tone says she already knows the answer to that: *No, I have work to do.*

"No," I say, refusing to add the rest. I've been working more and more since Amy started. No interest in dating, clubbing or going out. No interest in devoting more hours to working out, playing tennis or scuba diving. That leaves me with work as the only activity left to fill my free time. It's a good thing I enjoy working.

"Then...?" Wariness creeps into her gaze.

She has nothing to worry about. I'm saving her from a weekend in Hell Rustica. "I reviewed the projections you sent me. I think they're too optimistic, given the industry and some of the market indicators, which you should look up and incorporate into the model you've created. So. Can you adjust it, using more realistic scenarios?"

"Sure." A properly cooperative tone. "When do you need it?"

"Today. I need to review it to make sure it's ready for the meeting on Monday. Plus, it'd be great if you could find the pricing projections for the raw material needed for production of water filters, as well as labor costs in Vietnam and Thailand."

The bottom half of her face remains friendly and professional. The top half? It's shooting death laser through her furious eyes. If life were a cartoon, there would be a thought bubble over her head with a lot of *fuck you*s and *asshole*s.

Perversely enough, the notion heats my blood. I'm fucked up. But then, being normal would be a miracle, given my background.

"I know you'll be able to knock it out the park, no problem." I beam. "I'll wait for the updated Excel in my office. I have a few things to go over anyway."

See? I'm not a complete asshole. I'm not throwing work in her lap—thereby saving her from a weekend worse than death—then calling it a day and leaving. Not at all. I'll stay and work as well.

Of course, it's possible working isn't one of Amy's hobbies, but hey, we can't always do what we want.

Just like I can't do what I want with Amy.

4

AMY

Fuck my life.

No. Fuck my *boss*.

He has to be high to ask me to redo the projections with more "realistic" assumptions. All of them were already done with the most conservative outlook. He *knows* this. Hell, everyone at GrantEm knows this!

And yet he isn't happy.

What does he want? A financial apocalypse scenario?

I glare at the closed door to his office. I can't believe I ever found him hot.

Slowly, my anger builds to a raging fury. I'm an idiot, and all the fancy degrees I've collected haven't helped me see anything more than skin deep.

Because I *still* find him hot, dammit! Sometimes when I just let go of everything in my head and stare at him, I can feel myself melting like chocolate on an equatorial beach. And that, more than anything, adds to my irritation and frustration. I *should* find him hideous. Grotesque.

What's worse—I can't complain about working for Emmett to anybody. All my friends who graduated with me at Wharton and went into finance are insanely jealous. "You're so lucky! I'd give up a kidney to be able to work for Emmett Lasker!" And it's not just from my MBA pals, but everyone in the field.

So I shouldn't resent the fact that Emmett just torpedoed another of my romantic plans on the same day he asked me pick out a present for his lady friend. Once in a great while—when the stars from twenty galaxies go into alignment—he lets me go home early enough that I can grab a late dinner with Rick. Emmett's become more demanding in the last six months. He might be thinking I'm senior enough to rise to higher expectations. Or he's decided he needs to make me work harder to avoid the regret of hiring me. Or maybe he's realized his two-year carte blanche is about to expire, so he needs to kick it up a notch.

Regardless, these endless late nights *will* end. No matter how much Emmett regrets hiring me, the headhunters are going to focus on the fact that in the time I've worked for him I've overseen two IPOs and numerous ventures that got noticed by the national media. I'm going to get a*maz*ing job offers with more pay, more benefits and better hours over the next eight weeks. I'm probably going to have an orgasm right here on the office floor when I throw my resignation in Emmett's face and keep every last penny of my signing bonus.

For that, I can suck it up for the next two months.

I boot my laptop. As it comes back to life, my eye catches the five circles and a star on my calendar. *Please. I need to get the hell out of here.* Please *let the Blaire Group make me a juicy offer.*

Then I finally note the sad little 6MAT by the star. Damn it. Should've known the trip wasn't happening when Rick texted me this morning. Our relationship has been anything but smooth sailing. If I were superstitious, I'd suspect we were cursed.

Just look what happened today. I gave everything to Emmett before lunch, and he waited until now to ask for changes.

Stop being upset. Dig into the various markets and statistics and redo the model. Pull out the pricing projections Emmett asked for. The faster I do it, the sooner I can leave.

I open the Excel file I sent to Emmett. Even now, my projections seem fine. I can't make my assumptions worse than they are without making them about a crappy case of recession, which I don't think is coming anytime soon. Indicators don't support that.

Still...

He sees something I don't, I tell myself, taking a long, calming breath. *He sees something I don't.* If I don't force myself to believe this, I'm going to bash him over the head with my heavy-duty stapler.

Before I start digging into the spreadsheet, I shoot a quick text to Rick. I feel bad for letting him down because he was super excited this morning, but I have no choice. At least I'm not telling him through a Pulse post comment.

–Me: Something came up at work. I think I'm going to be late. Sorry!

After I hit send, I contemplate the huge model. Rick shouldn't have to wait for hours when he could be heading to Lake Tahoe and getting the maximum value out of the cabin rental. So I type another text and send it to him, all the while doing my best not to cry over the fact that I'm stuck in the office and will have to make the long-ass drive myself later. This seriously is *not* how I wanted my Friday evening to unfold.

–Me: Actually, this is going to take a while. Why don't you send me the address of the cabin? I'll drive out after I'm done. Thanks!

It takes ten hours or so to drive to Lake Tahoe. Shit. Maybe I should just fly, not for myself, but for the safety of other drivers on the road. I can't be sure I'll be able to stay awake.

I put the phone away and begin poring over the market data. Still can't see how my projections were wrong...

Nevertheless, I do manage to find enough indicators to support an absolute worst-case scenario and incorporate them into the model. This should make Emmett happy.

I'm a little over halfway done when my stomach starts to growl. I also can't suppress a yawn. The numbers in the Excel cells are beginning to blur, bleeding into each other like the Rorschach blots psychologists use for personality tests. Wonder what it means that what I'm seeing looks like... I squint. *Huh... Kind of like a penis.*

Maybe it's a sign that, deep inside, I think Excel is a dick, which doesn't make any sense. I actually like Excel. It makes my job a hundred times easier.

I blink and shake my head to wake myself up. It doesn't help much.

Need sugar. And more coffee.

I head over to the break room to grab a couple of candy bars and a latte from the fancy espresso machine Emmett's brother Grant put in for his birthday. Emmett and Grant both give presents to the office on their birthdays. It's a tradition. And probably tax deductible, if I know Emmett.

The floor's empty except for two other desks—a couple of first-year analysts who report to Grant. They probably screwed something up. Or maybe they were too bullish.

But now even they are closing their laptops. Lucky them. That leaves me alone in the office.

Actually, not alone. Emmett's still here. I know it because he hasn't come by my desk, which is on his way to the elevator bank.

I walk into the empty break room, take a large mug that reads SHORT YO MAMA, fill it with fresh latte and grab a Snickers bar and two bags of Skittles.

"Why are you still in the office? You aren't heading out?"

I turn, and there's Sasha. We met at Goldman, become friends, went to Wharton together and now are roommates while we work at GrantEm. Unlike me, she works for Grant Lasker, who is a nicer human being than Emmett. She must be ready to go home because she's carrying her laptop bag and purse.

"Emmett wants some adjustments," I say.

Sasha looks at my java with pity. "He knows it's Friday, right?"

"Yes, which is his most despised day of the week. The more he works, the more he thrives."

She shakes her head.

"And the stuff I'm doing is for the meeting Monday afternoon. It can't wait," I say, not to defend Emmett, but to soothe my disappointment over not being able to nap in Rick's car. Otherwise, I might just cry. Or scream. Or maybe do both at the same time—but not yet. I don't have a job offer secured, and I haven't hit the two-year mark, which means I can't throw my resignation in Emmett's face.

But in just fifty-six more days, I will. Gleefully.

She wrinkles her nose. "You couldn't pass it off to an analyst or two?"

"If I'm not seeing what's wrong, they aren't going to. And I don't want Emmett calling me in Tahoe and asking me to come in and redo it myself."

"Tahoe?"

I sigh. "Rick booked a surprised getaway."

Sasha raises both eyebrows. "*Nice.* I didn't know he had it in him."

"Yeah, me either. Let's just say it was indeed a surprise." And not in a good way, but I can't discuss boyfriend issues with Sasha right now because it will take time I don't have.

"That area has some really nice weekend rentals. Really swanky."

"He likes them *homey.*" No need to see pictures to know what he would've picked. "I told him I'd join him later today. After I'm done. But whatever. Why are *you* still here? I thought you were heading out to see Gage."

"We both had a few things to wrap up, so I moved my flight to tomorrow."

"Price you pay for dating a high-priced Bay Area lawyer." I haven't met Gage yet. But then, Sasha hasn't met most of my boyfriends, including Rick. We work too damn many hours.

"Yeah. Long distance sucks." She filches a bag of sour gummy worms—her favorite—and stuffs it into her purse. She always takes one from the break room before leaving. Says it helps her control herself. She claims if she goes to a supermarket hungry, she'll end up cleaning out the aisle. "But you know me. No working from home. Ever."

I nod. That's been her longstanding rule. Says it ensures that work doesn't encroach into her personal life. I adopted it too during my second year at Goldman. It helped avoid burnout while putting in hundred-hour weeks, so I've kept it.

"Hey, if you need help, let me know." She pats my arm in sympathy. Unlike some who might say it as a friendly but empty gesture, she means it.

"Thanks, girl. I will."

After wishing her a great weekend, I head to my desk. I consume the latte, and caffeine jolts through my system, pushing away the fogginess.

I unwrap the Snickers and pull my phone out of my purse to check for Rick's directions to the cabin. Multiple texts and five missed calls. This is unusual. He's never called me over missed or changed plans. Not that he's done much to hide how he felt. He can whine better than a three-year-old who missed his nap. But he never tries to compete with my career for my attention. That's the biggest reason we're still together, despite the times my gut whispered that I needed to cut my losses. Rick and I really aren't going anywhere. Rebounding with him seemed like a great idea six months ago, especially when my last boyfriend dumped me after I couldn't make two consecutive dinner dates and said that he needed a girlfriend who would put him first. He didn't understand that dinner dates won't pay off my debt.

–Rick: I didn't want to do this via text, but I guess you leave me no choice. This is ridiculous, Amy!

–Rick: Me or the job?

What? Where did this come from?

–Rick: Think real careful before you answer that.

–Rick: Are you listening?

–Rick: Are you ignoring me?

–Rick: Hello?

I stare incredulously at the texts. The time stamp on the "Are you listening?" is six thirty-four p.m.; "Are you ignoring me?" and "Hello?" are six thirty-five p.m. He went ballistic over me not texting back *within a minute*? Couldn't he see that I hadn't even read his messages?

Besides, I told him I'd join him after I was done. So what's up with the ultimatum?

He doesn't get to make threats after dumping this trip on me at the last minute! Especially when he knows the number of hours I work! I was clear about that from the beginning. Furthermore, I made it clear that I could only meet him around my work schedule.

And he said he was fine with that, no problem!

–Rick: Don't be a bitch.

Oh, hold on. Did he just call me a bitch because I told him *I have to work*?

–Rick: Me or the job?!!!!

Isn't the answer obvious? I didn't spend nearly half a million dollars on undergraduate and master's degrees to choose him and unemployment.

–Me: The job, BITCH!

I hit send with more force than necessary. Then I glare at the screen, fuming. *Who does he think he is?*

But every second I'm giving the phone a death stare is one more second I'm being unproductive. The projections won't populate themselves into Excel on their own. And besides, Rick can't even see my evil glare.

I put my phone away and turn back to my laptop. The calendar on my desk sits in my peripheral vision. I look at it and see the stupid 6MAT over today's date blowing a raspberry at me for bothering to try to accommodate Rick.

Screw that.

I reach into my drawer, pull out a black Sharpie and scribble out the 6MAT to erase the evidence of my relationship idiocy. Two seconds later, the area smells faintly of permanent marker ink. I put the marker away and go back to Excel.

I can probably get this done in the next hour or two, email it to Emmett and then go home. I'm going to splurge on an excellent bottle of Merlot and take a luxurious bubble bath. And then *sleep*. If everything goes well, I should be able to swing at least six hours rather than my usual four. The possibility is exciting.

That's me—living the high life!

I put together a document that lists the indicators and articles I've referenced. That way Emmett can't come back and ask me for exhibits to validate my projections and pricing of commodities and labor.

I hit save and reach for the Skittles. Boosting my blood sugar will be paramount to surviving the next two hours...

But the damn bag won't cooperate. I try to pull it apart a couple of times, fail, then snarl in anger and yank on the damn thi—

The little candies explode like a rainbow grenade. Some of them end up on the floor; most clatter around on my desk. I swipe those up and shove them into my mouth. Then I bend down to pick up the ones on the floor. We have janitors, but it's my mess.

After I grab all the contaminated candy and toss it into the trash, I park my butt back at my desk. The second my eyes fall on my laptop screen, horror sucker-punches me so hard I actually gasp.

Microsoft Excel is not responding
If you start or close the program, it will try to recover your information.
→ *Restart the program*
→ *Close the program*
→ *Wait for the program to respond*

"*No!* Oh, no, no, no, no..."

I click on "Wait for the program to respond" repeatedly. The error pop-up stays.

Why is it *not going away?* Does this mean my computer understood I'm going to wait or what? The engineers who designed Excel should've created a special alert that reassures panicked users that the "Wait for the program to respond" option has been chosen *and the program will respond.* The lack of such a feature is incredibly user-unfriendly!

Time slows. I gnaw on my nails, my eyes glued to the damned pop-up that refuses to go away. How long does it take before Excel deigns to respond?

I pull out my phone. There are more texts, probably from Rick, but I don't have the bandwidth for them. I open the timer app, go to the stopwatch tab and immediately hit start. The numbers on the screen whir past.

Please! God, oh please!

Two minutes. Three. Four...

... Ten minutes.

Panicked bitterness wells up, choking me. If the program hasn't responded after ten minutes, it isn't going to magically start now.

I give it another five minutes. Just in case.

Nothing.

Now all my hope is on this phrase: *If you start or close the program, it will try to recover your information.*

Don't you fucking fail me, Microsoft!

I force-close the program, then immediately restart it. I clasp my hands together in a desperate prayer, my eyes squeezed shut.

Please recover the file. Please, please, please! I'll sacrifice my left little toe.

The tension around my shoulders eases as Excel shows a recovered file in the left-hand pane. I click on it. Then press my hands to my mouth so I don't shriek with frustrated rage.

Screw you, computer! Screw you, life!

The damned program didn't recover the latest version. It recovered one from over an hour ago.

I look down at my phone. Eleven fifty-nine p.m.

In less than a minute, it's going to be *Saturday*. I was supposed to have an awesome job interview and hopefully make it to the surprise getaway to Lake Tahoe—not get stuck in the office, wrestle with Excel, break up with my boyfriend via text or have Excel crash and burn, forcing me to redo at least an hour's worth of work.

My fingers shake with fury and frustration. The lack of sleep over the last several weeks has left my head full of sludge. The gears in my brain refuse to turn, despite the fact that I had a huge latte less than two hours ago.

Whatever control I try to hang on to slips away. In its wake, a murderous rage erupts.

I jump to my feet. This is *all* Emmett Lasker's fault!

The projections I gave him earlier were *fine*. Wharton doesn't hand out MBAs just because you have a pretty smile. I deserve an explanation. And Emmett's going to give me one now!

I march toward his office. The gap between the bottom of the door and the floor is lit. He's probably in there panting, worn out from counting all the money he has. GrantEm is a venture capital firm. There could've been a major jackpot payout where the firm made its money back a thousand times over since he tossed this redo in my lap.

Now my resentment is boiling over. *He* has the pleasure of rolling around in a pile of cash like Scrooge McDuck. But me? I'm just a peon with an expensive degree I still need to pay for. And that payment seems to include giving up sleep and sanity, largely due to my boss.

It's time Emmett knows those two are a big no-no. The hell with suffering for another eight weeks!

I burst into his office. If he can make me work late, he has to deal with me confronting him about it. Furious words are loaded and ready, like bullets in a machine gun. But before I can fire them off—

"Amy..."

I freeze. That...didn't sounds like a reprimand. It sounded like a...moan. And not just any moan. A *sexual* moan. The kind you make when you're in a haze of lust.

It takes a while for my sleep-deprived, over-caffeinated brain to process the scene.

Emmett, reclining on a couch. His dick in his hand.

I just walked in on my boss's midnight masturbation.

5

AMY

The angry words in my head get jammed. I open and close my mouth, but not even a croak comes out.

Emmett's penis is *huge*. The biggest I've ever seen. And thick. Veins stand out, pulsing in his grip.

I drag my eyes up. He's fully clothed and properly covered, except for the crotch area. He's looking straight at me. No sign of embarrassment or oh-shit-I-got-caught panic.

Okay, I have to be dreaming. I know I'm exhausted. Maybe my latest Excel model *did* get saved. Maybe I emailed it to Emmett and had my wine and bath, and now I'm having a lucid dream.

Except... Why would it be about Emmett's penis?

God, I need to see a therapist.

My gaze drops again. Emmett is still erect. *Really* erect, showing off a daunting length and girth. But that isn't all. His penis is so well shaped that it could serve as a dildo mold. If Emmett sent unsolicited dick pics, women wouldn't complain. Hell, if Michelangelo had had Emmett as his model, *David* would be the proud owner of a much better-looking penis.

"Oh my God, could you put that thing away?" My words come out squeaky.

He pins me with a level look. "Why? It's my office."

"Yeah, but they're *my* eyes!"

"Which currently seem to be glued to a certain magnificent part of *my* anatomy."

I wrench my eyes off the member in question and direct my gaze to the ceiling. "Well, I'm not looking at it *now*." My face is so hot I feel like my makeup is melting.

"Too late. I still feel violated."

Violated? I lower my gaze again.

His hand is still wrapped around his dick, although it's not moving anymore. He's looking at me balefully. No, not balefully. I squint at him. It's hard to think clearly when my emotions are churning, the gears in my head are stuck in the sludge of six—or was it seven?—coffees and way too much sugar. After a moment, I decide he's gazing at me shamelessly. With a hint of God-I'm-hot arrogance.

"Usually that's reserved for the woman who's getting flashed." My brain is trying to sort out something he said that doesn't quite add up. It's material enough that I should worry.

"You aren't being flashed," he corrects me in a tone he often uses to provide feedback on my work. "You're helping yourself to the view."

"*I am not!*"

"Yes, you are. You barged into my office, completely uninvited. I don't recall you knocking, either. If you had, I would've told you to come back later." His you-know-I'm-right look grows more pointed.

I have absolutely no response to that because he is—irritatingly enough—correct. I did burst into the office, even if it was for reasons involving righteous anger. But now...

Well, this is *awkward*. And... *I sat on that couch when I came in to speak with him!* As a matter of fact, that's where I sat when I had my job interview...

I should be disgusted. Outraged. But the emotions churning inside aren't quite that easy to identify. It's all Emmett's fault that I'm too exhausted to sort myself out.

"Can you, uh, *cover* yourself?" I say, tilting my head heavenward. Lucid dream or not, this is embarrassing.

"What do you think I'm doing with my hand?"

I look down. His hand is wrapped firmly around his still-erect penis, his thumb resting on the tip. This has to be a nightmare. It was probably caused by the dick-shaped Excel blot I saw when my vision got blurry.

"Don't worry," he says magnanimously. "I won't take anything up with HR."

I can't even... I try to think of a response, but my brain just...fails. I focus on the fact that I'm in the office this late on Friday for a reason. It has nothing to do with Emmett's act of self-love.

No. It has everything to do with the fact that he's being an unreasonable son of a bitch, and I'm tired of it. What's worse is that while I've been working my ass off, he's been having dirty fun in the privacy of his office.

"HR? For what?" I snap. *I'm* the one who should complain!

"For this." He gestures between us. "You treating me like a sex object."

"You're treating your dick like a sex object!" He still has his hand wrapped around it, like a child guarding his favorite toy on a playground.

He puts the back of his free hand to his forehead. "I feel... cheap." His mouth turns down in dramatic dejection.

Cheap? A sex object? That's it! That's the *last damn straw!*

"I'll show you what being a cheap sex object feels like!" I snarl. Furious, I march over with my power heels punching the floor. I bend and fist the collar of his shirt, jerking him upward.

He braces his free hand on the couch, his eyes registering a flicker of shock. It further fans my rage. Does he think he can stomp all over me and I'll just take it meekly forever?

I crash my mouth against his in a rough, punishing kiss. No gentleness, just hot, searing rage and frustration.

But instead of pulling away like a properly stunned and chastised sex object, he kisses me back, his lips apart and his tongue licking, stealing a taste.

Something hot and needy explodes inside of me. My heart thuds as I take and take, trying to show him how cheaply I can treat him.

Our mouths fused, he cradles the back of my skull, then slides his hand down to the back of my neck. The touch is possessive. It fuels all the rage burning inside me and something else— something far more dangerous and volatile.

A low, thick moan tears from his throat, the sound muffled between our mouths. His naked need soothes some of the jagged edges I'm feeling, and shivers run through me. The tenor of the kiss shifts from anger to something else just as hot and raw.

Desire, my mind whispers. *Uncontrollable, scorching desire.*

It rolls through my veins, sends electric jolts along my nerves. My head spins as I strain for a control that keeps slipping out of reach.

The kiss is lush now. Emmett devours me like he's been starved for me since forever. And I devour him back, inhaling his sexy, masculine scent, feeling his hot, uneven breath on my skin. Lust grows until it seems to overwhelm what good sense I have left. I feel something snap inside. I want to kiss him until the world ends. Ease the ache between my legs.

He pulls me closer. Or maybe it's me who pressing against him. My breasts crush against his hard chest, my nipples puckering within the confines of my bra. The flesh between my thighs is slick. His warm, large hand slips under my skirt and pushes it up. I shiver and rock against him as the emptiness grows unbearable.

He feels so *good* against me. But I know there could be more. The fire burning inside me could grow hotter and bigger. And Emmett is the fuel I need.

I tug at his shirt, but there are too many buttons. Out of patience, I yank it apart, and those buttons fly. I breathe hard, my eyes on his naked torso. His chest is well developed, the abs tight and ridged. *Holy cow.* His physique is just as gorgeous as his face. And having it bared before my eyes makes me feel powerful. Utterly sexual.

I run my hands down his taut skin. His muscles tighten and flex at my touch. I bite my lip, focused on the task of exploring his body.

He tugs at my top, slithers his hand underneath the thin fabric and pushes my bra out of the way. My breast feels heavy as he cups it, brushing his thumb over the painfully tight nipple.

Sharp bliss streaks through me, ending between my legs. I moan and arch against his hand. A monstrous lust is riding me now, taking control. A vague voice in my head says this is a terrible idea, but I'm feeling too good to care.

He reclaims my mouth. Our kiss is brutal. He's holding me so tight, and the pleasure from his mouth is so searing, that I feel like my soul is burning. I sense something tear and realize it's my power thong, and then his clever fingers are touching my clit and the dripping flesh below. The starkly delightful sensation overwhelms me, setting every nerve on fire. And the torn thong doesn't seem important.

His fingers tugging and tweaking my nipple, his mouth fused over mine, he shifts until he's positioned underneath me. And then suddenly, smoothly, he's inside.

I clutch his shoulders, lost in the pleasure of animal friction. I'm riding him, but he's gripping my pelvis with his strong hands to move me up and down. He seems out of his mind with what's happening between us, his breathing rough, his movements hard and desperate.

Then he shifts a little, and his cock hits a spot I didn't know was inside me. Lightning starts flashing in my head and an orgasm crashes through me, the intensity enough to make me black out for a second. Blood roars in my head, and I feel like I'm going to rip in half from the pleasure exploding inside me. Air catches in my throat; I can't even scream.

Emmett tightens, then jerks as he pulls his dick out fast. Something hot squirts over my thigh as a tortured groan tears from his throat.

Collapsed over him, I struggle to catch my breath as my vision refocuses. Holy shit. That was technically a quickie, but it sure didn't feel like one. I've never come so hard, so fast. My brain's still sparking with lingering bliss. My muscles spasm in aftershock as my body recovers from the most intense orgasm of my life.

I had no clue this was possible. I shiver again as my body demands another round. I've never understood why people became addicted to sex, but now...

Emmett angles my head, then kisses me again. Tenderly at first, then growing more commanding. I let out a little whimper as heat pulses through me again, making me greedy for another orgasm.

A buzzing sound cuts through the layer of renewed need. I feel torn as sanity tries to wriggle way its way back into my mind.

Emmett pulls his mouth from mine a fraction, mumbles, "Ignore that," and then resumes the kiss. He presses his still-hard cock between my legs and moves, the damp friction sending another wave of dazzling bliss through me. My head spins, and I can't think of a single reason we should stop.

The buzzing goes off again and sanity finally slices through animal desire, seizing firm control of my mind. It slaps me with cold, lust-killing reality.

You just had sex with your boss. In his office.

Holy shit!

Nice going. Bet that really showed him what cheap feels like.

I jerk upright as dread starts sinking in.

Now he really can take it up with HR. For real.

I immediately jump off him, shoving my skirt down, then

reposition my bra properly. My face goes hot-cold-hot as embarrassment and horror battle for supremacy.

I feel Emmett's gaze boring into me. Horror wins. Panic surges through me, leaving me so cold I shiver.

"Amy?"

The buzzing. It's his phone on the table. I keep my eyes on it so I don't have to look at him. I simply can't right now. "You should answer that. Must be important."

I run out before he can respond.

6

AMY

I trot to my desk and grab my laptop and purse before Emmett can come out of his office. Dad told me that when you need to, you can overcome any obstacle in your way. He's right, because my wobbly heels are no match for my need to get the hell out of here immediately.

I dash to the elevator bank and hit the button out of reflex. But when I check the car displays, I realize there's nothing immediately available to take me to lobby. *No way am I waiting here like a sitting duck.*

I head right, open the emergency exit door and take the stairs. I can reach the floor below and catch an elevator from there. Improvise. Adapt. Overcome!

I reach the emergency door for the thirty-fourth floor and scan my employee badge over the security pad. The small light stays red.

Weird. I try again. It still doesn't turn green.

What the hell? Why isn't my badge working?

I push on the bar on the door. It doesn't budge. What's going on here?

Maybe the thirty-fourth-floor security pad is broken. I go to the thirty-third floor.

Still can't gain access.

Finally, it dawns on me that maybe it's because I don't work on those floors. The building has a law firm on the thirty-fourth floor and a tax advisory firm on the thirty-third. I study my employee badge. It has my photo on it—me smiling with a hint of nervous excitement—and my name, Amy Sand, in all caps. Underneath my name, it states GrantEm Capital.

Shit. If I want to get on an elevator, I'll have to go back up. To the office.

Where Emmett is.

Time to decide which is worse—taking the stairs all the way down to the lobby or possibly facing Emmett. Just thinking about my boss is making my lips tingle. Both sets.

Wait a minute... My thong! I left it in his office!

I slap my forehead. How could I have been so stupid! Oh my God! I want it back, but I can't possibly go up into his office again!

I breathe in and out deeply. *Think, Amy, think! You were overeducated for a reason!*

Okay, the thong is a loss. Even if I get it back, I can't wear it again. So what if it was my power thong, and I wore it every time I had something important planned for the day? I can buy a new one. And if Emmett ever mentions the old one or brings it up, I'll deny it's mine. It's not like it has my name on it.

Problem solved.

Taking a calmer breath, I move to the next issue: this endless rectangular spiral of stairs. Dad tells me I should exercise, but I never get the chance working in finance. I mean, I barely have any time to sleep. Maybe it's time I make my father happy. It's only thirty-three stories, not an eternity on a StairMaster. How bad can it be?

An hour or so later, I'm finally in the lobby. My legs are shaking, muscles I didn't know I had quivering like cello strings.

Sweat is pouring out of glands I didn't know existed. My lungs expand and contract unevenly, and my brain declares I'm an idiot.

I agree. By the time I reached the twentieth floor, I realized I'd made a huge mistake. But it was too late. I didn't have the energy to climb back up fifteen floors of stairs. Besides, it had to be easier going down than up.

It just didn't *feel* that way.

But now I'm finally, thankfully, rejoicingly *in the lobby*! I put my hands on my knees and suck air. If we ever have an earthquake and need to evacuate, I'm taking the elevator. I don't give a shit what the emergency manual says.

Once my breathing evens out a bit, I go to the garage across the street—the GrantEm building is great except for the lack of parking within the structure. As I start my car, I realize I've been a complete moron.

Running solved nothing. I'm still going to have to see Emmett. If not over the weekend—it's very possible he'll text me about the adjusted Excel model I *didn't* turn in—then definitely on Monday.

Covering my face, I let out a scream. What the hell am I going to do? Driving off a cliff sounds really good.

Except it wouldn't be practical. Besides, I love my dad too much to do that to him. And why should *I* die? I might've started the kiss, but Emmett put his dick in me.

Okay, Amy. Stop thinking. You're sleep-deprived, your blood sugar's too low and you can't be rational right now.

First things first. Go home. Sleep. Then *come up with a strategy.*

I drive home. It takes less than half an hour to reach the two-bedroom apartment I share with Sasha. That's almost magically fast in L.A. But then, the streets aren't crowded at one thirty-six a.m. on a Saturday. People are already clubbing and partying or staying home and doing productive things, like sleeping.

I slip off my shoes as I walk into my room and let out a sigh. If my feet could talk, they'd be groaning right now. Being stuck inside a pair of high-heeled sandals—even if they're my power shoes—for hours on end is a bitch. So is doing an unplanned cardio session in them. The bra's next to go. *So much better.* I don't know how ladies in the past functioned wearing corsets they couldn't get out of alone. Thank God I wasn't born back then.

After tossing my purse and laptop bag on the armchair near my bed, I check my phone for missed messages, just in case I didn't hear the notification pings or ringtone over the sound of my loud, desperate wheezing the entire time I was struggling on those damn stairs.

A million texts from Rick. I don't want to deal with him right now, so I ignore them.

How about Emmett, though? I wonder if my boss texted or called—and dread the possibility. He has reason to, and not just because of the sex. He could be thinking about the Excel model. After all, the man's a workaholic slave driver.

But—nothing from him. Something cold slithers its fingers along my shoulders and neck. What does this silence mean? Is he busy filling out an HR complaint form? Did he decide to take the call and then treat himself to another orgasm? He was hard when I ran out on him.

I press the heels of my hands against my temples and choke back a scream. Sasha's undoubtedly sleeping in her room, and I don't want to wake her up. For my own sanity, I'm just going to pretend that everything after eleven fifty-nine p.m. never happened. No matter how surreally weird and inappropriate it was, it's true that I did barge in, so it isn't one hundred percent Emmett's fault I got to see his penis...and everything else that happened.

On top of that, he spoke to me like he always does when he has his dick tucked appropriately away in his pants: annoying and sexy at the same time. So I'm going to assume he didn't particularly care about the whole...impropriety of the incident. In the nearly two years I've known Emmett, I've never seen him do anything inappropriate. Not a single whisper of a scandal or interoffice dating talk. The only thing I know is he is a workaholic, and since he spends almost every waking minute in his office, he probably does a lot of *personal* tasks there. It even has an en suite shower.

Yeah, but you had to kiss him!

I had to show him...then things got out of control. Oh my God. I can't think about that right now. The only thing I'm clearheaded enough to do is stick my phone into the charger and make a mental note never to sit on *that* couch in his office ever again.

I go to the bathroom and reach for a makeup wipe. The mirror shows an exhausted woman. I didn't bother to freshen up my makeup after Emmett asked me to redo the model, and my foundation and concealer no longer hide the dark circles.

Ah well. At least Dad won't know. As far as he's concerned, I'm super happy, super healthy and super awesome—enjoying life to the fullest.

Dad thinks not having a mother around left a mark on me, some kind of hole he can't fill. I know the idea gives him anxiety, which is why I date even though my life would be easier without a boyfriend. I want to show Dad that not having a maternal figure hasn't done *me* any harm.

Of course, that doesn't mean he's going to quit worrying or approve of my dates. He thinks I can do a hundred times better than the guys I've been with. Most men simply are not good enough for his little girl. He even said I'm dating *down*, and I really should date *up*. Aim high. Just like I aimed high when I applied to Harvard, went for Goldman Sachs and entered Wharton.

He doesn't buy my explanation that men aren't like schools and jobs. Having the stability of a family and the devotion of a man who loves me above all else is something Dad has always wanted for me. As far as he's concerned, I can have that with the

50

Harvards and Whartons of men, not the "averages" I've been "settling for."

Whatever. I run the wipe over my face, then take a quick shower to wash off the sweat and...other gunk. Then I put on a nightshirt and fall into bed, kill the bedside lamp and hug my teddy bear. *Okumasama*, who was given a butchered Japanese name because I was too young and didn't know any better.

One sheep... Two sheep...

My eyelids grow heavy. I close my eyes and sigh softly...

"Amy..."

The guttural moan tickles my senses. I imagine the scene...

Emmett. Reclining on a leather couch in his office. His cheeks flushed, his eyes glazed with desire.

"Amy..." He can barely get the word out amid his rough, uneven breathing.

His hand fists around his cock. His shirt sleeves are rolled; tendons flex under the taut skin. The muscles in his jaw bunch as he inhales, his hand moving faster. The buttons on his shirt are undone, revealing his gorgeous chest, which rapidly rises and falls.

I should be scandalized. Outraged. But I feel neither. He's raw and hedonistic as he chases his pleasure, my name nothing more than a soft moan tearing from his chest.

I walk into his office, his domain, licking suddenly dry lips. I can't look away from the tableau before me—lusty and sensual.

Our gazes collide. His mouth parts and his eyes darken.

A hot tingling sensation starts in my chest, making my nipples bead, and streaks down my torso. A whimper rises, and I press my lips together. But when the sensation ends at my clit, I can't contain the sound anymore. The flesh between my legs slickens.

"You're supposed to *work* in your office." I try for a reprimand, but my voice is too uneven and husky to be taken seriously.

"Work hard, play hard." He winks.

"Is that the rule?" I keep my gaze on his, then deliberately reach under my skirt and pull my underwear down my legs.

The hand around his shaft stops moving, but the muscles in his forearm quiver. I slowly skim my hands over my breasts, down my torso. The touch is light through my clothes. I shouldn't feel much, but hot shivers shimmy through me anyway. It's Emmett who's amplifying my pleasure, his increasingly rough breathing urging me to push boundaries.

"Do you want to touch me?" I whisper, mischief in my tone and a dare in my stare. The fact that I can sound like that surprises me. I'm never like this in bed.

"Yes." His eyes are pools of jet. "I wanted to touch you the second we met."

Desire heats my face. The intensity of his need is exciting, but also makes me a little apprehensive. I swallow my nerves, then stiffen my legs to stop from squirming. He's still on his back and I'm the one standing over him. I'm in charge. In control.

"I almost didn't hire you because you're too hot."

I laugh softly. "But I'm here now anyway. Do you often touch yourself thinking of me?"

"Always. I do it fantasizing about you using me for your pleasure."

Then he whispers all the things he imagines I'm doing to him and he's doing to me, every time he grabs his greedy dick. Filthy, dirty, completely inappropriate. The kind of things that would make HR scream in horror. The kind of things that make me even wetter.

My head spins with the raw words pouring out of him. He reaches for me, but I pull away playfully. I bend over his desk, making sure he has a view of my uptilted pelvis and ass. I slide my hand under my skirt—hidden from view, but he knows where it's going—and push my fingers into myself, pretending they're Emmett's thick, hard cock. I tell him what I'm doing, while sliding my other hand under my top, pushing the bra out of the way and cupping my breast.

I moan loudly, letting him know how good I'm feeling with the fingers inside me. Emmett's eyes are glued to what he can't actually see as he abruptly pumps his fist hard and fast. He fights for breath, and his teeth clench.

My own orgasm builds. I rein it back, wanting to see him succumb to pleasure first—

A white stream shoots out of his penis, landing wetly across his chest and belly. His entire body shakes uncontrollably with the aftermath, and the sight makes me feel powerful, in charge and sexy as hell.

The orgasm I've been holding at bay smashes past my control and booms through me, exploding like a bomb. My eyes squeezed shut, I twist and scream. Suddenly Emmett is behind me, flipping my skirt up and pulling my hand from between my thighs as he pushes himself into my slick depths.

He grabs my hips, his hands incredibly strong. I cover my mouth to contain a shriek as he s-l-o-w-l-y pumps in and out a couple of times, but it's no use. I struggle to breathe, then grind against him. I'm going to die if he doesn't—

Buzz. Buzz. Buzz.

Somewhere something keeps buzzing. Emmett curses.

I scrunch my face briefly, then open my eyes and look at the dim ceiling. Light is slicing through the gaps between the curtains. What the...?

I blink as reality reasserts itself. *Bedroom. My own bed. Home.*

Okay. Good. Thank God I didn't do anything inappropriate with Emmett *again*. Still... What kind of dream was *that*?

Nothing good, I decide. See the boss with his dick out, have a quickie with him and I'm having dreams with a whole new triple-X scenario? Good lord. He's hot, and the orgasm was phenomenal, but really? This is not going to help me figure out how to deal with him when we see each other again.

I fumble on the nightstand for my phone. The screen says two past ten a.m. And I have a few texts from Emmett.

Shit, shit, *shit!*

I sit up, feeling like a kid who got caught with her hand in a cookie jar. There's no way Emmett could know what kind of dream I had, but that doesn't make me feel any better.

Besides, now that my head and sanity aren't mired in the thick sludge of sleep deprivation and the peaks and troughs of blood sugar and caffeine, I'm beginning to see how reckless I was last night. I grabbed *Emmett Lasker* and *kissed* him. And not just a peck, but with a tongue down his throat!

Then I had his incredible dick in my very wet vagina.

I bury my face in my hands. I am so screwed.

He could be texting to fire me. The best I can hope for is for him to tell me he's going to call a meeting with HR to "discuss my behavior." I don't know if lack of sleep will be a valid defense. I should consult a lawyer specializing in HR matters.

But first, I should check the texts. Dread twisting my gut into pretzels, I swipe my phone.

–Emmett: We need to wrap up the model. I'm busy in the morning and early afternoon so let's meet at 4:30 to discuss.

"I can't" is not an option here. I read on.

–Emmett: Also send me all the references and data on the commodity and labor pricing so I can review those before our discussion.

–Emmett: You don't have to send the model early, but it should be ready for our meeting.

Huh? That's it? Not even a single word about what happened?

I wait for more texts, but...

My phone stays silent.

I drop my head back on the pillow with mixed emotions. Maybe he's decided to call it even. I mean, he *was* masturbating in the office. Besides, Emmett's been in finance for a long time. The man knows how to keep his mouth shut when necessary, and what happened between us last night isn't something you can talk about at dinner. Especially since it all started with his getting caught doing something inappropriate. There's a reason no scandal involving Emmett Lasker exists. The man is discreet.

Also, he doesn't know that I had a hyper-weird dream fueled by what happened last night. Nor that I'm uncomfortably wet and swollen between my legs after it. Most importantly, he has no clue I'm still feeling this awkward sexual frustration. Or the deep, aching emptiness that some perverted part of me wishes he could ease.

God, this is messed up. I have to see Emmett in less than seven hours.

My optimistic side says that it isn't *that* awful that I want to have sex with him again, even if I do feel like an idiot desperate for another bite of the forbidden fruit. After all, unlike men, if women have some clothes on there aren't any glaringly obvious physical reactions to indicate sexual arousal. So I just have to act calm and collected. As a matter of fact, he'll never find out I got wet dreaming about him because I'm going to wash that off right now.

Plus—and this is *the most* important thing—in less than eight weeks I won't be working for him anymore. All I need to survive seven weeks and six days is a little extra brazenness and shame-lessness. If Emmett can arm himself like that when he's caught in a scandalous situation, so can I.

Today is a new day. And like I decided earlier, everything that happened after eleven fifty-nine p.m. *didn't* happen.

7

EMMETT

It's after ten a.m., so Amy should be up by now. I fire off three texts to her while enjoying my first cup of coffee. I hope she's realized that she can't avoid me forever. She reports to me and no one else.

Sleep—if she got any after our awesome bout; she might've writhed in her bed all night wanting more—should help her reason logically enough to recognize the inevitability. She looked like she'd take about two seconds to conk out. That's the only explanation for why she ran like her skirt was on fire instead of cuddling with me. If she'd given me a moment, I would've turned the damned phone off so we could enjoy each other in peace. So I could lose myself in that addictive flavor of hers, the mesmerizing scent of her citrus body wash and her skin.

But no... She had to run. And who knew the woman could move so fast? By the time I got to my feet, pulled my pants up and made my way out the office to talk to her, she was already gone. I loitered for a few minutes at the elevator bank until it dawned on me she wasn't going to show, especially after a car came and went. And her desk was completely clean, confirming my suspicion.

Really annoying. Unfortunate, too. I wanted to take her to a late-night diner near the office that serves an absolutely awesome breakfast around the clock. Then talk about what happened like adults.

I'd also like to propose we continue to enjoy ourselves like adults. Only with a little more preparation. I had to pull out, since I didn't have a condom. Having sex unprepared isn't something I do, but when she was on me, I lost control. Being inside her felt more important than taking my next breath.

And it was hotter than my dirtiest fantasy. My cock's already hard with the memory of her clenching around it, hot and slick.

I shouldn't be too disappointed that we didn't get to have a talk about the future. I got to keep her thong, which she left behind in her rush. It's a hot black lacy item, and I'm a little sad I didn't really get to see her in it.

But there will be other chances. I'll see her again at four thirty. Earlier than that would be better, but I have a brunch with my brothers. But maybe the timing will work out for the best. I don't want to appear overeager or let her know I relived our hot encounter all night long...even if my dick has been hard for ten hours now.

The main strategy here is to play things cool and make her want to do it again, not have her think I'm obsessed with her, even though I am. Getting a taste of her last night only intensified my hunger.

Since I'm done texting Amy, I check the Pulse feed. And immediately burst out laughing.

Rick on Romance

Hey hey hey, what's up, Romancers? I know you guys have been waiting for the updates from my half-anniversary trip to surprise my girl. But due to some unfortunate technical difficulties, I wasn't able to film our drive to Tahoe.

"Technical difficulties"? Is that what influencers call getting their plans canceled these days?

I'm working on them right now to ensure you get a full view of how the trip goes as much as possible, so you too can surprise and treat your girl. Like always, I'm here to make a difference in your lives and would never leave you hanging.

Working on them. I laugh softly at the ridiculous lie.

What's he going to do? Charter a helicopter to fly Amy to Lake Tahoe after I'm done discussing the model with her? Ha!

He shouldn't call himself her boyfriend. Or act like he has any claim on her. He hasn't earned the right, even if Amy did put him in the boyfriend category.

Besides, from the utterly dazed look on her gorgeous face when she came last night, Rick must be terrible in bed. You don't have to be old to suffer from ED.

Amy got to sample what I have to offer. So after we go over the model, I plan to talk to her about *our* future. Which, number one, involves dumping Rick, if she hasn't decided to do that already. If it weren't for the fact that I kept missing the windows of opportunity when Amy was free, I would've already shown her how the man in her life ought to treat her.

I glance at the comments on Rick's Pulse update, then shake my head at all the *you'll get it done, bro*s and *we're behind you*s. If they only knew what a loser this guy is...!

I put my empty mug in the sink and drive to Huxley's mansion. My brother bought it a couple of years back, but didn't move in until last week because he wanted extensive remodeling done on the first two floors and the garden. He's particular about what he wants, and he doesn't like to settle. That's what makes him good at his job as an ad exec.

When I get to the mansion, I have to admit the upgrades look good. The garden's been ripped apart and redone with plants that won't guzzle up water. Huxley also put in a stone garden, the type he fell in love with during a trip to Japan five years ago. The swimming pool is wide and large, although I don't see the point of having one on the ground when there's one on the rooftop. His helicopter sits on the helipad—another addition.

I walk inside and note the walls have been covered with elegant and tastefully expensive textured wallpaper. The ceilings in different rooms have their own murals, and the living room features stained-glass windows. All in all, the place drips with a sensual opulence that demands to be noticed and admired while somehow avoiding a descent into vulgarity. But then, that's Huxley's forte. It's what makes his clients love him. Grant and I often hire his firm for the ventures GrantEm funds when they're ready to go public.

Some might call it nepotism. I call it hiring the best. If there's somebody who can do better than Huxley, I'm all for signing a contract with them.

My six brothers are already in the dining room. We got our dark hair and square jaws from our father—Ted Lasker. But that's where our facial similarities end. Which makes sense, since we have seven different mothers. On top of that, we're only four months apart in age, me being the oldest and Nicholas the youngest. Huxley is the second oldest, having been born three weeks after me.

A lot of people wonder how the hell something like this could happen, but it's quite simple:

Vasectomy fail.

During those months, Dad was sowing his wild oats with every young, willing woman he could find. And being a movie producer, he's always been able to find a lot. It's actually kind of surprising that he only impregnated seven of them. Statistical probability says there should've been more.

The rumor is that he tried to sue the doctor who performed the vasectomy, even though the man offered a redo for free. I don't blame Dad. I wouldn't go back to a doc who screwed up the first time, even for a freebie. Dad and I are similar in that regard—we prefer efficiency and competence over cost.

Since the second vasectomy, Dad hasn't fathered another child. He has instructed his assistants to select and send appropriate birthday and Christmas gifts to our moms, but he doesn't spend much time with any of them, since he's a busy man.

Trashy tabloid writers occasionally try to trip him up by asking which woman gave him which son. But faced with an impending offspring emergency, Dad came up with a plan: he named us after the women who bore us. My mother's name is Emma. Huxley's mother's last name is Huxley. Grant and Griffin are named for the same reason. Noah and Nicholas got their names because of their moms, Nora and Nicole. Sebastian is the only exception—his mother is a disowned heiress to the Sebastian Jewelry fortune.

Typical Ted Lasker efficiency. And naming us in that fashion saves him the potential embarrassment of not pairing us with the right mothers because he couldn't bother to actually remember anything about his sons. It's never occurred to him how self-centered and thoughtless that is. Other people's feelings are about as important to him as a penny is to a billionaire, even if those people happen to be his own children.

Huxley's dining room is huge, with a table big enough to host a large dinner party. Catered brunch food is spread out—crispy bacon, sausages, eggs benedict, French toast, pancakes and more. Huxley is talented in many things, but he can't cook. Actually, none of us really cooks. I'm about the best because I can fry eggs without setting the pan on fire. It's something Mom forced on me, and which I learned only with reluctance.

Housekeepers exist for a reason. I pay mine to do things for me that I don't want to do myself. It's a much more efficient use of time. And it keeps her gainfully employed with a good salary and benefits.

"Look who's here!" Huxley says, lifting his champagne glass. His blue eyes are sharp enough to cut, and he has a tongue mean enough to flay you mercilessly. Although he isn't the oldest, he takes being the second oldest seriously. Which means he's a bossy asshole.

Sebastian and Nicholas say he just likes to be in charge. I'm okay with that, since Huxley doesn't tell me what to do. He just likes to bitch about how I cheated by popping out of my mother's womb prematurely. But it isn't my fault I was hankering to build an empire of my own. He should blame himself for taking too long, considering he was two weeks late.

"Thought you were working," Grant says, pouring himself some champagne. "On that water filter project."

Noah raises his eyebrows. "You in the water filter business now?" His hair is sticking up like he hasn't combed it in ages. He's probably on some self-imposed deadline and—typically— decided to procrastinate. I don't know why he bothers to set deadlines when he never meets any of them. He's going to be working on his Magnum Opus for the rest of his life. He should give up on novel writing and stick to what he does best—wildlife photography.

"Nah. Just giving money and advice." I take an empty seat between Grant and Sebastian. Sebastian hands me a fresh flute. "I'm going into the office later to wrap up a few things."

"No bloodbath to come?" Nicholas jokes.

I help myself to some food. "What bloodbath?" The only bath I want in the office is a nice, warm one with Amy naked in the tub. But I keep that to myself, since Amy might bolt and try to work for another partner. Working for Sam Andersen would be a de facto demotion, but working for Grant would be considered a lateral move. Not only that, Grant would take her on to soothe her ruffled feathers. She's too damn good at her job. It's that competitive spirit of hers—unyielding and unstoppable.

So no innuendos until she and I have a discussion first. About us.

"There are rumors of associates at GrantEm quietly dying

from lack of sleep," Nicholas says. He owns many different businesses, one being a headhunting and recruiting agency.

"Untrue," Grant says. "Most of them complain loudly as they expire."

"Whatever," I say. "I never give more than they can handle."

Nicholas shakes his head. "If they were clones of you, sure. But they aren't."

He says that all the time. Apparently, I'm too smart and too quick. I resent that because I work damn hard. "I'm in too good of a mood to argue, so I'm going to pretend I didn't hear that."

"You? In good mood?" Huxley says. "Why?"

Because Amy and I had super-hot sex. Not that I plan to announce that in front of my brothers.

After a moment of consideration, he adds, "Did you already figure out what to get for Dad's birthday?"

Ah, shit. "It's his birthday already?" Marjorie hasn't said anything, so I figured I still had plenty of time to decide. Should've known better. She only works nine to five, and she is s-l-o-w. Plus, she hates giving me bad news, especially anything to do with my dad, so she procrastinates as long as she can.

"Five weeks," Grant says.

"Ugh." I *hate* buying stuff for Dad. He has everything a man could possibly want, including more money than me. He doesn't like waiting and isn't shy about voicing his displeasure when he gets something he doesn't want. The phrase "it's the thought that counts" doesn't exist in Dad's lexicon.

I know of one gift he wouldn't complain about: a stripper. But I'm not hiring a stripper for my father's birthday bash. The idea is simply too gross.

"Install one of those fancy filters you're funding in his pool," Noah says. "He'd like that."

"It's not that kind of filter," I say. Even if it were, no filter on earth can clean up what Dad does in his pool. It's disgusting.

"If you don't mind, I have the perfect gift idea," Sebastian says confidently, which scares me a little because Sebastian has a talent for choosing the perfect gift for everyone and every occasion. That's why his mother's side of the family plans to have him lead Sebastian Jewelry one day.

And yes, Sebastian giving us the perfect gift idea for Dad would be great, except it would have to involve something I won't like. Dad doesn't do tasteful.

"Do I want to hear this when I'm not done eating yet?" I ask.

"Sure. It isn't *that* gross. I guarantee he'll laugh and thank us."

"He never laughs or thanks anyone for a present," Nicholas says.

"He will for this one."

"Are we getting him cats?" Griffin says, dread etched on his pretty face. It must've made a lot of girls sign up for his econometrics course, not realizing the hell they were volunteering themselves for. If they got really lucky they ended up with him in behavioral economics, but he only teaches that once in a while.

Huxley snorts. "Pussies, maybe."

I'm skeptical, too. Nicholas is right; Dad basically appreciates nothing. When I got accepted to Stanford, he merely nodded and said, "Tell Joey how much you need for tuition and fees. He'll cut you a check and get you a Maserati. You can pick the color."

It wasn't personal, though. He did that to all of us. When we graduated, he didn't come to graduation for any of us. Said it'd be unfair to go to one and not the others. He booked first-class tickets for our mothers to attend the ceremonies and sent each of us a Lamborghini to replace the Maserati from four years earlier. And then he went and partied in the Bahamas with his harem.

It's just the way he is. And, viewed in a certain light, it's practical. What would I do with some praise from Dad? After a while, I'd probably just forget whatever he said. But his paying for college and giving me brand-new cars have a lasting impact. No student loans to worry about. And some sleek, sexy transportation I could rely on.

Of course, I don't have his Lamborghini anymore. I'm too old to drive Daddy's Lambo. I got myself a new one.

Sebastian leans forward. "Okay. Imagine your ideal type."

"Of what?" Noah says.

"Of woman, obviously."

I gaze beyond my brothers and let my mind wander. It doesn't take long to settle on my ideal type.

Long, soft golden hair I wanted to run my fingers through the moment I laid eyes on her. A lush red mouth that curves into a smile or purses when she thinks. Bright, intelligent blue eyes that never fail to jack up my pulse every time I look into them. A slim body with small, rounded breasts and long legs encased in monochromatic business outfits that beg to be ripped off her. Such sensuality shouldn't be hidden.

She can talk Excel and capitalization for hours without her eyes glazing over. A terrible taste in men, but nobody's perfect. I can overlook that little flaw. Even fix it.

"Now, imagine hiring somebody like that, seven different women, and putting them all into a fake cake," Sebastian says.

Amy in a cake. She should put on something sexy. A red dress. Maybe a bikini. Actually, forget that. Just a red ribbon around her neck.

"Afterward, we have the staff bring it out—"

Mmm, that's hot.

"—right before everyone sings 'Happy Birthday' and have the girls jump out at the end—"

I would *kill* to have Amy pop out of a cake and wish me happy birthday...

"—and give Dad a kiss on his cheek."

Record scratch!

"That's a terrible idea," I state flatly. I can just imagine the scene: Dad trying to sleep with all of them—at the same time. Or they with him. And drama. Lots and lots of drama because there will be other women at the party who want to bang him for reasons that have nothing to do with his personality.

"Oh, I agree it's totally inappropriate. But he'll love it, which means we'll have another year of peace," Sebastian says.

Grant nods. So does Griffin.

"Come on, Emmett," Sebastian says. "If he hates our gifts, he'll have a Christmas party and find some way to force us to attend."

I shudder. Dad's Christmas parties are a punishment. We've had to attend three of them so far. That's where we discovered a whole new meaning to *Santa's little helper* at the tender age of ten, and that's the least of what we learned.

"But giving him strippers in a cake is so...vulgar," Huxley says.

"Got a better idea? I'm open because I don't want to do strippers either, to be honest. Grandpa's going to be pissed if he sees it in the gossip rags." Sebastian's maternal grandparents are super traditional. I'm pretty sure that his mother getting pregnant—out of wedlock—by a marriage-hating serial womanizer is the reason she was disowned.

"He doesn't deserve all those girls," Griffin says morosely. "I wish he'd break something before the party, so none of us would have to go."

I'm not particularly religious, but I'd light a candle or two to make that come true. Unfortunately, Dad's healthy as a horse and he's never broken a bone in his life. The man's like Wolverine.

Huxley looks around the table. "I have a different idea. Might make things more palatable, and he won't complain too much, either."

I down the rest of my champagne, wishing I had something stronger. "Let's hear it."

8

AMY

After I'm done with my shower and am pouring myself a cup of coffee, Sasha comes out of her room, yawning. She's in nothing but a nightshirt, which shows off her long legs and arms. She walks like a ballerina, the result of taking ballet lessons from kindergarten to college.

She runs her fingers through messy hair, then blinks at me. "What are you doing here? I thought you were going to Lake Tahoe?"

"Rick and I broke up." I feel kind of flat about it. More important things from last night are occupying my mind at the moment.

Her jaw drops. "No way!"

"Way. And it happened over text, too." I give her my mug of coffee and pour myself another.

"Thanks." She wraps her slim fingers around the mug and takes the stool next to me. "So what happened?" she asks, obviously wanting to know everything she can about the breakup so she can lend me the moral support I deserve.

I tell her. She listens, her eyes gradually going feral as the story spins out and the caffeine starts to hit her system.

"Oh my *God*! What an asshole!"

"Exactly," I say, and sip my coffee.

"Who does he think he is? Elon Musk?"

I raise my eyebrows. "Elon Musk is your type?" I wonder if Gage looks like the ultra-rich billionaire.

"No. But multibillion bucks is." Sasha lifts her chin with the haughtiness of a prima ballerina. "A man's gotta be that rich before he gets to say, 'Me or the job.' But even that amount of cash wouldn't guarantee I'd pick him."

I laugh. "I can always count on you to make me feel better."

"Girlfriend, some men are junk bonds. Just not worth the investment." Sasha evaluates men like a rating agency. If they aren't investment grade, she won't even look at them. "We didn't put in all those hours and work at Goldman and Wharton to be somebody's girlfriend *for a while*. We're here to *go* to places. And get ourselves some triple-A guys."

I grin, pleased with her support, until a small part of me remembers what else I did last night—showing Emmett what being a cheap sex object feels like. Shit. That's what I really need advice and support on, more than the breakup with Rick.

I don't want to tell her everything straight, though. It's embarrassingly awkward. Plus, although she mainly works with Grant, she does see Emmett around the office. And that could make her feel weird. I certainly wouldn't want to know about Grant's penis or his bedroom—office?—performance.

All right. Time to keep this smooth. And share just enough details to get some guidance. "Hey, I got a question for you."

"I'm all ears."

"There's this girl I know…"

"Uh-huh." She takes a sip of her coffee.

"She kissed her boss." I say it in my most nonchalant voice.

Sasha blinks slowly. "Like a peck kiss? Or a *kiss* kiss with tongue action?"

"Tongue to tonsils. According to the girl."

Her eyes grow wide with curiosity. Sasha loves a good story, although she can be discreet when the situation calls for it. You have to know how to keep a secret to work in finance. People who can't keep their mouths shut ruin their reps or end up in jail. Sometimes both. "Is he hot?"

I recall how Emmett looks. An urge to lick my lips over-whelms me, so I drink my coffee instead. "Yeah. Uh, apparently."

"Did he object to the kiss?"

I think back on the encounter. A lot of it is sort of foggy from the lack of sleep and too much caffeine and low blood sugar, but Emmett did definitely put his tongue in my mouth. That isn't what someone does when they want to quit kissing. "I don't think so." Besides, we did a hell of a lot more than just kiss.

Sasha's dark eyes twinkle. "Does she want to sleep with him?"

Kind of a moot question now! But I pretend to give it some consideration. "No. I don't think so." A depressing and annoying thought pops into my head. "When a female subordinate sleeps with her boss, people assume she boinked her way up the corporate ladder, regardless of the truth." My résumé is freakin' awesome, and I don't want that kind of stain on my work history. Damn it.

"See, that's what's wrong with our culture." Sasha shakes her head. "People are narrow-minded. Nobody ever thinks that the boss could be paying *her* with sex, in addition to whatever salary, to stay at the company and continue to work for him. Bosses with benefits."

I almost spew my coffee. "That's not a thing."

"It should be. *Harvard Business Review* should do a case study on it. Women aren't the only ones who can use their bodies to get what they want." Sasha shrugs. Her attitude stuns me at times, but then, she was raised in France and she's very open about sexuality.

"Men don't offer sex as payment because women don't generally go for it," I point out, thinking about most men I know in my life, including all my ex-boyfriends. "*I* sure wouldn't."

"Obviously. We're more practical than men, and have higher standards. But if Chris Evans said, 'Hey, babe, I want to pay you with sex,' would you say no?"

"I actually prefer Thor." And she should know. Superhero flicks get only one viewing out of me—at most—but the Thor movies all got two despite my hellish schedule.

She rolls her eyes. "Fine. Chris Hemsworth."

I imagine the scenario, except it isn't Chris Hemsworth saying the line, but Emmett. He's sporting that sexy grin, his eyes sparkling silver-blue like moonlight off a river. His mouth slightly red and wet from a hot-as-hell kiss we just shared. While I'm trying to catch my breath, he says, "Hey, babe, I want to pay you with sex."

My cold, logical side says the only correct answer is "Hell no," but the other side—which currently makes up ninety percent —says I should pretend to give it some serious thought and then slowly say yes, so he knows it wasn't an easy yes. Men appreciate what they have to work for.

Oh, for God's sake, what's wrong with me? I slap a hand over my eyes. Given what happened last night, I'll be lucky if Emmett doesn't fire me. Or subject me to whatever his devious mind decides is a suitable punishment. On top of that, I need to see him later today, so I'd better get my head out of the gutter.

Next time I face him, I'm going to be on my best behavior. The perfectly professional Amy Sand, second-year associate at GrantEm Capital with only the purest financial thoughts in her brain.

"Well?" Sasha asks, her eyes glinting with determination. She won't back off until I give her an answer.

"I'd be flattered, but I don't know," I say finally, trying to hide my unsteady heartbeat, while my hormones scream, *Just say yes to Emmett! He can do you good!*

She sighs. "That's depressingly repressed. I'd totally do Thor."

"What about Gage?" I quip.

"He can watch." She laughs lightly, then sobers. "Look, I know you and Emmett have this weird chemistry." Her expression says I'm not fooling anybody.

"What?" My laughter is shaky, but I pray it just sounds light and dismissive to Sasha. "Girl, what are you *talking* about? Emmett and I aren't... You're being ridiculous. I was asking for somebody I know, not *me*. Geez, Sasha."

She gives me a look. "Come on. Everyone at the firm knows. There's a betting pool on when you guys are going to start going out."

"A *what*?"

"You heard me. It's been going on for over a year now."

"Over a *year*?"

She spreads her hands. "It started about two or three months after *we* started. I thought you knew."

"I had no idea! Oh my God! I can barely stand the man!" I didn't, by chance, shoot him a come-hither look without meaning to...did I? Do people think I'm getting ahead by flirting with my boss? Being sexually suggestive? A betting pool means people think Emmett and I haven't slept together, but that doesn't mean they won't speculate. Is that why Marion asked one too many questions about Emmett during the interview? Does he suspect—

"Uh-huh," Sasha says. "All that palpable love-hate. It's hard to hate a man with a face like that, so I understand. We all do."

Obviously, since every time I look at Emmett I'm struck by how hot he is, even while I want to strangle him for torpedoing another of my evenings. Especially when I haven't had much sleep for a while. God must've realized when He created Emmett to be such an asshole, He'd need to give the man something else to ensure his survival. I just wish God had chosen respect for his underlings' private time and need for sleep as the survival-enabling feature. Awe-inspiring male beauty is a problem.

Don't forget his magic orgasm penis, my mind whispers.

Shut the hell up!

Sasha puts a steadying hand out, like I'm a rabid dog frothing at the mouth. "Don't worry. Nobody thinks you're sleeping with him or anything. I mean, *yet.*"

"Yet? *Yet?* I'll have—"

"Yeah, yeah, settle down. Everyone knows you're where you are because you work your ass off. We all see the hours you put in, the deals you've executed. You're also starting to manage and support our portfolio companies, so... You're doing the work of somebody above you. And we saw the annual ranking."

That's a list of the top five performers the firm posts in the break room after the yearly evaluations are done. To make things fair, the grouping is done by rank and year, such as the top five first-year analysts, the top five second-year analysts and so on. The only people who aren't ranked are partners. Probably because their egos couldn't agree on who should be number one.

I was floored when I topped my list last year. Given that Emmett asks me to redo my work almost every day, I didn't expect to see my name up there.

"Everyone at the firm knows you deserve the top spot," Sasha says. "Actually, nobody will be surprised if you top the list again this June. A lot of people outside the firm know it, too. Venture capital is a small world, and people talk."

Sasha would know. She goes to a lot of those get-togethers, unlike me. I wish I could, but I almost never have time off. At least people aren't disparaging my work behind my back.

"You told me you planned to quit in two months," she says.

"Yep. That hasn't changed."

"So... If you want to go for it..." Sasha winks.

"No, no, no." My protest is too quick. So I add, "Even if I didn't work for him anymore, running into him could be awkward if we slept together."

You're a damn liar. His dick in your vagina counts as "sleeping together."

"But you kissed him," Sasha says.

"It wasn't *me*. It was *this girl* I know. I told you that already." Dear lord, I'm turning into Emmett. Utterly shameless. At least I don't have my hand over my bare crotch.

"And tongues were involved..."

Nope. Not admitting anything. "Yeah. Between the girl I know and the boss *she* kissed."

"And you must've liked it enough to talk to me about it."

"Not me. *Her.*"

She steamrolls on. "If you didn't care for it, you would've cut things off."

"I'll tell her that."

"*She* already knows. 'Cause that's how you were with all the guys you've dated."

"What? I'm not, like, unfeeling!"

"Didn't say you were," she says kindly. "But you don't like to waste energy on someone you've decided isn't worth it. You cut your losses and move on. If I hadn't asked you about the trip, you wouldn't have told me about breaking up with Rick until later. Anyway, I think it's admirable that you don't squander your time and focus that way. I could seriously learn some stuff from you."

She's overestimating my...cold-bloodedness. I just haven't met anybody I developed enough feelings for to care so deeply about. But when I do, I plan to get serious and marry the guy.

"Anyway, all I'm saying is if you want to do more than just explore Emmett's esophagus with your tongue, it's not going to hurt your rep. That's all." She taps the countertop with her fingers. "I would totally take advantage of him if I were in your shoes. The best time to do a hot dude from your office is right before you're about to quit. That way, if things don't go well, you don't have to see him again."

She makes great points. If I go to work for Marion Blaire, I definitely won't run into Emmett again anytime soon.

Sasha has no clue how tempting her suggestion sounds. Especially after that mind-destroying sex and my filthy dream involving Emmett and other positions we could try to see if the last night's orgasm was a fluke.

My hormones scream it is totally replicable—and I should do him again.

9

AMY

I'm in the lobby at four twenty-five p.m., waiting for one of the elevators to come down from the upper floors they've been at—some poor suckers are working the weekend like me—and grateful for the modern technology that enables me to effortlessly get to the thirty-fifth floor. If I had to climb that many stairs, I'd just collapse right here and cry.

The lobby is empty except for a few people who have the employee pass to bypass the main lock. Security's off today because expecting security to work on weekends is cruel and unusual, although expecting everyone else to do it is apparently totally fair.

I mentally chastise myself for being petty. The office is in the nicest part of the city. Nobody's going to come in to rob us on a weekend. Not that anybody tries to rob us during the week, either.

I pull out my phone to check messages. Nothing from Dad or Emmett. But there are over one hundred unread texts from Rick.

I've already made myself clear. There's nothing left between us that requires this many messages.

Out of morbid curiosity, I open the conversation thread.

74

–Rick: You can't do this to me!

Sure I can. This one came almost immediately after I told him I'd pick my career over him. He must've been glued to his phone to reply so fast.

–Rick: Our relationship can't be tossed out like garbage.

–Rick: Do you hear me?

–Rick: I can't believe this! Do you think you're going to get a nicer and more understanding boyfriend than me?

Wow. Doesn't he get tired of saying the same thing over a hundred times? He should at least consider copying and pasting to spare his thumbs.

–Rick: And I'll prove it right now. I'll give you another chance.

Seriously pathetic. Besides, he has to have some inkling that he isn't as into me as he claims. Every time we manage to go out, he's more interested in taking selfies and photos of the restaurants and food and posting them online than he is in me. He also makes sure to write a descriptive sentence or two and add all the appropriate hashtags. Half our time is spent updating his Pulse feed. That is not the behavior of a man who's into his girl.

I continue scrolling. Rick got a bit more creative after three a.m. Staying up that late text-bombing your ex is the privilege of a man who enjoys an overabundance of sleep.

He should have just gone to sleep in that nice, rustic cabin in Tahoe. He knows I don't stay up unless I absolutely have to. By three in the morning I'm dead to the world.

Except yesterday. While Rick was up messaging me, I was having my X-rated dream about Emmett—

Stop thinking about that dream!

Actually, I need to stop thinking about everything that happened *right now* if I'm going to face my boss.

I scroll through Rick's more recent texts. No other choice, since all the major markets are closed and there's no financial news to check.

—Rick: You think your job means something now, but at the end of day, jobs are nothing. Interchangeable. People are unique.

I purse my mouth. I've met people I later found to be boring and interchangeable. Mostly men who get upset when they realize my career is important to me.

—Rick: Jobs don't keep you warm at night, babe.

They keep me fed. They also pay for my student loans. Does he know student loans aren't dischargeable through bankruptcy? You have to be dead to be free of them. But I value my life too much to die, so I need a good-paying job. Like the one I have.

I don't bother to text my thoughts because Rick wouldn't understand. He dropped out of college and brags that was the best decision he's ever made. Of course, he also whines endlessly about the student loans he has to pay back.

Yeah, there's no refund if you quit, either.

—Rick: Jobs don't give you babies.

Does he think I want to have *his* babies?

—Rick: Nobody writes HERE LIES A CAPITALIST on their headstone!

"Nobody writes, 'Here lies some dude's girlfriend,' on their headstone, either," Emmett says from behind me.

I almost jump out of my shoes. Emmett sounds mildly amused and condescending. Of course, he's *exactly* the type of guy who'd write, "Here lies a capitalist," on his headstone.

"Are you reading my texts?" I ask, too dumbfounded at this behavior to pull off the cool and natural act I was hoping for. He's never done this—but then, we'd never kissed or had sex before. Does he think he's entitled to read my texts now because of what happened last night?

No! Nothing happened last night after eleven fifty-nine p.m.!

Praying Emmett can't sense my racing pulse, I watch closely for any sign of I-slept-with-you-heh-heh-heh or that things have changed between us. He isn't smirking or giving me a lusty look. Just behaving like he always does—with a sense of intellectual superiority over all of us mere mortals.

"In fact, I am." He leans closer to squint at my screen. I go still as his spicy, scent flows over me. There's a faint whiff of spearmint on his breath, a fresh, cool smell of soap on his skin. The heat from his body envelops me. The lust I felt during my dream stirs, warming my blood. My toes curl in my shoes. The emptiness inside me grows more intense, emptier.

I hold my breath to avoid inhaling any more of his addictive scent and stiffen my knees so I don't fidget. Based on his attitude, I'm almost certain he's more or less forgotten about the sex. It was great for me, but Emmett Lasker probably has great sex all the time. Pretty women are always on his arm at various social functions. And I'm not naïve enough to think that they only touch him up to his elbows.

Hold on a minute. That redhead! The one he was debating between diamonds and pearls for! Isn't he dating her?

But if he is, why did he say *my* name while having solo fun in his...?

Unless... *Her* name is Amy, too...

Oh *shit*. But I can't ask him now. If he's acting like nothing's happened, I'm certainly not going to drag us into that minefield.

"Doesn't he sleep?" Emmett's voice holds a hint of contempt. "Or have things to do? When did you break up with him?"

My gut tells me he's also saying, "I can't believe you stayed with him this long," which makes no sense—and, annoyingly enough, cranks up my shame and defensiveness. He doesn't know Rick. I've never discussed my personal life with Emmett. And I'd bet my bonus he didn't even know I was dating.

"Yesterday." The answer is clipped to discourage further discussion. I don't want to talk to Emmett about Rick. Doing so would be as embarrassing as discussing a finger painting I did in kindergarten with Picasso.

"Why?" Emmett says.

Guess he's going for his *shamelessly obtuse* tack again. I look at the elevators. A car is waiting.

I step up and press the button, and of course Emmett follows right after me. But there's nothing to be done about it. The doors shut, and the car starts to ascend.

Emmett is standing close enough to look at my screen if he wants. He smells even better in the enclosed space. The elevator, which is big enough to accommodate at least twelve adults, seems tiny. I feel like a trapped animal.

"So... You going to answer my question?" His tone says he will have his answer.

Demanding bosshole! "He was upset that I canceled our plans, so he was like, 'Me or the job,' and I said the job," I say very fast, praying he only catches maybe a quarter of what I'm saying but is satisfied anyway. Also, I didn't technically *cancel*, but I don't want to get into details with Emmett. It's already embarrassing enough that he's read those pathetic texts from Rick. Emmett's probably judging me for sure now—*how could you be so blind as to date somebody this awful?*

In my defense, I dumped Rick. Still... I should've known even before I started. Done my due diligence, like I always do when GrantEm is doing market and industry assessments. If I had, I would've known Rick was junk and not wasted my precious time on a doomed relationship.

Emmett beams like an athlete who just set a world record at the Olympic Games. "I didn't hear you. Say that again."

I squint up at him. He totally heard every word out of my mouth. Is this some kind of weird torment he's adopted because he's upset about me barging in on him last night? Or maybe he's annoyed about the kiss-turned-sex, which made him feel extra cheap?

I want to keep my mouth shut, but he looks too expectant. He hasn't okayed my Excel model. I should humor him until then.

"He was upset I canceled our plans on him, so he said, 'Me or the job,' and I said job," I repeat.

Emmett nods. By then, we're on our floor, thank God!

"My office," he says, all brisk and back to business.

I sag with relief at the change in demeanor. I can handle professional Emmett.

On the other hand... His office means the scene of crime. I just hope it doesn't remind him of what happened last night, especially when he's acting normal—irritating and bossy.

I also hope there's no sign of my thong.

Actually, scratch that. No sign would probably mean he picked it up, although I can't picture him bending down to pick up someone's already-worn underwear. Hopefully, I'll find it before he does and can subtly take care of it.

I follow him into his office, make sure to take the *other* couch and boot my laptop while surreptitiously scanning the area under the couch of shame.

Nothing. Did he fling it somewhere last night after ripping it off me? The details were lost in the haze of pleasure.

I hope it's in some dark corner of his office, to be discovered by a janitor. That would be less embarrassing than Emmett keeping it. And a janitor won't know who it belongs to. He'll just assume Emmett's a perv.

I steal a quick look in my boss's direction. Did he just smirk?

Oh yes he did. He might not have found my thong, but he hasn't forgotten a thing about last night. I inhale deeply. Gotta re-center myself.

Should we discuss what happened last night and set things straight? Nobody's in the office, so it's a perfect time. But he isn't hinting he wants to talk about it, which I guess means that we should pretend like it never happened.

More than fine by me.

Clinging to what's left of my sanity and professionalism, I pull up Excel. I quickly plug the missing projections and assumptions into the model. The work that took me over an hour last night only takes minutes with my brain functioning better. Why can't Emmett let me sleep more regularly?

He reviews the exhibits and projections I sent him this

morning while I tinker with Excel. I tell myself it doesn't matter what his verdict is. I plan on spending this evening working.

"Okay. This looks good," he says finally.

I freeze. *Did I hear that right?* This is the first time he's told me everything looks fine without asking for corrections. This is almost as surreal as me walking in on him and kissing him and... stuff last night.

Just to be sure, I say, "Really?"

"Yeah. Nice work."

I search for a sign that his response has something to do with the fact that we had sex. But he looks like he always does when he provides feedback on my work.

"Exactly what I expected," he says.

Oh wow. I should definitely buy a lottery ticket today. "Well...great. I'm glad."

He peers at me over his laptop screen. "Do you know why I needed them today?"

The way he looks at me makes me feel like a math-challenged high school senior in trig class. But I know better than to fake that I know. Emmett Lasker smells bullshit better than a shark smells blood. "Not really."

"It's important to have all the data and trends about manufacturing and distribution of the prototype before heading into a meeting with potential partners. It helps us get the best deal. Bernie has some good ideas, but he doesn't have a financial mindset. That's where we come in, and we can't go into a war without ammunition."

That makes sense. Unlike some venture capital firms, GrantEm Capital doesn't merely provide funding to entrepreneurs with big ideas. The firm also hand-holds them, making sure that everything they do meets all the regulatory requirements, the deals they make are fair and scalable and so on. Most ventures fail spectacularly. But our support ensures that the entrepreneurs we fund have the best possible chance at success.

"Do you think the portable water filter and desalination

device he wants to make are viable?" I ask, curious about exactly what Emmett envisions with this venture. Bernie Schumacher's idea is huge, and if it takes off, it'll change the world in ways I probably can't imagine, similar to how before Amazon came along people couldn't have visualized how online commerce and publishing would be transformed. I understand numbers and projections, but I don't always see how an idea, investment and timing can all mesh into a lever that revolutionizes an entire sector.

"No telling at this point, but I hope so. Clean water is scarce in a lot of the world, and easy access would make all the difference in a lot of people's lives. Just imagine what could happen if people don't have to waste their entire morning walking two miles down to a river to get water. I mean, *children* have to do this. If we have this, they could go to school instead." Emmett's eyes shine.

Anybody else, and I'd say he was thrilled with the possibility of making the world a better place. But with Emmett, I can't decide if he's excited about the vision of how this venture he's funding might improve the quality of people's lives or if it's all the money he could make if it succeeds. Given his demon-boss nature, probably the latter.

"Water doesn't sound sexy," he continues, "but only because people like you and me have enough. To someone who doesn't..."

He sounds like he truly believes in the idea. Despite knowing his profit drive as well as I do, even *I* buy into the vision he's weaving. It makes me want to be part of the team that makes it possible.

The man is a devil. He probably keeps a pitchfork somewhere in this office. But the late-afternoon sunlight pouring in through the windows behind him creates a gorgeous golden halo around his body. It's difficult not to just become mesmerized with him. He's so beautiful, like an angel. This is why even though he's a pain in the ass to deal with, he can still get my libido worked up.

I don't know how long I stare at him before he says, "So. The Excel model."

I shake myself, my cheeks heating with embarrassment. I clear my throat. "Yeah. Um...right here. Let me share it with you." I enable the collaboration tool so he can look at the file and make corrections at the same time and I can see what he's doing.

"No need for that." He comes to the couch and sits down next to me. "Let's just look it over together."

All my senses go on full alert. The blood in my veins heats, rushing faster, warming my skin despite the cool air in the office. I keep my hands steady and open the file.

He leans toward me, his body closing the gap even though I angled the laptop screen so he wouldn't have to lean *quite* this close. His hot scent revives and then begins to stoke the sexual frustration from my dream.

Good God, Amy. Be cool, girl, be cool!

So far he's been acting like nothing unusual happened last night, which probably means we're on the same page and he scrubbed it from his memory. I don't want to disrupt our mutual fake amnesia by doing anything that might remind him of *that* sex. It might annoy him enough to have him consider moving me to another team. His half-brother Grant Lasker's team is full, but there is a junior partner, Sam Andersen, who could use another associate working for him. That would be career suicide.

Not because there's anything wrong with Sam. But having Emmett Lasker dumping me in Sam's lap would signal to everyone that I didn't measure up to his expectations. It would shatter the reputation I've built from all the stellar deals I've executed. Everyone in the industry would pity me, and they'd whisper about what I must've done wrong to earn such a shocking demotion, barely an inch away from getting fired. People would question my ability, my dedication, and head-hunters—and interviewers at other firms—would want to know why.

"Emmett Lasker felt dirty and used because I caught him

doing something private at night, which led to us having sex, and afterward I ran out on him" isn't something I would ever be able to share. I wouldn't even be able to hide behind an NDA, because then they'd *really* speculate.

Think of something that will kill that empty achiness that's starting.

On cue, my mind flashes an image of Rick's naked penis. Smaller and not as impressive as Emmett's. Now that I think about it, not as well formed, either. And sort of pathetic and sad when it's limp, just hanging between his legs like a not-so-well-filled sausage.

I grimace, all the inappropriate thoughts about Emmett gone from my head. I forcibly push the disgusting image of Rick's penis out of my mind, too. *I'm in the office—what the hell is wrong with me?*

"Good," Emmett says slowly, as I click through all the tabs. "Good."

I relax. Maybe this is one of those rare weekends where the stars of twenty galaxies line up. Having tomorrow off is going to be amazing. Excitement is already bubbling, like I'm a kid before Christmas.

I'm definitely buying that lottery ticket!

"Glad you like it. So what's this version for?" I keep my tone smooth and professional. "To show the partners the venture's solid even if we have a recession?"

"Nah." Emmett reaches over and presses the save icon for the Excel file. It obediently responds—without giving him the attitude it gave me last night. "The one you gave me on Friday was great."

What...?

"This one is purely for your own good."

"My own good?" *Please tell me I misheard.*

"Yeah. It's good to redo models under various different scenarios. Helps you see the bigger picture. It's an excellent training exercise, and fun to do."

An excellent training exercise? Fun to do?

He had me stay past midnight on a Friday for a *training exercise?*

He's beaming at me like he's proud.

Oh, yes, he did. And he's *pleased.*

I take back what I said about him hot enough to work up my libido. I want to murder this son of a bitch.

"You look unhappy," Emmett says, the smile still on his I-don't-have-the-faintest-clue-why-that's-the-case face.

"Do you think that this *exercise* could maybe have waited until Monday?" I say in my calmest, deadliest voice, while fantasizing about wrapping my hands around his neck and squeezing. Emmett has a strong-looking neck, but I'll bet that right at the moment I could pop his head off it like a grape.

He seems oblivious to my mood. "No, it couldn't have. You've got a meeting to attend on Monday, and you're leading due diligence for the Drone project."

"So... The training *had* to happen on Friday. Right as I was about to leave."

He nods, wearing an expression that says he can't believe he needs to answer such an elementary question. "That's what I decided. Are you upset because you had to break up with your boyfriend?"

Is that what Emmett thinks? He's supposed to feel like a piece of shit for making me stay late to do something that wasn't essential or urgent! "No!"

But honestly, maybe *a little*, because breaking up is stressful, even though it was the right thing to do. With Rick's attitude the way it is, a breakup was inevitable. The fact that it happened last night actually saved me some time and effort. I don't want to invest in a relationship that's doomed to fail because my boyfriend doesn't respect what makes me *me*.

"Well, then. I don't see what the problem is." Emmett's tone says, *Do you?*

"The problem is the fact that the work wasn't needed for the meeting on Monday."

"But it's for your personal development."

I'm not going to win this argument. Besides, I only have seven weeks and six days left to go at GrantEm. Do I want to waste my time and energy arguing? "Fine," I say grudgingly.

He shoots me an expectant smile.

I stare back at him. I already handed over the exhibits and references. And the Excel model, which he seems satisfied with. What am I missing?

Maybe he wants to talk about sex now.

Nope. Not going there first.

"Aren't you going to thank me?" he says.

"*Thank* you?" It comes out as a whisper. No jumping to conclusions, since who knows what's going through that evil mind of his. I maintain a strained control over myself. "For what, exactly, would I be thanking you?"

He spreads his hands. "For the training! Unlike Wharton, I'm paying you to learn."

"Giving me on-the-job training is part of your responsibility as my boss." *So don't even think about wrangling undeserved "thank you" out of me.* I gather my things. "Do you need anything else?" I ask in my coldest and most professional tone. "Any more training on modeling and valuation, perhaps?"

He props his arm on the back of the couch and rests his temple on the tip of his index finger. A smug smile on his too-fucking-handsome face. "No, I don't believe so."

"Great. I'll see you on Monday."

Before he can say anything else, I open the door. The smile on his face has transformed, and he looks like a cat that just caught himself a bird he's been eyeing for ages.

10

AMY

I hit the button to call one of the elevators to take me to the lobby and try to focus on the positive. The meeting went *much* better than I expected. The review only took an hour, so I'm out of here before six. And he didn't ask for corrections or redos, which is a minor miracle. After I buy that lottery ticket, I should go to the beach, hold my arms out and see if the Pacific will part itself for me.

Now I just have to get into an elevator, *by myself,* and make my escape. And soon I'll be escaping from GrantEm Capital and Emmett Lasker as well.

It's going to be a long seven weeks and six days. But I can do it, and without murdering my infuriating boss for giving me busy-work for fun. He's not worth going to jail for.

Yeah, but he's worth another screw.

Shut up, shut up, shut up!

"You don't have to run out like I'm some plague carrier. I'm healthy as a horse—I mean, a stallion."

Emmett. *I knew it!* I knew things were going too well.

No parting of the sea. It's too late to take the emergency exit now, not that I'm capable of climbing down thirty-five stories' worth of stairs again. "I just want to get home and watch some Netflix." I smile, keeping my eyes on the closed doors in front of me.

Ding!

The doors open. Argh. Three seconds too late! I could've had the entire car to myself!

I gesture with a flourish. "After you."

He steps inside, then looks at me.

Oh no. I'm not making the same mistake again. "Have a good evening." I give him a small wave.

He pushes the button to keep the doors open. "It's big enough for us to share."

But I don't want to have another elevator ride with you. "I like the one on the right better. It's kind of a superstition."

He cocks an eyebrow. "I would've never guessed that by the number of times I've seen you riding here in the left one."

I doubt he's observed me that closely. More like he's going off a statistical probability. How annoying. "I ride the left one on even-numbered days."

"But you didn't yesterday."

"Yesterday was an exception. Wrong phase of the moon."

He gives me a what-bullshit smile. "Then I'll wait with you to see what's so special about the right elevator on odd-numbered days. Meanwhile, I might use the time productively and think of some extra training for you today."

For a fraction of a second I freeze, wondering if this is some kind of innuendo. But so far, his behavior has been completely professional.

Regardless, I absolutely refuse to spend the rest of the evening creating an Excel model for his amusement. "Is that a threat?" By all that is holy, I want to tie him up, toss him on the street and run him over a few times.

"No. I'm informing you of a possible training opportunity.

You'd have to give up Netflix, of course, but the training would be quite instructive."

"I wouldn't want to impose on you that way, especially after the brilliant training you came up with on Friday." I step into the elevator with him. Being stuck together for a few minutes is worth not having to do more bullshit "training."

"I always like it that you're considerate. And since I'm feeling agreeable, I won't ask you to draft the negotiation pointers and memos for Bernie so he can review them before the meeting on Monday." Emmett says it like a king granting a favor to a peasant.

He wouldn't have brought up something this specific if it wasn't something that needs to be done. "Who's going to do it?" *Whose work will I need to review over the weekend?*

"Me." His tone says, *Who else?*

Awesome. That means I won't have to review anything, but... "Don't you ever go home and just enjoy your free time?" I blurt out before I can catch myself.

"Sure." Emmett grins. "I do a lot of things in my free time."

"Like dating." I bite my tongue as soon as the words slip out. Why am I talking our conversation to something so personal? Is it his scent working on me again? Or maybe this is some kind of subconscious resentment and a need to talk to him because he shouldn't have done any of the things he did yesterday. Admittedly, I lost my head because of fury and a lack of sleep...but he shouldn't have responded to me. Or tried to go for a second helping when his phone kept buzzing.

He gives me a look. "Dating?"

Let's see how long you can play dumb. "You know. I saw a picture of you with some redhead at a gala earlier this month."

"Oh, her?" He shrugs. "We're not dating. We just attended the event together."

"Then why did you text me about 'diamonds or pearls'?"

"Did I?"

The elevator finally reaches the lobby. We walk out together, crossing the marble floor to the main entrance.

When Emmett still appears nonplussed, I roll my eyes inwardly and decide to help. "Yesterday morning?"

"Oh, that's right. No, that was for a market survey."

"Market survey?" I wait a few beats for him to elaborate. "Shouldn't you be delegating that sort of things to an analyst?"

"They can't handle it." He reaches for the huge, tinted glass door and holds it open for me.

I doubt that. I've never seen him talk to an analyst about a market survey, and none of the analysts have ever mentioned working on one, either. In addition, he's been asking me to pick this or that since I started at the firm. What market survey lasts that long? Of course, he could've just made up a series of market surveys for "fun" and "training."

This man needs a hobby. Something wholesome and harmless, like stamp collecting. He's so anal and exacting, it's precisely the kind of thing he'd enjoy. He can organize stamps by country, year, commemorative event and more. And quit asking me to pick between two different types of gemstones or vacation spots or clothes or whatever that happens to pop into his head.

As we exit the building, I open my mouth to suggest—

"I knew it! Working late, my ass!"

Rick's shriek pierces the air like an ice pick. I start, then swivel my head.

He's standing in front of the main door. He probably picked this location to loiter since it's the one closest to the garage on the other side of the street. His face is so red, his neck so stiff, he looks like he's about to pass out from hypertension.

"When did you get back from Tahoe?"

He rants like he hasn't heard me. "Job, really? You left me for this slick piece of shit?" He gestures at Emmett, who is observing the situation with eyes that are positively sparkling.

My stomach starts to hurt. When Emmett Lasker gets that look, nothing ends well.

"Who is this, Amy?" he asks.

"An *ex*-boyfriend."

Thank God I get to put Rick in the "ex" category. Still, it's embarrassing. He's making a scene in front of my office building. At least it's a Saturday.

I pray that nobody else from the office is working late today. I wish I'd checked. If anybody from GrantEm witnesses this, it'll hit gossip central faster than the speed of light. When you have no life of your own, you live vicariously through others. And nobody does that better than people in finance.

And then it happens. Valerie, a second-year analyst at the firm, walks by in a T-shirt and yoga pants. She lives in a studio apartment near the office and must have been at some fitness center nearby. Her hobby is gossip, which she claims is "networking." She takes out a phone and holds it in front of her. Shit!

"Ooooh... The guy you didn't get to spend time with because we were together yesterday evening...and last night," Emmett says, totally unhelpful. Not only that, he's painting the wrong kind of picture for Rick, which is seriously annoying. When I marched into his office, I was already through with Rick.

But Emmett isn't finished. "And I *think* we went into early Saturday morning. And just now, too, of course."

Argh! Why doesn't he just pour gasoline on the whole situation and fan the flames?

"You need to go home," I say to Rick. *And quit embarrassing me.* Ex-boyfriends are supposed to stay in the past, not the present.

Rick isn't listening, though. "You're picking *this*? Over *me*? Slick packaging over something genuine and real?"

"Yeah, Amy. Say it ain't so. Tell him neigh," Emmett says, putting a weird tremor into the last word, like he's a donkey.

Rick turns redder. "Picking your job over me, my ass! You were just looking for a way to end what we have so you could make me the villain. For this...this..." He points at Emmett, his finger quivering. "I don't even know what to call him."

Emmett smiles at Rick. "Don't worry, buddy. Happens all the time. I often strike people speechless with wonder and awe."

"Shouldn't you be in Tahoe?" I say to Rick, hoping to distract him before he gets any crazier. He might not care about his dignity, but I care about mine.

"I couldn't go with you cheating on me with this... this...*person*."

"I *never* cheated on you!"

Rick ignores me. He glares at Emmett, sizing him up—the expensive clothes, the watch that cost more than what most people make in a year, the four-figure haircut, and the towering height, a good five or six inches taller than Rick. My ex-boyfriend's eyes are bright with calculation. It doesn't take long for him to realize he comes up short. Way short.

That obviously isn't what he wanted in the situation. I was supposed to sink into misery and regret over losing him. Envious rage sparks behind his eyes.

"I should've known you were cheating," he says, obviously clinging to the belief that he's the poor victim. "And what kind of asshole steals another man's girlfriend?"

Fucking Rick. He's a talking cockroach!

Emmett looks at his watch. "We should get going. Our dinner reservation is at six."

What? There's no "dinner reservation" on my calendar!

Rick sticks his arms out, pointing accusingly at me and Emmett. "You fuckers! You aren't even trying to hide it!"

"Neigh." Emmett does that weird donkey thing again, although maybe it's a horse. "It's at Lux," he adds, like Rick hasn't yelled loud enough to alert every media outlet in the city. "I asked them for seven courses. You can pick the entrées once we get there, Amy."

What the hell is this? Something to make up for the Friday "incident"? A backhanded attempt to get me out on a date?

Rick is frowning like he's completely lost. Not surprising. Lux is one of those restaurants without a set menu or price. You pick the number of courses you want, tell them about any prefer-ences or allergies and the chef will create a culinary masterpiece.

Basically, if you have to ask about the price, you can't afford it. The only reason I know about the place at all is because GrantEm rented the entire restaurant for a Christmas party my first year at the firm.

I debate my options. One, ignore Rick, run back to the office and stay there until he goes away. But I have a feeling that would only embolden him.

Two, drag him away and talk some sense into him once he calms down. Make him accept that it's over between us. He should realize losing control only encourages my boss to be more outrageous. One of the reasons Emmett is a difficult man to work for is that he doesn't believe in de-escalation. When it amuses him, he'll pour gasoline by the metric ton onto any fire. The man needs therapy.

Three—

"Hey, man. Are you *ignoring* me?" Rick glares at Emmett, trying to turn the focus back on himself. He isn't totally stupid—he isn't getting physically violent with Emmett, who's both larger and taller. Rick isn't really out of shape, but he doesn't exactly exude male strength and power. "You think you're better than me because you've got some money?"

Emmett turns to me, his eyes lit with a devilish gleam.

Oh no...

"I assumed that my dominant personality was keeping him quiet, but I just realized that isn't it. Remember that earbud prototype we were working on? The one for muting idiots? I put it in this morning. Based on its performance so far, I'd say it's ready for mass production." He smiles happily.

I choke back a laugh. It's unexpected, and Rick deserves it, but unlike Emmett, I'm all for de-escalation.

Rick's jaw drops, his face now completely scarlet. "Are you calling me an idiot, you asshole?"

"No, I just think it's cute the way you part your teeth down the middle."

I cover my mouth as horror and amusement tug me in different directions.

Emmett pulls out his phone and starts texting.

Rick takes a step toward Emmett. I grab my hideous ex-boyfriend by the arm and pull.

"Come on," I say through clenched teeth. "Stop embarrassing yourself."

He snatches his arm out of my grip. "What have *I* got to be embarrassed about? I'm not the one in the wrong here!"

"Asking me to choose between you and my job was absolutely wrong. You knew I'd never choose you."

He looks like someone smacked him in the face with a rolled newspaper. "Never—? Of *course* you'd choose me! It's not like you have a bunch of other options. Nobody wants a woman who works all the time and only thinks about herself and what she wants. I was trying to *mold* you—"

"Into what? A Stepford wife?"

"No! Into a better, caring human being worthy of living on this precious planet."

Wow. Talk about telling me how he *really* feels. "Oh, okay. So I'm not worthy of living on the planet the way I am now."

He tilts his chin up. "Amy, you've got enormous potential. Just a little guidance and work and you'll be fine."

"I am *so* glad I dumped you. You're a piece of work, Rick."

"You made me—"

"No. I didn't make you do anything. You're just a pig, and I didn't see that until now."

Uniformed security guards appear from the building and hurry over, looking at Emmett questioningly. He points at me.

"Is everything okay, miss?" one of them says.

"No," I say, stunned that they're actually working on a weekend and annoyed that they didn't do something about Rick sooner. "This man is harassing me."

The security guards close in around a screaming Rick, who

threatens them with the dire consequence of having the entire encounter posted on social media.

Emmett gestures at Valerie. Under normal circumstances, I'd assume the boss was trying to get a subordinate to shut her mouth about what happened. But with Emmett, it's hard to tell what he'll do next to amuse himself.

I start walking toward my car. I've had my daily limit of shitshow.

"Amy, wait," Emmett calls from behind me.

I can't hear you! I keep on walking, doing my best to pretend that the confrontation with Rick didn't happen. What the world really needs is an earbud device that mutes bosses during personal time.

"I got the video."

That makes me stop and turn around so fast I actually wobble a bit. "What video?"

He waves his phone. "Valerie filmed the whole thing."

Oh no. "Did she upload it anywhere?"

"No. I stopped her before she could."

A good deed deserves recognition. "Thank you," I say. For this act of kindness, I suppose I can stop calling him bosshole or the boss from hell.

"And I told security to deal with your ex-boyfriend if he shows up again," Emmett says.

"Good. Thank you." I sigh. Hopefully, Rick won't return for round two, but you never know when an ex will decide to be an unhinged, sexist butthole. "Where were the guards?"

"They usually stay in the back on weekends, monitoring the cameras. Staffing is limited," Emmett says. "Anyway, want to get a drink?"

"Right now?"

"No, a year into the future. Yes, right now. You look like you could use one."

"I'll probably need a vat of alcohol to get over the trauma."

"That's fine. I'm buying."

I eye him suspiciously. *What's the catch?* He's being way too nice, and that's generally not a good sign.

On the other hand, why not? I won't turn it down, even though a little voice warns that there's no free lunch.

11

AMY

The bar, located close to the GrantEm offices, is one the firm often uses for happy hours. It's dimly lit and cozy without seeming small, and the guy serving us is a tall, morose-looking fellow named Satoshi. By the time he hands me my fifth cocktail, I'm feeling *much* better about the world. Emmett did good when he brought me here.

And the best and weirdest thing? My boss is actually behaving like a gentleman. He hasn't made a single suggestive comment. Nothing about us entering into a "merger" or how he'd like a chance to verify my "assets."

I can't decide if I'm disappointed or relieved. The fact that I'm conflicted probably means there's something wrong with me. Or maybe all this alcohol is impairing my logic. In Greek mythology, the god of wine is also the god of orgies. There's probably a reason...

"You aren't drinking wine," Emmett points out.

"I know." And I'm not thinking orgiastic sex with Emmett, either. That is *not* happening. We're both sharing that particular amnesia.

Emmett frowns. "I don't have amnesia."

"Not just you. Me too." For some reason, that's funny. "Our-nesia! Hahaha."

Emmett looks at me. "Good one. Maybe you—"

"Maybe I should get my vision checked. Things are looking a little blurry." Emmett isn't blurry, but then, he's sitting next to me at the bar. That's important. He needs to pay for all this. He said he'd pay, and I'm holding him to it.

"I was going to say, maybe you should make that your last drink." A corner of Emmett's mouth quirks up.

"Why?"

"Because you're already drunk?"

"Am not." I knock back the rest of my cosmopolitan. "Stop trying to cut me off. I'm getting my money's worth. 'Sides, if I get shitfaced after only five drinks, it's your fault." My recent lack of drinking practice has lowered my tolerance. I'm going to file an HR complaint for violation of my work-life balance!

"HR won't care," he says.

"How do you know?" I blink up at him. "Hey, are you reading my mind?"

"No. You just told me."

"Did not. Stop lying. I want another drink."

"I think you've had enough."

"Cheap is not sexy, Emmett." I gesture at my empty glass. "This is, like, one-millionth of your fortune. Not even. You could put your hand between your couch cushions and scoop up a couple hundred bucks in change."

He rolls his eyes. He's actually sort of cute when he's exasperated. I don't know why this is different from when he's upset at the office. Maybe it's being in a bar. Hard to take a guy who's buying you a drink or five seriously, although I have no idea why. It isn't the sex, because I took him very seriously in the office earlier today. I should talk to Sasha about that, without mentioning the sex part.

"I'm not cute, I'm hot. And that has nothing to do with money," he says.

"I think it does." *Cheapo!* If I'd known he was going to be this stingy, I would've gone to a bar by myself. It isn't like I asked him to pay off my student loan! He shouldn't act like I'm demanding so much. He's a billionaire. He can afford to buy more. I'm barely even tipsy.

He looks pained. "Do you realize you say everything out loud when you're drunk?"

"That's a very creative reason to cut me off before I've had my fill. But no, I do not," I say primly.

"Yes, you do. And you are. So why don't we make this your last dr—"

"You can't make me. We aren't working right now, so you can't boss me around. You're not the boss of me right now! You're just, you know..."

"What?"

"A guy paying for my drinks." And a guy I had angry sex with, but we aren't going to talk about that.

I gesture at Satoshi. He makes eye contact, but then glances at Emmett, who subtly draws a finger over his throat. Satoshi nods and turns his attention to another customer.

Bastard. Actually, *bastards.* I'm dealing with two bastards. But the bigger bastard is the bartender. He's choosing money— i.e., Emmett—over his customer's needs. He probably doesn't want to risk losing the firm's business.

But maybe that means *Emmett* is the real bastard. He's using his money and power to make people behave badly. The bastard behind the bastard.

"Three, actually," Emmett says.

"Three what?"

"Three bastards."

Emmett takes my arm and helps me up. I don't recall wanting to stand up, but why not? It's easier than getting to my feet on my own, although maybe he should've worried more about his own balance. He seems to be wavering a little. And he only had one whiskey!

But maybe—maybe!—he had something else behind my back. It *is* possible. The man is diabolically sneaky.

He's holding me close enough that I can smell his scent and feel his body heat. *Does he want to sleep with me?* My inner nympho says I should try to get another mind-blowing orgasm out of him. And it's hard to get her to shut up.

But Emmett isn't interested. He hasn't done a single thing to make a move. He hasn't tried to put his lips on me. Or hold my hand. Or caress my arm or brush his leg against mine under the counter.

He probably lost interest after our one-night stand. Actually, we can't even call it that. It was too short. Our fifteen-minute stand. And it was too, too...

Too *intense*. At least for me. One-night stands are supposed to be enjoyable and easily forgettable. Like a fast-food burger.

I hate it that I'm the only one obsessively thinking about *that* particular sexual episode. Emmett doesn't need a hobby, *I* do. *Like, uh...* I can't think of a good hobby. Reading, maybe. I can always reread *The Mathematics of Financial Derivatives*.

"You really need to stop talking." Emmett sounds pained.

"I wasn't talking. And *you* really need to pay," I say, hugging my purse to show him I'm not forking over a penny.

He sighs and signals the bartender, handing him a few crisp bills. Probably extra C-notes, old ones that he can't use to wipe away his tears when he's at home without any work to do. When I finally turn in my two-week notice, I'm going to get him an MP3 of the saddest violin solo piece I can find, so he can use it as background music for his times of work-free grief.

I told him I'd have a talk with HR about the lack of work-life balance, but he already has that covered. His work *is* his life...so there's balance.

"Wait," I say. "*Three* bastards?"

Emmett nods. "Looks that way."

"Who's the third bastard?"

"Your ex-boyfriend."

"Oh, yeah... That asshole." I try to nod, but my head feels a little woozy. I flap my hand up and down instead. "He's a special kind of asshole. *Camouflaged*. Acted like he supported my career. Do you know my previous ex didn't even try? He dumped me because I missed two dates. Two! You understand? Two!"

"Uh-huh. Two."

"Two! Another asshole! Who does that?"

"Wow," Emmett says as we step outside, his arm around my waist.

Since he's humoring me, I decide to let him hold me, ostensibly so he doesn't fall on his face. To be honest, I think he's hanging on to me to finally cop a feel, but I'm in a generous mood. And it's better that he's clinging. It stokes my female ego, which I think was grieving because Emmett thought I wasn't worth a second helping. Not that I should be going for that. Right?

It's hard to sort my emotions when I'm tipsy. Wondering about how I'm going to find another guy who can give me a similarly incredible orgasm is making my head hurt.

So I shut off my logic and just let myself enjoy having Emmett around. He's warm, and he smells amazing, seeping into my senses with all that sexy male pheromone stuff.

The air feels cooler and slightly smoggy. But I'm outside and I'm free! Yay, El Lay! There's a huge star above us. I stare at it, wondering why it's moving across the dark sky. Maybe it's alive!

No, wait. It's a plane. Man, I wanna fly somewhere warm and pretty. With a beach and plentiful pineapple margaritas.

And no Rick. Definitely not that bastard.

"Next time you see him, I hope you toss him out a window," Emmett says.

I giggle. For some reason, what he's saying is really funny. Maybe Emmett's right that I've had too much to drink. "No. No tossing people out of windows. I don't want to go to jail. But anyway, that's why I thought Rick cared. He didn't dump me just for missing a couple of dates."

"Rick doesn't care about you. He's been busy using photos and stories about dates he had with you to build his platform and make money."

I squint at Emmett. "What? Are you saying he's been using me to make money?"

He sighs. "That's exactly what I just said. You can probably sue him for some kind of alimony."

Ew. Alimony makes it sound like Rick is more than just a failed boyfriend to me. "We were dating, not married."

"Yes. And I'm pretty sure you didn't sign any release form or disclosure that would allow him to monetize your time together."

He's right! I try to snap my fingers but can't get them to work. So I just say it. "You're right." My throat feels parched. Damn it. Why do I have to be overcome with thirst when I'm not in a bar anymore? Wish I had something to drink...

Emmett puts me into a shiny Lamborghini. It's green, which has to be his favorite color because it represents money.

"No, it isn't an association with money." He makes sure I'm properly strapped in, then goes to take his seat behind the wheel and hands me a bottle of water.

"Heeeey, thanks! How did you know?"

"I can read minds, remember?"

"Oh yeah..." It doesn't hurt to indulge his quirky and cute insistence he can read my mind, especially when I'm in a pretty good mood. I struggle with the cap. Emmett takes the bottle, twists it open, then hands it back to me. "Thanks. Wonder if I can sue."

"Sue who? Me?" He starts the car.

"No, *Rick*." The engine roars like a dragon waking up. It makes me feel powerful. No wonder Daenerys Targaryen rode dragons in *Game of Thrones*. They were the ultimate power cars of the fantasy world. "For making money off me. What he's done is inequitable." There. Can't be *that* drunk, because I said the word without stumbling over it.

"Inequ—?" Emmett frowns, then shakes his head. "Never

mind. You should. Sue him, that is. By the way, where do you live?"

Does he want to come in? He isn't looking at me like he wants to devour me. And he's definitely not holding his dick in his hand and moaning my name.

So probably not.

"Directions?" he says. "To your place?"

Maybe I should drive *my* car. It's no dragon mobile, but it will do.

But oh wait... I had five drinks. If Dad hears that I drank that much and drove, he'll be *very* disappointed.

Resigned, I give Emmett directions. He starts maneuvering his car.

I suck down half my water and try not to think about the fact that I'm in a car with my boss/the dude I had a quickie with last night, who's now driving me home. A vague voice in my head says we need to talk about this, but...it's awkward.

Besides, Emmett wanted to talk about something else. What were we talking about before? Oh yeah. Rick using me to build his social media platform. And my suing him for that.

"I don't think I want to," I blurt out. "It's going to cost too much to sue, and—"

"Not that much."

"—I don't have money to burn." I bristle at Emmett for his dismissive tone. "I'm not rich like you."

"Being rich isn't a crime."

Probably not. But being a hot asshole is. Or at least, it should be.

"Did you just call me hot?" A corner of his mouth quirks up a little.

How is he able to keep reading my mind? We aren't in the bar anymore. "You missed the 'asshole' part."

"Hate it when that happens. But my mind only picks up the details worth remembering."

"That's why you have me. To remind you of details you're too arrogant to remember."

He laughs. Wonder what's so funny. Because my life isn't funny at all. No. Not even alcohol can save it.

Wow. That sounds depressing. "Emmett, do you know what's really unfair?"

"No, but I'm sure you'll tell me."

I will indeed. Anything for a man who drives me in a dragon of a car. "Ever since I started working in finance, I haven't been able to find an investment-grade date." That explains why the sex I had with Emmett was so good. If nothing else, his dick is triple-A.

"What are you talking about? You've been dating awful lot."

Is he judging me? He sounds mildly annoyed, but how dare he. *He* dates a lot, too! "Not really. Those were, you know, test drives. And they were all lemons. Not the kind you can put in a nice lemon bar dessert, but junk lemons. Sasha's right. She says most men are junk bonds."

A beat of silence. "What does that even mean?"

"It's a rating system. You should know. You're in finance!"

He gives me a look. "I know the system. I just have no idea how she would apply it to men. Not that I really care."

"Well, you should."

"Why? Sasha's opinions don't mean anything to me."

"Noo, the *rating* system," I say, quite annoyed that Emmett's being obtuse. If he keeps this up, *he* might get downgraded to junk. "Anyway, do you know lemons have inferior engines?"

"Lemons have engines?"

"Of course! Just because they're crappy, defective cars, that doesn't mean manufacturers can sell engineless cars!"

"Ah. Those lemons."

"Try to keep up. Anyway, I take them out for a test drive, and their engines die."

"How is that possible?" He pulls over and stops. "Your mouth alone could revive any dead engine."

I have no idea why he thinks my mouth has anything to do with ignition, but then, Emmett always sees something I don't. That's why he's a billionaire and I'm still paying off my student loans. "They're probably zombie engines."

Emmett gets out of the car, then walks around and opens the door for me. I realize that he's parked the car and we're in front of my apartment building. When did that happen?

"While you were talking," Emmett says.

"You need to stop doing that. It's getting creepy."

"Just part of my hot boss magic. Come on." He holds out a hand.

I debate a little about the wisdom of taking it because he's swaying again. Well... I guess he needs me to help keep him upright. The things I do for my boss.

I put my hand in his. The feel of skin on skin sends shivers up my arm. Despite the cool evening air, I start to feel hot. My heart beats quicker. Is my body recalling the sex from last night? Wanting to try a little bent-over-a-desk to see if it's as good as in the dream?

Please, don't. I don't need that right now. Not when Emmett's here.

I take a deep breath and heave myself out of the car, then smile like everything's great. "Thanks. By the way, are you okay to drive?" I say, belatedly realizing that he shouldn't have been behind the wheel any more than me.

"I'm fine. Totally sober."

Yeah, right. Let's see you count backward from one hundred! For some reason the idea is hilarious, and I start laughing.

"Are *you* okay?" he says.

He's being irresponsible. Must be that man pride. A frat boy from my undergraduate econ class totaled his car after a party once. Apparently he insisted on driving, despite everyone's objections that he was drunk. He was lucky that the only thing that perished was his Mustang—he hit a tree, and the tree survived—but Emmett might not be so lucky.

I don't want anything to happen to Emmett.

"I think you should come in," I say.

"Uh... Are you sure?"

I try to nod, but the attempt makes my head hurt. It was that encounter with Rick. He could give anyone a headache. I decide I should be specific about what I'm offering here so Emmett doesn't think I'm begging for more sex. Because I'm not. Wanting another great orgasm isn't begging it *specifically* from him.

"I'll make you some coffee." That should help him feel better. "Give you some water, too. Think I drank all yours." I gesture at the empty bottle, which is lying sadly in the pretty car. "Actually, lemme get that." I start to twist and bend.

"No, no, no, it's fine. I'll get it later." Strong hands close around my shoulders and haul me back upright. "Let's just get you to your door."

"What's the lush?"

"You mean *who's* the lush? That would be you at the moment."

"No, the *rush*."

"Don't want you to get sick."

He transfers his hands, one to my upper arm and the other around my waist, pulling me close and supporting me. His muscles are hard. He must work out, although when would he find the time? But the easy strength I'm feeling didn't come from sitting around in an executive chair all day.

"Not gonna get sick," I declare. "I'm *fab*ulous. But you can walk me to my door, heh heh heh."

Not because I need help, but this way he can't drive to his place under the influence. Suddenly we're in front of the elevator. And it's there! So we step inside together.

"What floor?" Emmett asks.

"Seven," I say. "Very lucky. Just lemme..."

Somehow my finger keeps missing the button. Emmett reaches past me and pushes it.

As the car takes us up, I remember what Sasha said about men paying women with sex. I said I liked Thor, but...

Yeah, *Emmett*...

If he offers me his body, is it like a retention bonus? To make sure I stay beyond the two-year mark?

"Are you going to quit?" Emmett asks suddenly.

Whaaat? Is he really reading my mind? Actually, he might've heard something from headhunters. He's tight with some of them. Well, everyone is tight with headhunters. Have to be, in this business. But that doesn't make any sense because I told all my headhunters to be discreet, and they're generally good about that sort of thing.

This is confusing. Wonder if he read my thought about the "retention bonus"...?

If he did, and he offers...should I go for it?

A wild and uninhibited voice inside me screams, "Yes!" And to be honest, I'm curious about whether Emmett was so amazing last night in the office because I wasn't myself. I'm slightly drunk at the moment, okay, but not too drunk to realize what Sasha said this morning is correct. There is this crazy, uncontrollable thing between me and Emmett. I just don't know what I'm going to do about it, and the indecision is killing me. I like to *make a firm plan* and *stick to it.*

The moment the door opens onto the seventh floor, we spill into the hallway. I lead him to my unit at the end—seven-oh-seven. I unlock the door and turn around in what I'm sure is an extremely seductive manner. "Come on in, the coffee's fine. A-hahaha."

"Uh-huh. You sure you want this?" Emmett's eyes search mine.

He's standing so close, his body emitting so much delicious heat. He smells good, all male and a hint of the whiskey he had at the bar. I want to lean closer and bury my nose against his chest, feel his heart beat against my cheek.

"Don't know, do ya?" Actually, I want to know if he's going to taste like the whiskey. Or something else.

He sighs and shakes his head. "I'm going to regret this."

I grin. It's funny he thinks that. I think so, too!

He cups my face. "You're entirely too drunk, but I want to kiss you."

"I'm not," I say. My logical side whispers that something about the current situation—Emmett cradling my cheeks like I'm something precious and desirable—is wrong. His mouth is so close. It's full and soft, and looks unbelievably yummy.

So I kick away my logic for the second night in a row.

12

EMMETT

As predicted, I regret the moment I said, "I want to kiss you." Not because I don't want to kiss Amy—I do. But because she's drunk. Utterly, adorably drunk.

And no matter how much I want her, I simply can't take advantage when she can barely stand straight.

Still, I don't mind being with her, indulging her drunk chatter. The more she drinks, the more she verbalizes her internal monologue. After her fourth cosmopolitan, she started saying basically everything that popped into her head.

So I know she thinks I'm hot. She also said I'm an asshole, but that isn't important. The key is focusing on the right things, because that's how dynasties are built.

Of course, I also noticed how she said something about quitting soon, but then suddenly she's all over me and her mouth is on mine.

Jesus. She tastes sweet, like all the cocktails she had. More important, she *feels* like all the hot fantasies that have been monopolizing my mind since the moment I laid eyes on her.

Her tongue flicks my lips. All the blood in my body seems to rush to my dick. Need thrums in my gut, ready to spin out of control.

She fists her hands in my shirt. All I have to do is take what she's offering. And it'd be so easy: just ignore that she's drunk and I'm sober.

Screw it. She wants it. You want it.

But that just wouldn't...

It takes more willpower than I thought I possessed, but I manage to pull away from her. She looks up, confusion clouding her glazed blue eyes.

"Our second time shouldn't be like this." My voice is rough. "When we do it again, you'll be sober and begging for it." And definitely not pulling a Cinderella at midnight and running like hell.

"Oh, *come on.* I'm not drunk." She sways slightly.

"You just don't *sound* drunk because you aren't slurring."

But there's no point in arguing. I turn her around so she can't kiss me again, not trusting myself to resist a second time. My dick's so hard it hurts. Resting my hands on her shoulders, I guide her gently into her apartment.

"Are you leaving?" She sounds a little whiny, like a child deprived of her favorite teddy bear.

"I really *can't* stay." I'm going to do something stupid if I do. I refuse to fuck this up and take advantage when she's too intoxicated to consent.

"But I don't want to be alone. And you shouldn't be driving tonight anyway."

"How come?"

"You're in no condition."

I think about saying that even *my* dick isn't quite large enough to interfere with a steering wheel. But I don't. "Uh, I drove us here."

"You did...?" She frowns. "When?"

"Never mind. My...condition is fine."

"You'll get into an accident." She points to a door. "That's *my* room." She takes a stumbling step toward it in her heels.

Damn it, she's going to fall and crack her head open. I step forward and escort her to her room. She opens the door and flips the light switch. I should turn around and go, but I can't resist the urge to peek into her private space. Her desk at work is utilitarian and clean. Nothing personal on it except a picture of someone I presume is her father—given the pronounced family resemblance—and a desktop calendar.

The room is modestly large. A queen-size bed sits flush against a wall with windows. Her sheets are pale cream with a small yellow flower print, feminine and charming. A small brown stuffed bear sits on one corner of the bed. Probably not a gift from her boyfriend because it's too old. The bear is wearing a shiny silver samurai helmet with a red Japanese character and a fierce Asian mythological beast, but the goofy smile on the bear's face makes it look harmless.

There's a plush armchair with a magenta cardigan draped over the back. A tiny vanity with some cosmetics strewn on top. A framed photo of her and her dad in a garden, both of them grinning.

The room is cozy, warm and smells like citrus. I like it, and for some odd reason find it comforting. Like home.

"Stay over there. I'm just going to wipe this gunk off my face." She tries to indicate her face but doesn't get much past her neck. "*So* annoying."

"What is?"

"Nobody's come up with makeup that auto-cleans off your face. Like, when you're ready to go to bed." She tries to snap her fingers. "Hey, you think we could come up with that?"

"Uh, it's not—"

"We're *in* venture capital. Bet we can make a fortune. Actually, *you* can make a fortune because you have the money."

She continues to totter on her heels. She's definitely going to trip and fall. I go down to one knee, place her hand on my shoulder so she won't overbalance and pull the stilettos off her feet.

I've never had any real opinion about a woman's feet before. Feet are just appendages designed to help people walk, nothing special. But Amy's are somehow fascinating. They're narrow, with cute little toes.

Maybe I'm developing a foot fetish. An Amy foot fetish.

Ah, fuck me.

"Thanks. I tried to slip them off earlier, but couldn't." Amy lowers her voice to a whisper. "They're very stubborn shoes."

I stand up. "It'll be our secret."

"Did you know Prince Charming put shoes on Cinderella?"

"Well, one shoe, anyway."

"But you did the opposite," she says. "Took my shoes *off*. Does this mean I'm supposed to vanish at midnight?" She frowns a little. "But where would I go? It's my home."

"It is. So you shouldn't go anywhere."

"Are you going to disappear instead?"

"No. Unlike you, I don't run when I'm uncomfortable. Also, there wouldn't be any point. You already know who I am."

Her eyes go wide and she wags a finger at me. "That's *true*." Then she weaves her way into the bathroom, swaying like a tree in a storm. Cursing under my breath, I follow her in. Bathrooms can be dangerous. All kinds of hard edges to slip and smack your head against. The vanity, a mirror, the toilet, the edge of the tub...

She plucks a sheet from a packet of wipes and runs it over her face. Then she reaches under her shirt and somehow manages to get her bra off by pulling it through the armholes. She flings it into a laundry basket in the corner and lets out a sigh. "Freedom..."

All my brain registers is that she's braless underneath her top. Actually, my dick registers it first because more blood's pooling there than up above.

She starts taking off her shirt. *Wouldn't it have been easier to just take the top off first,* then *the bra...?* Not that I get very far with that line of thought. Because *holy fucking shit, Amy's topless!*

Oblivious, she shimmies out of her skirt. But it isn't some sexy, seductive move. She's just taking it off. I *really* should leave now... But then her feet get caught trying to kick the skirt off and she starts to overbalance—

I step forward and catch her before she slams a knee against the toilet seat. She wraps her arms around me, her naked breasts crushed against my chest.

Her nipples poke me. A fire that starts from the touch blazes down to my dick.

This is both hot and frustrating as hell. I'm seeing more of her body now than I did yesterday when she was riding me.

"Hey, Emmett." She smiles, her eyes glazing over as residual alcohol is about to drown what little awareness she has remaining. "You haven't left."

"Not yet." *Revenge.* It has to be. And all because she's in a snit over the Excel training from Friday.

She nods—or tries to. Then she disentangles herself from my support, stumbles out of the bathroom and collapses onto her bed. The good thing: her position hides her tits from my view. The bad thing: it's showcasing that ass, which happens to be jack-knifed fetchingly over the edge of the mattress.

She said she wanted you. That's consent.

I put a hand over my eyes. *No, no, no...*

I go over, grab her around the waist and lift her completely onto the mattress, then tuck her in firmly. She doesn't resist. Actually, she's trying to cooperate. Maybe she's remembering that I write her performance evaluations.

As I start to pull away, she takes my hand. I freeze.

"Can you not go?" she whispers, her eyes nearly closed.

When I don't say anything—I can't because I'm fighting a hellish internal battle against my baser desires—she tugs a little harder. "Juss stay till I fall asleep."

The words are barely audible. Her mouth is set in a soft line, all vulnerable and sweet.

Just kill me now.

Sighing, I park my butt on the mattress next to her and try to think of new and creative ways to make money off credit default swaps.

13

AMY

My head feels like a million angry toddlers are pounding on my skull with spoons. *Ugh.* Why do I feel so awful?

I try to open my eyes but instantly give up. It's way too bright. *Didn't I close the curtains before going to sleep...?*

"Amy? You awake?"

Huh. Why am I hearing Emmett's voice? *Must be dreaming...*

"Some aspirin might make you feel better."

I open one eye a crack, just enough to get a blurry image. I squint, trying to focus...

Holy *shit.* Emmett Lasker. In the flesh. Leaning forward in my armchair and holding out a bottle of water and a couple of aspirin.

And that's not all. He's wearing a new shirt and shorts, which means he must've gone home—or something—because I don't have anything a guy can wear. But at the same time, I'm getting this sinking feeling he hasn't gone anywhere. His hair is damp, like he just took a shower, and he's looking extremely relaxed and *at home* in that chair.

I slowly—very slowly—look around. We're definitely in my

room. With Okumasama next to me, his head still covered by the samurai helmet I bought way back when, just for him.

I turn to look at Emmett and do my best to remember what happened yesterday after that embarrassing confrontation with Rick. It's surprisingly hard to dredge up. Emmett bought me drinks... I sort of got tipsy... And then...

And then...

Nothing. It's like somebody blew up that part of my memory. More likely it's buried, lost in the pounding in my head.

"How...?" I start, then stop, trying to figure out which topic is least embarrassing. "You changed clothes."

He looks down. "Oh. Yeah. From a gym bag I keep in my car. Always have a fresh set in there."

Okay, so he *has* been here all night. *And I'm...* Yeah, I'm practically naked. I didn't even put on a nightshirt. Oh my God, does this mean...?

I pull the sheet tighter around me and surreptitiously slide one hand down my body. Okay, at least I have panties on...but who the hell knows what really happened last night? I could've thrown myself at him. Or he could've taken out his most excellently shaped penis again, luring me with the promise of another super orgasm.

"What happened?" I blurt out. I need the facts before I react.

"Take these first." He pushes the water and the pills at me.

Okay, he's right about that. I down them and thank him.

"You're welcome," he says, sitting back.

A little personal distance. Good. "So. Um..." I clear my throat. "What happened?" *Please don't tell me I humiliated myself.*

"Don't you remember?" His tone says that every second of last night should be permanently etched in my memory.

Crap. "Um...not really?"

"You threw yourself at me."

"Oh, I did *not*." My denial is swift and firm, but inside I'm saying, *Oh fuck, fuck, fuck!*

He nods. "You did. Repeatedly. Called me hot, too. You also had what sounded like an especially filthy dream about me."

Did I moan his name while sleeping? "Again?"

His eyebrows almost hit his hairline. "Just how many filthy dreams have you had about me?"

"None! I misspoke."

"I doubt that. You have a tendency to say everything very frankly when you've been drinking."

Holy shit. Did I really tell him about the dream? And did I have *another* one? But... That doesn't add up. If I'd had another dirty dream, I should've woken up wet, even if I can't remember it now. I was soaked yesterday.

"You also get very explicit," he adds.

"No, you're lying, because I'm not—" I shut my mouth so hard that my teeth click.

Emmett waits a beat. "Not what?"

"Nothing." I refuse to discuss my vagina's moisture level with my boss on a Sunday morning when I'm naked except for panties under the sheet. Nope, no way.

What I need to do is find out why he's here, and why I'm in the state I'm in. But first, I need to make myself feel human again.

"Could you give me some privacy?" I say with all the cool nonchalance I can muster.

"Sure, I can do that." He gives me a small smirk, then gets out of my armchair and shuts the door behind him.

I sit up and immediately regret moving so fast. It feels like I'm going to *die*. My brain seems to actually jiggle inside my skull.

Isn't alcohol supposed to make your brain shrink? Okay, this is the last time I'm going to get greedy when somebody offers to pay for my drinks. There is no free lunch.

I cautiously make my way to the bathroom, pee, brush my teeth and shower. Thank God Sasha's out of town. Normally it'd be extremely rude, but I hope Emmett leaves without a word. But given my luck, I doubt that'll happen. I squeeze the water out of my hair, then towel it dry, since I don't have time to do anything

116

with it right now. There's no way I'm letting Emmett roam free in my living room and kitchen. He might discover something to find fault with—whether with me or Sasha. And then there will be the enormous inconvenience of some new "training" project. I swear, the man can suck the time out of anyone's life. He's like a boss who's really a time-vampire. *Bossferatu.*

But before I can face him again, I need to come up with a strategy. I can't ask him to tell me the truth about last night because he can just make up whatever he wants. He already claimed I was sexually into him, which I don't believe. Not even a little.

Alcohol has never made me want to sleep with a guy. Ever. It relaxes me, and it makes me laugh more than usual, but that's about it. Emmett's just making stuff up to get back at me for seeing him masturbate, then screwing him and running out. I thought he wanted to tacitly ignore that particular incident, but he must've changed his mind and decided to go on the offensive.

Which...isn't a bad idea. I can go on the offensive, too, and declare nothing happened last night. It's his word against mine. I shouldn't be naïve enough to trust that he's going to be honest about anything. He's the kind of boss who tells me my perfectly fine Excel models need adjustments, just for *fun.*

Satisfied for the moment with my plan of action, I put on a fitted shirt, denim shorts and flip-flops and step out of the bedroom. Emmett's large, masculine self is in the kitchen. He braces his hands against the edge of the sink and gives me a small scowl. "There's nothing to eat in this place."

"And you're surprised?"

"Well...yeah. Most women have *something* in their fridge."

"Most women probably have time to go to the grocery store and buy stuff." I give him a look. "They probably also have time to cook it."

"That explains why you've lost weight since starting the job," he mutters.

"I'm surprised you noticed. I only lost, like, two or three pounds."

"Two or three you didn't need to lose." He sighs.

"Well, don't make it sound like I'm starving myself on purpose. It's your fault." Normally, I wouldn't point such things out, but I have less than eight weeks left at GrantEm Capital. I view it as a public service to the person who'll be filling my position.

"Still, you should— Wait a minute. *My* fault?" He looks at me like I told him the moon is made of cheesecake.

Is this man for real? "Yes! I barely have time to sleep, much less eat."

His eyebrows arch. "Are you accusing *me* of overworking you?"

"Ding, ding, ding!"

"Nonsense. I just make sure you spend your time productively."

"Yeah, making *you* money."

"No, making *us* money. Which is *productive*."

Productive meaning profitable. I know corporate bullshit-speak. It's one of the things you learn while getting your MBA.

Besides, he seems annoyed as he looks around my kitchen, and I'm tired of this visual censure. "I have some coffee if you want."

"What I want is food with my coffee."

Bossy asshole. "Would you like me to feed you?" I say with a fake smile.

He smiles back, except he looks oddly...satisfied. And slightly teasing. My apartment feels too hot all of a sudden.

"It's the least you can do for what I had to suffer last night," he says.

It's unfair that I remember nothing. And he's going to hold that over me forever at the rate this is going. On the other hand, it looks like he brought me home safely and didn't try anything weird, so I probably *should* feed him something. Especially considering it's already after ten. I bet Sasha has some stale cereal in her section of the pantry I can filch.

"How about we get some brunch?" he says, before I can offer the cereal. "Come on."

14

AMY

Emmett drives. Strapped into the passenger seat, I keep my mouth shut. My head hurts too much to discuss anything tricky—like sex or sex-related stuff. The only thing I can talk about on autopilot is work, but that's the last thing I'm going to bring up. I'm not reminding the man of some task he can assign me. I plan to have this day fully off.

You know it's sad when the only thing you can think to talk about with your boss is work and sex.

I ignore the judgmental voice. It doesn't have eyes to see how gorgeous Emmett is.

He gives me a glance from time to time, but the only thing he can see is that my mouth is curved into a pat smile, since I'm wearing reflective sunglasses.

Emmett doesn't try to start a conversation, but that doesn't mean his mind is empty and calm. Or even innocent. He could be thinking about creative ways to make money in the bond market. Although fixed income security isn't exciting enough to be his thing, he "dabbles," according to some of the interviews I read about him.

Or he could be thinking about sex.

Of course, but it's probably sex in general, not sex with me specifically. Men supposedly think about sex every seven seconds. No man can think about specific sex with a specific person that often. Men prefer more variety.

He could be thinking about various positions with you.

That conjures up my dirty bent-over-in-his-office dream. I squeeze my eyes shut to force it out my head.

Emmett stops his Lamborghini in front of the Aylster Hotel. I eye the swanky building thinking, *Uh-oh.* Nieve, where I had my interview with Marion Blaire, is on the first floor. And it's famous for brunch. When Dad visited, I brought him here and we had the most fabulous time.

Unfortunately, I don't foresee a fabulous time with Emmett Lasker.

After handing his car off to the valet, Emmett leads me across the marble floor of the lobby. Chandeliers sparkle above us from the tall ceiling. Well-heeled guests lounge in cushy seats. The air smells faintly of the hotel's signature scent—something floral and slightly spicy that conjures up a feeling of opulent indulgence.

Emmett places a hand at my elbow like a gentleman. If it weren't for the fact that he's my boss and I've been dragged here like a hapless hamster to a snake cage, this would all be great.

Please don't go to Nieve. Not Nieve.

But, of course, we end up in front of the gorgeous ivory bistro. And also of course, the same maître d' from Friday is standing in the entrance with a warm, welcoming smile. *And he recognizes me.*

"Good morning. Welcome back." He beams at me.

"Hi."

Emmett gives me a sideways glance. "You come here often? We can try some other place..."

"No, no," I say hurriedly. "It was, like, last month."

"Last month?"

"With Rick." I cringe inwardly. I really should've said *with Dad*, except he doesn't visit that often and I had a brain fart.

Dates with Rick were always on budget. Nieve would've blown twenty dates' worth in one shot.

Now Emmett's staring at me like he can see straight down to the core of my lying soul. It's making me want to drop to my knees and confess.

Hold firm. Emmett has no clue what you're up to socially. You don't post anything on social media!

The maître d' gives me another smile. This time, it signals, *I understand.* "Would you like a table for two?"

"Please," I say most sincerely.

He signals one of the uniformed staff, and the man takes us to a table near the window. He pulls out one chair right as Emmett pulls out another. I hesitate for a second. My boss cocks an imperious eyebrow.

I take the chair Emmett offers, and then he sits down in the chair the server pulled out.

I open the white leather-bound menu and stare at the brunch options. Without touching his own menu, Emmett orders a pot of coffee and champagne.

"Anything to drink for you, miss?" the waiter asks.

My eyes fall on the sparkly silver page inset that explains their champagne brunch. You can add a glass of Dom Pérignon to your brunch to elevate it.

I don't know about elevating my meal, but I'm probably going to need alcohol to get through this brunch with Emmett. Besides, it isn't like I'll be knocking back cheap liquor. One thing about champagne—it's so elegant, it won't make you look like an alcoholic who starts drinking before noon.

"The same for me," I say. "And I'd like some French toast, with extra berries and whipped cream, and syrup on the side." I shut the menu.

"Three-cheese omelet with an extra order of bacon," Emmett says. "Whole wheat toast, butter and jam on the side."

The waiter repeats the order and leaves. I fidget a little, then down the icy water the waiter poured for me. The man returns with coffee in a gorgeous silver pot. He serves us, then leaves again.

I sip the liquid caffeine, my mind whirring. Emmett is silent, which is ratcheting up my anxiety level. This isn't like him. We don't have the kind of relationship that allows for a quiet, relaxed brunch on Sunday.

You also don't have the kind of relationship that allows for a quickie in the office. Or getting yourself plastered and having him drive you home.

It's like the universe somehow took a wrong turn on Friday and derailed my well-ordered life. Maybe I need to sacrifice an accountant to the Excel gods or something to get things back on track. A virgin accountant, which shouldn't be too hard to fin—

My phone buzzes. A text! Yay!

Thrilled with the distraction, I pull out my phone from the purse. "Sorry, I have to take this."

Emmett gives me a magnanimous go-ahead gesture.

–Dad: Hey, sweet pie, lots of love from Vegas! How you doing?

The text has Dad's new selfie. I smile.

–Me: I'm doing great. How are you?

–Dad: I'm doing fantastic. By the way, I'm going to be in L.A. at the end of next month.

–Me: Awesome!

–Dad: Xavier's getting married, and I told him I'd be there.

Xavier is Dad's dearest friend, and he moved to L.A. last year. He perpetually falls in and out of love, and this is his fifth marriage. Surprising he isn't going for an elopement in Vegas. You'd think the whole ceremony thing would lose its luster after the first few times.

–Dad: Thought I'd visit you for a couple of days, if that's okay.

If Emmett wasn't sitting right across from me, I'd be yelping with excitement.

–Me: That would be totally great!

Sasha's usually not around on weekends because she's jetting out to San Francisco. But I'll ping her later just to be sure. If she's staying in L.A. and doesn't feel comfortable having Dad around, I can always put him up in a hotel.

–Dad: Great. Looking forward to it!

–Me: Me too!

I send him a bazillion hearts. Since I'm not taking a selfie, I add the following:

–Me: At a business brunch with my boss right now.

–Dad: I understand. Man, that guy works you too hard. :(

Yeah, no kidding. But honesty would worry him, and it's unnecessary when I'm going to be done with Emmett Lasker soon.

–Me: That's why he pays me the big bucks. Anyway, gotta go. Love you! XOXO!

–Dad: Love you too, sweet pie!

"Someone from the firm?" Emmett says as I put away the phone.

"No, it was my father. He's going to visit at the end of next month." I smile, then sober a little. "By the way, you aren't going to make me work on that weekend, are you? I really want to spend some time with him."

Emmett looks a little surprised. "You'd rather hang out with your father than work?"

"Well...yes."

"Why?"

Because I'm normal, and don't love work above literally everything else in the universe? "Because I love him. He's the best dad ever." I give Emmett my most pleading look. "I'll work nonstop until then if that's what it takes."

The skin between his eyebrows furrows. "You don't have to do that. I'll let you have the time off. But if you change your mind, just let me know." His tone implies he won't be surprised if I do.

I look at him. In a way, it seems like it's for the first time. "Don't you love your father?"

He smiles. "Of course. I wouldn't be here with you if it weren't for one of his errant swimmers."

I can't decide if he's joking or not. The smile is a bit thin, but then, it isn't often that Emmett really lets go with a grin. And even somebody as vile as Emmett probably loves his dad. "So you understand why this is important to me."

"I suppose. But tell me what makes him special to you."

A direct question, in the same tone he uses to ask me to justify assumptions on the latest projections. It's almost like he can't imagine what would make a father special to anybody. "It'd take the entire day to tell you everything."

"Give me some highlights."

"Okay, well... He gave up so much for me, including a career in the military. You can't really be in the Marine Corps and raise a girl as a single parent."

He frowns a little. "What happened to your mother?"

"Gone," I say, not wanting to get into the sordid details of how she abandoned us.

"I see. Sorry to hear that."

I give him a tight smile. Most people assume my answer means she's dead. Which is pretty close to the truth, since she's dead *to me*. "It was a long time ago."

"Still. That's gotta hurt. I can't imagine not having my mother around." His expression changes. The eyes soften; the smile warms a bit. Even his tone turns...tender.

Which is weird, because all the tabloids and gossip sites basically labeled his mother a gold digger. But then, maybe he doesn't care about that. After all, she fulfilled the most basic of all motherly duties—sticking around. Mine didn't bother.

"Anyway, Dad didn't have a social life or anything. He was too busy learning a trade and taking care of me. He's a mechanic now. A really great one," I say proudly. "He taught me how to do basic repairs and change tires. Says a woman needs to know how to do that stuff more than men, since more bad things can happen to a woman who gets stuck because of a breakdown. Plus, some unscrupulous mechanics think it's okay to rip a woman off because they think we won't know." I shake my head. "Anyway, I wouldn't be at GrantEm Capital if it weren't for my dad cheering me on, believing in me and making sure I knew I was loved no matter what. So once I sort out my student loans, I'm buying him a beachfront cottage."

"He wants you to buy him a property?" Emmett sounds stunned.

"It's not that he wants me to. *I* want to. Because that's his dream retirement home, and he deserves it. I ran the numbers. I'll be able to afford it."

"Huh." Emmett looks like a college freshman listening to a lecture on how to valuate a startup. Fascinated, but a little surprised and confused.

"Don't you want to do things for your parents when they do something really nice for you?" I ask, taking pity on him.

He looks like he wants to shake his head, but doesn't go through with it. "No... But I buy them presents for important occasions, like birthdays and Christmas." He might as well be talking about having to vacuum a particularly shaggy rug.

Which is weird. He sounded like he cares about his mother. Is this about his dad? Like if his dad took off like my mom... But I know he didn't. Ted Lasker is a famous movie producer, and he's right here in Hollywood. He also acknowledged all his children, and—based on articles about Emmett's background—gave them the best childhood money could buy.

Our waiter comes with our food, set on elegant white china. The French toast looks amazing, all golden fluffiness. It smells even better, reminding me that I didn't have dinner last night. My mouth waters.

Suddenly starving, I dig in. I focus on eating, doing my best to not think too deeply about Emmett's personal life. Why should I be interested, anyway? I'm going to be gone soon. I drink my

Dom, which tastes like liquid gold, silently toasting to this successful nonsexual interaction with my boss.

"Can I ask you something?" Emmett says suddenly. "I couldn't figure this out on my own."

"There's something you can't figure out?" What could it possibly be? How to be a good boss? How to develop a warm, caring heart?

"It happens occasionally," he says blandly.

"But you're a god of finance. Everyone says so." *So ask yourself, rather than a mere mortal like me.*

"It's not about work."

Shocking that something other than work would bother him enough to cause him to ask.

"You mumbled something about it at the bar, but I want to talk about it while you're sober and actually going to remember what comes out of your mouth."

"Okay," I say warily. What wouldn't I give to remember exactly what I told him last night!

He looks at me straight, like he doesn't just want to look into my eyes but into my mind. "Why were you dating that guy?"

"I don't understand what you're asking." Ex-boyfriends aren't to be analyzed. They're to be put into a mental tar pit, to sink into the ooze and never be thought about again.

"That guy who came to the office. He must've had something going for him for you to date him. Some...aspect."

"Why do you want to know?" From anybody else, I might think it was sheer curiosity. With Emmett, I can sense landmines. Lots and lots of landmines.

"Just curious. I thought he was kinda awful."

My hackles rise. Not because I disagree with Emmett's judgment of Rick, but because it feels like he's judging my judgment. "Well. He wasn't this awful when we first started going out. He was better than the boyfriends I'd had before."

"Where did you find these guys? In a dumpster?"

"I just...met them," I say. "Not every person you date is going to be Mr. Right."

"You can do better. You're at least a nine."

Wow. I didn't know I rated that high. "Thank you...I think."

"That means you can have men who are a nine or ten or better."

"Ten *or better*? What's the scale here?"

"One to ten."

"So...?"

"Some guys get extra credit."

"Ah. The magic unicorn men."

"Exactly. With appropriate looks and assets." It's clear that he considers himself to be in this supernatural category.

"Uh-huh." I take a sip of my Dom. I'm not blurting out whatever just comes to my head, which at the moment is that Emmett Lasker could be a magic unicorn man—if he came with an *appropriate* heart. "I'm looking for more than just a man with a pretty face and money."

Emmett looks like he wants to add something to my list, but presses his lips together. Which is good. I don't want the distraction.

"I want a man with a heart and soul I can fall in love with."

"That isn't necessarily mutually exclusive to money and looks. Or better bedroom technique." Emmett speaks as though he's imparting the lost wisdom of the universe.

I don't miss the way his fingers subtly curl toward himself, either. Arrogant jerk. And *so* annoying, since his arrogance isn't totally unfounded. "I'm sure, but I don't want to make a snap judgment after looking only at the exterior."

"But you wouldn't have fallen for a guy who forced you to hike and cook and clean on your vacation. Would you?"

It's eerie to watch the contempt drip from Emmett as he describes what was essentially Rick's plan for the six-month anniversary trip. Not that I disagree. "Are you kidding? That'd be my idea of hell. The best vacation is one where I don't have to do anything. I want to lie there like a phone plugged into a charger and left in peace to reenergize."

Emmett nods and somehow makes the movement look smug. "Thought so."

I put my fork down, since every berry on my plate has been scooped up. I finish the Dom with a happy sigh. "Let me treat you to brunch."

"I don't let women pay for my meals."

He sounds slightly annoyed. I'm sure part of it has to do with the fact that I'm also his subordinate. Bosses pick up the tab. It's expected, especially in our profession. "What I mean is, to thank you for getting me home safely last night."

He waves it away. "Glad to help. Also, you stripped down to your panties right in front of me last night. So let's call it even."

I almost choke on my own spit. His tone is so dry that I can't tell if he's messing with me or what. But the way his gaze burns as he looks at me... My lady parts clench. I shift in my seat to relieve the uncomfortable achiness.

"Don't worry. I was a gentleman. I worked out a few new ways to make money off credit default and currency swaps instead. Which I plan to execute and make an ass-load of money off soon. So I don't mind."

The waiter appears with a white folio for the check. Emmett hands over his black AmEx but never takes his eyes off me.

I say nothing. This is my fault for trying to be nice. Nice doesn't go appreciated in Emmett's world.

"Thank you." The words come out stiff, despite my effort to remain unaffected—or at least project an unaffected mien.

"You're welcome."

He signs for the slip our waiter comes back, and we leave the bistro together. I start to head toward the main door, but Emmett moves toward the elevator bank, his hand at my elbow to guide me toward him.

"Where are we going?" I ask.

"To the seventh floor."

I swallow a gasp. "I'm not going to sleep with you," I hiss, in case he thought that's what we're doing next.

He stops abruptly. I almost bump into him.

"First of all, I never stay on the seventh floor," he says. "Penthouse suites all the way."

"Oh, right. The ones that come with a grand piano nobody plays."

"I never thought about them that way, but yes. Second, we both live in L.A., so we wouldn't have to get a room at a hotel for sex."

My face starts to heat. "Fine. So why do you want me to go to the seventh floor with you?"

"Because there's a spa there."

"A spa?" I say stupidly.

"Yes. You're familiar with the concept?"

"Of course I'm fami—"

"Good. Then come along."

15

AMY

There really is a spa on the seventh floor. A slim receptionist in a white and green uniform greets Emmett. He gives her his name and asks for a couple of massages like he expects to be catered to. I wait for her to say there's nothing available—you can't just show up and demand to be accommodated.

But no. She smiles, her lashes flutter and her cheeks turn pink. *Of course we have treatment rooms available for you and your guest. We're thrilled you're here again and thank you for your continued patronage.*

Meanwhile, I'm not sure if *I* should be thrilled about being up here with Emmett. A massage seems a bit random. Certainly, nobody has ever said, "Massage!" after a meal, in my experience. But Emmett is acting like this is totally normal, part of his standard agenda.

If my boss thinks something is normal, it probably isn't.

We're taken inside the quiet, gorgeous space. Fresh orchids have been placed around the room, perfuming the air. The table she takes us to is one elegant cross-section carved from a huge tree, and you can see the age rings on the surface. Another person brings us citrus water and warm hand towels that feel like heaven.

The menu options are quite extensive, with lots of information about each treatment. There's even a mud bath, although I don't know about sitting in mud for forty minutes at the prices they're charging. I don't care if the mud *is* supposed to be rejuvenating. It's dirt mixed with a little bit of water, not the elixir of life.

I tap the top edge of the menu. Honestly, I'm not sure what we're doing in the spa, exactly. The brunch, I understand. Emmett was hungry and so was I. But *this...*?

"The hot stone massage is really good," Emmett says.

"It is one of our most popular treatments. I recommend the eighty-minute option," the receptionist says.

I lean over and murmur into Emmett's ear, "I thought we were going home after brunch."

"Why? I never said that."

Spoken like a bossy bastard.

"Consider this a bonus," he says.

"For what?" Emmett is being *way* too nice. This isn't normal. I can't even imagine what he's trying to pull. I already said *no sex*.

"For work well done."

That only makes me more nervous. "Which, um, work in particular?"

"All of it. Since you joined the firm," he says, like he's talking to a confused toddler. "Don't you read your performance evaluations?"

"Yes, but... Do you take other associates for massages, too?"

"Nope. Just you. You're special."

He doesn't mean anything by it, surely. But somehow it punches my gut anyway, making my heart do that weird tumble it always does when I'm around him.

"Besides, *I* want a massage. And I doubt you want to sit around and wait for the next eighty minutes or so while I get the hot stone treatment. So stop acting like I'm setting you up for a session with Torquemada. Just lie back and try to enjoy yourself. Think of the empire."

I cannot believe *this man!* Still, he does owe me for all those hours I had to put in for his "fun training" bullshit. And I don't want to wait around for over an hour. So I feign nonchalance and accept. "Fine."

A Nordic blond guy with muscular forearms takes Emmett away, and I go with a cute brunette who leads me to a ladies' changing area. I strip down and put on a plush white robe, slip my phone into a pocket and follow her into a dimly lit room. Unlike the reception area, the space here smells faintly of lavender and something else I can't put a name to but is very soothing.

She asks me for my preference for oil, then any areas of concern. I ask her to focus on my neck and shoulders because they're always tense from being hunched over a laptop all the time.

Once I take off my robe and lie down on the bed, she starts. I hear some rocklike clacking, and then smooth, warm, heavenly pressure as the stones are slid over the knots I didn't know I had. Oh... Yeah... It's *so* much better than a regular massage. The stones are warmer than a masseuse's hands, and the heat relaxes all the tension from me. When she's done with a section of my body, she leaves a toasty stone or two resting on it, and my muscles go even gooier.

I sigh softly and close my eyes. Emmett's still a jerk, but this makes him less of one. It's probably the most luxurious, pampering experience of my life. It's an order of magnitude better than the spa day Sasha and I had to celebrate our graduation from Wharton and starting at GrantEm.

The eighty minutes pass in what seems like ten. When my masseuse gently taps my shoulder, I realize I've fallen asleep. I blink, then smile sheepishly.

"How are you feeling?" she asks.

I note her nametag. "I'm great. Thanks, Cat."

"My pleasure."

"Is Emmett done?"

"I think so. But take your time. He's probably in the resting area with some herbal tea. He likes to do that after a session."

She leaves, and I sit up slowly. Wow. My head is *much* clearer. And there's no tension anywhere in my body. I didn't know it was possible to feel this good.

I put on my robe and pull out my phone. This the perfect time to take a quick selfie with a big, happy smile and send it to Dad later. I should bring him here when he visits for Xavier's wedding. Just thinking about his being this relaxed and happy makes me smile.

I step out and make my way to the changing room. As I open my locker and begin to get dressed, I can overhear a couple of women gossiping on the other side.

"So who is he?" A breathless inquiry.

"Emmett Lasker. He comes by once or twice a month, depending."

I breathe more quietly.

"I thought he was a model when he walked by." She sounds like she's about to fan herself.

You and me both. I adjust my bra for better comfort.

"He's so *perfect*. That *body*." The other one sounds like she's swooning. "Every time he makes a reservation, I get excited. He always comes during my shift."

"Maybe he's coming here for you."

"Oh, please. He probably doesn't even know my name."

She shouldn't be that forlorn. Getting on Emmett's radar isn't always a positive thing.

"Ken's so lucky. He gets to massage that body."

I don't know if Ken feels lucky. But I'd like to touch that body again, if I could also somehow make Emmett not know I was the one touching it.

Oh my God, I sound like a creep...

"Seriously. Emmett Lasker won't make a reservation if Ken isn't available."

Ken must be really good. I should book him for Dad.

The two sigh and gab about my boss some more. As I finish dressing, I'm more or less forced to agree with every gushing word. If you don't work for him, he's pretty perfect. As a matter of fact, he gave me what I'd like to do to relax—an upscale brunch and massage. It's like he knew exactly what I'd love.

He wants to sleep with you again! Sasha's voice crows in my head.

If Emmett were just some guy I'd met, like Rick, I would've said yes to getting to know him on a personal level—including getting horizontal with him—while counting down my last days at the firm. I already know the man's great at sex, too. Not just great, but *The Best.*

But something's holding me back. Not all of my misgivings are due to his being my boss. I slip on flip-flops and wonder what's making me hesitate. I didn't second-guess myself when I applied to Harvard, or the position at Goldman Sachs, or Wharton or GrantEm. They were the best, and I wasn't going to settle for second best. It might have make me appear arrogant, but I knew what I was worth and capable of.

So why am I so indecisive about Emmett? I should be able to make up my mind.

Emmett Lasker is a person, not a school or a job.

And people are complicated. They don't always *seem* to be what they really *are.* Just look at my mom and dad. He thought she was worth it, did all the right things for her, but she ended up leaving him. The pretty outward packaging was exactly that— packaging. In the end, it couldn't conceal her selfish inner bitch.

There's nothing that says Emmett is going to be different from my mom.

Maybe what I need is a sign. It doesn't matter if it says a fling with Emmett is going to be fine or sleeping with Emmett again is going to be a terrible mistake. I just want *something* so I can decide.

And then I have to laugh at myself over how silly I'm being. I don't do *signs*. I must be really frazzled to want one. I believe in *facts*. And *planning*.

My phone buzzes. I look down, wondering if Emmett's texting me to see if I'm ready to head home.

But no. It's not Emmett. It's the sign I was hoping for.

16

AMY

–Marion: Hello, Amy. I'm thrilled to let you know the position's yours, should you still want it. HR is going to get in touch next week with the official offer, but I wanted to be the first to let you know.

I stop breathing for a second. I didn't expect the Blaire Group to make their decision this fast.

–Marion: Our compensation is generous, and there will be a relocation bonus as well. The details will be coming soon. Congratulations!

Smiling, I read both texts again. It's not a dream. *I have the job.*

–Me: Thank you! I look forward to speaking to your HR people next week!

This is a sign I should have a hot, discreet fling with Emmett Lasker for the next seven weeks and six days. If things get awkward or if he turns out to be some closet asshole, who cares? It's a fling! And the Blaire Group is in Virginia! Five hours away by plane!

Thank you, Marion Blaire. You're the best.

Feeling like the weight of the world has lifted off my shoulders, I sigh. *This* is the reward for all the things I've had to put up with.

I go to the resting area, where Emmett is back in his clothes and sitting at a table with some hot herbal tea. His wide shoulders seem loose and relaxed. The white porcelain cup looks dainty in his large hand, but he seems comfortable holding the fragile thing. He takes a ruminative sip and nods to himself. I can't remember a time when he was this free of tension.

Then he raises his eyes and our gazes meet. Something raw and hot coils in my belly.

Pretending I'm not feeling anything, I join him at the elegant table covered with white cloth.

"How was it?" he asks, a small smile curving his lips.

"Fantastic. Thank you." I choose the ginger lemon tea, which comes out almost immediately. I sip it. *So. Good.* "You're going to get me addicted to these massages."

"You should splurge. You received the highest bonus last year among your peers."

That part is no secret. Our rank is a big factor in the firm's compensation formula. I'm probably going to make the top again this fiscal year, which is in June.

"I would, but all my money's earmarked," I say.

"So is mine, but I allocate some of it to make myself feel good."

It's too bad he doesn't earmark some of his effort on being less of a dick to his employees. "I'm ready to head out if you are," I say, since I'm done with my tea and I don't want to tell him what I just decided here. The non-massage areas seem to be poorly soundproofed, and I don't want some receptionist hearing what I'm about to propose. "We can talk on the way."

Emmett raises an eyebrow, but we get up and he signs a slip for the service on our way out. The valet brings the Lamborghini around, and Emmett hands him a few bills. Then we're both in the car and off.

How should I broach this topic? Not romantically—we're

kind of past that. Not professionally, either. It seemed easy when I was playing it out in my head, but now that I'm alone with Emmett, I have no idea how to start.

"So. What do you want to talk about?" Emmett says, maneuvering onto La Cienega.

Guess he's tired of waiting. I thought men preferred to avoid we-need-to-talk talks. "Well... I've been thinking..."

"About?"

"Everything since...you know, Friday."

"Ah." He nods thoughtfully. "Friday."

"Anyway." I clear my throat. "I've decided that—if you're okay with it, of course—I'd, uh, be open to a very discreet fling."

A short pause. "A fling?" A corner of his mouth quirks.

"A *discreet* fling. Discreet being the key word here."

"Yeah, but you also said *fling*, which is more important."

Of course that's what he focused on. "Yes. I did say that. But there have to be some rules."

"Okay." He gestures at me to go ahead, his eyes on the road. "Give me the full disclosure."

Feeling like those drug commercials that have to list all the side effects, I start in. But at a normal speed so Emmett can remember *everything*, not just what's "important." "For one, we have to be totally professional at work. And I mean *totally*. One *hundred* percent. Nobody can know we're involved."

He nods. "Goes without saying."

"Good. I don't want to be the topic of gossip." Or have someone crow over winning that damn betting pool or some bullshit like that. Nobody's going to make money off my sex life if I can help it.

"FYI, GrantEm doesn't have a policy on interoffice dating, so long as there's no HR complaint," he says.

"I won't file a complaint." Then I move on to the second and final part. "No gifts. No dates." That should keep things clean and simple, since this isn't going to go anywhere with me leaving the firm in less than eight weeks. "Just sex."

He gives me a sidelong glance. "What's wrong with gifts and dates?"

I pause. "Why aren't you focusing on 'just sex'?"

"Oh, I'm focused on it. But gifts and dates are important, too."

"Well, yeah, normally. But that isn't our relationship."

"Don't treat me like one of your cheap, shitty ex-boyfriends."

"I'm not!"

"If I want to buy you something nice, I should be free to. It's my damn money."

"You said all your money's earmarked." Why is he arguing when he's going to get what he wants? He should just concentrate on "sex."

"I can always reallocate. That's the beauty of being a billionaire. I have lots of disposable funds to move around at my pleasure."

"I don't know why you're being difficult. It isn't like you aren't used to being an asshole." *There. I said it while completely sober.* I'm too peeved at his argumentative attitude to care if my choice of words pisses him off.

"I'm not an asshole."

I snort. "You crushed at least two people on Friday alone."

His eyes cut to me for a moment before going back to the road. "What? Who?"

"See? It's such a regular occurrence you don't even remember."

"If I crushed them, they deserved it."

I ignore that ridiculous self-justification. "I saw how Webber and Diana looked after leaving your office." Especially Diana, that poor child.

Emmett curses under his breath. "Did they complain to you?"

"No," I say quickly, not wanting to get them into trouble. We aren't close enough for that, and I'm usually too busy to gossip. "But I could tell."

"Have you ever reviewed their deliverables?"

"No."

"So you have no idea why I had to 'crush' them, as you put it."

"I don't know the specifics, but I can guess. You just wanted to give them *training for fun.*"

Emmett shakes his head. "Are you still holding a grudge?"

"Of course not. I'm a forgiving human being."

He heaves a sigh. "Okay. What I'm about to say is *strictly* between you and me."

"Okay." I want to hear how he plans to justify his treatment.

"Webber and Diana both fucked up. I gave Webber a handful of proposals and told him to rank them in order of viability. They aren't for profit. I wanted a preliminary report on which one to invest in for the most overreaching change in the world. For every hundred ideas we fund for profit, we take on one for simply making the world better."

"We do?" I blink. "I thought everything at GrantEm was for profit."

"We don't advertise it because we don't want them to receive different treatment. Not even Webber knows what they were really for. *Anyway.*" Emmett continues in a scary-calm tone, "What does he do? Not only does he trash every single proposal for being 'impractical,' he CCs the company founders who submitted the ideas in his email to me! I don't know where he got the balls to pull that kind of stunt, but he's lucky I didn't rip them off and shove them down his throat."

Wow. Emmett's right. Webber did fuck up, and he's lucky he didn't get fired.

"As for Diana, she's sloppy. I told her she needs to QA her work with more care, but she just won't do it. You can turn in a sloppy projection to your professor. It's a class assignment, and the only thing you're risking is your grade. But in real life, you're risking millions of dollars and the livelihoods of people who work at the firm and the portfolio companies."

I wince because that is also a screwup. I make a mental note to see if I can help Diana do better. Webber's close enough to my rank and year that he might not want it, but she would.

"Don't bother," Emmett says.

"Huh?"

"You're thinking about helping. Right? They wouldn't appreciate it."

"How do you know?"

"They badmouth people who are doing better than them. They think the break room is private." Emmett smiles coldly. "It's not."

I'm glad I rarely gossip anywhere in the company, the break room included. But...does this mean Emmett knows about the betting pool about us? Or maybe not, because he hasn't done a thing to indicate that he's aware.

He continues, "Anyway, back to the gifts and dates. They're a must. Non-negotiable."

"More important than sex?" I ask, stunned that he's stuck on this point. I can't picture any of my ex-boyfriends arguing this vociferously about gifts and dates when they could have sex. Gifts and dates were things they did to *get* laid—the means to a happy end.

"Why does your mind go to that extreme? I never said sex didn't matter. It's the trifecta."

"It's a *fling*. Besides, when would we be able to date? I never leave early enough for that, and it'll look suspicious if I start."

"And on the eighth day, after a nice little rest, God created the weekend."

"Am I going to have free weekends?" I ask sarcastically.

"Thankfully, I control your assignments." He smiles.

And it'll only be for a few weekends. Probably not worth an argument. "Fine."

"Good." He smiles. "Now that we've settled that, move in with me."

"*What?* No!"

"Why not?"

"Gifts and dates doesn't mean moving in together!"

"How are we going to spend time together if you're there"—he gestures in the general direction of my place—"and I'm there?" He gestures elsewhere—probably where his place is. "I don't want to limit our time to just weekends."

"That's not the point," I say, feeling like I'm talking to a brick wall. The man's smart, but when he's got an idea in his head, it's impossible to budge him. So I go for the argument that might make a dent. "And even if I were willing to move in with you, I room with Sasha. She would know."

He sighs a must-I-come-up-with-all-the-solutions? sigh. "Tell her you're moving in with your boyfriend."

I have to laugh. "Emmett, get real. She knows I broke up with Rick. Nobody moves in with a rebound the next day."

"Sure they do, if their rebound can reignite their libido the way I can. I know that equine ex-boyfriend of yours gutted your sex drive."

I'm not discussing Rick's effect on my sex drive with Emmett, mainly because he's right, and I refuse to concede any point. You give an inch; he takes a mile. "It doesn't matter what you say. The answer is a big, fat no. To use your word, it's *non-negotiable*."

He drums his fingers on the steering wheel for a moment. "I guess I'll need to open a satellite office in Alaska and send Sasha there..."

I choke back another laugh, then shake my head. "Even if you do, my answer won't change."

He shakes his head. "Fine. Then can you at least *come* to my place? Or do I need to get a separate love nest just for us?"

"Your place is fine."

17

EMMETT

Amy seems to be into privacy, so it's a good thing I live in a mansion. Still, part of me is annoyed that she refused to move in, because that would've made things easier. It isn't like we're strangers. We've known each other for almost two years now! That has to count for something.

From the way she reacted, she doesn't want me to show up at her apartment, either, since she doesn't want Sasha to know that we're sleeping together. *Irritating.* We pay more than enough for our associates to get their own places.

I'll see if I can do something about that later. For now, all I can think about is Amy. How nice she smells. How relaxed she seems after the massage. How she's smiling more easily.

My dick's so hard it's painful. But this isn't the time to hurry. I need to do my due diligence and find all the spots that drive her crazy.

I steer past the gates, secured by codes, and cruise through the green garden with topiaries of animals I inherited from the previous owner. When we reach the main entrance, I kill the engine, and she's already out of the car.

Trying to conceal how pounce-ready I am, I walk over and

open the door to the sprawling two-story structure for her. She breathes out, "Wow," as she looks around. I guess the place is impressive enough. I wouldn't know how it looks from a woman's point of view, since I've never brought one home. My mother doesn't count.

No time for a tour, though. Later, when the beastly lust is quenched.

"Come here." I pull Amy into my arms and claim her mouth. It's soft and sweet, tastes faintly of lemon and ginger. And is one hundred percent pure Amy. Infuriating, smart, cocky, determined, driven... Everything I like about her.

I thread my fingers into her warm, silken hair, cradling the curve of her head. I skim my free hand down her body, breast to flank to the flaring curve of her butt.

She responds like she can't get enough of me. Our tongues glide past each other, then tangle. My breathing grows louder and rougher; she plunges her hands into my hair, gripping my head for a deeper kiss. A small moan tears from her.

Jesus, she's addictive. If she was hot on Friday, now she's nuclear. Knowing she wants me as much as I want her makes my blood simmer.

I pull my mouth from hers for an unbearable second. "Hold on." I lift her up bridal style and carry her upstairs to my bedroom, where the door is ajar. I toe it open, carry her in and place her on the bed. The sight of her lying there, hair spread on the sheet like spun gold, is...perfect. It feels *right* to have her in my bed, her blue eyes dark and glazed with desire. Her lips are starkly red and wet from the kiss, and the desire to have her mouth on my cock makes my vision go hazy.

She looks up at me and licks her lips. *Jesus.* I place my hands on either side of her head and kiss her again, forcing myself to be tender and take it slow. She wraps a hand around the back of my waist and pulls me closer, sucking gently on my tongue.

Clinging to control, I slip a hand under her shirt. She reaches from the other side and unhooks her bra.

I give a fervent, silent thanks to whomever invented the front clasp as I cup her breast, feel the soft, warm weight against my bare palm and rub my thumb against the blunt, stiffened tip.

I push her shirt up and take her nipple into my mouth. She grips my hair as I suck, the tip of my tongue flicking over the hard little nub.

"Emmett, Emmett..."

Her mindless chant is an aphrodisiac. I lavish the other nipple with the same attention, and she cries out, her hips bucking.

Blood roars in my head. I pull the shirt over her head and toss it. I cover her neck with kisses and hear her breath hitch when I press my mouth against the skin behind her ears. A kiss with lips and tongue placed dead center between her collarbones makes her shiver. Fondling her breasts while layering her belly with kisses earns me a needy whimper that frays the already threadbare reins of my self-control.

She's incredibly responsive, her entire body open to sensual torment. But she's reacting with uncertainty every time I explore a new part of her gorgeous body, like she's unsure about my touch there. It's a crime nobody loved her thoroughly, showed her how her whole body can be used to make her feel good.

Their loss is my gain, I think with vicious satisfaction as I pull her pants and underwear down her legs, placing kisses along the path. She's lost her flip-flops somewhere between the foyer and the bedroom. I press my thumb against the arch of her foot. She moans in bliss. Smiling, I nip the skin at her ankle, then run my mouth along her calves and kiss the skin behind her knees. It makes her squirm, the muscles in her ass tightening as she lifts her hips impatiently. I lave the spot, just to be sure, and her fingers dig into the sheets.

"Mmm-hmmm. So soft and sensitive everywhere. We're going to have so much fun."

"Yes, yes," she whispers breathlessly. I don't know if she

understands half what I said or what she's agreeing to. She's feeling too good to know or care.

Excited at her reaction, I take her mouth in another lush, carnal kiss, our tongues tangling. I slip my hand between her legs. Feel the liquid heat. She's so slick, so wet.

My thumb against her clit, I push a finger into her. She makes a sound between bliss and dissatisfaction. After a couple of drives, I push two more fingers in and feel her clench around them desperately. I take a moment, inhaling and exhaling to regain my slippery grip on control. I experiment with the angle of the thrust, feel the way her inner muscles respond. My fingers bump against a small spot inside, and she screams against my mouth, digging her fingers into my shoulders.

"Do you like that, Amy?" I demand, elation driving me.

"*Yes!*" she yells.

Then, before she can let out another loud moan, I kiss her, fucking her with my fingers and letting her clit grind against the pad of my thumb. She braces her feet on the mattress and rocks against me, her back arching. Her leg and arm muscles shake as she tries to hang on.

But I'm going to watch her break as she hits the peak.

And she does, her mouth open in a soundless scream, her whole body tighter than an overwound spring, then suddenly relaxing into a puddle of bliss. Air rushes in and out her lungs, and I place tender kisses on her mouth and her breasts, then on her belly. I love everything about her orgasm. How it makes her lose herself. How it makes me want to drive her harder and higher.

I spread her legs. She's too overcome to care. Her pink flesh glistens, like a glazed treat. I wanted to lick it, suck on her clit until she comes again. But my dick's too hard and throbbing.

I rip my clothes off roughly, then reach over to the night table and pull out a condom from the drawer.

Once I'm properly sheathed, I position myself and thrust into her until I'm buried all the way to my balls.

Holy Christ. She feels amazing. And it actually feels hotter than on Friday when I drove into her bare.

I grip her hips and begin to move. *Oh yes.*

It's an effort not to just immediately go full speed, but I should wait. See if she like it that way, too...

...but the sliver of control I've been hanging on to vanishes like a snowflake in my grip, and I power into her. She clings to me hard. She whispers my name endlessly, breathlessly.

Her growing pleasure feeds mine, and I'm now out of my mind with searing need for her. My skin is tight and hot, my lungs struggling to draw in air as I plunge into her.

She arches against me, clinging to me, her voice an aria of ecstasy. I bury my face in the crook of her neck and inhale her sweet scent—mixed with clean, misted sweat and arousal. And I erupt, my arms wrapped around her like she's the only thing that matters in my world.

18

EMMETT

Amy passes out after the last orgasm. I hold her, feeling more at peace than I can ever remember.

It's the sex, my dick says.

It's not the sex. Well, okay, it's partly the sex. But I've never felt this way after sex with another woman.

It's Amy.

Making her lose herself isn't just fun, it's *satisfying*. I could spend the rest of my life doing it. Cash out my stake in GrantEm, let Grant take over the firm. Or maybe provide capital, but stay out of day-to-day management.

On the other hand, that probably isn't something Amy would want. She's too driven to be with a man who doesn't have some ambition of his own.

Somewhere, my phone buzzes.

It's Sunday. Can't be anything that important.

I let it go to voicemail, but a few moments later, it buzzes again.

Amy's brows start to pinch.

Fucking asshole. I don't know who's on the phone, but it has to be an asshole to be calling on Sunday when I'm trying to have some quality time with the woman I've been obsessing over for almost two years.

I pull away gently and tuck her in, making sure sheets are covering her all the way to her chin. I find my pants on the floor and pull out my phone, then tiptoe out of the room, ready to ream the butthole.

The screen says: Dad.

I feel my face scrunch. What the hell is going on?

He never contacts us. Not for holidays. Not for birthdays—ours, not his. It's kind of a shock that he even knows my number. Whenever he wants to convey a message, he has Joey gets in touch via texts.

Probably a butt dial. Or maybe Dad has decided to dispense with assistants and harass me directly.

Dad calls *again.* I'm tempted to ignore him, but he might go nuclear, call Mom on her well-deserved luxury Mediterranean cruise and ruin her vacation because nobody should be happy when he isn't. Or come over to confront me in person. And I'd rather eat my shoes than risk having Amy meet him. It'd be too embarrassing.

Suck it up and answer it. Humoring him is easier than fighting him.

I wait until I'm at the bottom of the staircase so I don't bother Amy. "*What?*"

"Son of a bitch. That took a while."

"I was napping," I snap, then reach into the fridge and grab a bottle of water.

"I'm calling about my birthday."

"Okay."

"I've decided what you all can give me this year."

"Okay..."

"I want a baby."

What the *fuck*? I'm glad I was in the process of twisting the cap open, not actually drinking the water. "Well, Dad, you know what to do. Just have another vasectomy fail. The baby won't come in time for this birthday, but next year you'll have a new little human to bounce on your knee."

"Not my baby! *Your* baby!" Dad booms.

The planet seems to stop spinning for a moment. "What?"

"You heard me. I want a grandbaby. That fuckin' Josh Singer's bragging about his grandson." Contempt drips from the last word.

Josh Singer is, in my father's mind, the Arch-Nemesis. There doesn't seem to be any real reason, but then, Dad doesn't need a reason to hate someone.

"Fuck him and his bragging," Dad grouses.

"Okay, let's back up a bit. Number one, Josh's kids are married. Grandchildren are what happen when your *children are married*." Why do I have to be the one to unruffle his feathers? Some young, nubile thing should be on that. He's surrounded by women all the time.

"You don't need to be married to make a baby!"

"Yeah, well, I'm not doing it your way." When I have a baby, I'm going to marry the mother of my child first. Do things properly.

"I just want one, not seven! *Just one!* What does a man need to do to get what he wants for his damn birthday?"

Oh for God's sake! I'm not having a baby just to give him something to rub it into Josh Singer's face. "I gotta go. I have an *urgent* call."

"Nothing's more urgent than this!"

"Actually, everything is." I hang up, turn my phone off and let out a rough breath.

"Um. You okay?" comes Amy's voice from behind me.

Oh, fuck. Rubbing my forehead, I turn around. She's standing at the bottom of the stairs, looking gorgeous and sexy as hell in her shirt and shorts, her long legs and feet bare. "How much did you hear?"

She rolls her eyes left and right in a slightly amused do-you-really-wanna-know expression. "Something about an urgent call? Did you mean a call of nature?"

I laugh. "No, don't worry. Nothing *that* urgent."

"If you say so. But don't deny yourself just because I'm here." A corner of her lips twitches, then she lets out a small giggle. "By the way, who was that?"

"My dad."

"Oh. Do you two...um...get along?"

With another woman, I'd just shrug and smile. No need to go into detail about my personal life. With Amy, I want to answer... but honesty would be embarrassing. Dad is one of the things that my brothers and I pretend don't exist as much as possible.

"We get along great." *As long as we don't have any contact.* I grin, determined to move the conversation into more pleasant territory. "Wanna see the place? I haven't given you a tour."

19

AMY

Emmett doesn't seem that interested in talking about his father, so I decide not to probe. Just because he gave me more soul-destroying orgasms today than all of my past boyfriends combined doesn't give me the right to dig into his personal life.

Especially after I said that what we're doing is a fling—just sex. So I focus on the tour of his mansion.

Emmett's home is rich. But not gaudy-new-money rich. It's understated and classy, an interesting combination of marble, wood and crystal. The furniture is contemporary and expensive, but it doesn't have a don't-touch museum vibe that you see in some homes. It invites you to relax and let your guard down, which isn't so easy to pull off in a place that's dripping with money. Original paintings hang from walls. No family photos with his dad, although I do spot a couple of shots with Grant and a few other guys Emmett's age. There are also several photos of Emmett with a well-preserved brunette, whose similarities to Emmett are so striking that she has to be his mom. Lots of pretty flower arrangements everywhere—and they're fresh. Can't be more than a day old.

"I'm surprised you have so many flowers." We settle on a

plush couch in the living room opposite a huge TV. Since our situation is mainly about sex, I don't want to get too personal.

"Why is that so surprising?"

"When do you have the time to enjoy them?" Besides, Emmett doesn't strike me as the type to buy flowers just because.

"I don't, but there's a local florist my mom likes. It makes her happy that I support him."

Emmett must adore his mother. He's spending a fortune on flowers he doesn't care for, and he didn't become rich by wasting money. Maybe those nasty articles about his mom's mercenary ways weren't exactly true. Lowbrow publications aren't generally interested in the truth, just whatever gets the most clicks.

"You've seen his work before," he says.

"I have?" My ex-boyfriends never bought me flowers, and GrantEm doesn't invest in ventures as small and ordinary as flower shops.

"Larry does the flowers for the GrantEm events. Those roses you got for making the top five among your peers came from his place."

Huh. I remember them being exceptionally large and fresh. Still, there has to be more to Emmett's mom's liking the florist than just his thumbs being intensely green. "So what did he do? Save your mom from a mugger?"

"Not quite that dramatic. But Mom did have her purse snatched. While everyone was busy digging out their phones to film the event, he offered to call Mom an Uber and gave her some cash so she could get home safely. He told Mom he'd offer to drive, but that might not make her feel comfortable, considering."

"Wow. That was nice of him." It sounds like a meet-cute from a romantic comedy.

"He'd just opened his shop, and it was doing okay. But when I heard about it from Mom, I wanted to do something."

It makes sense. If somebody ever did something similar for me, Dad would fix the man's car for free for life.

"Before I forget..." Emmett reaches into a drawer underneath the coffee table and pulls out a sleek black key card with a long series of numbers stamped on it. "Here. For you."

"What is it?"

"A guest access key to the garage. You can also scan it over the door there to get inside. And if you lose the card, you can input the first three and last three digits directly into the system to get in. So you should memorize those."

"Oh." I continue to stare at the shiny plastic. I've never exchanged keys with any of my ex-boyfriends. It always felt too personal and involved. Like *mi casa es tu casa*, but more invasive. My bed is your bed. My time is your time.

"Here," Emmett says. "Take it."

No way to gracefully escape. I wrap stiff fingers around the card. "Um. Does this mean you want a key to my place...?"

He shakes his head. "I remember what you said about living with Sasha. But it'll be easier if you can come here anytime, rather than wait for me to get home first or ask the housekeeper to let you in."

"Thanks," I say, pleased that he isn't being difficult about the whole thing. "But you aren't worried about letting me in here? What if I come over and rob you blind?"

"You would never do that. I wouldn't have asked you to move in with me earlier if I couldn't trust you."

Wow. That's the nicest thing Emmett has ever said to me. Well, he's said other stuff, like how hot he thought I was, but he's complimenting my *character*—and we're both fully clothed at the moment. I should mark the date on a calendar.

"Besides, I know where you work." He winks. "Hey, are you hungry?"

"No, but I could use a drink."

He moves to the kitchen, me following. He reaches into the fridge and pulls out a bottle of sparkling pink lemonade from a local beverage company.

"How did you know that's my favorite?"

"How could I not know? Other than coffee, it's the only thing you drink in the office." He uncaps it and hands it to me.

Surprised he noticed. "Thanks." I take a sip and sigh. It's so, so good. I'm going to miss this when I move to Virginia.

"Can you keep next weekend free?" Emmett asks.

"Why?"

"I want to take you to La Jolla. I have a vacation home there, so we can spend the weekend in San Diego. Maybe scuba dive, if you're certified. If not, we'll think of something."

"Actually, I am certified. Got my license in high school." When I graduated, Dad and I went on a scuba tour in the Caribbean. We loved it, although we never got a chance to try again because I've been so busy. Diving in San Diego sounds fantastic.

"Awesome! There's this amazing kelp forest. You'll love it." He smiles, his eyes twinkling, making him look a hundred times hotter and more approachable. "If we're lucky, we might get to see some seals, too."

I grin. "Wow. Is there anything I need to bring for this trip?"

He shakes his head. "I'll prep everything. All you have to do is show up at the airport on Friday looking pretty. I'll text you the details."

20

AMY

The week's going great. *Much* better than I expected.

Although Emmett agreed to keep our fling a secret, I worried a little that he might change the way he treats me, which would let the more observant gossipmongers in the office figure out something's up.

But nope. He doesn't do any of that.

He still texts me this-or-that questions, which is fine. I don't mind helping him out with his *market survey*. He also tells me to redo my Excel models, probably for "fun training." But instead of waiting until it's five fifty-five p.m., he asks between two thirty and three thirty, which is an improvement so massive it brings appreciative yet slightly peeved tears to my eyes. The annoyance being that he could've done this *before*.

Still, I get to leave by nine o'clock. A true miracle.

Of course, Sasha notices. "Did you tell Emmett he'd better let you go home early because you aren't going to stick around much longer?" she whispers in the break room on Wednesday. She and I haven't had a chance to talk since my fling with Emmett started. She came back from San Francisco late on Sunday, and she's been super busy since then with urgent deadlines from Grant, only coming home to shower and change, then head straight back to office. She's been living on nothing but gummy worms and coffee for the last three days. "You've never gone home before eleven back to back before."

I start to answer, then remember what Emmett said about this room being not so private. "No. But I think he's finally realized I do better work with at least seven hours of sleep."

The extra sleep has other side effects. Like quadrupling Emmett's attractiveness. The man is already hot as hell, but when my brain is crystal clear with sufficient rest, the impact of his sparkling blue-gray eyes and smiling mouth hits me like TNT detonating.

Thankfully, nobody seems to have noticed anything's different. Emmett hasn't eased up on cracking hearts and crushing souls. Webber still walks around looking dejected, and Diana still seems like she's ready to burst into tears at any time.

Anyway, since Sasha *did* notice my changed schedule, I decide to stay late and get some extra work done. No need to get on her finely honed suspicion radar.

I review the models and memos that the analyst working with me on the Drone project sent. Janey went too conservative. A very gloomy outlook. Her explanatory notes aren't bad, but they show that she disregarded data that contradicts her position. Not good.

Her job is to look at *all* the data and then make a judgment call. She's been with the firm for the last eleven months, so somebody should've taught her that by now. Who was she working with before?

I look up her profile on the intranet database... *Webber*.

I shake my head. He should've mentored her better. I send a quick email to Janey, asking her to redo her model. The server syncs; the email disappears from the outbox.

I feel vaguely annoyed. And...a little weird. Like I just pulled an Emmett Lasker bosshole maneuver. Well, not quite *that* bad. Unlike Emmett, I didn't tell her to stay up until two a.m. to get it done. Besides, this is for her benefit. She has at least one more year to go at GrantEm.

My phone buzzes.

–Emmett: Can you come over to my office?

Hopefully he hasn't found some Excel model that requires an immediate redo.

Maybe it's karma.

Shut up.

I stop myself from running my fingers through my hair and stand up. *Emmett and I established a firm rule that we're going to be professional in the office. Remember that. No need to primp.*

I take a deep breath and make my way toward his office. It's a little after ten, and the floor is empty. The cleaning crew doesn't come in until four thirty a.m. Plus I guess everyone's having a slow day, since we usually have some people at desk on Wednesday nights. Even Sasha and her team went home by ten. Grant ordered them all to get six hours of sleep, since they've been dragging their feet like zombies.

I knock on the door, like a good, professional employee, even though nobody's around to see.

"Come in," Emmett calls out.

I open the door and walk inside. Before I can take a breath, the door slams behind me, and Emmett's mouth crashes down on mine.

You're in the office! Kissing is not professional! Sadly, the voice of judgment is no match for the hot lust my boss's mouth arouses in me.

His tongue invades my mouth, and I grip his arms. The muscles are taut and hard, and I whimper at how much I've missed this kiss, missed tasting him and feeling his need for me growing more intense as our mouths tango.

He pulls me tight. His large erection presses against my belly; my body zings with lust, but I put a hand on his chest and push back, gulping for some cool air to reorient myself.

NADIA LEE

"You're still here." He places his forehead on mine. "You should've gone to my place. I was waiting to follow you home."

"I was *working*. Sasha thinks it's weird I left early two days in a row. She would've gotten really suspicious if I left early again."

"Forget her. Let's go home." Clearly, the *home* in question is his.

This must be how Eve felt when the snake offered her the forbidden fruit. *Trust me, it's perfectly fine.* But I stay strong and shake my head. "No."

He raises his eyebrows.

My mouth dries as heat spreads through me. "If it's anything like Sunday, we won't be done until two in the morning. At least." The sex on Sunday was the best ever. It drove me insane how he wouldn't relent, just kept going and going, submerging me in one tsunami of pleasure after another. "And I'm going to want to roll over and fall asleep."

"So? My bed's big enough for two of us."

"*So?* So what do I say to Sasha when she wants to know why I didn't come home?"

"I thought she was a roommate, not a cockblocker." He lets out an irritated sigh. "Let's get you a place of your own."

"No. I'm not leaving her in the lurch." Besides, she already knows I'm moving out soon to take a new job. It's going to look really weird if I tell her I need my own apartment.

Emmett waves a hand. "I'll cover your portion of the rent." Mr. Problem Solver.

"No!" Even if I weren't moving away, I wouldn't agree to this. "There will be no money exchange between us here. If you insist, we won't do this at all." I want his body, but not enough to disrupt my entire life.

He gives me a thoughtful look, although his darkening eyes hint at growing frustration. "Well, if you aren't coming to my place—"

I put a finger over his mouth, still wet from our kiss. "We

160

don't have to do it at your place. In case you haven't noticed, the office is empty now."

The dream I had on Friday simply *refuses* to let me alone. *Me bent over the desk. My ass lifted for Emmett.*

Slick heat gathers between my legs. I want to know how good it's going to feel. *Probably mind-blowing.* For some reason, every sexual thing I try with Emmett is amazing.

The man isn't just a god of finance. He's also a god of sex.

I tunnel my fingers into his hair, pulling him down for another kiss. He wraps his arms around me. This time, when his cock presses against my belly, I rock against him, my mouth fused to his.

"Tell me you have a condom on you," I murmur against his mouth.

"Of course. I *am* the CEO."

"What does being CEO have to—"

"Condoms Eternally On-hand."

I laugh into our kiss, lost in the taste of him, all heat and Emmett. His heart booms hard and fast against the hand I place over it. His excitement is infectiously, exhilaratingly hot.

I maneuver us around in gentle, dance-like circles until my ass bumps against the edge of his desk, exactly where I want to be. He unzips the professional ivory and gray dress and pushes it down until I'm in nothing but my bra and thong.

"I will never get enough of this view," he says.

His reaction ratchets up my confidence. I'm enjoying the view, too, of his thick cock pressed against his slacks. Smiling, my eyes on his, I unhook my bra and let it fall. He takes a nipple into his mouth with an impatient groan and drags my thong down my legs. Then he travels south, his mouth leaving a hot trail down my belly. He spreads my knees and positions himself between my thighs, his breath tickling my skin, raising shivery goosebumps.

I should feel vulnerable and weak, standing in his office naked while he's fully clothed. But the erotic worship in his eyes makes me feel bold. Empowered.

"You smell great," he rasps.

My face heats. When men go down on you, it's usually because they want you to suck their cock later. A little quid pro quo extra-credit work, rather than something they're doing because they really want to. And they make sure you know it, if not explicitly then by overtly hinting at it, in case you're—God forbid—too obtuse.

But not Emmett. He sighs appreciatively and closes his mouth over my lady parts like he's dying for it. I gasp as his tongue flicks around, his hands sliding up, up, up until they cup my breasts, his fingers toying with the beaded nipples.

Intense bliss radiates all over—from my nipples, my clit...from the absolute core of who I am. Everywhere he touches turns into an erogenous zone.

A climax builds abruptly, slamming into me with a force that leaves me punch-drunk. Air catches in my lungs and my vision dims. Even as I struggle for breath, he rises and kisses me, his tongue invading my mouth. I kiss him back, desperate for more of him. For the pleasure only he can give.

He grips my ass, digging his fingers in, kneading possessively. I love the rough handling. It says so much about how little control he has left.

"Your ass is killing me," he whispers between kisses.

"I think *my everything* is killing you."

He lets out a laugh, dark with need.

Shooting him a saucy grin, I turn around and bend over the desk, my arms stretched out, my hands together. I tilt my pelvis, giving him a view of the ass he loves so much.

He curses under his breath. Bet his underwear is wet with precum.

"Put your cock in me." My voice is dreamy with anticipation.

"You telling me what to do? Who's the boss here, anyway?" He slaps my ass, the sting wringing a gasp out of me; I'm half surprised and half turned on. "Patience."

He undoes his buckles and fastener. There's the hiss of a

zipper and the ripping of foil. Then his cock is pushing at the entrance of my dripping pussy.

I expected him to drive in hard, like on Sunday. But his movements are unhurried. Smooth. Each leisurely thrust lays another film of honey-sweet pleasure over me, until I'm drowning in the simple, hot joy of having him inside. Sweat mists over my bare skin, and I arch my back, pressing against him, wanting him to up the tempo.

Instead, he grips my hips and controls the pace completely. His absolute dominance over both himself and my body drives me crazy, until I'm whimpering and begging.

An orgasm begins to shimmer like the sun rising on the horizon. He drives me toward it as I reach for it. When it finally breaks over me, it isn't frenzied like before, but as deep and powerful as the vast ocean. And I cry out his name endlessly.

No matter what happens, I'm never going to regret this fling with Emmett Lasker.

21

AMY

Emmett and I disembark from his jet on Friday at three forty p.m. "I still can't believe you told everyone in the office this was a work trip," I say.

"You don't want anybody to know what we're really up to, right? And I didn't feel like waiting until evening. The view's prettier at sunset."

Emmett isn't showing the least bit of guilt over the lies he fed everyone about needing to do an in-depth review of the distribution partners for Bernie's water filter venture. There are two in San Diego that Bernie's considering.

"Do I need to make a PowerPoint presentation or draft an executive memo?"

He gives me a blank look. "For what?"

"So we have some work deliverables to show on Monday? I can probably mock something up that looks decent enough in a couple of hours, as long as you don't expect perfection from a prop."

He waves away my offer. "That's already taken care of. I told you, all you have to do is show up."

Wow. He really meant what he said.

Well, in that case, I'm just going to sit back and relax. Since he's a perfectionist, whatever he's put together probably looks amazing. I'll just soak up the atmosphere here and think about our dive adventure. I googled some underwater photos, and they looked great. In person should be incredible.

The drive to La Jolla takes less than half an hour once we load our rental SUV, waiting for us on the tarmac by the runway. I've never been to San Diego before—no time—and love how different it feels. A lot more casual and relaxed.

Emmett's "vacation home" is more like a mansion. Located on a beach, it has two pools and hot tubs and walls with enormous windows to maximize a gorgeous view of the Pacific.

I look around the place like a gawking tourist, taking in everything from the cool marble floors to the walls in a shade somewhere between cream and peach. The furniture is mainly ivory, with teal and yellow accents. A spiral staircase sits to the left, and a huge open kitchen to the right. Straight ahead of me is a giant deck.

I walk out onto the deck and have to put a hand over my eyes despite my sunglasses. The sky is cloudless and an absolutely perfect blue. A gentle breeze carries the scent of salt and ocean. The water moves constantly, reflecting the sun from every possible angle.

Placing my hands on the warm wooden balustrade, I practice some deep breathing. It's like emotional toxins that I didn't know were accumulating inside me are being expelled with every exhalation.

"Enjoying the scene?" Emmett says, a smile in his voice. He walks up next to me and looks out at the ocean.

"Love it. I can totally see why Dad wants the view."

"He's thinking about retiring in La Jolla?"

I shake my head. "No, way too pricey. Florida. He loves the beaches there after living in a landlocked state for so long. And he deserves it. He's done so much."

I shoot Emmett a smile, then take a quick selfie to send to Dad.

"For a woman who doesn't do social media, you seem to take selfies pretty seriously," Emmett says.

"No, it's this thing I have with my dad. He doesn't like it when I send him emojis. Says he prefers to see my face." I smile. "And I like to make him happy. It's the least I can do. How about your father?" I ask, stepping over the boundaries into a more personal territory. I know I shouldn't, especially after telling Emmett repeatedly this is just a sex-only fling. But I can't seem to stop myself. Maybe it's because Emmett's looking at me like every word out of my mouth is fascinating. Or maybe it's the view. Or maybe it's this weird tingling sensation in my soul that feels regenerative.

"Well..." Emmett shrugs. "He bought us Maseratis and Lamborghinis, but doesn't expect any selfies in return. I think he'd be horrified if we started doing that." Another shrug.

"So your Lamborghini was from him?"

"The one I've got now? Hell no. I bought myself a new one. Mom took the old one, even though I told her I'd buy her whatever she wanted." His expression softens. "She did a lot for me."

"Oh." I don't know what to say. It feels weird to hear someone talk about his mother as a person who's capable of putting somebody else's needs first. I mean, I know such moms must exist, but the idea seems sort of surreal. Like a lottery everyone but me can win.

But Emmett takes my "oh" as an encouragement to continue.

"She gave up on love because she kept falling in love with poor guys."

That sounds kind of gold-diggerish, but there's probably more to the story.

"Dad's child support was set to end when she married someone," Emmett adds.

"You're a little old for child support..."

"I mean in the past. Now... Yeah, she thinks love isn't going to happen for her at this point. There was a painter in Paris she loved when I was in high school, but they broke up because he wanted to marry her, and she couldn't. When he got engaged to somebody else, she was devastated, although she did her best to hide it." He sighs, then shrugs like he's not going to let it bother him.

"That sounds awful." His mom's struggle is like my dad's— giving up what could make her happy to provide a better life for her child. "But there are billions of men out there. She can find one who's right for her."

The smile on his face is a little tight. "Maybe, if she can find someone who can look past her rep. Social media makes it hard to keep your private affairs private."

He's standing in sunlight with a gorgeous backdrop, but there's a hint of melancholy. My heart aches for him and his mother. I always thought if you had the kind of money Emmett does, life would be easy. Good things just rolling into your lap while you wipe your nonexistent tears with hundred-dollar bills.

Knowing that he has worries and feelings like everyone else makes him seem a hundred times more approachable.

I place my palm over his cheek and go up on my toes. My lips find his in a soft, loving kiss, barely brushing against each other, while we share the same air, endlessly, achingly.

Our hearts seem to beat in unison. Heat rises, but there's much more underneath. Something infinitely sweet and lovely that I don't dare put a name to because it's too scary. Too life-changing.

This is just for a few weeks until I go off to another state, three time zones away from SoCal.

Emmett lifts me and takes me upstairs, where we hold each other and make slow, gentle love that breaks my soul.

22

AMY

"Sleepyhead..."

I put a pillow over my head.

"Sleepyyyheeeead..."

"I'm on vacation," I grumble.

"Even so. Time to get up."

Emmett sounds entirely too cheery, which is better than the gloomy mood from yesterday when he was talking about his mom. But I make it a rule not to get up early on vacation if I can help it. Having to get up early and hustle is something work makes me do.

"Give me one good reason," I mumble.

He kisses my bare shoulder. "Don't you want to see the kelp forest?"

I crack my eyes open. "The kelp forest?"

"Yup."

I gasp and come fully awake. "Scuba diving!"

He grins. "Exactly."

"Yes, yes, yes." I hop off the bed and rush to the bathroom. "I'm dying to see it."

He laughs. "Well, you can't go naked. So get ready."

"Okay."

I take a light-speed shower and get dressed. No makeup other than lip gloss, since we're going to be in the water. Then I toss a cardigan—ocean temperatures tend to be low—and a bottle of sunscreen—because the sun will be high—into my beach tote bag and rush down to meet Emmett on the first floor.

He hands me a small latte and a light breakfast of toast and banana chunks. Gotta get some carbs to keep my energy up before the dive. "Should we pack some snacks and drinks too?" I ask. The air you breathe while diving is dry, which sucks the moisture out of you.

"I already packed everything. And I hired a guide for our dive."

"You did?" I thought it'd be more private. On the other hand, it isn't like we can do anything naughty underwater. *Can we?*

"We probably won't need her, but it can't hurt. Besides, it keeps her employed for the day. And I want somebody to take pictures of us." He grins. "I already briefed her."

"Good call." The only thing I regret about my dive tour with Dad is that we have only two pictures of us together underwater.

We drive to the beach. The guide, a lean blond woman named Jessie, is already waiting with my gear. Emmet unloads his own scuba set from the SUV as she helps me put mine on. Surprisingly, there's no boat in sight.

"Can't take a boat out," Jessie tells us when I ask. "It's, like, totally against the rules here. Gotta protect the marine life, right? But you can take one out if you dive in another spot."

"The kelp bed is only a quarter mile offshore," Emmet says. "It's worth the effort. And the water seems pretty calm today."

"Okay." I can probably swing a quarter-mile swim. It can't be any worse than thirty-five flights of GrantEm stairs.

We change into our gear, check to make sure everything's in order and enter the surf, holding our fins. My heart thumps with excitement as my feet dig into the sand. Once the water's slapping our chests, we put on the fins and start snorkeling out. The visibility is excellent in the blue-green water: fish darting, bits of seaweed dancing.

The water's calm, like Emmett said, and the fins make it easy to swim. So it doesn't take too long before we're at the kelp bed. We put on the regulators and dive.

A gorgeous vista unfolds. If I weren't underwater, I would be sighing with admiration.

The kelp strands are huge, stretching from the ocean floor all the way to the surface fifty feet above. Their leaves spread out and sway to the current, creating a beautiful light show in the sunlit-filtered water.

Bright red, orange and gold schools of fish dart among the towering columns of kelp like they're playing hide-and-seek. They don't panic or scatter away from us, seemingly not afraid of people at all.

A turtle glides by, swimming with the cutest and blandest expression on its face, like it's too cool to care about anything or anybody. I tug at Emmett, who seems to be totally at home in the water, and point.

He turns, gives me the "OK" signal and then points at something to his left. I stare, mesmerized, as seals cut through the water like living bullets, their bodies sleek and streamlined as they playfully twist and turn. They're stunning. I've seen nature documentaries about wild seals, but watching them on TV simply doesn't compare.

None of the sea creatures swim away as we lazily propel ourselves among them, until I spot a small, lobster-looking thing on a rock. It dances back a little, like it can't decide if we're harmless or not, raising its tiny claws in challenge. I wish I could communicate that we're totally harmless.

Jessie floats by, camera in hand, and takes a couple of shots. Emmett swims up and slips an arm around my waist, which has to be difficult under the circumstances. He signals Jessie, and she takes our picture from several angles.

More time goes by, and it's almost like I'm dreaming. The

pressure of the water around me and the regular sound of my own breathing, combined with the green-filtered light, make everything seem surreal. Then something that feels a bit too substantial to be a kelp leaf brushes my leg. I turn a little and see an open mouth full of teeth...and a dorsal fin.

Holy shit! Shark!

My heart races. A shark in open water can be bad news. An article I read about shark attacks flashes through my head while the ominous theme from *Jaws* plays in the background. Although the shark isn't really big enough to eat me, it's big enough to take a good chunk out of my thigh. And it looks hungry.

Now I *really* wish I could speak shark, so I could tell the thing that I'm not very tasty. Plus, I'm covered in a rubber wet suit, which has to taste bad—even to a shark. I swim away, but it lazily circles back around to follow. Another one moves closer as well.

Can sharks signal their buddies to come join them for feeding? I thought only dolphins could communicate with each other with their clicking sounds.

Feeling a little panicked, I tug on Emmett's arm.

He looks back, and I point at the sharks.

He waves, not at the shark, but at me. What's he trying to say?

I shrug helplessly, but he reaches over and squeezes my hand. The simple motion soothes my frayed nerves. Suddenly, my heart is no longer racing. Emmett puts his free hand out as the shark glides by and strokes its flank. The fish doesn't show any reaction, content to share its domain with us, and the adrenaline spiking in my veins settles down.

I feel safe.

I stare at our linked hands, then at Emmett. And here, in this alien, aquamarine realm, I realize there's something more between us than just his bossholehood and sex.

23

AMY

Eventually, we have to surface and swim back to shore. Jessie strips me out of my gear with casual competence and promises to send us our photos in the next day or two.

After changing, we grab lunch at a casual seafood restaurant with a view of the ocean we just emerged from. Emmett teases me about my reaction to the sharks, which, it turns out, are actually harmless.

"Okay, but how could I have known? They didn't have a we-don't-eat-humans sign on their backs."

"Because they were too small?" he says. "They were barely as long as you are."

"They could've eaten my thigh. Or an arm. Taken it off right at the elbow."

"Amy wings, with barbecue sauce?"

"Right! I mean, a shark will eat anything."

After lunch, Emmett and I come home, shower and chill. It didn't seem like much in the way of exercise, going so leisurely through the water, but the dive took it out of me. If I weren't in San Diego for the first time, I'd probably just get a pizza delivered for dinner later. But I want to see more of this gorgeous city.

So we go a drive. Emmett knows all the beautiful, interesting spots we can hit. We don't go to SeaWorld or the zoo, because SeaWorld would be anemic after our dive and the zoo is enormous and would take literally an entire day. But we hit Balboa Park and stroll through the gardens and the Botanical Building, with more lush flora than I've seen in my entire life. Thankfully, there are no potentially man-eating animal encounters.

Afterward, we take a drive along the coast. I take tons of photos, and we laugh and smile as we take silly selfies and eat ice cream by the beach. The sunset is stunning, gold and orange from the sky bleeding into the restless blue ocean until the Pacific looks like it's on fire.

I've been on beaches at sunset before, but this feels different. The vibe is more easygoing. And I'm holding Emmett's hand, our fingers threaded and linked. The breeze tousles our hair, and I can't recall the last time I was this happy. Or had this strong of a need humming through my veins.

I tilt my head. Emmett turns at the same moment and our eyes meet. And then our mouths do.

He kisses me tenderly, sweetly, like we have all the time in the world. I soak in his flavor, his texture. I love the way he carries me off to another universe where it's just me and him and our desire for each other.

More than sex, more than sex, a voice in my head sings.

Part of me wonders if he feels it too. Or maybe this is how he treats all his girls, and I'm trying to read something that doesn't exist because none of my ex-boyfriends did anything this nice. After all, all that "diamonds or pearls" or "rubies or sapphires" or "beach or mountain cabin" stuff must've been for some woman or other. Just because he's amazing now doesn't mean he's going to stay that way forever.

The thought leaves me bereft, like an abandoned child.

I pull back under the darkening sky before I do anything stupid. "We should get back."

"We have to go get dinner first," he says, his eyes unreadable.

He drives us to an upscale seafood and steak restaurant and gives the smiling hostess his name. She checks her system and nods. "Yes, we have you right here. Your table's ready."

"When did you make the reservation?" I ask in surprise.

"Friday before we left. I thought you'd like it here."

I smile with appreciation at his thorough planning. He's making me feel special, like this is more than just sex. Like I matter.

Don't get too comfortable, girlfriend. There's a deadline on this thing. One you set.

But that doesn't mean my heart doesn't melt. I'm not a robot.

The hostess takes us to a table set in the balcony overlooking the beach. She leaves us with our menu and water.

"Wow, it's so pretty," I say, looking out at the view.

"It's got its own charm at night. The moon's out, too."

I tilt my head. Sure enough, a full moon is sitting low in the velvety black sky, the silver light dancing over the rolling ocean.

Suddenly, something jars the table. The water in our glasses sloshes over, leaving wet spots on the table cloth.

As I turn to see what's going on, a brunette in a red dress pushes herself from our table. A strong smell of alcohol wafts from her, and she's barely standing straight.

"Are you okay?" I look around to see if she has a friend or date or someone. And sure enough, a man is hurrying over—

Marion Blaire? Oh shit!

What's he doing in San Diego? He lives in Virginia, five freakin' flight hours away!

"Sorry," he says, putting his arms around her.

Should I look away and pretend I have no idea who he is? Yeah, that's going to go over real well, when he's going to be my next boss. Not to mention, I can't pull that off gracefully anyway.

Before I can decide on what to do, he pulls back a little. "Amy?" A grin splits his face. "Hey, how are you?"

"Hi," I squeak.

"Sorry. This is my fiancée, Brandie. She's been out in the sun

174

for too long and had one drink too many on an empty stomach." He gives me a sheepish what-can-you-do? smile.

"You two know each other?" Emmett says. His voice is glass smooth.

Damn it! That's the tone he gets when he's upset. He's only talked like that in the office, about deliverables. But I guess it also applies to non-office settings too.

"You're here with *him?*" Marion points at Emmett, his gaze sweeping my boss up and down, almost too thoroughly to be polite. Emmett's dressed casually, and so am I, although Marion isn't inspecting me to compare, thank God!

Emmett shoots him a razor-edged look. "Yes, she is. We're on business."

"On a Saturday evening?" Marion's tone says *bullshit*. His fiancée is still swaying on his arm, but he doesn't make a move to take her back to their table.

"Some of the best deals are done on weekends. Those of us who had to climb the ladder on our own know this." Emmett blinks innocently.

"Well. Dragging an associate out on a weekend for a job." Marion tsks and turns to me, hooking a thumb at Emmett. "He can't possibly be worth this level of personal sacrifice."

I give him an awkward smile and take the fifth.

"Loyalty," Emmett says. "You wouldn't understand."

Time to defuse the situation! "It's my job," I announce.

Marion ignores Emmett. "Loyalty is a two-way street. And this guy won't be there for you when you need him. If I were you, I'd be choosy about who I gave my loyalty to."

My God. Emmett's my boss, not the man I gave my heart and soul to! But from the way Marion's talking, Emmett and I are about to tie the knot and make a baseball team's worth of babies.

"I don't feel so goooo..." Brandie whines. Her head droops and sways back and forth, hair hanging like seaweed.

"Maybe you should take her back to your table?" I say, half

standing to catch her in case she collapses. "Or a bathroom?" I'm also *desperate* to have Marion go away.

"Very classy, holding a conversation while holding a nearly passed-out woman," Emmett says. "I guess this would be your version of multitasking?"

Marion turns with a retort, but Brandie's face plops on his chest, then slowly slides down, her eyes closed.

Cursing, he carries her away.

I let out a soft breath. "You didn't have to be so mean about the fiancée. I had a drunk incident, too."

"Yeah, but A, you aren't my fiancée, and B, you were highly entertaining. If you're going to be drunk, you have to be fun. Otherwise, it's just crass." Emmett taps his fingers on the menu. "How do you know that idiot, anyway?"

"Oh, I interviewed with his firm once. When I was, uh, looking for a job during my second year at Wharton."

Emmett's eyes turn flinty. Like Dirty Harry about to shoot a scumbag. "Fucker," he mutters finally. "Should've known. You must've made an impression for him to remember you after all these years."

Crap. "I guess." I give him what I hope is an innocent smile.

"At least I don't think he noticed anything about us. Second teamer for sure." He picks up his menu. "Let's order dinner."

Relieved that he's dropping the topic, I nod. And make a mental note to be more careful.

24

EMMETT

"Okay, you Martian body snatcher. Where's my brother and what have you done with him?" Grant says, strolling into my office on Monday before the floor starts teeming with analysts and associates.

"What do you want? I have a lot of stuff to get through." Gotta make up for the work I didn't do over the weekend.

He peers at me. "When you talk like that, you sound like the brother I know, but..."

"Yesss...?"

"You've been too cheery," he says in the same tone a doctor might say, "Your condition is terminal."

That brings me up short. "*Cheery...?*"

"Well, you know. Relatively speaking. You didn't make anybody cry last week."

"What is it with—? I don't make people cry! I merely show them the error of their ways. How they decide to react is on them."

"Ha. Show them in a way that has them in the emergency stairwell sobbing." He drags his index fingers down his face.

"And since when do you care about how I handle the staff?

You know the rule. If you can't move up..." I make a cutting motion across the neck.

"Obviously. But there's something wrong when you aren't making HR sweat, wondering what bullshit they need to feed everyone to get them to not hate you."

I roll my eyes. HR has never had to do that. "They don't hate me. They instantly forgive me when I talk about the ten percent of the workforce that does anything meaningful at GrantEm and the other ninety that are sheer deadweight." For whatever reason, everyone believes they're the ten percent.

"That's mean. Even Paulson said twenty percent does the real work."

"Things are tougher here than at Goldman, and you better realize that sooner rather than later if you don't want to be part of the ninety percent. Anyway, I'm busy. I need to get all this stuff"—I gesture at my laptop, which unfortunately doesn't increase its size in proportion to the number of tasks on my to-do list—"done before lunch."

"So? Delegate it. That's why we pay them"—Grant inclines his head toward the floor—"the big bucks."

"I can't delegate everything. So come on. What do you want?"

Grant folds his arms across his chest, his eyes narrowed. "There's seriously something wrong. It's like...you got laid. The best sex of your life."

"Don't be absurd. I always have great sex." Time to change the subject, *fast*. If he goes any further in this direction, he might even realize that Amy's the one I'm sleeping with. Grant is a genius at this sort of thing. "What's your problem?"

"Did you find the perfect woman to impregnate?"

"Did I *what*?"

"Or maybe there's already a bun in one of your ovens. Tell me it's true."

"Did Dad call you about wanting a grandkid for his birthday, too?"

His face scrunches worse than an empty beer can somebody stepped on.

"Jesus." I shake my head. "You should know me better than that. I already said no."

"And he didn't do anything to you?" Grant stares at me like I'm the one he wants to be when he grows up.

"Not that I've noticed." I was too busy with Amy. Besides, it sounds like he moved on to my brothers after I refused him.

"He called my mom after I told him I couldn't give him a grandkid."

Ah jeez. Dad and his drama.

Grant continues, "He said he'd buy us hookers for the job unless she does something about it."

Grant's mother tells him everything because she's slightly needy and fragile and wants her son to comfort her every time she's upset. It reassures her of his love. A lot of her "upset" comes from her personality, but I doubt she's being melodramatic this time. Dad would absolutely believe that bought-and-paid-for women would make great mothers for his grandbabies. To him, a child is something to be popped out into the world and shown around when it suits his mood. Loving, caring for, giving guidance and nurturing are all functions to be contracted out. If he could bypass women and just grab our sperm himself to get a grandchild, he'd do it.

"I'm not doing a hooker," I state flatly.

"I'd bet my entire portfolio he's going to FedEx one to each of us."

"Refuse the package. Do I have to come up with a solution to every Dad problem?"

"Should I adopt a baby?" Grant says, obviously not listening. "Or maybe Huxley or Griffin would agree to..."

"Don't even think about ruining some poor child's life," I say. "If you can't love them the way they deserve, you shouldn't have them in the first place. And frankly, I think none of you are ready for that kind of commitment."

"And *you* are?"

"No. Which is why none of us are going to humor Dad on this point. We're going to go ahead with the gift idea we came up with at Huxley's, and that's that. Huxley can lay on some bullshit about how Josh Singer never got the kind of gift we prepared." He's an ad exec. He can come up with suitable lies.

"Yeah." Grant nods morosely. "But it'd still be better if you just got somebody pregnant."

"Shut up and get out." I point at the door, but my voice lacks anger. My brother's wish sounds selfish, but I understand where he's coming from. He doesn't like to have his mother get hysterical over Dad's calls.

He leaves. Instead of turning to the work awaiting my attention, I text Mom to make sure she's okay. She's tougher than Grant's mother, but that doesn't mean her emotions are immune to Dad's manipulative abuse.

She doesn't answer. Then I remember she's in Europe. She could be getting ready to head out to enjoy her evening.

Sighing, I put the phone down and get back to work. I can only solve what I can solve.

25

AMY

When the elevator dumps me out on the floor at work, Grant is coming out of Emmett's office. Emmett's being here early—even before me—isn't unusual. But Grant is another matter. He usually arrives later.

He and Emmett don't look much alike. The only similarities are the dark hair and the jaw. The rest must've come from elsewhere. Still, he's a handsome man. It's just that the only thing he inspires in me is a mildly pleasant feeling one might harbor for a non-asshole partner at work.

"Hi, Amy," he says. "How'd the trip to La Jolla go?"

I tilt my head. Grant was just in Emmett's office. Did he hear something? When I said I wanted to keep our fling discreet, I meant we needed to keep it secret from *everyone*, including brothers and best friends. I'll probably tell Sasha later—but if I do, it'll be after I'm gone from this company.

"It was good. Very productive." A standard, boring response that doesn't give away anything.

"Good." He nods distractedly and goes to his office.

Hmm. Maybe Emmett didn't tell him, and he was only asking

because he wanted to know I'm working hard to make money for the firm.

I've booted my laptop and am checking my inbox when my phone pings.

–Marion: Amy, I wanted to reach out and apologize for what happened on Saturday.

–Marion: I got a bit emotional there after a long day. Hope you aren't upset about the interruption.

I tap my desk. Why would he be texting me *now*? If he really wanted to apologize, he would've done so before. Was his fiancée embarrassed when she sobered up enough to realize she'd made a fool of herself in front of someone who could be working for him?

–Marion: I also realized that HR was remiss in not sending you the official offer. It'll be rectified immediately, and the official offer in writing will arrive soon.

Okay, maybe this is the real issue. Maybe he thinks I'm not going to accept the offer because of the scene on Saturday. But I was too distracted last week to even think about the written offer —or lack thereof—although I would've noticed if it hadn't arrived by the end of the week.

–Marion: And because we want you so much, we're increasing the signing bonus.

He names a figure that makes me raise my eyebrows. As tempting as the sum is, I don't want to take it if I'm going to get stuck there for two years. Been there, done that. I need a bit more flexibility.

–Marion: The other terms are all the same.

Wow. It's like he's reading my mind. Being tied at the Blaire Group for a year at that amount is an excellent deal.

Still, I can't shake off this vague discomfiture. I've got skills I bring to the table and will be an asset to whatever firm I work for...but he's being a bit *too* eager to have me say yes. I was dying to, too, until I witnessed that weird tension between him and Emmett.

Granted, Emmett probably has some enemies and people he

doesn't get along with. I have a list of people I don't care for, and I'm sure there are people who call me a bitch—or worse—behind my back. It's inevitable.

At the same time, the enmity between Emmett and Marion seemed a little too intense. Almost personal. Emmett didn't talk to me about it, and I didn't probe because I didn't want to slip up and say something stupid.

After mulling for a bit, I decide on a neutral response.

–Me: Thanks for reaching out, Marion. I understand. I look forward to the letter, and I hope your fiancée is feeling better.

That accomplished, I confirm a couple of Zoom interviews, one with a venture capital firm in Boston and the other with a private equity firm in New York. Just because I have an offer doesn't mean I shouldn't explore other options. I discover a headhunter's email about an opportunity in London in the mountains of unread messages in my inbox, but I turn her down. I don't want to be that far from Dad, even if it is a great chance to work overseas.

After I'm done with a couple of meetings, Sasha comes over.

"Hey, wanna grab some lunch? I actually have time to eat."

"You sure you don't want to grab a power nap instead?" I ask. She's sporting dark circles not even concealer can hide. There are nap rooms at the firm, and she could doze off for an hour.

"I just had coffee to stay awake for a call. Let's lunch. We haven't talked in ages."

"In that case, sure. Let's go!"

We head to a sandwich shop nearby. The sandwiches are a little above average, but their coffee is to die for. Since an addiction to caffeine is an integral part of professional success in finance, the place does good business.

I order a turkey and avocado sandwich and an iced Americano, and Sasha grabs a BLT with extra bacon and an iced latte.

We find an empty booth and sit down. Sasha eyes her food like she's in heaven.

"You almost done with the work Grant dumped on you?" I ask.

"Almost. What's left isn't super urgent. I'll actually leave by midnight tonight." She drinks her latte like an elixir.

"Yay," I say.

She sighs. "Yeah, but I'd rather have a day or two off. I want to see my nephew."

"Nephew?" Sasha's never mentioned having a nephew.

"Yup. Fresh from the factory. My sister just had her first baby."

Oooh. She did say something about her sister being pregnant a while back.

"Look." Sasha pulls out her phone, taps it a few times and flips it around.

The photo shows an adorable little baby, a pale blue cap over his head. His eyes are closed, his tiny mouth slightly open. It looks like he's about to yawn with all his might. "He's an angel."

Sasha takes the phone and places it on the table. "He is. I really want to knit something for him, but..." She sighs.

I wince with sympathy. Nobody has time for that sort of thing at GrantEm. If you do, you aren't working hard enough. Or worse, nobody wants to give you anything to do because you're incompetent.

Incompetence is a death sentence. It makes you undesirable, un-hirable, unwanted. People in our industry would rather hang out with a leper than an incompetent.

"I wanna go see him." Sasha sighs. "I didn't get to see him in person or hold him. It's not fair."

"Can you go this weekend? Your sister's still in Orange County, right?"

"Yeah, but I doubt I'll be able to stop by. I have to work." Sasha sighs again, this time like the world is ending. "At least she's sending me photos and videos. I'm probably going to do a video call, but it's not the same. At least it's not my own child I'm not there for."

"Yeah." There isn't much I can say to cheer her up. "Don missed his kid's birthday two years in a row. He said his daughter was inconsolable."

"At least Peggy doesn't seem to have it that bad," Sasha says. "Her husband doesn't cry when she misses their appointments."

"Lucky her. Well, relatively. It's kinda sad when you actually have to schedule meetings with your own spouse."

"And they just got married last year! But like she said, at least it prolongs the honeymoon phase. Hard to get sick of your husband when you almost never see him."

"And he's in investment banking, so he gets it."

"Right. Otherwise... Boom." Sasha snaps her fingers. "Divorce."

Broken marriages and relationships litter the industry. Now that I think about it, I'm a statistic, too. It'd be a job in itself to count up the number of boyfriends who left me because I work too much. "So our options are limited to people in VC, PE and IB?"

"Even private equity is kinda iffy. I don't think they work as much as we do."

"Probably not." Right now I'm having a casual fling with Emmett, who's in venture capital, so it's sort of a moot point to whine about. But suddenly my future seems to have a pall cast over it. I don't want to limit myself to dating and marrying a man I have to make an appointment to see. And I certainly don't want to miss our kids' birthdays and plays and all the other special occasions.

"Or we have to quit."

That's even more depressing. I need the money to pay off student loans and buy Dad his dream retirement home in Florida. Can't do that if I quit, no matter what the reason might be.

So stick to VC, PE and IB. It isn't like you have a choice, since you were the one canceling on your boyfriends all the time. They had to make appointments to see you.

"Just look at the people who haven't burned out yet," Sasha

says. "Nobody has kids unless they have a spouse who works nine to five and does the parent stuff. Peggy said she has no plans for kids."

I blink. "Ever?"

"Ever."

"How come? She adores children." She has pictures of her twin nieces all over her desk.

"Student loans. She still owes enough to buy a house. So does her husband." Sasha thinks for a second. "Not around here, obviously. But somewhere in the Midwest or Texas? Definitely."

Hearing this from Sasha is crushing. It's making me accept something I've been in denial about for years—that I'm not going to be able to have it all, unless I can clone myself. "It's unfair. I thought we could do the superwoman thing if we just put our minds to it."

"No kidding." Sasha swallows the last bite of her BLT. "What we have is a crap-ton of student loans and busy careers. If we want more, we need to change our plans and expectations. And then adjust accordingly. Except most of us can't or don't want to, so..." She sighs again, then gives me a small smile. "Sorry, I'm being so gloomy when we're finally catching up. I just feel crummy about not seeing my nephew."

"Totally understandable," I say, patting her arm. But a small voice in the back of my mind whispers it isn't understandable or okay that the plan I've made—and been sticking to all along—could be totally wrong.

26

AMY

The week is jinxed. That's the only explanation.

My laptop crashes on Tuesday, making me lose hours of work. Since I'm in charge of the deliverable, I redo the entire model—*which Excel didn't save!*

At two thirty-four a.m. the laptop decides that *playing* dead isn't enough. It goes ahead and *actually* dies. Of course, the IT department is gone. Unlike us, they only work nine to five.

"Argh!" I clench my hands around the edges of my husk of a laptop. It's all I can do not hurl the thing across the empty office. Pressing my thumb against the throbbing spot between my eyebrows, I pull out my phone.

–Me: The model you asked for this morning is going to be late. My laptop died, and I don't know if the server backed up the new file or not.

I send it and huff out an annoyed breath. Emmett left at seven for a business dinner, and didn't come back. Which means he's home now, either sleeping or working. I put the odds at fifty-fifty, given his workaholic nature.

I should've waited until tomorrow morning to text him. But old habits die hard. I'm used to updating him regularly. When I was hired, Emmett told me he hates surprises. Of course, no boss likes surprises, even if they're good ones.

–Emmett: Go home. Have IT give you a new laptop tomorrow morning.

His text is professional. Bossy. Like it always is. It's comforting that he hasn't let our fling change our work dynamics. But a part of me is weirdly sad that he hasn't said anything personal.

Get a grip, Amy. You're just tired.

Shaking myself mentally, I type up a very venture capitalist response.

–Me: Got it. I'll give you a new ETA once I get the replacement.

–Emmett: As long as I can have the file by tomorrow COB, it should be fine.

I can probably swing it by five.

–Emmett: Sleep tight.

That's new. Like ice melting on a heated frying pan, the odd blue feeling from just moments ago disappears.

–Me: You too.

It's too late to stop by Emmett's, so I head home. Plus I need what little sleep I can manage before I wrestle with Excel—again —tomorrow.

The laptop I get on Wednesday morning works okay, although it randomly produces a loud whirring noise that makes me nervous. It sounds like something's dying underneath the hard casing, but I don't have the time to ask for yet another unit. It takes two hours for the IT department to configure a new laptop and migrate all the data that's been backed up to GrantEm's cloud. I can't lose more time on getting another replacement, especially when I'm going to be gone in less than six weeks.

On Thursday, Webber leaves Emmett's office looking positively ashen. Even his lips are bloodless. Within an hour, we get a short farewell email from him. He said he was resigning, but we all knew he was being "counseled out," which is the euphemism for being canned. Guess he crossed Emmett for the last time.

The mood in the office is subdued. Regardless of how you feel about Webber, seeing him getting fired isn't something to celebrate openly, even if he officially *resigned*. It isn't like people don't know what really happened.

Meanwhile, many of us groan silently. Webber's sudden departure means whatever he's been doing will be divvied up among those left under Emmett. Not that anybody will be dumb enough to whine out loud. Emmett wouldn't blink before exiling them to the Land of the Canned.

Since I also work for Emmett, a lot of crap from Webber's plate splat-lands on mine.

I tap my fingers on the desk, staring at the mountain of tasks to be completed. If Emmett wanted, he could reduce my workload and ask me to come over to his place...

The second the thought pops into my head, I push it away. What the hell is wrong with me? That would be a gross abuse of power on his part, and everyone would know for sure something was up between us if Emmett started letting me leave earlier than normal. *Especially* if everyone else is staying late to make up for Webber's absence.

If Emmett wants to have a bedroom tango with me, he needs to make an appointment. Just like Peggy needs to do to see her husband. And I'll have to do the same to see him personally. The man's schedule is booked solid.

The thought is somewhat depressing. Not sure why. It's like...

I sigh. I'm not thinking about anything logically. Not since my lunch with Sasha. My phone pings.

–Emmett: How about a short trip to Napa this weekend?

Great minds think alike. I was just musing about needing appointments. But... I look at my dauntingly long to-do list.

–Me: I'll need to work late tomorrow.

–Emmett: We can leave on Saturday. Spend the night at a resort up there.

I restudy my to-do list. I can probably swing it... No? I'm going to need to come into work a couple of hours earlier than usual on Monday, but if I really push myself this week...

When I don't respond immediately, he sends another text.

–Emmett: It has a spa, too.

I smile, recalling the hot stone massage he treated me to and how amazing it felt.

–Me: You're awfully into massages.

–Emmett: They feel awesome. Work hard, get pampered hard.

I bite back a laugh.

–Emmett: If you don't take care of yourself, who will?

Touché. It's not like Dad's nearby, not that I'd ask him to take care of me. It's now my job to take care of myself *and* him.

–Me: Okay. That should be fine.

Sasha's working straight through the weekend, and it's likely she won't be coming home. Just because things eased up a little last week doesn't mean anything. An associate is out of office after she lost her mother in a car crash Tuesday night, and Sasha needs to do two people's work for a while. I haven't seen her since our lunch, but I notice a small carry-on underneath her desk at work, which is a sign that she's going DEFCON 1—shower and sleep in the office. The nap rooms at GrantEm are quite nice, with a bathroom attached to each.

At two a.m., I shut down my laptop and gather my things. Emmett's office door is open, lights still on. He's not there, though. He walked out about ten minutes ago, but hasn't returned.

I hesitate, feeling like I should say goodbye before leaving. Odd, since I've never had the same urge before.

I don't want to text him to say bye. That's a bit too...weird. Out of my standard routine.

It's the week getting to me. I've been working late, and Webber getting fired dampened my mood, even though I'm sure he'll be fine. Some firm will snap him up. I force myself to resume the march toward the elevator.

I should've known the day wouldn't end on a high note. By the time I reach the lobby, it's pouring, like somebody punched a hole in the heavens right above Los Angeles.

"Fuck me," I mutter. I have to run to the garage across the street to get into my car, and I, of course, don't have an umbrella.

Above the rain, low, angry clouds reflect the nighttime lights of the city. It doesn't look like the downpour is going to cease anytime soon. I don't want to stay trapped in the lobby because of rain.

It's just water, not poison.

I inhale deeply and dash out, getting soaked through in less than ten steps. By the time I reach my car, I'm breathing hard, water dripping. I squeeze the rain from my hair, then lean against the driver's-side door for a bit, waiting for my breathing to settle. I shouldn't have bothered to run. I couldn't be more drenched if I'd taken a nap in the downpour.

I climb into the car and drive carefully. Half an hour or less to my place...

Or not.

Traffic's a mess. People in Los Angeles can't drive for crap in the rain. On top of that, there are two accidents on the way. So the trip takes two hours.

How delightful. Soggy clothes add to my boundless joy.

By the time I'm home, it's after four and a chill has settled all the way to my bones. I take a hot shower and fall flat on bed, trying to get at least two hours of good sleep.

I fail miserably. I'm too uncomfortable. Not sure why.

Friday doesn't go any better. I wake up, my head full of squishy cotton balls. I'm not feverish or anything, though. At least, I don't think so. It's just the lack of sleep and general stress and annoyance.

By the time I'm in the office, I feel like I've already put in a full day's work. Dad texts me hello. I text back with a smiling selfie, hoping he doesn't notice that I'm exhausted.

I have two meetings. Thank God I don't have to present, because I understand very little of what's being said. Not because the material is too technical or complicated. My brain just can't seem to keep up with anything, even when the topic is on something as simple as projected risks and interest rates in Japan and China.

Thankfully, Emmett's off-site today, which means he isn't there to ask questions to attendees. I might say something stupid and embarrass myself.

After lunch, I stare at the model for hours. Nothing makes sense on the spreadsheet. I don't know why. It made perfect sense just last night.

Instead of sorting it out, I just want to place my head on the desk and close my eyes.

And join Webber, yay!

Just because we're sleeping together doesn't mean Emmett won't fire me if I start getting lazy.

I place my elbow in front of my laptop and prop my chin in my hand. If I stare at the numbers with more focus, they'll start making sense. *Actually, I should grab coffee and a Snickers first. Oil the gears in my head that have decided to creak and get stuck today.*

I stand up, and the floor tilts under my feet. The office spins for a moment. I blink, then the eerie sensation goes away. What was *that?* Low blood sugar?

I go to the break room and grab a coffee and Snickers. Down both fast.

They don't resolve the matter of my suboptimal brain function. *For God's sake.* My laptop died last night, and now my damned head wants to die, too.

By six, I feel like absolute shit. Another Snickers would be a bad idea because now I'm not just foggy, but queasy. I wish I could throw up, but I know that won't happen because unless I'm food poisoned, my stomach hangs on to every ounce of food that makes its way into it.

Go home early and get some rest. The model isn't due today.

Great idea, but I can't leave this early, especially when I'm so close to finishing. Just because something isn't due today doesn't mean I can wait on it—there's always something *else* I could be doing.

When it's nine, I finally feel comfortable enough to leave. I manage the short drive home. Thank God it isn't raining and the traffic is okay.

The official written offer from the Blaire Group is waiting in my mailbox. *Took 'em long enough.* Something about the way it arrived feels wrong, but I'm too tired to figure it out. Right now, all that matters is that I have the offer in hand.

Since I'm getting the mail anyway, I grab everything else as well. I toss it all on the dining table without bothering to sort it out, then strip and land face-first on my bed. Once horizontal, I instantly feel a hundred times better.

My eyelids grow heavy, but I'm too cold to sleep. I pull the sheets closer and hug Okumasama.

A loud banging at my door wakes me up. I blink, rub my bleary eyes and check the alarm clock. *Noon.* Shit! I can't believe it's this late already.

The banging continues. I stay in bed, hoping Sasha will answer it because I really don't want to leave my bed this weekend—

Wait. She's slaving away at the office.

More banging. It can't be a delivery—no delivery person is this insistent.

Ah, shit! Emmett! I was supposed to meet him at the airport more than an hour ago for our trip to Napa! Shock and guilt race through me. How could I have forgotten?

I hop out of bed, then freeze with one hand braced on the wall as my bedroom does the same eerie waltz that the office did yesterday. When the room quits spinning, I start to reach for my purse so I can call Emmett, but the banging on the door won't stop.

"*All right already!*" Take care of this first, then call Emmett.

Shrugging into a robe, I stumble toward the door. "Who is it?" I call out.

"It's me!"

Emmett...?

27

EMMETT

When Amy doesn't show at the airport at ten thirty, I figure it's the traffic. It's L.A., and shit happens.

When she doesn't show by ten forty-five, I start to worry.

The worry turns to panic when she doesn't answer my texts or calls.

I stride out of the terminal. It isn't like Amy to ghost someone. She's one of the most responsible people I know. Unlike some of the women I've dated, she also wouldn't say yes to something she wasn't too keen on and then show her displeasure by canceling the last minute or not showing. The only time she canceled on her ex-boyfriends was when I dumped so much work on her that she couldn't make it to their dates.

And I made sure she *didn't* have any urgent deadlines from Friday to Sunday.

After tossing my carry-on into the car, I drive to Amy's place. Her car is in the lot. So she's home.

What's going on?

I go up and bang on the door. There's no immediate answer.

Is she okay? She lives in a safe neighborhood, but...

With someone else, I might assume she's being passive-aggressive. But this is Amy. Miss Upfront. A woman who is candid enough to say all she wants is sex—and list her terms— wouldn't play games.

I knock harder and wonder if the super's available to let me in. Normally they'd refuse, but if I make a compelling case that she might be hurt...

"Who is it?" she finally calls out.

Oh, thank God. But the relief only lasts a moment. Her voice is a little off. "It's me!"

The door opens. Amy stands there, her hair sticking up and pillow creases on the left side of her face. Her cheeks are flushed —but not in a healthy way. Her eyes are glazed, and she's crossing her arms tightly, hands wrapped around biceps like she's cold.

"Oh." She blinks a few times. "Oh crap. I was about to call you. I'm so sorry. I totally overslept."

I put a hand to her forehead. "You're burning up. You should be in bed."

"Uh. I should...?" She looks dazed.

I nod and put my arm around her. She must really be sick to be this messed up. "Mind if I come in?"

She starts. "Oh. Yeah. Sure."

I walk in and push the door closed.

"I'm really sorry," she says. "I didn't mean to make you come all the way out here. I should've called to let you know I can't go. But you can. You should go to Napa and have a good time."

Just what kind of dick does she think I am than I could "go to Napa and have a good time" while she's sick? I may be a demanding boss, but that doesn't mean I'm a shitty human being.

"In fact," she says, "if you go now, you can still ma—"

I put a hand over her mouth. "I'm not sorry I'm here instead of Napa."

She stares at me blankly, then pulls back. "But you were really looking forward to the trip."

"Yes, but with you."

She continues to stare. But she doesn't refute what I said, or claim that what we have is just sex like she would if she weren't sick. She's scrupulous about sticking to deadlines and parameters. Actually, she's meticulous about executing plans exactly as laid out.

She has no plans to move us beyond fuck buddies. But I want more, and I'm not above taking advantage of her weakened state.

"Let's get you back in bed," I say.

"But I really—"

"Now. Rest."

"Are you sure?"

"Yes." Since she isn't moving on her own, I start pushing her gently toward her bedroom.

"But the trip—"

"Canceled. We have new plans for the weekend. Nursing you back to health."

"But...it's your time off."

We reach the bed. I put my hands on her shoulders to have her sit down. Then I move her until she's lying there with her samurai teddy bear.

"You should use it more productively," she says. "Or for fun."

I tuck her in, pulling the sheets all the way to her chin. "It'll be both, taking care of you."

"Um...okay. Feels a little weird, though."

"How come?"

She frowns. "Nobody's ever nursed me back to health. I mean, except my father."

Either she's been exceptionally healthy or her ex-boyfriends were shit. I put my money on the latter. I've been sick before, and my ex-girlfriends never did anything.

"Well, your dad isn't here," I say. "So you're stuck with me. Let's see what we can do to make you feel better soon. You have anything for the fever?" There must be some Tylenol or Advil around.

"Chicken noodle soup," Amy says.

"Huh?"

"That's what I want." Her eyebrows pull together. "That's what I get when I'm sick."

"Comfort food?" I wonder where I can get some soup. There's always Campbell's, but I don't know if that's what she has in mind. And nothing's sadder than getting not-quite-right comfort food when you're sick.

"Yeah. Dad used to make it for me from scratch."

From scratch? She looks at me like I can single-handedly butcher a plump chicken and turn it into soup in the next hour. But I don't want to burn the building down. "I can't do home-made soup, but I know someone who can."

28

AMY

I don't have to wait long before Emmett has piping-hot chicken noodle soup delivered and brings a tray of it into my bedroom. It isn't homemade, obviously, but it doesn't seem to be from a can, either.

The broth is richly flavored, full of shredded chicken meat, noodles and veggies. It isn't exactly like how my dad makes it, but it's pretty close.

"Good?" Emmett asks.

"Yes. Thank you." I smile a little. The soup tastes like warmth and love. But most importantly, it shows he cares.

Since I left home for college, I've put pressure on myself to do well and be self-sufficient. When I got sick—which happened occasionally—I fended for myself and did my best to avoid letting Dad know because I didn't want him to worry. He's done so much for me already that I don't want to be a burden anymore. I want to be a daughter he can be proud of, an adult he can count on.

And some of my ex-boyfriends didn't want to do much when I was sick because dealing with a sick person is never fun. Sasha can't stick around when I'm sick; she's way too busy, which I totally understand. We've sort of mutually agreed to bring each other OTC meds and some snacks, but that's about where things end.

Emmett is the first person since Dad to not only hover but insist on taking care of me. Our relationship is supposed to be just about sex, but his solicitousness makes me feel good anyway. Part of me wants to lean just a little bit more. A small voice in my head warns that that's a terrible idea. But I can't figure out why it's so bad when it feels so nice.

After I finish the soup, Emmett tucks me in and takes the tray away. I watch him read a printed report—he's always working—and we talk a little bit about the project. Then I start to get tired. He looks at me and shuts his mouth. I doze off.

When I open my eyes again, it's dark in my room. My head is no longer full of wet cotton balls and molasses. The chicken noodle soup Emmett brought me must've done the trick. If it hadn't been for that, I would've gotten a can of Campbell's. Sasha thinks it's weird, but when I feel this awful, nothing but chicken noodle soup will do. Placebo effect, maybe, but it works.

I stand up carefully. The room doesn't whirl.

Feeling optimistic, I start to stretch my arms above my head. I wonder if Emmett's gone home. It's not like he has anything to do around here. If he goes home, he could work...

Work!

Holy shit! The offer from the Blaire Group! I left it on the dining table last night!

Sheer, unadulterated panic surges. I rush out into the dining room and freeze at the sight of Emmett at the table.

He is typing away on his laptop, but that isn't the point. The manila envelope is the second one from the top, right below some grocery store leaflet. Is that how I left the mail last night? I can't remember. There's no reason for him to go through my mail, but if he accidently knocks the stack over... Or... Or...

There are billion perfectly innocent scenarios in which he might discover the written offer. The envelope doesn't have anything to indicate it's about a *job*, although he might wonder why the Blaire Group sent me a thick manila envelope.

"Well, hello," Emmett says.

"Hi."

"You must be feeling better."

"Yeah. Sort of." I try to read his face and fail. He's wearing his inscrutable business expression, which means whatever he's been tinkering with on his laptop is work-related and not necessarily good news. "Thank you."

"You're welcome." He closes his laptop and props his chin in his hand. "So. Do you want more soup, or something else?"

He's *way* too close to that envelope. I want him as far from it as possible. "Why don't we go out and get something to eat?" I can probably manage an hour or so of outing.

"Actually, I thought we should do delivery." He comes over, puts a hand on my forehead and nods. "Better. But I don't want you to overexert yourself."

"No, no, it's really no problem. At all. Really. I just want to make sure the weekend isn't a total loss for you."

He looks insulted. "Why would staying here with you be a total loss?"

"Isn't it?" Rick certainly would've been annoyed. Actually, any of my ex-boyfriends would've been less than thrilled if I got sick and they had to cancel a trip. They'd also hint—if not outright whine—about the fact that they lost money, since it was a same-day cancellation. And they'd expect me to do something to make up for it, which I would, since I'd feel guilty. I feel bad about Emmett missing out on the trip, so I should do something—or at least encourage him to enjoy Napa on his own or something.

"No. You make me sound like a, a..." He thinks for a moment. "A soulless *insurance adjuster* or something."

Shame comes over me. Emmett deserves better. But I also need to pull him away from that package from the Blaire Group. And getting delivery will mean spreading food out on the table. So...

"Why don't we order a pizza, and we can watch a movie while eating?" I give him my most winning smile. *Perfect*. It'll force him to park himself on a couch in front of the TV and give me an opportunity to hide the mail.

"Okay."

Whew.

He stands up, and his hand brushes the pile. Everything falls, landing in complete disarray.

Shit!

"Sorry," he says, bending down.

"No, no!" I fall over the mess like a football player diving for a fumbled ball. Since I don't have any athletic grace, I land on my face. My whole body jars at the impact. But it doesn't matter. I manage to block Emmett's view.

"Are you okay?" His tone says that he's now worried about my mental health.

"Yeah, fine. Totally good. Lemme just, uh, pick these up, and why don't you order the pizza?"

"Um. Yeah. Okay. What do you want?"

"Anything," I say. "I'm not picky."

"Pepperoni good?"

"Perfect. Excellent."

He pulls out his phone. While he's tinkering with a delivery app, I grab every piece of mail under my torso, dump it into Sasha's bedroom and shut the door firmly.

Disaster averted.

I wouldn't be as happy, though, if I knew another disaster was just around the corner.

29

AMY

I hear Sasha curse from the next room on Tuesday morning. We're both getting ready for work when her "Shit!" comes through the wall quite clearly.

Did she forget something at the office? She came home with her carry-on last night, which means she plans to actually start sleeping in her bed.

There's a knock on my bedroom door. I lower my lipstick. "Come on in."

Sasha appears. "Can I borrow a couple of tampons?" she says, exasperated. "I thought I had some, but I'm out."

"Yeah, sure." I go to the bathroom and grab a handful for her.

"Thanks. You're the best!" She rushes out.

I watch her go, then look down at myself. Sasha and I have the same cycle, more or less. Sometimes she's a day early; sometimes I am. But after having lived together for almost two years, we're basically synced.

But I'm not feeling anything that indicates I'm about to start mine anytime soon. Sometimes I'm late when I'm stressed or not sleeping well, but I haven't had any of that. I mean... I was sick over the weekend, but that wouldn't be enough to delay my period... Would it?

Well, Aunt Flo is a fickle bitch. I try to shrug it off, since it's not like I can force myself to start menstruating. Thankfully, I don't have to think much about anything except work. Emmett spent the entire weekend taking care of me while I recovered, then left early on Monday for a Chicago business trip. So I'm the one in charge of the small water filter company team. Also, I need to wrap up the next phase of the Drone work. Which means I don't have time mull over why I'm not bleeding like a stuck pig.

After lunch, I get a text from Marion.

–Marion: I hope you got the offer letter.

–Me: I did. Thanks.

–Marion: Did you have a chance to review the terms?

–Me: Not yet.

I wasn't opening that envelope while Emmett was around.

–Marion: If you have questions, you can always reach out to me.

–Me: Okay. I appreciate that.

–Marion: I know you're interviewing elsewhere, and you're a candidate in high demand.

–Marion: Before you accept an offer from a different firm, I want you to contact me. We can always match or do better for you.

I blink a little. That's...flexible of them. Maybe they *really* need a new body at the Blaire Group.

–Me: Okay. Thanks!

I make a mental note to review the offer in more detail later and go back to work. A little after two thirty, Emmett texts me. I smile as I read it.

–Emmett: Everything going well?

–Me: Yeah. Everything's on track. How are the meetings?

–Emmett: Boring. Wish I'd brought you with me.

I try not to laugh. I can picture him sighing with annoyance. All right. Time to cheer him up a little.

—Me: You have Jerry with you. Didn't he amuse you with 2000 pictures of his daughter?

—Emmett: The baby's cute, but I'm not into other people's kids, especially when the stories are about drool and diaper changes. Plus, he's not you. You're more fun to be around.

I can feel my smile widen. It isn't every day somebody says I'm more fun to be around. Most would say I'm more practical or methodical or preplanned or something.

Still, I don't mind. It's sort of nice to hear somebody say I'm fun.

He's a guy. He's thinking sex.

Yes, but I can be sexy *and* fun at the same time.

—Me: I'll still be here when you come back.

—Emmett: Can't wait. I wish I could move all the meetings to tomorrow so I could be in L.A. by Thursday morning.

—Me: Thursday would be tough, but I'll go over to your place Friday after you land. How about that?

Hopefully, my period will have started by then, so we'll be limited in what we can do, but I'm sure I'll manage something. I'm a creative problem solver!

—Emmett: Deal. That'll be the perfect incentive for slogging through this trip. Let me know if you need anything.

—Me: Will do. Don't work too hard. Don't want you all exhausted when we get together. ;)

I put my phone away. Maybe my period is late because Emmett isn't around and I'm down about waiting until Friday to see him. Stress is a killer.

Still, it'll start any day. Look how miserable Sasha is. All that cramping, and the hormonal rollercoaster. I'll be joining her at Club Misery soon.

Wednesday goes by. Nothing.

Thursday. Nothing.

Friday. *Still* nothing.

I even wait until after lunch. But no. Not even a fleck of blood.

Good God. What does it take for my period to start? A virgin sacrifice?

Since I'm getting a decent amount of sleep and eating three squares a day, it can't be that. Then again, maybe it's *because* I'm getting decent sleep and nutrition for once. My body simply can't adjust.

The only other explanation would be pregnancy, except that's ludicrous. Emmet and I have been very careful. Neither of us wants to have a baby off a sex-only fling. We've always used condoms...

A shiver runs down my spine. Time slows; the air in my lungs thins.

We didn't use one that first time. When I caught him masturbating in his office.

Oh *shit.*

But he pulled out. So... Um... The little swimmers couldn't have wriggled across my skin, into my vag and squirmed their way up until they ran into my unguarded, foolishly welcoming egg.

Could they?

I glance around to make sure nobody's watching and quickly Google "effectiveness of the pullout method."

Say it's one hundred percent. Say it's one hundred percent!

But no. When done perfectly it's only ninety-six percent effective. In real life it's only about *seventy-eight percent effective in preventing unwanted pregnancy.*

I stare at the screen, frozen in horror. That's basically *one in five.*

I look down at my belly with horrified shock.

Be positive! You could be one of the four in five who avoided pregnancy!

Emmett has to have had a lot of experience, I think, clenching and unclenching my trembling hands. It's not like he doesn't know what he's doing in bed.

Experience with sex. Don't know if he's done a lot of

pulling out, a contrary voice argues. *How often could he have been taken by surprise while masturbating, then jumped by a horny—*

Shut up, shut up!

I look at my phone, then shake my head. There's no way I'm texting him about this.

He's flying home tonight. I drive home after nine, willing myself to bleed. *Now.*

But nope. My underwear feels drier than midday in Vegas. Fuck it.

I pull into the lot of the Target closest to my place, then walk in and buy a pregnancy test. Not that I think it's going to come back positive. But I need to eliminate the possibility.

I use the self-checkout and scan the box myself, breathing hard. I think about all the reasons a woman might miss her period —other than pregnancy—then remember Mrs. Ashworth, my tenth-grade gym teacher. She wasn't even forty, but had an early onset menopause.

I perk up. There's a *great* possibility. I'm only twenty-eight, but it could be, like, ultra-early onset. That'd make it hard for me to get pregnant later, but medical science is a beautiful thing. I'm sure they can discover a way to fix me up. Pump me full of estrogen and resuscitate dear dead Auntie Flo.

Feeling marginally better, I shove the test into my purse and go home. Then, to confirm that what I have is just an early onset menopause, nothing serious, I pee on the stick.

Then wait.

And wait.

If I'm pacing, it's only because I need the exercise, not because I'm nervous.

Because I know *I'm not pregnant.* No way, no how.

Except...

The stick slowly reveals two lines.

I put a hand over my mouth. My head goes blank—just a barren white space with nothing. I'm sure I'm supposed to feel or think *something,* but I just can't. Not when the stick says I'm pregnant.

How can I be pregnant? I have job interviews! And an offer in Virginia! A job that will require I put in close to a hundred hours a week. Does the Blaire Group have a twenty-four-seven daycare center for its employees?

My knees start to shake. I stumble into the sink and knock a few things off. Something made with glass falls on the floor and shatters. But it's hard to care when my life just got upended.

Not just upended. Fucking *nuked.* Above me, a mushroom cloud is rising.

I plop down on my butt on the bathroom floor. My womb feels perfectly at peace.

The door bursts open behind me.

"Hey, are you okay?" Sasha says, her eyes wide. She's still in her office clothes, her laptop bag hanging from her shoulder.

I turn and blink up at her.

"I heard something crash." She comes over and puts a hand on my shoulder. "Why are you sitting on the floor?"

Do I want to get up? I mean, I guess I should. I lift a hand.

She starts to bend down to help, then stops. "Oh. My. God."

"What?"

She lets out a gasping breath. "You're *pregnant?*"

30

AMY

Oh, crap. *The test!*

I didn't mean for Sasha to see it. Not when I have no idea what I'm going to do about my new medical condition. "Hey, at least it's not early onset menopause."

My best friend looks at me like I've just lost my mind. When I merely stare back at her, her expression shifts to worry. "Um... yay...?" she says.

"I guess. Yeah. Yay."

She parks herself next to me on the bathroom floor. She's probably decided mental intervention is more urgent. "Okay. What's going on?"

"Well, unless this stick is defective..." I gesture.

"Is it?" Her tone reminds me of my kindergarten teacher talking to a child in denial.

"Probably not...?" The last part comes out in an oh-my-God-what-do-I-do whine.

"Do you know who the father is?"

I nod slowly. *Emmett Lasker. Holy shit. I'm pregnant with Emmett's baby!*

The fact is sinking in, heavier than a stone descending into the oceanic abyss.

"So...are you going to talk to him about it?"

"I don't know." This pregnancy is a *major* surprise, the kind Emmett will hate to hear about.

Sasha thinks for a moment. "It's not Rick's, is it?"

I almost gag. "Hell no! I had my period since the last time I had sex with Rick, so I'm safe."

"Sorry. Had to make sure. I'm glad it isn't his."

"*You're* glad...?"

We both start laughing. But if the child were his, I wouldn't be this conflicted, since there's no way I'd let him back into my life.

But does Emmett want to be a dad? If so, can he be a good one?

He's intelligent. Rich. And surprisingly fun. But he's also contrary, arbitrary, unpredictable and loves to escalate just for the hell of it. He also has no problem sticking a knife into your heart and twisting it if he doesn't think you measure up.

Hmm...

A child is going to need a dad who's going to be there, in their corner no matter what. At the same time, the dad has to be firm and teach the kid right from wrong, instill good moral character and discipline. To be empathetic yet fair, be kind without getting taken advantage of. A dad who will provide the stability the child needs to feel secure.

Emmett can probably pull all that off *if* he's willing and puts his mind to it. But that's a big if.

"Okay. The first thing you should decide is if you want to keep the child," Sasha says.

I turn to look at her.

"All this is moot if you don't want to keep it."

I run a trembling hand through my hair. "You're right. It's just... Not keeping the baby never crossed my mind."

"You're in shock." Sasha pats my hand.

"No kidding." The words are unsteady. "This was *not* part of the plan. Damn it, I have a job offer and interviews. A career." A career that requires you make appointments to see your significant other. "You can't work in finance with a baby."

Sasha's quiet for a while. "It's certainly going to be challenging, unless you have an understanding boss."

Which Marion Blaire probably isn't going to be. Nobody wants a new hire who requires coddling. And maternity leave within a year.

"Regardless, if you plan to keep the baby, you should talk to the guy. Even if you don't plan to marry him or anything, he should at least do his part. Pay for child support and all that."

"I guess." It's my fault. *I should've just walked away* when I caught Emmett masturbating in his office. I squeeze my eyes shut. Why didn't I do that? And the worst of it all, how am I going to tell him?

She wraps her arms around my shoulders. "Hey, girl. No matter what you decide, I'm on your side. And my mouth is zipped until you announce your impending motherhood."

I hug her back. "You're the *best*."

"Let me know if you need anything, okay? You don't have to try to figure this out on your own."

"Okay. And thanks."

Sasha helps me clean up the bathroom. What made the biggest ruckus and noise was a jar of cream that fell on the floor and broke. The cream exploded on impact and splattered everywhere, kind of like my life.

When we're done, Sasha returns to her room to change. I pick up my phone and stare at the screen.

I should tell Emmett. I don't want to keep something this big from him. At the same time, I don't know how to begin the conversation...or if it's something I can text or should call him about.

Maybe I should talk to him in person. Except...

My hands grow clammy. Face to face sounds even more difficult.

The phone vibrates in my hand. I look down and see a text. Must be Emmett telling me he is in L.A.

–Emmett: Hey, my flight got delayed. Won't get in until midnight.

I let out a shaky breath. The news feels like a stay of execution.

–Me: How about if I go over to your place tomorrow at

I think for a second. What would be a good time?

–Emmett: How about you come over at ten?

Well. I guess he made the decision, since I can't think of a single objection.

–Me: Sounds great.

–Emmett: Awesome! Can't wait to see you.

I exhale. Awesome isn't what he's going to feel when I drop the P-bomb on him.

31

AMY

Okay, time to get proactive. I go out to Target and buy ten more pregnancy tests, all different brands. I also check the batch numbers to make sure they aren't all the same. Statistical probabilities say I don't need that many or be this paranoid, but I have to be *sure*.

Since my bladder is refusing to empty itself, I drink four cups of water and pace around the apartment until nature calls.

All ten tests come back positive.

Fuck. Me.

There's no way I'm *not* pregnant. Which means I need to prep for tomorrow's conversation.

I create a PowerPoint presentation to help collect my thoughts and create some props for the upcoming talk. They take forever, even though I can usually make one in an hour or less. The presentation formula is simple:

Warm up the audience.

State the agenda.

Iterate the importance of what I'm about to say.

Storyboard the material for the greatest impact.

Closing remarks.

Q&A.

Except... How do I warm Emmett up to the news? No matter how I begin, it's going to go over as well as an exploding landmine.

And the greatest impact? I doubt he needs or wants a greater impact than what just telling him will provide.

Argh! I shove my fingers into my hair. This is worse than telling Dad I crashed my car in high school.

Still, I manage to put something together, mainly focusing on pros of the baby and options available to him, such as joint custody and reasonable child support as determined by an attorney. I don't want Emmett to think I'm angling for some kind of commitment between us because of the baby, since that isn't what we agreed to in the first place.

Just in case the PowerPoint is a bust—I might change my mind tomorrow—I also draft three executive memos. They read dry and professional.

Good. Good.

Since I might possibly need it, I create an Excel model of what the cost of raising a child would look like. Except... How do you quantify the time investment necessary? Maybe I can do it the way some of my friends who went into management consulting do—create a blended rate for me and Emmett and use that to put a price on parental involvement.

I sigh as I stare at the model, my whole body collapsing like a sandcastle under an unforgiving wave. How the hell am I going to put a price tag on my plan—paying off my student loans and buying Dad the retirement home of his dreams? I make the money I make because I put in the hours I put in. If I want to pull back, then I'm going to have to make a career switch, which would pay far less but allow more free time.

Hey, at least you're going to give your dad a grandbaby to bounce on his knee!

Some silver lining. I'm certain a surprise accident baby isn't what Dad has in mind for me.

I toss and turn all night, getting up three more times to tinker with the presentation, memos and model.

The next morning, I don't feel any better. Would it be bad if I canceled on Emmett?

Yes. Yes, it would. He'd want to know why, and I don't want to lie to him. Besides, telling him I'm sick won't work, either. He'll just come over with a vat of chicken noodle soup.

Why couldn't he be a little bit more selfish? Like Rick?

Of course, if he were like Rick, I would've broken up with him by now.

I make a cup of coffee to fortify myself before I go, but Sasha stops me. "You might want to limit your coffee and tea. Caffeine is supposed to be bad for babies."

I look down at the fresh brew. *You gotta be kidding me.* But I don't want to do anything that could hurt the baby, so I sigh, resigned to the fact that I'll have to go cold turkey on coffee for a while. "Life is so unfair. You want this?"

She gives me an apologetic look. "Sorry, but...yeah. Thanks."

It takes me a long time to pick out clothes. I don't want to wear something super casual, but I don't want to look like I'm going into the office to talk to the boss, since it isn't that kind of rendezvous. I settle on a white cotton shirt and dark jeans. Then I slip on my favorite high-heel sandals. Half casual, half serious.

By the time I park in Emmett's driveway, I'm quivering with nerves. My hands are clammy around the steering wheel, and I'm honestly surprised I was able to drive here.

I'm also probably starting caffeine withdrawal. And I have to throw Emmett into a minefield.

After taking several deep breaths to calm myself—which doesn't work—I sling the biggest purse I could find in my closet over a shoulder. It contains my laptop. I didn't want to bring my laptop bag because that might look weird.

I ring the doorbell and wait. Emmett opens the door with a wide grin that would normally make my heart flutter. Right now

I'm too nervous to appreciate how hot he is in his gray V-neck shirt and black shorts.

He puts a hand on my shoulder and sweetly pulls me inside. "Missed you." His lips brush over mine.

I pull back with a smile that I hope looks relaxed and happy. "Me too. How was the trip?"

"Went well. Surprisingly so."

I nod. "You were just well prepared for it." Far better than me right now, because now the PowerPoint presentation and memos and Excel model I made last night seem stupid.

"Do you want—"

My belly growls.

He stops, and my face heats. My stomach's too knotted for food. Why is it embarrassing me?

"I slept in," I say as smoothly as I can manage. "Late."

"Let's get you fed, then," he says.

I open my mouth, about to turn him down, then catch myself. Breakfast is going to take at least half an hour. People shouldn't talk about uncomfortable topics while eating, to avoid indigestion.

"Sure," I say with a smile, hoping he offers me saltines or dry toast. My gut can't handle anything more than that, and not because pregnancy-related nausea has started.

"Okay. Let's go." He picks up his keys.

We can't go out because he's going to want to go someplace fancy, like another champagne brunch. I'm not ready to tell him why I can't drink. *Yet.* Especially not in public. "No, we should stay in."

"We should? Why?"

"I don't want anything rich."

He nods slowly. "Okay. No problem. We can do something quick and light, although that doesn't give us a lot of options. I don't really cook."

"I wouldn't expect you to." I wouldn't be able to eat a bite anyway.

He walks into his pantry and gazes at the shelves, one hand on his chin. "Well... I have bagels."

"That'd be great." I sit at the counter and paste an expectant expression on my face. *Yum. Bagels.*

"Plain or egg?" he calls out.

"Plain, please." Nothing that reminds me of *eggs*, fertilized or otherwise.

Emmett brings out a couple of toasted bagels and cream cheese. "Coffee?"

I squelch a sense of resignation. "Just some orange juice, thanks." Vitamin C is supposed to be good for you, so it's probably good for fetuses, too.

I nibble on the bagel, sans cream cheese. When should I broach the subject of the baby? And how am I supposed to smoothly pull out my laptop, boot it and start in with PowerPoint? Or Excel?

Instead of sitting and worrying last night, I should've dropped by the office and printed everything out. That way, I could take it out of my purse, all slick and ready.

Maybe we should talk about it tomorrow. It isn't like I have to tell him *now*.

"... Amy?"

I start. "Huh?"

"I asked you what you think about the plan."

"The, uh, plan?"

He gives me a look. "Were you listening?"

"Sorry. I was just...thinking about the Drone due diligence."

"I said we should do the wine country tour we were going to do last weekend."

"When?" I ask, out of reflex.

"*This* weekend." Now he's frowning at me.

"Oh. Well." Shit. This is going to be the second time I'm torching his plan. Well, the baby's going to torch his life, too, but... *Crap.* "Maybe not this weekend."

"It's no big deal. There are tons of flights, and I can book the resort right now."

I swallow. He obviously thinks I'm worried about the logistics. But planning a sudden trip is the least of it. When you have the kind of money he does, nothing's out of reach.

On the other hand... Maybe this is the opening I need. I can turn down the trip and tell him why I can't go drink a bunch of wine. I just have to do it all cool and calm.

"Emmett, there's, um—"

An alarm suddenly blares and lights start flashing above us. Emmett curses and picks up his phone from the counter. He taps the screen a couple of times, and the alarm dies.

"What was that?"

"Somebody just jumped the fence."

"What?" Emmett's home has a high wrought-iron fence. Plus it's in a safe, wealthy neighborhood. And it's not even eleven a.m. Who'd do something so crazy in broad daylight? "Maybe it's a false alarm?"

His eyebrows pinch as he glares at the phone screen. "No. We have an intruder."

"Seriously? Should I call 911?"

"No." Emmett seems totally calm, which is comforting.

The doorbell rings. He sighs deeply, stands up and walks past me to the foyer.

I sling my purse over my shoulder—in case I need my phone or the pepper spray Dad sends me every Christmas—then grab the butter knife and fork off my bagel plate, too, just in case. Now properly armed, I follow him.

The hi-res security panel next to the door shows the person on the other side. A redhead looks up and smiles at the camera. She's gorgeous, with sharp, high cheekbones that belong in a fashion magazine. Careful makeup covers her face, her eyes edged with long, curly lashes. Her hair is thick and glossy, shining like burning copper.

The only thing strange about her is the clothes—a beige

trench coat. The weather's too warm for that. But still, facially, anyway, she's a ten.

And compared to her, I'm quite ordinary. Just mascara and lip gloss. A white shirt and jeans. My sandals are cute, with nice heels, but that's about it.

"Who's that?" I ask.

He shakes his head slowly. "I...have no idea."

The redhead waves then starts banging on the door.

"Maybe you shouldn't open it." *I have a bad feeling about this.* Not because I suspect he and she have some history. But my instinct says she's bad news. "She could be unhinged."

"Mmm."

"Just because she's pretty doesn't mean she's sane."

"I know," he says, squinting at the woman.

"Hello?" she calls out from the other side. "I know you're home. Ted Lasker sent me!"

Emmett's *dad* sent this woman? Why did she jump over the wall, then?

Emmett yanks his hand away like the door turned into a viper. He'd take a step back if I weren't in his way.

"Shouldn't you answer that?"

"Two seconds ago, you didn't want me to."

"Yeah, but that was before I knew she works for your dad." Who knows what Hollywood people think is normal?

"Yoo-hoo!" she says. "Hel-lo-oh! Your father sent me! It's important."

I elbow Emmett gently. "You should probably see what she wants."

He sighs, then opens the door.

"Hi," she says chirpily, standing hipshot. "I'm Brenda. Are you Emmett Lasker?"

"Yes," he says slowly.

"Oh, wow. Cool that you're so *hot*. Hahaha! That was a joke. But seriously, I was kinda worried you might not be."

I stare at her. What a bizarre way to talk to someone you just met. Whether Emmett's dad sent her or not, she seems one wheel short of a hamster cage.

"I really wanted a hot costar," she adds with a winsome smile that says she's not crazy.

"Ooookay." Emmett clears his throat. "So, uh. What are you here about?"

"It isn't about what *I'm* about, but what *we're* about." She undoes the belt around the trench coat and shrugs it off her shoulders. She's completely naked underneath. *And completely shaved,* I note. She raises both arms like a game show hostess showcasing the best and final prize of the night. "Ta-da!"

32

AMY

Oh my God. Holy cow. I try to look away, but only manage to raise a loose hand in front of my eyes.

Emmett is staring, too, his gaze unblinking. Couldn't *he* at least put a hand up or something as well? He doesn't seem to really be *interested*, but he isn't showing any annoyance, either. His expression is a weird combination of I-knew-it and I-can't-keep-my-eyes-off-her.

The latter part bothers me more than anything. She might be hot, but has she read *The Mathematics of Financial Derivatives?* I don't think so.

Okay, snap out of it. I'm being ridiculous. If I didn't know better, I'd say I'm jealous, except I shouldn't be because technically Emmett and I are having a sex-only fling.

"What the hell are you doing?" Emmett says finally.

"An audition," she says like it's completely normal to stand on somebody's doorstep buck naked on a sunny Saturday. "For Ted's next movie."

"Your dad makes porn on the side?" I ask, flabbergasted. Ted Lasker has produced countless hits—the kind of movies you watch in theaters—but maybe he does other things, too. After all, sex sells.

"*No*." Emmett's response is immediate and firm.

"But she's naked and..." Something else she said earlier pops into my head, scattering confusion like confetti. "She said you're her costar. When do you find the time?"

"I don't. And I'm not her *any* star. I don't act, and I have no desire to act."

"Sure you do," she cuts in. She sounds breathless, which has to be fake. Nobody gets breathless just standing there. "Your dad said so."

"So?"

Confusion ripples over her. "Everyone wants to be a star!"

Emmett shakes his head.

Brenda looks lost. Maybe she doesn't realize Emmett is already a star—just not in Hollywood.

"But you have to! I need my big break!" she whines loudly. "He said you do auditions all the time!"

He does?

I don't think Emmett notices me staring, though. He's too busy letting out an exasperated sigh. "Look, you need to leave. I'm not doing this *audition*."

"How come?" she says.

"I'm busy. I have company." He points at me.

"You can finish the audition with her. I can wait," she says.

Instead of correcting her, he says, "No, you can't. But if you leave now, I'll open the gates so you won't have to jump the wall again. Wouldn't want you to break a nail or anything."

She looks down at her hands with a gasp as though she's just realized the horrible possibility. "Fine. I'll come back when you aren't in an audition with somebody else." She flicks her eyes over me—and doesn't seem too impressed—before she turns to Emmett with a smile. "Bye!"

She shrugs on her trench coat and walks away, hips swinging. She has to know we're watching her.

As she moves off into the distance, I turn to Emmett. "Does this happen often?"

"No."

No elaboration. His answer could mean this sort of things happens *occasionally*, or that it never happens.

I study him closely. He is entirely too calm and collected. Plus, he had that I-knew-it expression earlier, like this is something he's done before many times. He didn't react with much shock when she took off her coat, either.

When we were in La Jolla, Emmett told me he got along fine with his dad. So he must be at least somewhat comfortable with this kind of incident.

Just like that, all my anxiety over telling him about my pregnancy vanishes. I feel deflated. And that sensation's soon replaced by annoyance and a vague sense of betrayal. I didn't realize he and his dad have this kind of weird...relationship.

"I think I'm going to go home now," I say finally. I'm pleased at how calm I sound.

Emmett peers at me. "Are you upset?"

"A naked woman showing up on your doorstep? Why should such a minor thing upset me?"

"Come on," he says, spreading his hands. "She's just some girl Dad sent over. I've never met her, and I don't particularly want to meet her again."

If he's trying to make me feel like I'm overreacting, he's succeeding. But I know I'm not being unreasonable. Maybe it's normal to him for his father to send a woman over and have her get naked on his doorstep, but it isn't in my world. "That doesn't change how I feel about the situation." I raise my hands as I move toward my car. "I need some space, okay?"

He follows me out. "For how long?"

"I don't know. I haven't thought about it."

A beat. "Ten minutes?"

Men. "A day or two."

"A *day or two?*" He gestures in the direction Brenda ran off. "Amy, come on. She's not worth that."

You're blowing it out of proportion. You aren't being cool.

"She might not be, but I need that much time to sort my thoughts." I need to decide if I can partner with a man, who has random naked women popping up at home, to raise a child. Dad didn't even *date* when I was growing up.

"Amy, you're being unreasonable," Emmett says.

Too late. I'm already in my car. With lots to stew over.

33

EMMETT

Fury erupts as I watch Amy drive away. What the hell? It was going so well until that woman showed up.

Fucking Dad. He knew FedExing a hooker wouldn't work, even if he paid her handsomely for her trouble. So he's resorting to sending some poor woman desperate for a break in Hollywood.

I slam the door shut and pick up my phone. If Dad thought he was going to get away with this, he has another think coming.

After five rings, our call is connected.

"Who the hell do you think you are? You sent me a girl auditioning for porn and think that's going to get you a grandbaby? I'd rather get vasectomy!"

"I'm sorry you feel that way," comes Joey's dry, professional voice. "Would you like the name of the doctor who did Ted's first vasectomy? He's still practicing."

I want to rip a hole into Dad, not his assistant. "Where's. My. Father."

"Busy."

I narrow my eyes. "Oh, I get it. He sends me his 'actress' and is hiding now because he knows I'm going to ream him out."

"Just like gods don't need to hide, Ted Lasker never hides. You know that."

"Bullshit!"

"He is busy, as he often is, making a movie that will entertain millions. On top of that, everyone knows you're a good son. You'd never be disrespectful to your father." Joey sounds like a shitty actor at an audition—soulless and unconvincing.

"Can't you hire a writer for better lines?" Not that my criticism is going to make a dent in Joey's relentless desire to make sure Dad gets whatever he wants. Joey would be nothing in Hollywood without his job as my dad's assistant, and he knows it.

"Ted knows you're busy with work, and he just wants to help you along with the grandbaby production."

"I'm not some baby-making widget! And you—along with my super entertainer father—embarrassed me in front of my girlfriend!"

Joey perks up. "You have a girlfriend?"

Shit. "No," I say, annoyed with myself. Now he'll hire somebody to figure out who my girlfriend is and try to work on her. Amy doesn't need that kind of static.

"Is she pregnant?" Joey asks, his words brimming with excitement.

"No! There's no girlfriend, pregnant or otherwise."

"Ah, but you said there was. Can you *get* her pregnant? Like with a doctored condom?"

"You are the most vile, underhan—"

"If you feel squeamish about putting holes in condoms, I can provide some that are pre-perforated. They look slick. She won't suspect anything, I promise."

"*No, no, no!*" I say it three times so that maybe one will get through. Joey has highly selective hearing, a trait he picked up from Dad.

"I hope she's a redhead," he adds. "Ted wants a redheaded girl for his grandchild."

"Well, he can father one himself!"

"You can't father your own grandchild, Emmett." Joey speaks like I'm intellectually challenged. "Even if biology wasn't your best subject, you should know that. It's just common sense."

"If you don't stop, I'm going to kill you and dump you into one of those medieval common graves."

"No, you won't, because you'd hate the prison lifestyle. Anyway, expect some condoms in the mail." He hangs up just as I'm about to burst a vein.

There's a reason Dad likes him. Horses have blinders for their eyes. Joey has them for his ears. He only hears what he wants to hear and ignores the rest. He only conveys what Dad wants to convey, nothing else.

My phone buzzes. Hopefully it's Amy, done with her thinking. After all, what Brenda did doesn't deserve even a second.

But it's a text from Huxley. I sigh.

–Huxley: I'm going to build a penal colony on your anus. Who wants to chip in?

He sent it to me and the five other brothers. What's he talking about?

–Sebastian: I don't want anything on my anus, but if it's on yours, I'm in.

–Huxley: I meant your anus! Duck!

I roll my eyes. It's obvious what the problem is.

–Me: Are you having Siri text us?

–Huxley: Yes. She's terrible at this.

–Sebastian: Use your fingers.

–Huxley: Can't. I'm driving.

–Me: Then stop texting until you can.

–Grant: What's your anus supposed to be?

–Huxley: A planet.

–Me: Uranus?

–Huxley: Yes! Thank you! Ducking Siri.

I shake my head. What did he expect? It's an imperfect technology.

–Noah: Are we putting Dad in the colony?

–Huxley: Yes. Exactly.

–Noah: Well, I'm all for that.

–Sebastian: Can we make it farther away?

–Nicholas: And colder?

–Griffin: What did he do now?

–Nicholas: What do you mean, what did he do now? He didn't do anything to you?

–Griffin: Nope.

Lucky bastard.

–Huxley: Some chick tried to break into my place. She was naked under a trench coat.

–Nicholas: If she'd done that when I was in my home in Texas, I would've shot her dead. SMH.

–Me: He sent me one, too!

Which ruined my plans for the weekend. Amy is most definitely *not* going to be in a romantic weekend mood while she's processing Brenda. But why does she need a day or two to think about it, anyway? A few minutes should've been plenty of time. Then we could've gone to Napa and had our belated wine country tour.

I hope Amy wraps up her thinking quickly. Nothing good will come of her obsessing over what Dad did. The only thing he's good at is throwing money around and making movies. Anything else turns to shit.

–Griffin: Wow. Guess I dodged a bullet.

Maybe Joey overlooked Griffin. Why couldn't he have overlooked me, too? It isn't like I'm that important to Dad.

–Noah: He sent me a redhead. And she wasn't that hot.

–Huxley: Is that what got you upset?

Palpable disapproval pours from Huxley's text.

–Me: I'm disappointed in you, Noah. She could be the reincarnation of Marilyn Monroe, and I'd still say no.

–Noah: Of course. But you can have sex with her, then say no afterward.

Spoken like a true player.

–Grant: You'd get Dad cooties. I'll bet you my Bugatti that he slept with the girls he sent us.

My face scrunches, but Grant is right. It'd be a typically Dad thing to do.

–Sebastian: Excuse me while I go throw up.

–Huxley: Keep the gross details to yourself, Grant.

–Grant: It's for Noah's own good. In case Dad sends a hotter woman next time.

–Noah: He's not gonna waste his time like that when he's failed.

–Me: Guys, Dad is serious about wanting a grandkid. Joey offered to send me punctured condoms.

–Griffin: Maybe he's just sending you a box. I haven't talked to Joey since I got my PhD.

–Sebastian: I'm gonna kick his ass if he sends any to me.

–Me: Get in line. But we have to figure something out to stop this nonsense. All this sending women is disrupting my routine.

And upsetting Amy. She doesn't deserve this kind of aggravation.

–Grant: Like what? He won't stop until he gets what he wants.

–Nicholas: I'm getting myself huge guard dogs. Gonna leave them unleashed on my property.

My brothers toss out more ideas, but they're all temporary measures. We need a more permanent solution to the problem. And soon. I'm not having another fight with Amy over some trick Dad pulls to get what he wants.

34

AMY

Sasha isn't home when I arrive back from Emmett's place. So instead of getting to talk to somebody trustworthy about what happened, I spend the day cleaning my room and bathroom twice. I scrub the toilet until you could perform surgery on it. I wipe the kitchen counter probably two dozen times. Do four loads of laundry.

By late Sunday morning, all the clothes have been washed and folded and I've run out of things to clean. Sasha isn't going to be home until late—if at all—which means I'm sitting on a now-pristine floor, tired and alone with too many thoughts spinning in my mind, a state I absolutely despise. It's unproductive and makes you confused and stupid.

So what's a girl to do when she doesn't want to think?

I try Netflix. But its AI must be spying on me because it's recommending me nothing but baby shows. How many movies and dramas about pregnancy can you make? Is it a thing to run away from your boyfriend while you're carrying his baby? At least four shows say it is...*if he's a sociopath.*

Maybe this is Netflix's way of making me feel better about

my life. Emmett might have a naked woman stopping by, but at least he's not a serial killer.

Wow, Amy. Set the bar low, why don't you?

Okay. How about Prime videos?

Let's see... Movies and shows about baby showers... Surprise pregnancy... Maternity leave...

Ugh. What kind of excitement can you possibly generate from a show about *maternity leave*?

I turn the TV off and throw my hands in the air. There's gotta be something else more fun to do... Like... Like...

My eyes slide to the bathroom. The toilet gleams at me.

Fuck. My. Life.

Expelling a long sigh, I drag myself to the closet and change into an office outfit. It's Sunday, but it doesn't matter. It's my rule not to do work at home.

My phone pings. I brace myself, since I have no clue if it's going to be Emmett the Boss or Emmett the Fling.

But happily enough, it's Dad!

–Dad: Hey, sweetie pie! How are you?

I'm pregnant and might end up a single mom, but hey, my bathroom is really *clean.*

–Me: I'm doing awesome. How about you?

–Dad: Great! Just great!

We exchange selfies. He looks happy, and I look okay. It helps that I'm not in my frumpy cleaning T-shirt and shorts anymore.

–Dad: Hey, remember how I said I'd be in SoCal for Xavier's wedding and would stop by?

–Me: Yeah.

–Dad: Well, it got canceled.

–Me: What happened?

–Dad: Xavier decided he's better off single.

Shocking. I mean, I agree with Xavier's assessment, given that this would be his fifth marriage. But I honestly didn't think he'd come to that conclusion on his own. Most people can't see their own situations clearly.

—Me: How come?

—Dad: His fiancée got pregnant.

Asshole. That's a terrible reason to dump your fiancée. My empathy doubles, since I understand *exactly* how she's feeling right now. Emmett hasn't dumped me, but then, he doesn't know. And based on what happened yesterday, he might. A baby would get in the way of him doing "auditions."

—Dad: Turns out it's not his baby.

I take it back. *What a bitch.*

—Me: How did he find out?

—Dad: He had an accident a couple of years ago, which makes him shoot blanks, you know?

—Me: Wow. That's awful.

—Dad: She tried to pass it off as his, but it didn't work. And get this—she cheated on him with his younger brother!

—Me: OMG!

—Dad: She figured he wouldn't know, given the family resemblance.

Who needs Netflix and Prime videos when you have my father's friends?

—Dad: Xavier's heartbroken and pissed off, but I think it's best this way. It's better to find out sooner than later that the person you're with isn't going to work out.

—Me: Absolutely. Cut your losses.

As I hit send, my heart stings because I'm wondering if I'm going to have to my cut *my* losses. I don't know how to explain Emmett why I was unhappy on Saturday if that sort of thing is normal to him.

—Dad: Exactly. How do you live with somebody you can't trust, much less share the same values with?

After unknowingly sowing more uncertainty and doubt into my head, Dad gossips about his life and buddies for a minute or so, which keeps me entertained. At the same time, I start to wonder why he's so text-y. Normally, he doesn't type this much.

Does he have something he wants to say, but doesn't know how to start?

Part of me wants to prompt him, but I rein myself in. I'm the one who should be telling him about my pregnancy, since it is going to impact his life, too. But I can't bring myself to do it when I haven't told Emmett—or even know if I *want* to tell him in the first place.

Finally, Dad wraps up his gossip.

–Dad: You take it easy, you hear?

–Me: Yes, sir! Have a great Sunday, Dad. Love you!

–Dad: Love you, sweetie pie!

I can almost hear his hearty voice and even heartier hug, and feel the love swell in my heart. He's truly the best there is. I put the phone into my purse and head to the office.

A few people are working at their desks, including Sasha. She waves when she notices me. I wave back, glancing at Emmett's office door. It's closed, but that doesn't mean anything, since he could have decided to spend his unexpected free time catching up on work.

Now that the shock of the naked redhead has worn off, I realize I haven't done anything to fix the problem, a.k.a. my secret pregnancy.

Don't rush into anything, I tell myself. I need to be sure about my next move. So while my subconscious tackles the issue, I review an Excel model I made—not on the baby but on a real company we're funding. I already went over it on Friday, but you can never go over a model enough times. Or so I tell myself.

The task takes longer than it should. My head is foggy with a mild headache throbbing like background static. Coffee withdrawal is real. *Please, God, just one iced Americano.* Or latte. Or plain drip. Any variety will do.

Be a responsible adult, Amy.

Yeah. That's why fifteen minutes later, I'm in the break room, going over the non-caffeinated herbal tea options, hoping something will look appealing.

"Hey, I didn't know you were working this weekend," says Sasha, walking in. She helps herself to a huge mug of coffee, and it's an effort not to drool.

"Just some stuff I need to review. Nothing super urgent or anything."

She peers at me. "How are you feeling?"

"So-so." I really want to whine about coffee, but I don't want her to feel bad.

"Uh-huh. Well, I guess that's good, considering. So how did he react?"

"I, uh, kinda didn't..."

"What? A bun in the oven and you didn't say anything—"

"What bun?" comes Emmett's eerily calm voice from behind us.

Shit.

Sasha's neck and head sink until her shoulders are nearly touching her ears. Her expression says, *Sorry!*

I squeeze my eyes shut for a second. This is *not* how I wanted him to find out. I inhale, then hold my breath for a moment. My heart starts racing.

Settle the hell down. I paste on a fake smile, the same one I put on when I'm trying to look happy about Emmett dumping a last-minute task on my desk.

"I'm waiting," Emmett says, still in that scarily calm voice.

I turn to him, the smile still firmly glued to my face. "Emmett! What are you doing here?"

"It's my firm."

Right.

His gaze flicks to Sasha, then snaps back to me. "My office, please."

Without waiting for a response, he turns and walks out. He didn't grab whatever he came to the break room for, damn it. I wish he'd gotten a snack or coffee or whatever, because that might improve his mood.

Right now, he most definitely feels like finding fault with me.

He won't have missed the fact that my roommate knew about my pregnancy and he didn't.

"I am *so* sorry," Sasha whispers, her whole face pinched.

I pat her shoulder. "It's fine. Might as well get this over with."

"Are you going to tell him about the...you know?" she whispers, without mentioning the word "resignation."

I shake my head. "I'm still thinking about the offer." I also have two more second-round interviews. "I'll be fine." *I hope.*

I straighten my spine and walk purposefully to Emmett's office. He left his door ajar, so I walk in and close it behind me.

He's leaning against the edge of his desk, his expression unreadable. "Take a seat."

I do.

"So." His cool gaze drops to my belly briefly before meeting my eyes. "The bun."

"Yeah, um..." I exhale, feeling like a prisoner about to be executed. "I found out on Friday."

"Is it Rick's?" he asks with a small frown.

"No." I'm not offended by the question. Sasha asked the same thing. "It's most definitely not his."

Is it me, or did the tension in Emmett's shoulders ease a little? He doesn't ask me how I know, just nods.

So I feel compelled to add, "My guess is that it happened that first time...here. We didn't use a condom."

"Why didn't you say something earlier?"

His calm attitude makes me twitchy with anxiety. Shouldn't he react with more...emotion? Accuse me of getting pregnant on purpose to entrap him or something? "It didn't seem like something I should text."

"But on Saturday?"

"Brenda showed up," I remind him.

He closes his eyes briefly and curses under his breath.

He probably feels inconvenienced. Hard to audition naked women with a baby around. I don't want to force him into doing something he might not want just because I'm carrying his child.

People who are forced into decisions rarely honor them. And if they do, they resent the hell out of it. Neither the baby nor I deserve that.

"You don't have to do anything you don't want to do, except to provide child support because that's what a baby should be able expect from its father."

"*What?*"

"Take time to think it over," I say, giving him a graceful way to back off and process it. "I know you're probably in shock. This wasn't part of our plan."

"What plan?"

"A sex-only fling?" Shock seems to have temporarily halved his IQ.

"That was not a 'plan.' Asking me to hand over money to pay for the cost of raising a baby isn't much of a plan, either."

That annoys the hell out of me. I'm not some irresponsible non-planner! "I made an Excel model on what it takes to raise a child." I don't bring up the PowerPoint or memos, since he seems to be focused on the financial aspect.

"I'd like to see it. I'm sure I'm going to want changes."

Ha. I'm not staying up until two a.m. to redo it!

He continues, "Regardless, I can't remain uninvolved." He narrows his eyes. "We'll get married."

"*What?*"

He spreads his hands. "We'll get married."

I stare at him, trying to process why in the world he's saying this. My heart is racing, my belly all fluttery. Marriage never occurred to me, and the idea is scary as hell because I like it far too much. *Somebody wants me enough to make the commitment!*

Until cold reality slaps me hard. *Girlfriend, he didn't say the M-word until you got pregnant. And remember Xavier? Weddings can be called off just like that.* Cold reality snaps its frigid fingers in demonstration.

"Are you out of your mind?" I croak.

"I'm perfectly rational," Emmett says calmly.

"No, you aren't. If you were, you wouldn't have thrown out marriage as an option. Your judgment is clouded by the confusion of the moment."

"I am *not* confused. Just like you have definite ideas about how a fling should go, I also have definite ideas about how *my* baby should be raised."

"Which is...?"

"In a *household*. With *two* parents. Who are *married*."

Wow. I didn't expect Emmett to be this traditional. He was raised in Europe for a while—which is supposed to be more liberal than the States when it comes to stuff like this—and his father is a Hollywood producer who *never* married.

"Emmett, we're not getting married just because I'm pregnant."

"May I remind you that *that*"—he points at my belly—"is *my* baby you're carrying?"

"Yes, but marriage! It's a big step."

He squints at me, then closes his eyes and nods. "You want to be romanced. Of course. Flowers, chocolate, jewelry..."

"No, it isn't about stuff like that! I'm not marrying someone who I can't be sure will stick around no matter how rough things might get. If you marry me for the baby, you're committing yourself for at least eighteen years. I don't want you to get bored and leave in the middle of it." As the words slip from my mouth, I realize the chances of him getting bored are significant. The man's too smart and too rich not to, or put up with a situation when it's no longer amusing. I can't risk my future happiness—or my baby's—on his mood. I deserve a dependable man who wants me for myself. "If you feel like you have to have some stake in the baby, we can do some kind of joint custody."

"Tell you what. Let's just temporarily put marriage aside. Until you're sure." It's like he didn't hear my joint custody offer and is confident I'm going to change *my* mind.

I can tell from his expression that he isn't going to budge on this. Well, I'm not budging either. I'm not letting my child feel the same sense of abandonment and pain I felt when I was old enough to realize my mom didn't want me enough to stick around.

"Fine," I say, since it isn't productive to argue. Once he has some time to think a bit, he'll realize I'm right. "Can I go back to the due diligence I was doing?"

"No, you can go home. You don't have anything urgent on your plate. There's no reason you have to do that today."

I hesitate. I have nothing to do at home except stew.

He gives me a firm look. "If you don't, I'll find a lot of *training* for everyone in the office to do and make sure they know it's all due to your amazing effort."

"You are *such* a jerk."

"A jerk who wants you to not work on Sunday." He bares his teeth in a smile. "Sue me."

35

AMY

The second I walk into my apartment, my phone pings. Maybe it's Emmett texting to let me know he's seen the light—and I'm right.

But no. It's actually Sasha.

–Sasha: Is everything okay? I stopped by your desk after I thought you'd be out of the big, bad boss's office, but you'd left. Did Emmett get really pissy about your upcoming maternity leave?

Oh crap. I should've expected her to be upset. Now she'll be angsty about getting me into trouble for the rest of the day if I don't set her straight.

I put my stuff at the foot of my bed and sit on the edge of the mattress.

–Me: Not really.

He isn't upset about the maternity leave, but the fact that I'm not sure about marrying him over the pregnancy. The more I think about it, the odder it seems. Aren't guys generally happy about *not* being forced into commitment? I'm giving him a graceful way out.

–Sasha: It's illegal for him to do that. I'm sure of it. You're

239

entitled to your leave, unless you told him you quit.

Obviously my bestie is operating under a different assumption.

—Me: Not like that. It's complicated.

—Sasha: What's complicated? You're so close to hitting 2 years anyway. If you wanna sue, let me know. I can ask around for some lawyer recs.

I can already picture her asking her boyfriend. No. Just no.

—Me: Please don't. A lawsuit isn't the way to go here.

But even as I hit send, I know she isn't going to listen. She's like a pit bull when somebody in her circle's threatened.

—Me: You can't tell anybody what I'm about to say.

—Sasha: You known I can keep my mouth shut. But you're scaring me here.

I inhale slowly, and exhale even more slowly.

—Me: I didn't want to tell you like this, but put a hand over your mouth and clench your teeth together.

—Sasha: Why?

—Me: I don't want you making any strange sounds! You're still in the office, right?

—Sasha: Fine. Done!

—Me: Okay. Here's the super secret. The baby is Emmett's.

Two beats and no response. Did she faint from shock? Do I need to call 911?

—Me: Hello? You there?

Three dots appear on the screen. I wait.

—Sasha: HOLY SHIT! Fuck! I dropped my phone and banged my head on the desk when I bent down to grab it.

—Me: Ouch. Are you okay?

—Sasha: NO! You're pregnant with Emmett's baby? Emmett Lasker?

—Me: Yeah.

—Sasha: Ack! We need to talk about this.

—Me: I knew you'd say that.

—Sasha: Why did you have to tell me this when I have a shit-ton of work to do?

–Me: Ask Grant for an extension?

It's a feeble attempt at a joke.

–Sasha: He wants the baby, right?

Boy, does he ever.

–Me: Yes.

–Sasha: I don't have to poison his coffee, then.

–Me: In case you feel the urge to spit in his coffee instead, he told me to go home and rest.

–Sasha: Ooooh. I like that. You deserve a break.

–Me: He wants to marry me for the baby. I'm not sure.

–Sasha: Wait. He's offering marriage?

–Me: Yeah, but you know how I have my life planned out. Marrying a guy just because I'm pregnant with his baby isn't part of that plan.

I want to marry a guy who's sure about being with *me*, no matter what.

–Sasha: But you liked him enough to sleep with him, so maybe you can at least think about it? Emmett can be a little weird, but then, all geniuses are. But he doesn't strike me as the type to throw something that serious out there just on impulse.

–Me: Yeah, that's true.

And that's what's making it hard for me to think clearly about what Emmett said. On top of that, he seemed determined.

–Sasha: I have tons of shit I have to do, but I will do everything in my power to leave the office by 9 so we can talk tonight.

–Me: Okay. I'll wait for you.

–Sasha: Thanks, but if you feel tired, don't wait up for me. Just go to bed. That's more important.

–Me: Thanks, girl.

I put my phone down, then lie on my bed and stare at the ceiling. Sasha's loyal support soothes my nerves, which have been raw since I had that confrontation with Emmett. Maybe...just maybe I can be the tiniest bit more open-minded about what he proposed.

36

EMMETT

Books on pregnancy and child rearing. *Check.*

Prenatal vitamins for Amy. *Check.*

Lunch massages for Amy at the Aylster. *Check.*

What am I missing? I tap my fingers on the desk and gaze at the laptop. A PowerPoint presentation is open for my review, but I'm too distracted to look at it. Even though it's Monday at eleven, when I should be fully ramped up.

But I'm not. What the hell do I need to do to convince Amy I'm right about getting married? My gut has never led me astray, and it's unlikely to start now.

Marriage as a concept is nebulous and unexciting. But marriage *with Amy* is electrifying. A woman who is smart, gorgeous and hot as hell? Yes, please. The baby will be a bonus, especially if it's a girl who looks like her mom. But for some reason, Amy doesn't see the same thing I do. I can't believe she said I'd get bored.

I don't waste my time and energy on people I find boring.

Except telling her, "I would have never slept with you if I thought you were boring," probably isn't going to work. Women need more solid reassurance.

Diamonds...? Sparkly, elegant and expensive... That's pretty good reassurance. On the other hand, can she be bought like that? She might be more impressed if I did something for her instead.

Maybe *I* should make a PowerPoint presentation on all the things I can provide for her and the baby. She has to know it's nearly impossible to raise an infant alone while working in venture capital. She's going to need a team of nannies and some kind of in-house staff for grocery shopping and cooking. I'll also pay for the kid's education, all the way to whatever degree they want. At the rate college tuition's rising, it's going to cost a billion bucks to get a four-year degree by the time the kid's old enough to enter.

But is that going to be enough to convince her? She probably has more immediate concerns. She's pregnant right now. It has to be taxing for her body to turn a few cells into a fully grown human baby. One of the books I ordered probably has some advice on what to do for Amy. I pick up a pink one and start reading. Thankfully, I'm a speed reader, so it shouldn't take more than a couple of hours to get through the five-hundred-page volume.

Somebody knocks on the door.

"Yeah?" I call out, my eyes still on the pages.

The door opens. "Wow. You decided to take one for the team?"

I glance up. Grant is giving me a look of sheer gratitude and admiration. "No," I say. Amy only told me about the pregnancy because she got caught red-handed. I'm not letting anybody know until Amy and I get a chance to discuss how we're going to break the news to our families.

"But the books—"

"Are for an industry analysis I'm doing. A proposal on a new kind of service for pregnant women."

"Ah." Grant nods, taking a seat on the other side of the desk. "It's important to know your customers."

"Exactly. How else can I judge the viability?"

"And since you're going to know so much about pregnancy, you can also take one for the team. You are the oldest, after all."

"Might be the oldest, but I'm not senile." I'm not letting Dad anywhere near Amy or my kid. The baby isn't some prop Dad can use to feel superior to Josh Singer. "You aren't that much younger." I'm not finding the answer I'm looking for on the pages. "Hey, did your mom ever happen to mention when she started puking in the morning?"

"For what?"

"Either due to morning sickness...or the sickening sinking feeling in her gut that her kid was an idiot."

Grant laughs. In fact, he has the highest IQ out of all of us. "No and no."

A text arrives on my phone. Grant reaches for his at the same time.

–Griffin: WTF! He sent me a damn hooker at the university! During my office hours!

I arch an eyebrow. He doesn't have to elaborate.

–Me: Calm down before you do something you'll regret. Probably nobody noticed. It isn't like anybody goes to office hours after the first month.

Not because Griffin's class is easy. But when a subject is too far beyond your comprehension, you can't even ask a question because you know so little. Plus, girls who have the hots for him tend to give up after about four to five weeks because he *never* sleeps with his students.

–Griffin: WRONG! I had a bunch of econ majors outside my office to protest their midterm grades.

–Grant: Does it matter? You're the envy of all the frat boys.

Grant and my phones ring. It's Huxley, doing a group call.

"Griff, I know you're mad. But you're tenured, so who cares?" he says in a feeble attempt to cheer our brother up.

Griffin is seething. If Dad were in his office, he'd give him a flying knee to the face. Although he's a professor of a subject as unexciting as econometrics, he's done years of kickboxing.

"He's right," I say. "It isn't like *you* hired her."

"The fucking head of the department cares, that's who. He wants me to, quote, 'restore the dignity of the economics department,' unquote, by doing some bullshit case he couldn't get anybody else to do because it's stupid. It's a tech firm that couldn't make it in Silicon Valley." If Griffin were a cat, all his hair would be raised. "It's a failing company with poor capitalization and cash flow."

"It'll be fine," Grant says. "Just go through the motions. It isn't like anybody expects you to work a miracle. Shoddily run companies fail all the time."

I nod. "Exactly."

Grant leans backs in his seat. His gaze flicks to the tower of pregnancy-related books on my desk, and a smirk tugs at his mouth. "By the way, guys, guess what Emmett's reading now?"

"*How to Anal-Rape Wall Street for Profit in Three Easy Steps?*" Noah says.

"Pregnancy and baby books."

My brothers erupt. I give Grant a dry look. "They're for market research," I say, while Grant snickers.

"He wants to know about *morning sickness*," Grant says.

"Yeah, I hear there's a booming market for pregnancy puke," Sebastian says.

I sigh. They clearly don't believe me about the market research, not even a little. Excess protest on my part would only cement their disbelief.

"Just make sure she stays near a toilet," says Huxley, Mr. Practical. "But the real problem isn't morning sickness, it's the weird cravings. One of the assistants in my office got knocked up a little while back. She ate canned tuna mixed with mustard and chopped green olives for three months."

"That sounds disgusting." Hopefully Amy will like something a bit more normal and dignified. Like tacos or pizza. "But the books really are for an industry analysis. Grant doesn't know what he's talking about." Time for a change of topic. "How's the birthday gift coming along?"

"All good," Sebastian says. "But you know Dad's going to whine that it isn't what he asked for."

Nicholas mimics Dad: "'What does a man need to do to get the birthday gift he wants?'"

"He needs to get over it. We're going to show up, aren't we?" Huxley says.

"Exactly," I say. "Besides, you don't get what you want when you give almost zero notice. The party's only two weeks away."

"Are you guys bringing anybody to the party?" Noah asks. "I'm bringing a date."

"Are you trying to break up with her?" Huxley says.

"She wants to get into movies," Noah says. "And insisted."

"I have nobody," Griffin says. "I wish I didn't have to go."

"Me either. There's nobody I'd bring to Dad's birthday party." I'm not subjecting Amy to what will undoubtedly turn into a massive clusterfuck. "Too damn embarrassing."

Three knocks at the door. "Come in," I say, then turn to my phone, relieved I don't have to continue the conversation. "Kids, I gotta go. Work."

"Likewise."

We hang up. Grant stands as Amy walks in. Just the woman who's been endlessly occupying my thoughts.

37

AMY

Grant and I greet each other, all professional. Emmett's eyes skim me carefully, so I paste on a smile and pretend I'm fine.

There's nobody I'd bring to Dad's birthday party. Too damn embarrassing.

If Emmett and his dad didn't get along, I might assume he was embarrassed about his dad. But I know that isn't true, so maybe Emmett's embarrassed about me. The notion is like a hot knife stuck in my chest. I force a smile and feel the corners of my lips twitch a little.

When Grant closes the door behind him, I take a seat.

"How are you feeling?" Emmett asks, all solicitous.

How much of that warmth is real? "I'm fine. You?"

"Good." He clears his throat. "So. Have you thought about what I said yesterday?"

I start to answer until the books on his desk catch my attention. "Did your brother see those books?" *Did you tell Grant?*

"Yeah, but I told him they're for an industry analysis. He has no clue."

"I see." I nod slowly, trying to decide how I feel about that.

"So, about what I said yesterday..."

Did you mean I am embarrassing when you said, "Too damn embarrassing," or was it something else? The words form in my mouth, then get stuck. I was an idiot for thinking I should keep an open mind about his proposal. "What about it?"

"What do you think?"

"Shouldn't we meet each other's families first?" I throw that out instead of the *real* question I want to ask.

He shakes his head. He's trying to keep his expression neutral, but I catch the wince fleeting across his handsome face. "I don't think that's necessary."

Too damn embarrassing. Emmett's voice echoes in my head. The queasiness I'm feeling has nothing to do with morning sickness.

"It isn't like we're marrying each other's families," he adds.

My hands shake, and I clench them. I'll be damned if I let him know how hurt I am. "Let's talk about the Drone project."

"But we didn't get to finish—"

"I need more time." *To compose myself.* It's going to be humiliating if I end up crying, even though I can feel my face heating.

He peers at me. "Are you okay?"

"I'm fine. Just a little nauseated."

"Morning sickness?"

I shrug. Let him think it's the pregnancy. That's better than having him see my bruised heart.

Even though he's giving me a look I can't quite decipher, he goes over the project with me. The company's almost ready for its IPO.

I mechanically write down what he says, but my mind is whirring about why he asked me to marry him if he's too embarrassed to take me to his father's birthday party or introduce me to his family. Now that I think about it, he didn't seem that enthused about meeting my dad, either.

When I return to my desk and sit down, I note the Amazon box under the drawers. It's full of different brands of prenatal vitamins. There's a note inside that reads:

Wasn't sure what was the best, so I ordered a bunch.

It's an act of somebody who's trying to do the right thing and take care of the mother of his child and the baby itself.

Come on, Amy. You only heard one side of the conversation. Maybe somebody on the other side made some weird comment.

Not very convincing, because there was hardly enough pause for somebody to say something, but I have to shake this off until I'm emotionally and mentally ready to talk to him about it.

As I sit in front of my laptop, I have a text from Emmett.

–Emmett: FYI you have a 30-min lunch massage at the Aylster spa from M-F.

I stare at the message. *He didn't even hint about a massage.* Once the shock wears off, confusion follows. This is another example of him acting like he cares.

So why did he say, "Too damn embarrassing"? I just can't imagine who or what he could be talking about, except me.

Part of me wants to reject this massage offer, but I change my mind. It'll be good to do something to de-stress myself. Not just for me, but for the baby, too.

–Me: Thanks.

–Emmett: You may not have time for lunch, so they're going to buy whatever you want and have it ready for you when you leave. Give the spa receptionist your order before they start the massage.

–Emmett: And you don't have to limit yourself to the hotel restaurants. They can get you stuff from outside if you want.

He's thought of everything. Maybe he was embarrassed about something else. Maybe he's feeling awkward about meeting the father of a woman he knocked up without meaning to. Maybe he'll come around after a few days and realize we can't just get married in a vacuum. We might not be marrying each other's families, but that doesn't mean they won't be an important part of our lives. If nothing else, our baby deserves to know its uncles and grandparents.

But as the hours pass, I don't get anything that indicates Emmett's changed his mind about keeping our families separate and uninvolved. What I get instead are incessant texts from him. Like this one after lunch.

–Emmett: Sage or sunflower yellow?

Two shades pop up on my phone. Both are lovely, but sage feels a bit too dark.

–Me: Sunflower yellow.

Or this one midafternoon.

–Emmett: White or oak?

–Me: Oak.

–Emmett: Why?

–Me: Warmer.

–Emmett: How about oak or cherry?

–Me: Oak.

Then before he can ask why, I add:

–Me: Cherry's too dark.

–Me: Can I come by after work?

I want to talk to him about what I'd like *if* I agree to marry him—that I want our families to be part of our lives, since it was just me and Dad when I was growing up. And I want to have a good relationship with his father, since he's important to Emmett. Everyone needs to get along and support each other. Maybe I should make that clear to him, in case he somehow doesn't realize this. Then we can discuss how we're going to announce the news to our families.

–Emmett: I have a late meeting, and I don't want you to stay up. See you tomorrow?

–Me: Okay.

The next morning, he texts again.

–Emmett: Sea creatures or land creatures?

I frown. Does he want to go diving again? Is that even safe if you're pregnant? Or is this a hint he'd like to do a safari or something before the baby's born? I have my first doctor's appointment at the end of this month—she couldn't fit me in earlier—and I don't want to commit to anything until she clears me.

–Me: Sea creatures.

–Emmett: Why?

–Me: They remind me of our diving trip in La Jolla.

And I'll never forget how I felt there, sharing the stunning underwater vistas with him.

After my Tuesday lunch massage, I leave the hotel with a takeout beef burrito that the concierge got for me. My phone pings, and it's Dad.

–Dad: Hey, sweetie! When you get a chance, can you give me a call? Thanks!

I bite my lip as I read the text. He almost never asks me to call because he knows I'm usually busy. This must be important.

Trying to control a shiver of apprehension, I call him.

38

AMY

"Hi, Dad!" I say in my cheeriest voice.

"Hey, sweetie." The brightness in Dad's tone feels forced. "I didn't interrupt anything, did I?"

"No, I've got a few minutes," I say, checking the time. My meeting isn't until one thirty.

"Oh, good."

I wait, but he doesn't say anything else. An awkward silence stretches. "Are you still there?" I ask.

"Yeah, yeah. Um. I was just calling to see if everything's good."

"It's great. Everything okay with you?"

"Yeah, um. Well. It's about Renée."

Shock punches me in the gut. Of all the things I imagined, the topic of my mom wasn't anywhere near the top of the list. "What about her?" I try for some calm, but my voice is shaky.

"Well, uh, she contacted me."

"After all these years?" This is infuriating. "What does she want? Money?"

"No, no, nothing like that." He gives a short laugh. "She knows I'll never give her a penny."

True. Dad's no fool.

"But she wants to connect with you," he says.

Bitterness surges, until it's all I can taste in my mouth. "She doesn't think it's too late?"

"I think that's why she tried to follow you on Pulse, but she couldn't see any photos, so she sent a friend request. I guess you ignored it."

"I don't do social media. I only have an account there because..." I sigh impatiently. "Anyway, no. I'm not interested."

"Then you don't have to deal with her, Amy. I only wanted to tell you in case you wanted to talk to your mother." Underneath the calm is a hint of sorrow. He's always felt he couldn't fulfill all my needs.

"I do not." I inhale deeply, hold the breath for a moment, then exhale. "I don't need a mother. I have you, Dad. You're the one who loved me and raised me. She doesn't get to show up now and take any of the credit."

"Okay," he says gently.

I soften my voice. "I love you."

"Love you too, sweet pie."

We hang up. I stay where I am for a few seconds to gather my spiraling emotions and slowly unclench my hand from around my phone. I have to return to the office, eat lunch and go to the meeting.

But the fact that Mom wants to reconnect after all these years keeps nagging at me. It's like a dog that won't quit nipping at your heels.

After the meeting, I go back to my desk and pull out my phone. I stare at the Pulse icon. Why should I want to be her social media buddy now?

I put my phone down on the desk. I should ignore her. She doesn't matter. She can't just quit on me and then show up later when it's convenient.

But I find myself picking up the phone again and tapping the Pulse icon.

Sure enough, the request is the first thing that pops up.

Renée Wilson wants to share mutual friendship with you.

Confirm | Decline

I click on the X to close it. What *I* want to do is check out her profile. See the kind of life she's had after she dumped me and Dad. To be honest, I don't know what I expect to see. Maybe I want to see her regret her decision to split. I know it's going to feel like I'm being disemboweled if I see her with a new family... especially if there are children around my age.

Do you really want to see that?

But I'm already on her profile. Her face shot is excellent. Either it's one from ten or fifteen years back or she's done a lot of work to preserve her youth. Single. No kids. The gut tension eases, and I can breathe more easily.

That confirmed, I go through her posts, photos and videos. Contrary to my wish that she regretted abandoning me, she's had a *great* life, I note with bitterness.

Images of her bouncing around topless by pools with beers and cheap sparkling wines spraying around her. Her licking white syrup all over her hand in a suggestive manner, her eyes on the camera, her mouth parted in a lascivious smile. Men gyrating against her, rubbing their dicks against her butt. She might as well star in a soft-core porn.

Parties. More wild parties that stretch for years on end, from the day she joined Pulse. I guess I should be relieved she didn't post any orgy videos, not that that would really shock me.

No wonder she didn't want me around. She might've been able to lead a degenerate life just being with Dad, but not me. I'm an inconvenience—or was when I was younger and needed her. But now... Maybe she thinks I'd make a great "girlfriend" to take to her repulsive parties. After all, she's getting old. In the latest photos, her skin's starting to show her age—and the decades of depraved lifestyle and choices. Maybe she needs younger meat to gain entrée. Who knows?

I can't decide if I'm relieved and happy that I've been right all along that I'm better off without her. Or if I'm sad that the person who contributed half my genetic material is such a pathetic human being. Maybe it's a little bit of both.

I type a quick personal message for her through the app.

I heard from Dad. You know, the parent who actually stuck around and raised me. FYI, I never use Pulse, and I'm not interested in connecting. Don't bother Dad again.

I stare at the sentences for a while. Part of me wonders if I should soften it up a little...but no. Was she sweet and kind when she decided to dump me and Dad? She didn't look back. Never made an effort to call or send a birthday card or any of those things. She doesn't get to wake up one day and decide to play mother because she feels like it.

I hit send, then delete the app. People like Mom don't deserve my time or energy.

"Amy, are you okay?" Emmett asks, pausing on his way back to his office.

I force a quick smile. "Yeah. It's all good." As I speak, I realize I haven't seen him since I spoke to him about the deliverable yesterday. It's crazy how busy we are that we don't see each other much, even while we're on the same floor. If we worked for different firms like Peggy and her husband, we really would have to make appointments.

The baby's going to need its father, and taking the offer from the Blaire Group is going to be a bad move for both of you.

Well, yeah. I'll have to stay here if I decide to marry Emmett.

He looks around, then lowers his voice. "Can you stop by my place when you're done?"

Finally a chance to talk about what's on my mind. "Yes. I'd like that very much."

39

EMMETT

I'm standing in front of the elevators at six p.m. Grant raises his eyebrows as he passes by.

"Not ordering in tonight?" he says.

"Nope. Heading home."

He stops in mid-stride. "You feeling okay?"

"Sure. Why?"

"It's barely six. Fever? Upset stomach? There must be something."

"I'm not sick. Just wanted to practice a little work-life balance today."

"Good lord, the world is ending. I should check the news, see if some giant meteor is about to destroy us all."

I sigh and step into the waiting elevator. Grant doesn't have to act like Armageddon has arrived just because I'm leaving a little early. Although honestly, it does feel strange. But I need to prep my home before Amy comes over, so I can make my case.

I know we both work a lot, and our lifestyle might not be conducive for raising a child. I've seen how things are in our profession.

On the other hand, I'm not going to let her take on the full burden. It's my kid, too. Plus, money can solve a lot of problems, often in ways that she might not be aware of. I want to have her focus a little more on that. Let her know she's not on her own, whether she marries me or not, although I prefer that she does. It's just a logical step.

Is that all? my mind whispers.

What else do I need? Love? I have no clue what love is or what it should feel like. Isn't it enough that Amy and I have amazing chemistry, we're both smart, we understand each other's careers and we get along? That's more important than something as vague as love.

Once I'm home and in the living room, I text her.

–Me: When do you think you'll be coming by?

–Amy: Half an hour. I just left the office.

–Me: What do you want for dinner?

–Amy: Pepperoni pizza?

–Me: Done!

I place an order, then check the fridge to make sure I have her favorite sparkling pink lemonade. There's an entire case.

Perfect.

Amy pulls in a minute after the pizza arrives. She walks breezily through the door, her purse slung over her shoulder. She looks gorgeous, her eyes bright and her mouth sweet and full. The pregnancy books all said the glow doesn't happen until later, but she already looks like she swallowed a banquet full of stars.

"Wanna eat first?" She's pregnant and eating for one and a half. Some say you eat for two when you're pregnant, but according to the books, the baby's the size of a poppy seed. It's just too small to get full personhood yet.

"Yes! I'm famished."

We dig into the pizza. She can't drink, so I content myself with a glass of Coke while she sips her lemonade and we talk about the water filter project. I don't want to ambush her with my prepared statement about the baby yet. It's always best to broach a sensitive topic when the audience is in a receptive mood.

"Since it's not your typical for-profit venture, what's going to happen if it's really successful?"

"We'll toast with the best champagne, and I'll continue to be involved with Bernie and make sure he doesn't let some hedge fund or private equity firm take it over."

"I thought that was the exit strategy."

"Normally, yes, but not after the botched one with the Blaire Group."

Her fingers flex and unflex around her lemonade. "The Blaire Group botched one?"

"It was a couple of years back, but yeah. The whole thing was a clusterfuck. To be honest, I should've known better than to say yes when Marion Blaire wanted to be in charge of the deal. He has an overinflated sense of his own competence. And it bothers the hell out of him he's only where he is because of his daddy."

There's more to our enmity than that. His ongoing attempts to mess with me professionally and personally are more than irritating. He regards us as rivals, which is ridiculous. Rivals would mean we had the same level of talent and drive. The reality is that he just tries to steal my employees. Well, former employees. I hear that he's snapped Webber up. He's welcome to that unwanted dreck.

Amy sips her lemonade, her eyes lowered. "So. Are we only here to share a pizza and talk about Marion Blaire?"

Here it comes. I shift in my seat, mentally checking through my plan to make my case. "No," I say. "I want to show you something, if you're done eating."

"I'm done." She wipes her fingers on the napkin.

I lead her upstairs to the bedroom between my bedroom and an office. The door and one window have been left open, and the smell has dissipated a lot.

I gesture into the room with a flourish. "What do you think?"

She stops at the entrance and stares. The walls are painted shades of blue-green that look like the La Jolla water. Sea turtles and seals and towering kelp columns occupy two walls, while the others have unfinished murals of the marine world. An oak crib is already put together and sitting in the corner.

She walks inside slowly. She doesn't speak, just turns slowly, looking around the huge room, her eyes wide.

Finally, I can't stand the tension. "Do you like it?"

"Yes! Wow. It's...gorgeous," she whispers. "I love everything."

Thank God. "It's the nursery."

"When did you prep all this?" she asks. "You didn't know what I was going to text back to your questions, did you? I'd like to believe I'm not that transparent."

I laugh. "No, you aren't that transparent." *I wish.* "I started yesterday."

"But you were in the office the whole time."

"Yeah, but I'm home at night. I put together the crib."

She looks at me like I just single-handedly cured cancer. *Oh yeah.*

"But I can't take all the credit. I hired a crew to do the painting and supervised them over the phone."

She blinks a few times. "I'm not sure what to say. I wasn't... I haven't even thought about a nursery yet."

"Well, you've been busy." She's adorable when she's flustered. "I figured it was something I could take care of."

"Thank you."

So far, so good. "Listen. I know what you said on Sunday, but I want you to consider that raising this baby on your own isn't going to be as easy as you think. I don't want to be the kind of father who ignores and abandons his children." Like Dad. He gave us money, but nothing else. If he could go back in time to ensure his vasectomy didn't fail, he absolutely would. Or at least contact the women quickly and ask them to get abortions. "Same thing with you being the mother. We're already compatible in a lot of ways. We both understand the demands our careers place on us. We're both smart, and we want to do the right thing for the baby. Marriages have been built on a lot less."

Thoughts fleet through her softening eyes. A small smile curves her lips. She's at least halfway convinced.

Then her eyebrows snap together into a V.

Damn it. What's the sticking point?

"I don't want you to take this the wrong way," she says.

Uh-oh... Women say this when they're about to give you some really bad news. "I don't want you to take this the wrong way, but your dick's small" or "but you smell funny" or "but you just aren't my type."

Nothing to do but feign cool nonchalance. "Okay."

"I overheard you and Grant talk about your dad's birthday party."

Fuck.

"And you said something about not taking anybody there." There's a hint of hurt in her gaze, vulnerability. "You also said, 'Too damn embarrassing.'"

Well, obviously. Dad's parties are *always* awful. Meeting him one on one is even worse. At least at parties, his attention's split. In more private gatherings, you get all of his insufferableness.

"You also told me you didn't want us to introduce each other to our families. I don't think you should make a commitment to somebody you feel that way about," she continues haltingly, her cheeks turning red. "Um. You should probably commit to someone you don't mind introducing to your family, you know? And frankly, I deserve a man who is proud of me. At the very least."

Shit. I had no idea this is how she took that off-the-cuff comment. I have to fix this *now*. Dad isn't worth the angst.

I press my lips firmly on her forehead, like a stamp with my name on it. "Amy, I thought you were awesome when you came to your first interview. And I haven't changed my mind since."

"Thanks, but you don't have to lie," she says, her frown deepening. "I heard what you said when you hired me."

40

AMY

Emmett looks puzzled. *But how could he have forgotten?*

"You said, 'I'm going to regret this,' before you offered me the job." My voice is sarcastic and resentful over the fact that he's making me relive an old humiliation. Maybe he says it to everyone he hires, which is why he can't remember.

Yup. A total bosshole move.

He stares. If he were a cartoon character, a bright light bulb would pop up over his head. "You thought I said that because I didn't really want to hire you?"

"Why else would you say it?"

"I wouldn't have hired you if I thought you couldn't hack it," he says in an I-can't-believe-I-have-to-explain-this voice.

"You hired Webber," I point out.

"No, *I* didn't. Someone else interviewed him. Anyway, forget Webber. The reason I said that is because I wasn't sure I could remain purely professional. You were too attractive."

Hmm... He could be lying. After all, we're sleeping together, and he probably doesn't want to piss me off with something he said a couple of years ago.

"Stop giving me that look. You know I don't think you're

some freeloader whose slack we have to pull. Your work speaks for itself. Along with your annual review."

Okay, *that* alleviates my doubts. "And all this time, I was working like mad to prove you wrong," I mutter.

"I don't know how you could've proven you weren't hot. I was annoyed as hell you were dating all those losers." He huffs.

I have to agree, I dated some really bad options.

He adds, "You deserve better."

"Like you?"

A corner of his mouth quirks upward. "Hey, if the shoe fits..."

I can't help smiling. "What if I find someone even better?"

"Better than *me*?" He looks genuinely confused. "Nah."

I have to laugh. This man is absolutely impossible.

"And just to make sure we're clear, I was *not* talking about you when I said, 'Too damn embarrassing.' It was something else my brothers brought up." He puts his hands on my shoulders. "I'm never embarrassed by being with you, Amy."

I search his face. See earnestness. Warmth unfurls in my heart. "Okay."

"If you really want, I'll take you to Dad's party. Just don't be too shocked, okay? His events can be...unorthodox."

I smile, hugely relieved and happy to have that cleared up. "If a party isn't the best way to meet your family, we can do it some other time. Maybe a small dinner or something?"

"There isn't any good time." He frowns. "He's...uh...busy, among other things. So let's just do the party. It'll probably be better that way."

"Okay."

"So are we all good? Nothing else you want to talk about? No other misunderstandings?"

"Nope." I wrap my arms around his neck and kiss him. He feels so, so good against me, all hard and lean strength. I missed him—being with him, tasting him, hearing his voice, smelling his intoxicating scent. I used to think pheromones were fake, some

BS created to sell perfume or explain why people do stupid things when it comes to the opposite sex.

But I'm not so sure anymore. The heat Emmett induces, the way he invades my mind and shatters my focus at odd intervals—it can't be explained any other way.

Still, none of that would be enough to convince me to think really long term. It's knowing that he cares—that he's excited about our baby, our future. The effort he put into creating this nursery, the way he's taking ownership of a shared life.

A man who was planning on a short-term fling wouldn't bother putting together a crib himself, much less hiring an entire painting crew and giving them detailed instructions. He could've simply painted the walls a standard off-white, put in a prefab crib, filled it with carelessly chosen toys and called it finished. If he even bothered to do that much.

I feel my body shifting and moving with his in a slow dance across the nursery and into the hall. Our mouths are fused, my fingers digging into his hair. The kiss grows carnal, his lips and tongue plundering me.

He pushes a door behind him open with the back of his heel. We circle into his bedroom, my head spinning lazily to match our tempo. Need flutters inside like sweet butterflies.

My world tilts as he lays me gently on the bed. The cool sheets feel fabulous against my heated skin. Cradling his face, I pull him down for more kisses. He obliges as he fumbles with the buttons on my blouse and spreads the clothes, then undoes the front clasp of my bra. He tugs at the zipper on the back of my skirt. I lift my hips to help, then relax when he pulls my skirt and underwear down in one long, sensuous glide.

Then he strips naked and makes my body sing. His mouth closing over the tip of my breast wrings out a soft sigh. Strong suction elicits a groan. His hands are everywhere, leaving trails that tingle. He is taking his time, adding one layer of hot liquid pleasure after another until I feel like I'm drowning in languid bliss.

I dig my fingers into his shoulders, slick with sweat. The rough sound of his breathing is the best aphrodisiac to my ear. His erection presses against me, and I squirm, wanting him to fill me, until we're joined, as close as we can be to each other.

When he reaches for a condom, I take his wrist. "You don't have to," I whisper. My heart flutters at the significance—the commitment and trust I'm placing in him. "I'm already pregnant. And I want to feel you—just you—inside me tonight."

His eyes darken with burning need. I spread my thighs in silent invitation, then rock my slick folds against his erection.

He groans, squeezing his eyes shut. "You're killing me."

The laugh tearing from my throat is low and seductive. I didn't know I could sound like that, but Emmett makes me feel like a goddess of sex and desire. "Shut up and deal."

He does, gliding all the way in with one smooth stroke. I gasp at the pleasure of having him inside. We've had sex many times before, but this feels different. More connected. More intimate. Our fingers thread, link. We hold on to each other as we move, both of us contributing to a hot, sweet rhythm until a climax shatters over us.

And when our breathing settles, I know I'm open to giving us a chance as a family.

41

AMY

Over the next week or two, Emmett sends more pictures and options for me to look at for the nursery, while I look for a present for his father. Emmett said just showing up would be enough, but it *is* his dad's birthday. I want to make a good first impression, and that means not arriving empty-handed.

So while working, I browse the Internet for options. Finally, I settle on a set of gorgeous onyx cuff links with Ted Lasker's initials—something he can wear when he has to dress up for an award ceremony or something.

Emmett told me it's a pool party, so I should either have a bathing suit on underneath my outfit or else avoid the pool area completely, because otherwise people will drag me into the water for fun. So I put on a pink bikini under a sundress, stuff a beach wrap and sunscreen in my waterproof tote bag and head over to Emmett's.

"If my dad talks to you, just nod and say as little as possible in return," Emmett says as he drives us to his father's place. "The more you talk to him, the worse it gets."

"How come?"

"You'll see. Dad can get a bit too...rowdy when he has a lot of alcohol in him, and there'll be tons of booze at the party."

Emmett must be worried about his father making a bad impression on me, especially since they're tight.

"Don't worry," I say with a smile. I'm not going to make a snap judgment based on a few drunk comments. We've all said things we wished we hadn't while under the influence.

"And ignore his friends, too. Or—if you have to interact —just smile."

"I can do that." I sigh as anxiety starts to rachet up. "I wish I'd watched more movies."

"Why?"

"So I could fit in better? Won't people at the party be talking about them? I mean, they're all movie people. I think I've only seen, like, two of your dad's films. I should've at least tried to watch them all."

"You'll need more than watching movies to blend in," he murmurs.

Probably, but I decide the party won't be as bad as Emmett makes it sound. My guess is he's trying to set my expectations low so I'll be pleasantly surprised. Besides, it's for somebody my father's age. Probably something fun, dignified and expensive. Maybe with a stripper in a cake or something similarly "risqué." I'm sure I can handle it.

Emmett pulls in to a gigantic mansion, a huge, shiny ivory structure that looks like a château with turrets and balustraded terraces. The windows are arched and spotless. The landscaping is immaculate, green and lush with precision-cut lawns and bushes. Bronze and marble statues dot the green. They don't seem contemporary because they are in the shapes of people who are recognizable. But they're all nude and in sexually suggestive poses, although the crotches are strategically hidden. I don't know much about art, but they're probably expensive, the kind of pieces that would be gracing museums if Ted Lasker hadn't bought them.

All sorts of fancy European cars line the driveway. Emmett squints at a couple of them. "Huxley and Griffin are here—two of my other brothers. I'll introduce you later. They're great."

"Awesome." I smile, happy to note Emmett and his brothers seem close.

We get out of his Lamborghini. Music throbs in the air, with high-pitched squeals cutting through the beat from time to time. The guests must be having a good time, which is perfect. Meeting his family is going to go smoothly.

Emmett and I make our way to the main entrance. A slim orange-haired man in a teal shirt and jeans stands guard. He's of average height and slightly below average attractiveness, but his mossy-green eyes are alert and his short, stubby fingers are fast over his tablet.

"Emmett, so good of you to come." Without giving him a chance to respond, the man turns to me. "And who is this young woman?"

"My date," Emmett says.

I wave and give the man a pat smile.

The man looks me over, taking in my sundress and hair and makeup. "I didn't know you were bringing one. Is she going to make Ted—"

"You're not my mother, Joey." Emmett's tone says, *Shut up.*

"And thank God for that. You couldn't pay me enough." Joey smiles thinly and turns to me. "I'm Joey Martin, Ted Lasker's assistant."

"Amy Sand. Nice to meet you." I extend a hand, which goes ignored because Joey is too busy tapping his tablet screen.

Emmett sighs. "So rude."

I agree, and smile a blatantly fake smile.

Joey looks up, then blinks at my hand. "*Sor*-ry. Just busy." He shakes my hand perfunctorily. "The party's that way. And presents go over there, if you brought anything." He points to a huge pile right behind him.

I place mine on the pile as Emmett shakes his head. "You didn't have to get something."

"Bribes *do* work," Joey says.

"It's a gift," I say.

Joey waves us away. Since I don't want to deal with him any more than I have to, I link my arm with Emmett's and move toward the party.

The inside of the home is cool, with lots of black and white tiles that make the floor look like a chessboard. Suits of armor and alabaster horse heads sit in the corners like chess pieces. There are murals on the ceiling, but I can't make out exactly what they are because the ceiling is too high, and the light from the windows up there make everything appear hazy. All I know for sure is there are lots of flesh tones.

Emmett takes me upstairs to a huge bedroom. "This is my room. We can change here," he says.

While he starts taking off his shirt, I look around for any hint of what his childhood was like. But the room is sterile. A bed, a landscape painting that looks like an original, an empty closet. The room doesn't even smell like him. It's nothing like mine in Vegas, which still has posters of hot actors and bands from my teen years taped to the walls, the pink sheets I loved when I was growing up, my old clothes in the closet and the trophies I won sparkling next to stacks of worn paperbacks of my favorite YA romance novels.

"Did your dad redo the room after you moved out?" I ask, disappointed.

"No. I never really lived here." There's a strange sense of relief in his tone. "It's 'my room' as in, Dad told me I could use it when I visit."

Well... That's an odd arrangement when Emmett has his own place in the city, but then, maybe it's for those rare occasions he can drag himself away from the office and spend time bonding with his dad. The house in Switzerland where Emmett grew up probably has a room that could shed more light on Emmett's past. I wish I could see it one day, assuming his parents kept the place.

Emmett has stripped down to black trunks, and I'm in my bikini, which I will put with an almost-sheer wrap.

"Do you need some sunscreen?" I ask, smearing some on my arms, legs and belly.

"Sure." He helps himself to the bottle, then rubs it all over my back, lingering and massaging.

I sigh, loving the way he finds small ways to pamper me. "You're so good at this."

"Applying sunscreen isn't really *that* difficult."

"You know what I mean." I turn around when he's covered every inch of my back. "Let me return the favor."

I squirt a dollop of sunscreen and spread it all over the lean expanse of his back. The repetitive motion is soothing and helps me calm my mind before meeting his dad.

"Okay, so we're going to go out to the pool now."

"Okay." I laugh. "Is that some kind of warning?"

"Just try not to be shocked, no matter what you see," Emmett says.

"It's just a birthday party by a pool, not an orgy. Why are you being so serious?" It's like he's a Catholic priest about to perform last rites.

He opens his mouth, then shrugs. "Okay. Hopefully it won't be that bad."

I pat his shoulder. "I'm sure it'll be fine."

Emmett and I go downstairs and walk through the house to reach the pool that's on the other side. Apparently, the place is built in a U around the pool for maximum privacy.

Arches and more arches. Ted Lasker's residence is almost like a castle, just slicker and more contemporary. Finally we reach the pool.

Holy mother of God...

42

AMY

Balloons in deep red, purple, silver and gold float everywhere. Every single one is shaped like an open mouth with a tongue hanging out, a penis or a vagina—although maybe those last ones are supposed to be orchids. A gentle breeze stirs the balloons, and the X-rated decorations bob cheerily as music vibrates in the air, the bass booming.

Ted Lasker must film porn on the side. Or maybe his party planner didn't get the memo that it was a *birthday* party.

Emmett has a small smile on his face, like he's enjoying the scene. Maybe this is how his dad likes to celebrate his birthday. I mean…it's Hollywood, right?

I try to hide my discomfort. Everyone else is laughing and cheering, and who am I to ruin the fun, especially when I asked to have Emmett introduce me to his family? Besides, the attendees are adults. Emmett's dad wouldn't have thrown a party like this if there were little kids present.

At least it's not an actual orgy. Ms. Positivity, that's me.

As Emmett and I enter the area, there is a pair of what look to be large, salmon-colored exercise balls in front of us. Emmett smacks one of them hard. Cheers erupt from the crowd several yards away.

White liquid shoots out from a huge, curved shaft attached to the double balls, and I realize that it's an erect penis. He isn't the first to have smacked it, either. There are wet spots everywhere. The apparatus in front of us isn't the only giant dick present. There are nine more, set to the left and right of the entrance, like a line of porno arches. Some people have the red balloons that I saw earlier—the ones that look like mouths or vaginas—wrapped around their torso. They're covered with the white goo.

"Do it again, Emmett!" a blonde in a barely-there thong calls out. She doesn't have a top on, but she has a vagina balloon. The white liquid is in her hair and on her left shoulder. Ew.

Emmett shrugs. "Already did it. Don't blink or you'll miss the action."

"Oh come on!" a redhead whines. At least she isn't topless. She has a mouth balloon.

"Em-mett! Em-mett!" The blonde starts a chant, waving her fist.

Others join in. I can do nothing but watch. Shock wrecks what thoughts or emotions I might be capable of.

Emmett laughs. "If you insist." He smacks the other ball, and white liquid arcs in the sky again.

"Yeah!" The crowd whoops with laughter.

The blonde shuffles left and right as partygoers scream instructions at her. The milky thing splats, hits some, misses some. But the blonde manages to position the vagina so that some goo lands on it.

"Score one for Team V!" a guy calls out.

More whooping. Somebody showers the people with champagne.

"Your turn," Emmett says to me.

The question jolts me out of my stupor. "What? Are you high?"

"Everyone has to hit it when they enter the pool area for the first time."

I look at the balls and the eagerly waiting mouths and vaginas dubiously. "I don't think I can hit that hard."

"Don't have to. There are sensors inside." He gestures at the curved shaft above us.

I can't believe I'm about to do this. "Okay..." I make a fist and hit the ball.

Another squirt of white from the tip of the shaft. "Score one for Team M!" More cheering and hollering.

"Great shot!" a middle-aged man says, while taking me in from head to toe. I don't care for the lasciviousness in his gaze, which is glazed with too much alcohol or drugs or something. "I'm Sean." He says his name like I should recognize it. He's probably somebody famous in movie business. Wonder if he's going to be ego-bruised if I tell him I have no clue who he is.

"Amy," I say politely. Just because I'm surrounded by porno stuff and dealing with an obnoxious drunk doesn't mean I have to lose my manners.

"My girl," Emmett adds as he wraps an arm around my waist, giving the guy a back-off-creep look.

The man raises his hands. The gesture is innocent, but his eyes are anything but. "Hey, no problem. Just being friendly."

"There are other women to be friendly with," Emmett says.

I don't try to soothe the tension between them since I'm not too crazy about being *friendly* with the man.

I turn my attention to the party. Emmett and I are still standing in front of the entrance. To get to the main section, we'll have to walk through the, um, dick arch colonnade. A bunch of people are congregated around the balls to shoot the fake cum, while the people with the vagina and mouth balloons are trying to catch it. I don't want to have that crud all over me before I've even had a chance to say hello to Emmett's family.

The breeze blows in our direction, carrying the scent of the mess on the floor. I wrinkle my nose. I thought the giant dicks

272

were shooting syrup, but the smell is weird. It's almost like...*real* ejaculate.

As Sean stalks off to impress people with his name, I tug at Emmett, slightly worried about our next move. "We're not walking through that, are we?"

"We don't have to," Emmett says.

I sigh with relief. Emmett leads me through a narrow side path I didn't see when we came out of the house.

"Did the party planner rob a sperm bank?" I ask.

"What?"

"That..." I gesture at the mess under the arch. "That *stuff*. The smell."

"Oh." He shakes his head, wrinkling his nose. "It's some kind of starch solution mixed with chestnut pollen. Chestnut flowers have a very distinctive scent."

"Well! Learn something new every day."

"Yeah. Dad's a guy who can teach you many things."

Emmett looks at me, and I give him a smile like I'm perfectly fine. This party is probably sedate by Hollywood standards. Besides, the arch setup might not have been Emmett's dad's idea. One of the guests—some wild, coke-snorting director or producer —could've brought it in for "fun" and Emmett's dad didn't want to upset them by turning it down. I shouldn't make assumptions.

The path takes us to the other side of the pool. A buffet is laid out with lobster, shrimp, steak and more, with everything cut into bite-size pieces and skewered on bamboo picks. Seven fountains are set up. From the way they smell, they're all laced with strong alcohol.

"Want something to drink?" Emmett asks.

"Yeah, sure. Water would be great."

"There won't be any water out here. Let me see if I can go find some." He looks around. "You, ah, going to be okay on your own?"

I don't want to make a big deal about how bothered I am by the party setup. His dad is a Hollywood guy, and this sort of public display is probably something I'll just have to tolerate. He'll probably turn out to be a nice man with lots of positive attributes once I get to know him better. "I'll be fine."

Emmett talks to somebody manning the drink station, then walks away.

Trying to act cool, like attending this kind of Hollywood bash is something I do every weekend, I stand by the table and study the people. About half of them are dancing, gyrating against each other. The other half are standing around with drinks in their hands and chatting. I look for Emmett's dad—I know what he looks like from publicity pictures—but can't spot him. He's probably surrounded by friends and colleagues. I should wait for Emmett to make an introduction to avoid any awkward misunderstandings, in case his dad assumes I'm a wannabe actress or something.

"Hey, want to try the lemonade?" a bleached blonde says. Her dark roots show a little as she flips her hair.

"Where is it?" Holding a drink would give me something to do with my hands.

"Right there." She gestures at one of the fountains. "Sarah makes the best lemonade. Want a sip of mine?" She moves her clear plastic cup closer to me.

The waft of alcohol is so strong that I can't smell any lemon. "No, thanks."

"You sure? Bummer." She frowns, then brightens. "You can try the cherry-ade, then."

I'd bet my degree that that's heavily laced with alcohol as well. "I'm okay. Really."

"Okay. So who are you? I haven't seen you around," she says.

"This is my first time at Ted's birthday party."

She looks at me, up and down, but not unkindly. More like confused—maybe trying to pin me down. "I don't remember seeing you elsewhere, either. Are you new? You haven't done anything, have you?"

I've gotten an MBA, worked for a major investment bank and

am working at a venture capital firm, but my gut says that isn't what she's referring to. "Probably not."

She pats my arm. "Everyone has to wait for their moment."

"That's true."

"Hey, Mellie, why aren't you giving our new guest something to drink?" a brunette says, coming over with a whole bottle of champagne. "This isn't some cheap shit. Ted doesn't do cheap. It's *Dom*." She raises the bottle she's holding. "You'll love it."

"I'm good," I say.

"What's your preference?" the brunette says, her free hand on her hip. "I can't imagine anybody who doesn't like Dom, but hey, first time for everything, am I right?"

"Nothing. I'm waiting for my water." *Where is Emmett?*

Mellie and the brunette gasp in unison. "Nobody drinks *water* at a Ted Lasker's party! You might as well insult the man."

"I'm not—"

"Honey, if you want to be a star, you have to *act* like one," Mellie says. "Stars don't drink water when they can down some Dom."

The brunette nods.

"Unless you're pregnant," comes a high voice from down around my waist.

I look down and see a boy who can't be more than five or six. He's in *Finding Nemo* swim trunks, his platinum hair slicked back. Black sunglasses cover his eyes, and he's smiling like he's done something clever.

Shock tugs at me from two different directions. First, that he correctly guessed why I'm not drinking. And second, that there's a *child* at a party with a penis gallery. Did he hit one of the balls, too?

I look in the direction of the entrance. You can see those giant dicks—and the genitalia balloons—clearly from everywhere.

"Are you lost?" I say to the kid.

"No. I'm here with my mom."

What kind of mother brings a child to... But maybe she didn't know. "Where is she?"

"Good question."

"Maybe you should call somebody?" I suggest.

"Why?"

"Because... You know. This isn't really the kind of place a child should be."

Mellie and the brunette titter. "You are hi-*lar*-ious. Are you trying to break out as a comic?"

"No." *Just how drunk are they?*

Emmett finally reappears from the pool house nearby. "Amy, here's your water. Took forever to find it in the fridges." He hands me a cold bottle of Evian.

"Hi, Emmett," the boy says.

"Hey, George." Emmett puts an arm around me.

Maybe he's going to take George to some wholesome area where other kids are hanging around. But Emmett doesn't do anything. Actually, he's acting like it isn't particularly shocking to see George at a party like this.

"Hi, Emmett," the girls say, waving.

"Ladies." Emmett inclines his head with a smile.

"So. Is she your girlfriend?" Mellie asks.

"Yes. Amy, meet Mellie and Sunshine."

I give a little wave. "Hi."

"By the way, I think she's pregnant," Sunshine says. "She's not drinking anything. I even offered her some Dom." She lifts the bottle.

"Are you getting hitched?" Mellie says, her eyes wide. "I want an invite."

"Um..." Okay, I should've met his family at a smaller gathering. Like a private dinner.

"I'm trying to convince her," Emmett says with a wink. "Now, if you'll excuse us, we're going to see if we can find my parents."

"Oh, I saw your mom over there." Sunshine gestures toward the other side of the pool where people are gathered with drinks.

Emmett thanks her and links his fingers through mine. I look back at George, who's hanging back by the buffet.

"Shouldn't we do something about the kid?" I ask.

"No. His mom will flip out and make a scene if anybody tries to intervene. She calls it meddling, and it's best for George if we leave him alone."

That poor child! "Is she an actress?"

Emmett shakes his head. "She works with actors to help with their speech—mainly accents. Some other stuff, too, but she prefers to work on movie sets. More prestige and glamour."

"Isn't there a space for kids? Away from all the, you know...dicks?"

A corner of Emmett's mouth quirks upward. "A space for kids? Not really on the priority list here. But George is used to it. He gets really uncomfortable when you try to move him elsewhere. He likes to think he's a mature individual."

"Did your dad *know* about the kid coming?" I can't imagine his father being okay with this. If this were my dad's party—although I can't imagine him throwing anything like this—he'd make sure there was something age-appropriate for children.

Emmett's eyebrows dip in disapproval. Is he upset I'm asking too many questions about George? I just met him, but I can't seem to shrug him off like others. What about *our* baby? I don't want our child to be subjected to dick arches and genitalia balloons and so on when he visits his grandfather. The other option is to get together someplace neutral, but that doesn't seem right, either. They're going to feel left out if they aren't invited to celebrate their granddad's birthdays and so on.

Finally, Emmett sighs. "Yes. But he doesn't stop George's mom from bringing him."

Before I can ask another question, a tall, lithe brunette in an ivory bikini and translucent azure beach kimono comes over. She's stunning, her facial features delicate and carefully sculpted, the long, dark hair framing her heart-shaped face perfectly. Her skin is smooth, her body firm and lean enough to grace a magazine cover, but there's a maturity about her that says she isn't one of those young, desperate-to-break-into-movie-business women. Something about her feels familiar, although I don't remember seeing her in any movies, TV shows or magazines—not that I have a ton of time to look at those.

Emmett's face splits into a brilliant smile. "Mom!"

That's his *mother?* I blink and look again. Only then do I realize she's the same person I saw in some of the photos at Emmett's home. She looks even younger in person. Shocking, since most use camera filters to take years off their age.

"Baby! I missed you so much." Wrapping her slim arms around him, she kisses him on both cheeks.

"You look good," he says with a laugh.

"Thanks to you. The cruise was amazing."

"Mom, meet Amy Sand, my girlfriend. Amy, this is my mother."

"Ma'am," I say, extending my hand.

Instead of taking my hand, she pulls me in for air kisses. "Oh, please. Call me Emma. 'Ma'am' makes me sound so old."

"Of course. Emma." I smile, somewhat relieved she seems warm and friendly. And normal.

She gives me a quick once-over. Nothing overt or rude, but more like innocent curiosity over her son's date.

"I can't believe Emmett hasn't said anything, not that we get to speak much," she says. "How did you meet?"

"We work together," Emmett says.

Emma raises her eyebrows as she regards me. "Oh! Then you must be smart."

"Well, I don't know about that," I say. "But thank you."

"The things Emmett talks about make *zero* sense to me." She notices the water in my hand. "Emmett, dear, why don't you get your date something better to drink? Ted's gone all out for this party. He's determined to outdo everyone, including himself."

"I'm fine," I say. Emmett and I should probably announce the baby at some other time, without so many genital balloons and topless women around. Just wholesome pink and blue balloons, everyone fully clothed. Plus, family only.

"Are you sure?"

"I've already witnessed a lot of the going-all-outness."

The impeccably shaped eyebrows arch again. "Oh, the decorations? You get used to them. They'll probably be even more outrageous next year."

If she's trying to make me feel better, it's not working. Emmett squeezes my hand, but that doesn't help much either.

"Ted has certain things he enjoys. As long as we laugh and go along with him, he's happy," she adds. "So have you met Emmett's brothers? Other than Grant?"

"Not yet."

She nods, then waves at a couple of men some distance away. They begin to walk over.

The men have Emmett's dark hair and square jaw. Plus they're tall. But they also look remarkably different—from the shapes of their noses to mouths and the way they project themselves.

Emma turns to deal with a waiter who's brought her another drink and some young woman who seems overeager to talk to her, so Emmett does the introductions when the men get to us.

"Amy. This is Huxley. He's in advertising." Emmett indicates a man who has to be marketing spices he hates from the vaguely annoyed look on his face.

But he smiles as he shakes my hand. "Hi." The smile makes him seem friendlier.

"And Noah. He's a wildlife photographer."

"I also write fiction," Noah adds with a wink—a light flirt and laid-back, nothing like Huxley.

"One book that's been in progress ever since any of us can remember," Huxley adds dryly, like not having finished a book is the greatest sin.

"I'd love to read it when you're done," I say.

"Oh, for sure," Noah says. "It'll have all the good stuff. Nobel-worthy."

Emmett sighs with affection and exasperation, while Huxley looks skyward.

"Where are the others?" Emmett asks.

"Seb said he'd be late. Griff's late, too. No idea why. Maybe debating if he should bring poison."

Poison?

Huxley leans in. "Rat poison."

There cannot possibly be rats in this mansion. But Emmett, Huxley and Noah all seem unfazed.

"Nicholas has some kind of stomach bug, but he'll be here soon," Noah says. "Didn't get sick enough to be hospitalized."

He almost sounds mournful, which is weird. Why would he want Nicholas to be hospitalized?

I make a mental note to talk to Emmett and see what the deal is with his brothers. Maybe there's bad blood between some of them? If so, I want to know about it.

"So how did you two meet?" Huxley asks me. "I had no idea Emmett was dating."

"Well—" My answer is cut short when a man slaps Emmett's shoulder hard enough to make him take a step forward for balance.

I turn and see Ted Lasker, in the flesh. The man's bigger than I imagined—he's as tall as Emmett, his bare chest solid, a pair of wet black trunks sticking to his hips, his legs thick. Fine lines have etched some aged roughness onto his face, and there's silver at his temples. His appearance gives a clue as to how Emmett will look when he gets older, but the eyes are different. They're hard and calculating.

"Well, well, well! Heard you got your girl pregnant!" Ted announces loudly. He gives Emmett another clap on the back.

Crap! How did he find out? And this is really, totally *not* how I envisioned everyone learning about my pregnancy!

Emmett's expression says it isn't his preferred method, either. Huxley and Noah's eyes widen as they stare at Ted, then at Emmett and me. Emma cuts her conversation with the party attendee and comes closer.

"You are?" Huxley and Noah finally say in unison, although I'm not sure if they're talking to me or Emmett, because their eyes are on him.

Emmett unclenches his teeth and turns to his dad. "Look—"

"If you'd told me, I would've put a water fountain in at the buffet." Ted speaks so loudly it's like he can't hear anybody else. His eyes gleam with satisfaction. "I *knew* you'd come through when I said I wanted a grandbaby! You never let me down!" He turns to me. "So. You're the baby carrier."

Baby carrier? That makes me sound like some kind of fertility machine!

"Just wait until I show Josh Singer my grandbaby. He's going to be pissed!" He laughs triumphantly and claps his hands. I can't believe that's the first thing going through his mind. My baby isn't some *thing* he can use to piss people off!

He turns to Emmett while hooking a thumb at me. "This girl's smart, right? I don't want a dumb grandbaby. At least not one dumber than Josh Singer's."

"Uh, you can ask me directly if you're curious about my IQ," I say.

Ted Lasker finally turns to me. "I'd never do that. If your IQ was low, how would you know? Emmett, maybe you should take this one back and get a new one."

It takes me a second to process what he's saying through the haze of outrage.

Emmett wraps his arm around his dad's shoulders. "Why don't we go inside and talk this over like rational people?"

"I suppose. But I want a cigar! Where's Joey?"

43

EMMETT

God damn it!

I get Dad away from Amy as quickly as possible without appearing like I'm angry or embarrassed. He isn't drunk enough not to notice, and he'd whine, complain and make everyone's life miserable over the perceived slight.

And I don't need any more humiliation in front of Amy. I still want to kick my own ass for agreeing with my brothers to give Dad the cock canon last year. It was our collective way of calling him a dick, but of course Dad's too self-centered and vain to understand the unspoken message. He thought it was a testament to his virility. Which explains why he decided to make more and use them for a game at this year's party.

"Can you text Joey?" Dad says.

"No. We need to talk first."

"With cigars."

"Thanks, but I'm not really in the mood."

"Why not? Is the baby carrier difficult about things like that? It's just a cigar."

"Can you stop calling her 'the baby carrier'? Her name is Amy. She and I work together, and I like her."

Dad looks at me like I'm an undercover Martian. "So?"

"I plan to marry her," I say, frustrated and pushed to my limit.

"Now hold on, Emmett." He puts a hand over his heart. "You don't have to *marry* her. I wouldn't ask you for that kind of a sacrifice."

"Didn't you hear what I said about me liking her?"

"Is she richer than you? Maybe well connected in some way that could help your business? That's the only reason to marry somebody."

I actually feel sorry for all the women who dated Dad. He's awful, too self-centered. He wouldn't know what a true emotion was if it came and kicked him in the balls. God must've been in an ironic mood when He gave Dad the ability to stir deep feelings through movies.

"I don't want to marry her for money or connections," I say quietly.

He looks truly confused. "So you're doing it for the baby?"

"The baby needs its mother and father, who love and care about its wellbeing."

"That still doesn't mean you have to *marry* her." He gestures in the general direction where we left Amy with Mom and my brothers. "You don't have to do any of that to make sure your kid doesn't starve on the streets!"

This must be some fucked-up way that he's trying to actually be a good dad. The sole fatherly intervention he's decided to force upon me.

He's right—I don't have to marry Amy. She already offered joint custody. But I don't want the possibility of her marrying somebody else, having that other guy be the father figure my kid sees every day.

Actually, forget the baby. The idea that knots my gut is simply Amy with somebody else. It's been going on ever since she joined GrantEm Capital. That's why I made her work late so often, especially on the days and weekends she had plans.

"Look, I'll get you a good lawyer. I'll even pay for it. You can take the calf without the cow, no problem," Dad says.

"As magnanimous as that offer is, no. You aren't going to do that. As a matter of fact, you aren't going to go anywhere near Amy or me or our baby."

"What?" He stares at me like I just called his latest movie boring.

"We're done, Dad. If you can't respect me—or my girl—I don't want you around."

44

AMY

I stay rooted to the spot while Emmett and Ted Lasker walk away. Huxley and Noah continue to stare, and Emma looks at me with pity. My face burns, embarrassment churning in my gut.

I slowly go over what Emmett's dad said and did. He doesn't want to know me—*at all*. The only thing he's interested in is the fact that I'm pregnant with Emmett's baby.

No, it's more than that. He said *he knew Emmett would come through*. When did he ask Emmett to make a grandbaby? Is that why Emmett didn't use the condom that time?

But that doesn't make sense, because he used them every other time. Then again, they could have been expired or compromised in some way.

I squeeze my eyes shut for a moment. My head is throbbing painfully, and I need a moment to gather my thoughts. *I can't do it here.* Not while Emmett's family is watching. Not while this crowd is hollering and cheering and yelling.

I want to go home, shower, get under the covers, hug Okumasama and lick my emotional wounds while I figure out what the hell has really happened between me and Emmett.

Since Emmett drove me here, I need to call an Uber. I start to pull out my phone, but Emma is quicker.

"Do you want to stay and wait for my son or do you prefer to jet out?" Her tone is gentle—no judgment, just sympathy.

It's easy to respond honestly. "I'd like to go home."

"Let me give you a ride, then."

"You should stay. Won't Ted want you around?"

"Oh, I already said hello. He won't care if I leave." She shrugs.

I want to turn her down and take an Uber driven by a stranger who has no idea what the heck just happened here.

"Ubers aren't allowed to come to the main door. You'll have to make a long walk through the garden to the main gate," Emma says, clearly reading my reluctance.

I don't want to make that walk, just get the hell out of here before Emmett and his dad come back. I don't have the emotional energy for that sort of encounter right now. If Emma wants to chat during the ride...

Well, I can just deflect or say something vague, although I have a feeling she's too perceptive and compassionate to probe very hard. "Okay. Thank you."

She nods and takes me back into the house. I put the sundress back on, and she just ties the sash around her kimono more tightly before we go to her Escalade and head out.

The sound system plays soothing strains of classical music. It doesn't do much for my current state of mind.

"I'm sorry you were forced to endure Ted's party," Emma says. "It's no easy feat, even if you aren't pregnant."

"I thought it would be a good chance to meet his family." Her sympathy makes it easier for me to open up, despite my earlier resolve. I place a hand over my belly, which is churning ominously—like a warning to stay away from the madness I just witnessed.

"Who told you that?"

"Emmett. I suggested a more private setting, but he thought the party would be better."

Emma frowns, then sighs. "You probably won't believe this, but he's right. It isn't easy to be at the receiving end of Ted's nearly undivided attention. He can be very charming when he wants, but generally he's...difficult."

"Do you think it's true? About what he said about telling Emmett he wants a grandbaby?"

Please, God, let this be a simple misunderstanding. I don't want this baby to be something Emmett wants just to make his dad happy. What if Ted decides he doesn't care for the baby after all? Will Emmett lose interest, too? The notion sends a shudder through me. I want our future to be based on something more than Ted's wish list.

"Probably. Isabella—Grant's mother—said Ted asked for a grandbaby for his birthday this year. Of course, he asked so late there's no way a baby could be born in time." Emma rolls her eyes.

"Like how late?" The question is more than painful—it gnaws at me. But I have to know in case the timing doesn't make sense. I want proof that Emmett didn't say or do all those sweet things just to make his dad happy.

"He asked a few weeks ago."

The answer knocks the breath out of me. The timing works out with our affair. But I cling to the fact that I'm the one who proposed the no-sex fling to Emmett after our massage at the spa.

"But his sons could just ignore him, right?" I ask, shaky but hopeful. They seem successful and wealthy. Do they really need Ted Lasker's money or approval?

"Probably, but he apparently contacted some of the mothers to put pressure on the boys. Isabella was a bit distraught."

Emma doesn't seem distraught. Actually, more like the opposite: totally Zen. Maybe Emmett already told her he was on it. He gets along with his dad, which probably means he wants to give him

287

the grandbaby the old man desires. And I understand the impulse—I've always wanted to give my dad grandchildren, too. He loves kids, and beyond that, I want to show him he did an awesome job raising me to be a well-adjusted, happy woman without Mom around.

"I don't suppose Emmett told you all this," Emma says gently.

"No." And I'm furious he didn't, leaving me to be ambushed like this.

She sighs a little, the sound full of pity. She doesn't mean to make me feel awful, obviously, but that doesn't lessen my humiliation. A lot of what Emmett did makes no sense to me. He didn't want to announce the pregnancy to his family—maybe he only wanted to let his father know for some weird reason—and he didn't want to meet my dad—which is understandable if he isn't serious about us. But the nursery? The way he made sure to have it reflect what I want more than what he wants?

Maybe he's just really inconsistent—hot and cold, hot and cold. Don't forget how he drove you crazy ever since you joined the firm. You aren't the only one who thinks he's brilliant but impossible, and personality doesn't compartmentalize. Assholes are assholes in all aspects of their lives.

"How much does his dad want a grandbaby?" I want to confirm how far Emmett would go for his dad.

"At the moment? It's his sole desire in life." Emma chooses her words with care. "Ted is rich, powerful and isn't used to being made to wait. And if you didn't notice, he's not exactly shy about what he wants. We all know he wants one."

I don't know exactly who she means by "we," but I can guess it includes Mellie and Sunshine, because they were there when I turned down the alcohol and then little George announced I was pregnant. They must have told Ted, which is why he dropped by the way he did.

He also said he wants a *smart* child, so it makes sense Emmett would settle on me. I might not be a financial genius like him, but I do have two degrees from Ivy League schools.

Maybe he didn't want me around his family for a reason. I don't fit in with the crowd, and I don't—

Wait...

I blink, swallowing a gasp as a sudden realization strikes me. Ted's party was eerily like Mom's parties, if hers had the luster and slickness money can provide. Worse, actually, because *a child was there* and people seemed okay with it. Would Emmett's family insist on having my baby there? It might be normal for a Hollywood infant to grow up watching something like that, but it isn't normal in *my* world. I want my baby to keep its innocence as long as possible.

Clearly, I was premature in offering joint custody or considering Emmett's marriage proposal seriously. The best course of action now is taking my baby as far away from that environment as possible, before Emmett realizes he can't have fun at parties like that with a kid around. I'm not putting myself or my baby through the heartache of being tossed aside like a piece of old Styrofoam.

Emma stops the car in front of my apartment building.

"Sorry the party turned out to be such a disappointment," she says softly.

"Don't be. It was enlightening." I force a smile. "Thanks for the ride."

I hop out of the car, not looking back. Once I'm back in my apartment, I shower, then draft an email to Emmett.

45

EMMETT

The pool area is a heaving mass of humanity, and I can't spot Amy in the milling, drunken crowd. They're still playing the ridiculous spooge game, and their loud cheers and yells grate on my nerves. If I were in charge, I'd end the party *now* and throw everyone out.

I text her, but she doesn't answer. *Probably can't hear the notification in this noise.*

Okay, I need to get her out of this mess. I run into Huxley, who's chatting with a redhead who is clinging to him like a silicone-enhanced octopus. "Have you seen Amy anywhere?"

He frowns, doing his best to pull away from the woman. "She's around here somewhere. I saw her with your mom not too long ago."

That brings my anxiety down a notch. Mom has undoubtedly explained to her that all the idiocy at this party is Dad's idea. She's good at smoothing ruffled feathers.

I pull out my phone and text Mom.

–Me: Is Amy with you?

There's no immediate response. Either she can't hear the notification or she's too busy talking to Amy. I hope it's the latter.

Mom has a calm style of communication, which is exactly what Amy needs at the moment.

Trying to settle my anger and nerves, I finish a beer. My phone vibrates in my hand.

–Mom: I just dropped her off at her place.

Shit. *She left without telling me?* Then again, it might be for the best that Amy is away from this clusterfuck.

–Me: Did you talk to her?

–Mom: A little.

–Me: How did she take it?

–Mom: Hard to tell. She didn't say much.

I shove my fingers into my hair and clench it. The prickling pain helps me gather my thoughts.

Amy is probably stewing. She's smart as hell and has good instincts, but beyond that, she's careful. She likes to take time to make plans that are most likely to lead to success and then stick to them. Most importantly, she doesn't like taking risks in her personal life.

Engaging in a "sex-only fling" with me was probably a huge gamble for her. I don't want anything to happen that will make her regret that choice.

I start toward my car. I'm done with this damned party. Dad can prance around and have fun, but I'm going to Amy's place to make sure she's okay.

Just as I climb inside my Lamborghini, another text arrives. I check the phone immediately, hoping it's Amy. But nope.

–Mom: I think she needs some time to herself to process what happened. I don't suppose you warned her?

–Me: No.

–Mom: You should have.

–Me: Yeah. But I didn't know how to talk about Dad with her.

Regret, annoyance and self-recrimination wage a battle in my mind. He's one topic I avoid discussing with people. My brothers don't count because they already know what kind of human being he is. But I don't talk about him to my dates, to reporters, to anybody lured by the glamour of the movie business who is curious enough to ask. When I have to make conversation about him, I keep it superficial and vague, hiding all the dirty laundry. It's just too humiliating to talk about his behavior.

My gut says I should go see Amy right now. But Mom's text is holding me back. Perhaps giving Amy a day to think about what happened might be a good idea. And I can use the time to come up with a good in-person apology.

–Me: Amy, I heard Mom gave you a ride home. I'm sorry about the party, and I'll talk with you on Monday.

I grimace as I stare at the text. "Sorry" seems so anemic. But I can't think of anything better, so I hit send and pray I can find a way to make it up to her.

46

EMMETT

On Monday, I arrive at the office earlier than usual. I want to get some stuff out of the way before Amy shows up, so I can smooth things out with her. But I'm feeling optimistic. After turning things over in my head for several hours, I know exactly how to approach the situation.

The floor is empty except for a few folks who stayed and pulled all-nighters through the weekend. While my laptop boots, I grab myself a coffee and stop at Amy's desk on my way back. It's neatly arranged, with a calendar and a few manila folders with papers inside. Although the firm's going paperless, a lot of associates, including Amy, still like to go over some items holding something in their hands.

Still not here. I run a finger along the top of her calendar, then go park myself at my desk with the door open so I can see when she comes in.

But until she does, it's time to work. I double-click on Outlook, and the server vomits hundreds of emails into my inbox. I shake my head as I skim the subjects—almost seventy percent are either irrelevant or FYI only. People need to quit looping me in when I don't need to be involved. I'm not reading their emails just because they land in my inbox.

But then there's an email from Amy.

The subject says *Notice*. Nothing to indicate which portfolio company it's about, which is generally how Amy labels all her emails. My heart thuds, pumping something acrid through me. I gulp down half the coffee. She must've been really pissed off about what happened yesterday to write an email and send it to me at one fifty-six a.m. She's never sent me a personal email before. Knowing her, I can imagine her drafting multiple versions before settling on this one.

Come on. You know you deserve it. Man up, read it and make your apology even better.

Girding my loins, I click it open.

From: Amy Sand
To: Emmett Lasker
Subject: Notice
Sent: Today 1:56 a.m.

Dear Emmett,

Please accept this letter as formal notification that I am resigning from my position as Associate with GrantEm Capital. My last day will be two weeks from now.

Thank you so much for the opportunity to work in this position and grow in the past two years. I've greatly enjoyed being a part of bringing GrantEm's revolutionary services and offerings to life.

I'll be wrapping up all my duties and transferring them to another associate for transition.

I wish GrantEm Capital all future success.

Sincerely,

Amy Sand

Huh?

Formal notification? Last day? Transition?

Resigning?

This is one of the most generic resignation letters I've ever read. Hell, she didn't even add the usual "Love to stay in touch."

I finish the remaining coffee in my mug and read the notice again, in case I was hallucinating. But nope. Amy is still quitting the firm. And by quitting the firm, she's also quitting *me*.

Fuck! She isn't going to give me a chance to explain?

The hair on the back of my neck bristles, and I look up to see Amy walking out of the elevator. I jump to my feet and signal her.

"In my office." Despite my best attempt to appear calm and collected, my voice sounds brittle.

"Sure."

Her eyes stay cool, her mouth unsmiling, as she places her purse and laptop bag on her desk and comes over. She shuts the door and takes a seat, crossing her legs.

"I understand that you're mad, but don't you think it's a bit dramatic to quit your job?" I say, not caring about preliminaries. The two-week notice changed everything.

"No. I've given it a lot of thought."

"It hasn't even been twenty-four hours." She thought about it for a few days before deciding to have a fling with me. She should at least devote that much time to her resignation!

"They've been quality hours," she says thinly.

"How are you going to take care of the baby without a job? And pay for all those doctor's visits?" I cast about for more expenses. "Your student loans. You know you can't get rid of those."

"Thanks, but you don't have to worry about any of that. I've already accepted another offer."

"Another..." When did she interview for another job? Before or after she decided to start dating me? "Where?"

"At the Blaire Group."

"You gotta be shitting me!"

"Nope. So you don't have to worry about my financial situation. They offered the most benefits and money." She says the words like she's reading cooking instructions.

The skin under my eye starts twitching. "Let me guess. It was Marion Blaire who offered, right? In person?"

She nods. "He seems like a reasonable guy."

"When did he approach you?"

"A few weeks ago."

It's a vague answer, but it means she had this fucking offer at least by the time we went to La Jolla...

"Jesus, I've been a dumbass," I mutter.

Her impassive façade cracks. "What?"

"You acted like you didn't really know Marion at the restaurant in La Jolla. But you'd already had your interview with him."

Guilt flickers in her gaze.

Her betrayal sucker-punches me, and I clench my teeth. "He probably decided to offer for sure after that incident, if he hadn't already."

"It wasn't like that."

Too late for explanation. If she didn't feel comfortable in La Jolla, she could've mentioned the offer later when I brought up the Blaire Group snapping up Webber.

"If you wanted to stay with me—were serious about joint custody or even getting married—you would've told me about Marion's offer. Hell, even if there was no baby, you should've tried to leverage it to get more money out of GrantEm." The fact that she stayed quiet means she was plotting to dump the firm—and me—and jet off to Virginia as soon as she hit the two-year mark with GrantEm so she wouldn't have to pay back her signing bonus. I'd wager my Lamborghini the last day specified in her notice is her seven hundred and thirtieth day at the firm.

She looks away briefly.

Confirmation!

It guts me. And the fact that I'm hurting makes me hate myself. Why did I let anybody have this much power over me? "You know what? Forget the two weeks. No need to come in. Pack your stuff and get out now. I don't let traitors work at the firm."

She stares at me like she's the injured party. Somehow that makes me want to go hold her, which is bullshit. She's the one who brought this on herself and me.

"Emmett—"

"My lawyer will be in touch about the baby," I spit out through the bitter lump lodged in my throat. I don't want to hear what she has to say. She's forcing me to turn into my father—a father who won't be married to his baby's mother or do any of the things a father should do except provide money.

She clicks her mouth shut. Exhaling a barely audible sigh, she turns around and walks out, closing the door firmly, leaving me behind.

47

AMY

"Hey, girl, were you out sick?" Sasha calls out as she walks in at ten p.m. Since she's been busy for weeks, coming home later than me or not at all, Grant must've told her to leave early and catch up on some sleep, like he did before.

"No," I say from the kitchen. The microwave dings, and I pull a mug of hot chocolate out. "You want some?"

She looks me up and down, taking in my T-shirt and shorts. "What happened?"

"That." I gesture at the box I left on the table. It's open, my stuff from the office clearly visible inside.

She stares at it, her jaw going slack, then swings back to face me. "Did Emmett *fire* you?"

"No. It's complicated." I want to cry, but also don't want to. My life is already a mess; no need to make my face match.

"Let's sit down, and you tell me everything."

Sasha wraps her arm around me and leads me to the couch. I follow, holding on to the hot chocolate. I've already gone through a box of caramel truffles, but I need more comfort.

"What happened?" she asks once we're seated. "I thought things were okay between the two of you."

"We were okay, and then we weren't."

I sip the hot chocolate to give myself time to gather my thoughts. Right now, all my emotions—including ones I didn't know I was capable of—are having a no-holds-barred battle royale.

"I turned in my resignation," I say. "And he didn't take it well."

Sasha blinks, then her gaze flickers to my belly. "I thought you weren't going to quit because of the baby. Didn't you and Emmett decide to raise it together?"

"Yeah, but...not anymore." I sniffle.

"That *asshole!*"

I shake my head. "It was my decision." *And the right one, too.*

She looks stunned. "How come?"

"It's *really* complicated..." I sigh, hating the way Emmett made me feel this morning—like I backstabbed him. "Please don't share this with anybody because it's private, and I don't know if Emmett or Grant wants this to be public."

She makes an of-course-not gesture.

I tell her about the birthday party. The awkwardness and discomfort plaguing me. Seeing a child there. His father's buoyant reaction to my pregnancy. And the realization that having fun at a party like that is something my irresponsible I-only-care-about-me mother would love.

"Given how well Emmett seemed to fit in, I can't help but wonder if there are aspects of him that I don't know about. Ones that would make him a terrible partner and father to my baby." My voice cracks.

"Oh, honey." Sasha squeezes my hand. "That's awful. Did he try to explain what happened?"

"No. I turned in my resignation, and he basically told me to pack my stuff and get out."

The callous order sucker-punched me. Even though I know I did what's best for my baby, I thought he'd try to explain himself. But he reacted like *I'm* the one who ruined our relationship.

"He didn't take it well that I'm going to work for the Blaire Group." I already texted Marion to let him know I was taking the offer. I had a final interview with another firm, but didn't want to wait. And given my situation, I absolutely *cannot* be without insurance.

"How come? He couldn't expect you to not work somewhere."

"He considers it a betrayal." But somehow he doesn't seem to think it was a betrayal for him to not tell me about his dad's burning desire for a grandbaby and let me be ambushed at the party in front of his brothers. "He and Marion Blaire have this stupid competition thing going. Apparently Marion has a way of trying to take whatever Emmett has. He took Webber."

"So? Is he implying that you only got a job at the Blaire Group because of Marion Blaire's weird hang-up with him?" Her voice bristles with annoyance.

"I don't know. Maybe." I haven't been able to think too clearly about Emmett's reaction since I left the office.

"I don't give a shit how betrayed he felt. It's still no reason for him to treat you like that, not even giving you a chance to send a goodbye email to anybody. Even worthless Webber got to send one."

"Only goes to show I made the right call." I sip my hot chocolate, wishing it were something stronger.

"You did. There's no reason for you to stay with a man with an ego problem. It isn't like he has a monopoly on you or your ambition."

"No. No, he doesn't."

But he made me dream for a moment that maybe I could have it all—the career, the baby and a supportive life partner—only to yank it away. That won't be so easy to forgive.

48

EMMETT

Grant doesn't nag at me. None of my brothers give me crap for bailing at the dreaded birthday party, which is unusual. Must be this damned Monday being so dreadful for everyone.

Or maybe they can sense I need to be left alone.

I wish I could get to the break room for coffee without going past Amy's empty desk. Every time I walk by it, I feel like a fist is slamming into my gut, and another wave of anger and betrayal washes over me.

Still, I manage to get some work done. Our startups depend on me doing my job.

Nine o'clock comes, and I leave so I don't have to see Amy's desk anymore. But as I walk into my home, I realize I haven't gotten away from her at all. The kitchen counter reminds me of the breakfast we shared. My mind's eye sees how sweet and sexy Amy looked coming down the stairs...

The doorbell rings. My heart jumps to my throat. It could be Amy, here to tell me she messed up—*I'm sorry, can you take me back?*

But the image on the security panel immediately shatters my fantasy. It's actually my brothers gathered there. *Shit*. It's clear now why they haven't bugged me with texts about ditching the party. They plan to bug me in person!

I really don't want to talk to them. What I need is a stiff drink and some sleep. Preferably in a guest bedroom, since I don't want to sleep in the bed Amy slept in. At least not until the sheet are changed.

"Open up!" Grant yells. "We know you're in there!"

"Don't make us kick the door in," Noah says, sounding entirely too happy about the possibility. He likes to think he's a tough guy.

I sigh, go to the door and yank it open. "What are you doing here? Don't you have things to do, money to make?"

They look at each other.

"I made enough for the day," Huxley says.

Noah shrugs. "I never do nine to five."

Sebastian says, "Never work this late at the office. You know that."

"We're worried about you. You left us with Dad and never called or texted." Nicholas gestures at the bags they're holding. "We brought food and alcohol."

They aren't going to leave. Not until we talk. To be honest, if the situation were reversed, I'd be worried, too.

Still, I can't stop a sigh from forcing its way out. "Fine. Come on in."

My brothers walk right in, like they knew all along they'd win.

They take over the dining table and spread out food from Manny's Tacos. Sebastian brings plates and forks from the kitchen, and Griffin passes napkins around. Huxley hands out beers.

And soon, a late dinner is ready.

Since I'm not saying anything first, I start eating. A beef and guac burrito I would normally love tastes like sawdust. I wash it down with the beer, which is bland and flavorless.

"So you got Amy Sand pregnant," Grant says.

302

My eyes on him, I shovel more sawdust—I mean *burrito*—into my mouth. Should've known this "dinner" is about Amy.

"Is it true you fired her?" Nicholas asks.

"Of course not! *She* quit."

"What did you do?" Huxley asks. "Or was it Dad?"

"No idea. Seriously. I didn't do anything, and I pulled him away from her, so I don't think it was anything he did, either. Maybe it was the shock of the party." I shake my head. "But she didn't *talk* to me. Just gave me a generic two-week notice."

"At least it was civilized," Noah says. "My last girlfriend threw the nearest thing she could find at me. Thankfully, it was just cold water."

"You're doing a shitty job of trying to make me feel better." I wish Amy had thrown her desk stapler at me. At least that would mean she felt something for me.

"What are you going to do about the baby?" Sebastian asks.

"I don't know yet." I told her my lawyers would be in touch, but that was in the heat of the moment. I want to do more than just pay for school tuition and living expenses. I want to be there for the kid. Have shared moments, create memories.

"It's your kid." When I say nothing, Grant gives me a look. "Right?"

"Of course it's my kid!" Amy might betray me and plot to go work for Marion Blaire behind my back, but she wouldn't lie about something this big. That just isn't her.

"Look, anybody would be shocked into temporary insanity after attending one of Dad's parties for the first time," Huxley says. "Give her some time to regain her sanity. She'll come back."

I snort. "I wish. She's moving to Virginia."

"Isn't that overdramatic?" Sebastian says.

"She *is* pregnant," Grant says.

There's a general murmur of understanding around the table.

Noah rolls his eyes. "It isn't like she's moving to another galaxy. It's just a domestic flight, no big deal."

"She's going to be working for *Marion Blaire*," I say.

My brothers all wince. Grant in particular looks extra pained. He hates Marion almost as much as I do.

"Extremely poor judgment," Grant says, shaking his head.

"So are you just going to let that dickhead take her?" Sebastian asks. "Shouldn't you go kick his ass and drag her back to L.A.?"

"And then what? Take away her cell phone and keep her in a cage? If she doesn't want to stay, she won't. She's too smart and resourceful to remain in a situation she hates." And I want her to *choose* to stay with me, not be forced into it because of money or the baby or anything else. I've always wanted her to choose me.

Perhaps that's the reason I'm so bitter right now. She chose somebody else over me, when I'd choose her over anyone. It burns my gut to know she doesn't feel even half of what I feel for her. If she did, she wouldn't have left.

49

EMMETT

"You work entirely too much," Mom says when I join her for lunch on Tuesday at her favorite French bistro. A soothing melody from "Claire de lune" floats in the air, all elegant and ethereal. Just the kind of relaxed scene she likes.

"I do not," I say, then kiss her cheek before taking my seat. Mom looks great with the light tan she's recently acquired. Her cream-colored dress accentuates the golden undertones.

"It is a sign you're overworking when you can't find the time to have dinner with your mother before she takes off for Japan."

She's doing another trip to Japan, mainly because she misses Kyoto. She says it's too charming a city to not visit regularly. None of the bustle and slickness of Tokyo. Just calm tranquility with a long history and culture.

"I'm here, aren't I?"

The waiter arrives, and I order a martini and the special. Mom decides to have lemon water and the fish of the day.

"Isn't it a bit early for a martini? It *is* a workday," she says.

"I deserve it." What happened with Amy is still driving me crazy. My emotions are too jagged. Raw. I need something to soothe the pain, and a single martini at lunch isn't going to kill me.

"At least your girlfriend isn't here to watch you enjoy a drink. Pregnancy is when you need alcohol the most."

I don't want to talk about Amy or pregnancy, but despite myself, I'm curious. "How come?"

"Oh, hormones and stress. Your body's going through so many changes, and all you're feeling is anxiety and doubt."

"I thought women were happy and excited when they're pregnant."

Yeah, but Amy is on her own right now. Probably not that happy.

I push the unwelcome thought away. It was her choice, not mine.

"That, too, but things are hard." Mom sips her lemon water. "Babies represent a huge responsibility. Once they're born, there's no going back. You have to love them and nurture them for the rest of your life."

No refunds. No do-overs. Once the baby's out in the world, that's it. Stuck. Except I didn't feel stuck when Amy told me she was pregnant. Our baby feels like a blessing—like a winning lottery ticket.

I study Mom. She looks serene. But I wonder...

The waiter brings our lunch, interrupting our conversation. After he places our plates in front of us and disappears, I pick up my utensils.

"Did you ever regret being pregnant with me?" I ask.

Mom gives me a what-is-this-about look.

"You can tell me honestly," I add. "I'm too old to get scarred at this point."

She cuts her artichoke. "Of course not. Never. But I regret that you didn't have a better father."

"Eh. Who cares about that asshole?" I hate that she feels bad about the situation when Dad doesn't. "I had you. You've always been the best mom anyone could ask for."

"Well, thank you. But I couldn't give you what a good father could. So I'm glad you and Amy are going to be involved together in raising your baby. I'm certain you'll both make great parents."

Guilt. "Actually, she and I had a fight. We aren't, uh, together anymore."

"*What?*" Mom puts down her fork and knife. "Emmett Alexander Lasker!"

I wince. Full-grown adult or not, Mom still has the power to send shivers of apprehension through me by calling me by my full name.

"I am *shocked!*"

"It couldn't be helped," I say defensively. "She backstabbed me. Instead of talking to me after the party, she submitted a letter of resignation. What was I supposed to do?"

"Talk to her? Nothing was stopping you, wasn't it?"

"It isn't that simple. She didn't just quit. She's going over to the enemy."

Mom gives me a withering look. "North Korea?"

"Worse. *Marion Blaire.*" Mom knows that creep's weird obsession with "beating" me.

"All the more the reason for you to talk to her, Emmett! She doesn't know the situation between you and Marion. She was hurt and traumatized at the party. You didn't tell her about your father's ridiculous demand for a grandbaby, did you?"

A beat.

"No," I say, my voice a tad lower. "But only because I didn't think it was relevant."

"Of course it's relevant! Ted is going to be her child's grandfather."

"He'll be interested for, like, two seconds and then move on. I'll be shocked if he remembers the kid's name."

Mom shakes her head. Her expression screams, *Where did I go wrong with you?* "I know you're embarrassed about your dad and his behavior. And I understand exactly where you're coming from. But that doesn't mean you get to hide him or pretend he can't affect you anymore. He can and does. If he really meant nothing, you wouldn't be so resistant to talking to her."

Why is she trying to make me the villain here? And not just any villain, but a dumb villain. "I already told you why I didn't talk to her."

"For God's sake, Emmett. Marion Blaire is nothing to you. He annoys you the way a fruit fly annoys you. It's just an excuse not to confront the fact that you don't want to discuss your father with her, so you've decided to shut your mouth about it, even if it means losing her and the baby."

"But—"

She raises a finger. "Would you have behaved any different if she didn't quit and only wanted to discuss your dad and what happened at the party with you?"

"Well...yeah. I mean, I wouldn't have told her to pack her stuff and get out," I say, refusing to admit she's right. I don't give Dad that much power over me.

"Oh my lord. You're so smart in some ways, but blind in others. If she'd only wanted to talk, you would've found a way to gloss over everything. You always do when it comes to the topic of your father. You'd say how everything was fine and offer to talk to your father if it'd make her feel better. But every time you do reach out to him, both of you end up talking past each other rather than talking to each other. And so the exact same issue she had at the party and with your father would surface again and again." She pauses. "Just like it does for you."

I stare at Mom. She's speaking quietly, but each word hits like a bullet.

"For some reason, you won't cut your father out of your life, even though you know he's toxic. I've heard you threaten to do it, but you don't follow through. And he knows that. I suspect it's because you want to pretend he doesn't affect you and you're perfectly fine around him."

She reaches across the table and holds my hand.

"I know you want to be a good parent to the baby you've

made with Amy. But being a good parent sometimes means making hard choices, including blocking out people who don't add anything to your life. Amy's reaction at the party isn't unusual. What's abnormal is acting like your dad's behavior is perfectly fine. I'm glad she's sensible enough to see the rot underneath his glitzy, moneyed veneer. Not everyone does." She sighs softly. "I know the topic of your dad is hard. So I'm not going to say you have to talk to her about it. But if you love her and want to keep her, you need to. Now leave that martini alone and eat your food."

Back in the office after lunch, concentrating on work proves to be impossible. Mom's words keep circling in my head.

Is she right? Did I let my pride get in the way of smoothing things out with Amy?

Until I learned she resigned, I did plan on talking to her. But I wasn't *really* going to discuss my dad. Just say that he likes to throw wild parties and tell her sorry if she felt uncomfortable. And I was planning on apologizing for Dad's behavior over finding out that she's pregnant—saying that he's been whining about wanting a grandchild for a while and just got carried away in his excitement.

But I wasn't planning on getting to the root of the problem.

Fuck. Mom *is* right. Everything I planned was merely glossing over the real issue, and Amy deserves better than some bullshit rationalization. If I'd told her the truth about Dad from the beginning, maybe she wouldn't have left or taken the job with Marion.

I look out the open door. Amy's desk is there—its tan surface, clear of her things, somehow reminds me of a desert.

There's a hole in my heart that's growing bigger and more painful. I miss her. Her smiles—fake, professional, genuine, all of them. Her scent—the fresh body wash over the sweet, feminine aroma underneath. Her mouth—which can say the funniest things or kiss me until my whole body is burning.

No other woman ever touched me the way she has. No other

woman made me long to hold her in my arms the way she did. When I think of Amy, I see a concrete vision of our future—us growing old together, holding hands and smiling as we gaze into each other's eyes.

You're in love with her, you moron.

And you drove her away out of pride.

50

AMY

Once Marion receives my text about taking the offer, he moves quickly to have me fly out to Virginia to actually see the office and meet some of the people I'll be working with.

The Wednesday flight is tediously long—five hours—but the airline bumps me up to first class. Although I'm not a particularly superstitious type, the upgrade feels like the universe saying, "Virginia is where you belong."

Of course, it could also be Satan pulling me into the pits of hellfire. The devil probably doesn't trick you into going to hell by making the trip difficult and unpleasant.

Be positive. It's a new chapter in life.

True. Right. No need to be so morose about it already.

I spend the night in a Hyatt. It feels strange to have my phone stay quiet. It used to buzz constantly with notifications from Emmett regarding work or the nursery or things for our baby.

Did he get rid of the nursery? Maybe throw away the crib and blankets? I hope he donated them. Just because we aren't going to use them, doesn't mean somebody won't.

Thinking about that gorgeous room sends a pang through me,

but I shake it off. I can't be with somebody just because of a pretty nursery.

Right now, I need to figure out how I'm going to raise this baby on my own. Emmett's offer to hire an army of people to help raise the baby so I can still pursue my career isn't likely to be on the table anymore.

So, let's see... The Blaire Group's salary is much higher than GrantEm's. Arlington isn't a cheap city, but it isn't as expensive as L.A. If I'm careful, I can probably still pay off my loans, save money to buy Dad his retirement home in Florida and have money left over to hire a nanny to watch over the baby while I work. I should run some numbers, create an expense spreadsheet to double-check my thinking.

The next morning, Dad texts me. I respond without telling him about my life imploding in L.A. I hate to keep things from him, but I just don't know how to tell him everything. I eat some dry cereal in the hotel lounge and go straight to the office. En route, I text Marion to let him know I'm on my way.

The Blaire Group is headquartered in a tall blue building that sparkles like a column of sapphire. The lobby is huge, with a pine tree in the center. The golden plaque underneath it states it's a tree that the founder of the group planted in hopes that the firm would grow strong and stay true to its mission.

People in business casual scan IDs to get through turnstiles. The sight of a paper copy of the *Washington Post* on the security desk hits me hard—*I'm really in Virginia. I'm leaving L.A.*—and all that entails, including Emmett and Sasha—behind.

"Amy!"

I turn around and see Marion smiling and waving as he walks past the turnstiles.

"Hope you haven't been waiting long," he says, all friendly.

"No. I just got here."

"Aces. Let's get you up to the office."

He helps me get a visitor's pass, and we take the elevator to the twentieth floor. The Blaire Group office is already a beehive of activity. The space is minimalistic and contemporary, with lots of chrome and glass.

"We don't have cubicles or an open-space design," Marion explains. "For group work, we have the atrium and conference rooms, but otherwise, you get your own office. That way it's easier to focus on your own work without people interrupting you."

He pauses like he's waiting for praise, so I smile as though being confined to one walled-off space is the most thrilling thing ever. "Super!"

"Right?" He grins.

A few people passing by say hello to Marion and give me a curious look. When he introduces me as a new colleague from L.A., something flickers over their faces. What's with the odd reaction?

But the tour continues in this fashion, with everyone behaving the same way. If I didn't know better, I might think the office sent out an internal memo yesterday telling everyone to act weird to prank the new hire. But private equity people are too busy for that sort of stuff.

The worst part is that Marion seems oblivious. An uneasy feeling starts in my gut, but it's too late to change my mind about the job. I already declined all the other interviews I had lined up, and I have to have medical for all my prenatal stuff—not to mention when the baby finally comes.

Marion finally shows me into HR, which is tucked in the back. We walk into the director's office.

"Hi, I'm Heather. Nice to meet you."

"Hi, Heather. I'm Amy."

"Welcome to the Blaire Group. We're so happy to have you here." The words roll from her mouth smoothly and perfunctorily, like she's rehearsed them hundreds of times. "Marion's incredibly excited." Her gaze flicks to Marion with a hint of derision, then back to me.

He laughs, apparently missing the disdain in her eyes. And she specifically said, "Marion's incredibly excited," as though she herself couldn't care less. I note she hasn't offered me or Marion a seat, making us stand when she has three empty chairs on the other side of her desk.

His phone pings. "Excuse me. I need to take this call." Marion walks off, leaving me with Heather.

"Do you have any questions?" she asks with a polite smile that says she's busy.

"Actually, I do. Could I have a copy of your maternity leave policy? It was missing in the packet I received with my offer."

Her eyebrow arches. "Are you starting family soon?"

"Well. I want to be prepared."

"It's on the intranet. We're paperless for things like that. But I wouldn't worry too much about taking a few weeks off."

"You're very flexible," I say, surprised.

"Well. It isn't hard to be flexible in certain cases."

There it is again. Sarcasm and judgment.

Enough is enough. I don't have time for bullshit or intraoffice drama. "If this is supposed to be a prank, it honestly isn't funny."

Genuine confusion pushes out the sarcasm and judgment. "What do you mean?"

"You and a bunch of people in the office have been acting strange around me," I say. "I find it off-putting."

She frowns. "Nobody ever asked about it before."

I cross my arms. "Maybe they were more tolerant of unjustified censure. I'm not."

"It's just..." She sighs, betraying her discomfiture. "Well. *Marion's* excited."

"You told me that already."

"*We* aren't."

Who is this "we," and what the hell is this about? My colleagues and I have never had any strong feelings about hiring decisions at GrantEm, unless the new hire turns to be a mistake. But none of the people here had a chance to work with me or get to know me, so that can't be it.

"How come?" I ask.

She sighs softly, then speaks matter-of-factly. "Because when you're busy and you know your new colleague isn't going to pull her weight, it's bound to be irritating. And usually, I'm the one who has to step in and mediate the conflict that arises from such situations."

"What a— That's ridiculous! None of you know me well enough to decide that."

She shrugs. "We know Marion hired you."

"Just because he might've made a few hiring mistakes before—"

"From GrantEm Capital," she says. "Look. You only need to stay here long enough to put in the time to keep your signing and relocation bonuses. I'm sure you can pull that off. Now, I need to get back to my real work. If you tell Marion any of this, I'll deny it, so don't even think about it." She gives me a level look before turning to her laptop.

I'm speechless as I process what she just said. It matches what Emmett told me about Marion before. It dawns on me—painfully—that Marion might've hired me not because he was actually impressed with me, but because he wants to have something that used to belong to Emmett. I never considered the possibility because I know I'm one of the best.

The awful realization that almost everyone at the Blaire Group views me as an unworthy hire stabs into me. I wince, my pride in tatters. If I come here, I'm never going to get a chance to shine. People will exclude me, ensure I'm not involved in projects and initiatives that will help me grow. Sure, I could still come anyway and prove myself so everyone is sorry they were mean to me. That'd make a great movie script, but this is real life. I nearly killed myself trying to show Emmett when I started at GrantEm. I don't want to have to do the same here, especially not with a baby on the way.

Maybe if your coworkers don't expect anything of you, you might not have to put in the hours, which means more time for your baby.

Yeah, but that also equates no chances to advance, no pay increases or bonuses. And if there's a layoff, I'll be first on the chopping block. Then what will happen to me and my baby?

Marion comes back, putting away his phone, and takes me to lunch. The whole time he goes on about how happy he is and what a great career decision I've made.

But all I can think is: *Have I?*

My doubts linger the entire time I'm in Virginia and on my flight back home to L.A.

This time, the airline doesn't upgrade me.

51

AMY

"How did the office visit go?" Sasha asks early next morning. She didn't come home until I went to sleep, so we didn't get to catch up yesterday after I landed.

"A complete disaster." I prop my chin in my hand, my elbow resting on the kitchen counter. I heave a long, hard sigh.

She checks her phone to make sure the battery's full, pulls it off the charger and tucks it into her purse. "How come? Is your new boss a werewolf with chunks of meat stuck between his teeth?"

I laugh. "I wish."

"That bad?" She makes a face, then checks her watch. "I have five minutes if you need to vent."

I shove my fingers into my hair. "It's just... I feel like such a fool! He doesn't really want me."

"Sure he does. He made the offer for you. He even reached out to you a few times. He has to want *you*." She makes a finger gun and points it at me.

"I mean he doesn't care who he hires. He didn't hire me because I'm brilliant."

"Did his mom drop him on his head when he was born?"

"No. He apparently hires anyone who's ever worked at GrantEm. Specifically, anybody who's ever worked for Emmett."

Sasha purses her lips. "That isn't a terrible hiring criterion. GrantEm has great people."

"Yeah, because GrantEm retains all the good ones. But what about the others, the ones that can't cut it? Sasha, Marion hired *Webber*."

"Okay, well... Yeah, that's indiscriminate."

"Right? So everyone at the Blaire Group figures I'm like Webber. Maybe worse." My pride is still trying to recover.

"Holy shit."

"Yeah." The basic problem is that I'm in L.A. and the Blaire Group is in Virginia. What good reputation I have among my peers at GrantEm hasn't percolated across the entire country. I'm not a big fish like Emmett or the other partners.

"I'm so sorry. What are your options, then? Can you get another job?"

"I don't know. I have, like, seven days until my last official day at GrantEm." Emmett might've *unofficially* fired me, but I'm still getting paid and my medical is still valid. "I put out some feelers, but I don't want to go without medical if I can help it."

"That makes sense." She looks at my belly briefly. "You know what? Let me also ping some people and see what's out there."

"Thanks, girl." I appreciate her effort, although I'm not sure if it's going to be fruitful. It won't be easy to get another job in seven days.

"Hey, what are friends for? I'm always on Team Amy."

She hugs me hard, then takes off so she won't be late for work.

I watch the door close. It feels so weird to be home alone on a Friday. I even got up early because my brain refused to sleep past five a.m. on a weekday.

My phone buzzes with a notification. I look at the screen.

–Dad: Hey, sweetie! Happy Friday!

He attached a selfie—hale and hearty with a huge smile and

crinkling eyes. It makes me smile in return. He is truly the center of my universe, my rock.

I inhale deeply. It's time to come clean about the baby and everything, but telling him through texts seems a little cold. It's the kind of conversation that requires a call. I'll try to be calm and steady, and come across like I'm in control. Then he won't worry.

–Me: Is it okay if we talk?

–Dad: Of course!

Good old Dad. He picks up instantly when I call.

"Hey, sweetie pie!" he says.

"Dad..." I bite my lip, shocked at how shaky I sound. I thought I could talk about this without getting emotional.

"What's wrong?" He's serious now, with an overt I'm-gonna-kick-the-ass-of-whoever-made-you-cry tone.

"I'm pregnant," I blurt out, then cover my eyes. I didn't mean to announce it like this. He's going to be so disappointed.

"Uh... Did you... The guy didn't force you or anything, did he? I just want to be sure, since...you're so upset."

"No!" *That's where his mind went?* "We both wanted to do it." That part was for sure, although I don't know about the rest.

"Okay. Well, uh, good. I guess." There's a pause. "And the baby...?"

"I want to keep it."

"Okay." His tone says, *I respect your decision.*

"I'm sorry." My voice is brittle and small.

"For what, sweetie?"

"I feel like I've disappointed you."

"Amy, no. Never. You've never disappointed me. I've always been proud of you."

I sniffle.

"Honey, I'm already in love with your baby. And I'll always be in your corner, no matter what."

"Thank you, Dad," I manage through the hot lump in my throat. This is how my father *always* is. And I want my baby to have it, too.

"So. Is your new job going to be less demanding, Give you some time to take care of the baby? Or do you want me there?"

His immediate offer to help out chokes me up, and I fan my hot face. I don't have to be a fortune-teller to know the Blaire Group isn't going to be flexible about my situation. Most firms aren't, contrary to what their fancy HR-generated brochures claim. But somehow I can't tell him that, not because I want to lie about it, but because I don't see a future for myself at the Blaire Group yet.

"I don't know," I say.

"The new place didn't tell you?"

"They kind of did, but...it's in Virginia. And it's private equity. The people there work a lot. And honestly, I don't know if I belong there." As I say that, it dawns on me that I had that sense of belonging at GrantEm. Sure, I was upset over what Emmett said when he hired me, but the people at the firm respected me. They knew I was the best associate—

"Sure you do!" Dad says. "Who told you that you don't belong? You went to Harvard! Got an MBA at Wharton! You're the smartest person I know!"

I smile through the hot unshed tears. "Thanks, Dad. But it's complicated."

Then I proceed to unload everything Heather told me.

"I just feel so torn," I add. "Going there is the smart, safe thing to do."

"But you don't want to go," he says, cutting through all my messy emotions.

"I don't know if I want to be surrounded by people who won't like me just because of where I worked before or who my new boss is."

"Then don't go."

"But I can't be without a job. Especially now."

"Amy, sometimes in life you have to take risks."

"Risks? I have a baby on the way."

"Your child won't want to see you get beat down by jerks who already made up their mind about you." He sighs. "Honey, I know you. You're careful—you always make sure what you're about to do isn't going to have a negative impact on your life, even if it doesn't turn out so well. I've never seen anybody plan out an exit strategy as well as you do, and that's something coming from a Marine.

"I'm going to tell you something, okay? I've always wanted to tell you, but never got to because you seem to have your life so well in order. But this seems to be the time.

"You can't have the perfect exit strategy for everything. There's no contingency plan that can eliminate *all* the risks. You can only do your best. And it sounds like if you go to this place in Virginia, you won't be doing your best. You'll be settling. You'll be going into a situation where people won't give you a fair chance and will treat you badly. You know you deserve better, and this would be a major step backward in that career you worked so hard for. That's why you told me you couldn't be without a job, without any of the excitement you had when you had an offer from your current place or that bank before you started your MBA." He pauses for a moment. "You *can* be without a job for a few weeks until you find something that puts fire in your blood. I already told you I'm in your corner, sweetie. If money's what's holding you back, I can help out."

"*Dad!* I can't take your money!"

"Of course you can. I'm your father. Taking care of you, no matter how old or how independent you think you are, is what I'm supposed to do—what I *love* to do. I love you, Amy, and don't forget it. You're not alone in this."

Tears streak my face. I wipe them with my fingers, then try to breathe evenly so he doesn't know I'm crying.

"Follow your heart, sweetie. Do what feels right. Don't spend all your life worrying about risks and contingencies. Most of the time, the worst things you think can happen don't."

"But didn't it? When you had to quit being a marine to raise me and Mom split? Wasn't it the worst thing ever?" I say, still feeling guilty about the sacrifice he made.

"Are you kidding? I have my health, I have my brain and good sense—and I have the most beautiful girl in the world in my care. What's so awful about that? Could things have been better? Yeah, sure. But it wasn't even close to the worst thing ever, Amy. You're a blessing. You deserve everything good in life, and I wish you'd have a bit more faith in the world and yourself that things will work out for the best. The world isn't as dangerous or terrible as you think."

As I take his words in, all the weight and pressure I've been carrying start to float away. I feel like I can finally breathe freely.

I sniffle. "Thank you, Dad. I love you so much."

"I love you too. Don't do anything I wouldn't do, and do all the things I would do, but better."

I laugh a little. "Thanks."

We hang up. I blow my nose and have a glass of water. Then I take my phone and type up an email for Marion.

To: Marion Blaire
From: Amy Sand
Subject: About the offer

Dear Marion,

After careful consideration, I've decided it will be best if I look for opportunities elsewhere. Thank you for taking the time to interview and meet with me. I hope we can stay in touch.

Sincerely,

Amy Sand

I stare at the email for a second, making sure it sounds okay. Then I go back and delete "I hope we can touch in touch." If I didn't put that phrase in my GrantEm resignation, I'm not putting it on my letter to Marion.

My heart does a massive tumble, and my belly twists and churns like laundry in a spin cycle. I clench and unclench my shaking fingers and hit send.

The email vanishes, and my heart starts beating normally again.

I made the right decision.

Then I think about what Dad said. About my fear of something bad happening, and my need for an exit plan. Compared to my coworkers, I *can* be overly careful. I make plans and I stick to them.

That's why I didn't act on my attraction to Emmett. I dated *safe* guys—who all ended up not working out. I only went for Emmett when I thought it didn't matter how our affair ended because I wasn't going to be around for long.

You were planning to fail, which is why the relationship between you and Emmett failed.

I close my eyes briefly. I don't know if I was actually *planning* to fail, but my mind was focused on the relationship failing. Even as Emmett romanced me and took me on that amazing dive and cared for me when I was sick, I was thinking about the end.

So when the horrible party happened... I just...assumed he would be like Mom and never told him why I was upset. Never gave him a chance to explain his side. But what could've been the worst outcome of talking to him? Nothing that bad. I would've learned that he really was a jerk or there was a big misunderstanding that needed to be cleared up.

I've been *really* emotional since finding out about my pregnancy. I presumed my life was becoming messy because I didn't stick to the plan and made the impulsive decision to sleep with him.

But that decision brought me some amazing memories with Emmett. And this baby, who is unexpected but whom I couldn't love more. I constantly think about the precious little life inside me—worrying about whether I can be a good mother. I want to give this new human all the love and support I was blessed enough to receive growing up.

Okay, so I've totally screwed up. But maybe it isn't too late to talk to Emmett. To be really open about my fears and hopes and dreams.

Like Dad said—what's the worst that can happen? Emmett refusing to listen? That wouldn't be any worse than my current situation.

I have nothing to lose.

Bolstered with renewed optimism and bravery, I text Sasha for some tips on how to approach an ex-boyfriend after a fight. She has far more experience dating than me.

Her answer comes after a few minutes. And the advice nearly makes me fall off the kitchen counter stool.

–Me: Are you sure that's a good idea?

–Sasha: Trust me. I've never NOT gotten a guy's attention with this tactic. Plus, it's going to be extremely convenient when you make up and need to celebrate.

–Me: I don't know. It didn't work on him before.

–Sasha: Wait! You tried it already?

–Me: Not ME. You know how I am.

–Sasha: Yeah, you need more sass and confidence. Anyway, the other girl must've done it all wrong. You have to have the right attitude to pull it off, which I expect you to have.

–Me: If you say so.

I'm doubtful, since I'm going there to apologize and talk, not impress him with my *attitude*.

–Sasha: Look, if you're that skeptical, let's make a bet. $500.

–Me: Okay. I could really use the money.

–Sasha: Haha, very funny! Now if you'll excuse me, I need to work and think about what I'm going to do with the five Benjis you're gonna hand over. Hehehe.

52

AMY

To say that I'm skeptical would be a very large understatement, but I follow Sasha's advice. She's right about it catching a man's attention, of course. But this is Emmett—who is no ordinary man.

Sasha says that *the right attitude* is *owning the entire space.* Keep my shoulders back, chest out and spine straight. Strut like I'm the queen of the world.

I can do most of that. But strutting like the queen of the world is going to take a lot of faking. I guess all there is to do is try my best.

I debate between the office and his home. He's always at the office, but then, so are other people. I don't want to wait until everyone's gone except him. Logistically speaking...

Actually, never mind. I don't have a GrantEm employee badge anymore.

His place is the only option. We'll have all the privacy we need. And if our discussion doesn't go the way I hope, at least I won't have to walk past other people and pretend I'm okay.

So at nine in the evening, I drive to Emmett's place. He doesn't usually leave this early, but there's always the possibility. Best to be prepared.

Surprisingly enough, my passcode still works to open the gates. So I pull my car up to the driveway in front of the main entrance. The lights, triggered by sensors along the way, start glowing at my approach. His car isn't anywhere in sight, and none of the windows in his home are lit.

I cut the engine and wait in silence, mentally going over what I'm going to say. But eventually, that isn't enough to keep me engaged.

I take out my phone. No wonder people do social media. It's gotta be awful to be in your own head all the time when you have downtime. I haven't *had* much downtime, so this is new.

A new email notification pops up from Marion.

To: Amy Sand
From: Marion Blaire
Subject: Re: About the offer

Amy,

I don't understand. Are you turning down the offer? If so, can I ask why?

Regards,

Marion

Sigh. I don't suppose "no" is going to be enough. Why do people ask yes/no questions when they don't want a yes/no answer?

But I should probably tell him. It's obvious that nobody at the Blaire Group is going to clue him in about his ridiculous HR decisions.

To: Marion Blaire
From: Amy Sand

Subject: Re: About the offer

Marion,

I don't think the culture would work for me. People seem uncomfortable about the fact that I'd be working for you after having worked at GrantEm Capital under Emmett Lasker. I prefer to work with colleagues who are congenial and friendly, and I hope you understand.

Sincerely,

Amy

I hope this provides enough clues for him to figure things out. If not, he's too oblivious, and nothing can help somebody that unaware.

The lights along the driveway die, and I'm plunged into darkness. I look for more emails to respond to, but they're all junk. I put my phone away and stare at the driveway. How late is Emmett going to work? Should I have made an appointment? But if I tried, he might've said no. For all I know, he might've blocked my number already.

He didn't block the code for the gates...

Yeah, but he could've forgotten that.

I wrap my arms around the steering wheel and rest my head there. It isn't too bad a position—I'll still be able to see Emmett's headlights when he drives up.

I'm actually pretty comfortable. I stay like that for...a while.

And then, suddenly, there are a couple of light taps on my window. I jerk up, wincing as I feel a burn in the side of my neck —*ow!*—and stiffness in my shoulders. My arms are numb from a lack of circulation.

"Amy?" Emmett's voice sounds muffled through the window.

Oh. So he's finally ho—

Oh shit.

Getting caught sleeping in my car isn't the opening I envisioned. I look up to read his expression, but the light is behind him, keeping his face in the dark.

Since I don't want to yell, I try opening the door. It isn't easy with numb arms and hands. After four flopping attempts, I manage to step out of the car, then instantly bend over and put a hand to my back at the tightness.

So much for attitude! The space is owning *me*. If Emmett's feeling charitable, he might call 911 for an ambulance.

"Are you okay?" He lays a hand on my shoulder. His touch is tentative, like he's worried he might cause me further pain.

And that, more than anything else, makes me want to cry, which is ridiculous. Why are my emotions all over the map? "Yeah, I'm fine. Just...give me a second. I think I sat in the same position for too long. What time is it?"

"A little after three."

No wonder I'm so stiff! I can't believe I slept for so long. "You've been working late."

"It's about normal. Do you need to sit down?"

"No. I need to..." I slowly straighten. My back is still tight, but loosening. "I need to talk to you."

"Out here?"

I look around. Or try to, then give up. My neck's in too much pain. I must've pulled a muscle when I woke up. Ugh.

"No. Let's go..." I'm about to say "inside," but realize that maybe he doesn't want to invite me in anymore. If Rick ever shows up on my doorstep wanting to talk...

"Come on."

Emmett points his chin toward his home and puts his hand at my elbow. The gesture loosens a little of the anxiety that's been knotted inside me.

We go into his mansion, the lights coming on as we step inside. Memories of our time together flow through my mind— eating together, chatting and laughing, sharing our bodies and making each other feel good, seeing the nursery he created. So many good moments, so many sweet emotions.

And I realize I was right to come back, to try to hold on to him. Because no matter what drama might exist in his life, what we had was real.

The love I feel for him is real.

He leads me to the living room, then gently seats me on a couch. He takes the sectional to my right. Emmett looks as gorgeous as ever, but a little exhausted. His gray-blue eyes are slightly bloodshot, and his cheeks seem hollower than before. Something like determination fleets through his face as he studies me.

"So," I begin, since I'm the one who came by and said I had to talk to him. But the next part doesn't come. I don't know why. I had some words that sounded good in my apartment, but they seem so prepared and phony now. Panic rises like a wave.

Your planned speech is no good.

Shit. This means I need to wing it. And I hate winging it. But as I look at Emmett, I hate the possibility of wasting this opportunity more.

"Okay. Um, first of all, I'm not going to the Blaire Group. Actually, I went out to Virginia, but turned the offer down after visiting their office. So, there's that. Um... If you're wondering whether I have another job lined up, I don't. But I'm okay with that."

Emmett frowns. "What about your plan?"

I raise one hand and release an imaginary balloon. "Poof. Gone like the wind."

His eyes grow curious.

I decide to take that as a positive sign. "I'll probably have to make a new one."

"I suppose you will," he says.

"But I still want the things I want. That isn't changing."

His expression shutters a bit.

I need to get to the point before he gets bored and throws me out. Emmett Lasker can't stand people who bore him.

"Things like a family—a husband who loves me, and children he and I both adore. I thought I'd get around to that once I was more advanced in my career. Done with my student loans and had more savings. But the, uh, timelines have changed." I put a hand over our baby growing in my womb.

"Yeah," he says slowly.

"I have issues, Emmett. I don't..." I sigh. "My mother ran away when she decided she wasn't going to have the kind of excitement she wanted in her life if she had a baby to be responsible for. Settling down wasn't for her. I like to act like that didn't impact me—or hurt me—but I think it did. She reached out to me on social media a little while back, and when I saw the pictures she posted... They were of her partying, drinking, smoking joints, that whole scene. Basically a forty-something woman acting like a teenager, and it just...hit me the wrong way." I swallow and inhale a shuddering breath. "So when we went to your father's party, I started to doubt, especially when your dad came and said the things he said about wanting a grandbaby. I..."

The words trail off as my courage starts to fail. *I really should've made a PowerPoint presentation.* Or *some* kind of prop with timelines and plans and things. Emmett's just staring at me, his gaze intense, and I'm too nervous to interpret his reaction.

When I stay quiet, Emmett sighs a little. "Thank you for explaining. I was actually planning on calling you or stopping by. Because, well... I lied while we were together." He looks overly somber.

My gut tightens unbearably, and I feel like I'm about to throw up. Just how bad is this lie going to be?

"I don't get along with Dad at all."

Huh...?

"He's more like a sperm donor. Well, a sperm donor who paid for things, but I think he did that to make sure my brothers and I weren't around to bug him. He shipped us all off to a boarding school in Switzerland when we were three."

"Oh my God... *Three?* You were so little!"

Emmett shrugs. "Mom and all the other mothers of my brothers came with us. But it was obvious that Dad didn't really want his kids. We were a group of vasectomy-fail babies to him. Nothing more—"

"Wait, *what?*"

"Yeah. He only ended up with us because a vasectomy he thought would keep him child-free failed, and seven of the women he was banging got pregnant."

"*Seven* women? All at the same time?"

"More or less at the same time. And yeah, seven. That we know of."

I cover my mouth with a hand. This is *crazy.* And here I thought my situation with Mom was awful.

Emmett continues in a wry tone, "He only contacts us when he wants something, and we only go see him on his birthday. We try to avoid him as much as possible because nothing good ever comes out of the encounters. There are more scandals attached to his name than anyone wants to count, and frankly, I find them—and him—embarrassing. I didn't want to have you meet him, ever, which is why I didn't want to take you to the party. I didn't want us to have a private dinner or something with him either, because spending that much time with him, in such close quarters..." Emmett shudders.

He doesn't have to say more. Now his reactions make much more sense. I wish he'd told me the truth—at least the part about not getting along with his dad—so I wouldn't have put so much pressure on him to make the introduction and so on. I would *die* if Emmett ever met my mom.

"You didn't want to talk about it because it's...embarrassing."

"...embarrassing," he says in unison with me.

Sympathy wells up. "I'm so sorry."

"Yeah, me too. I should've said something, but it was just

easier not to. It's a habit—I'm not used to talking about Dad with anybody, especially given his celebrity status." He smiles a little. "And because I don't want people feeling sorry for me or saying something flippant like 'At least your dad paid child support.'"

Ugh. People can be so judgmental about others, and they rarely know all the facts.

"I was hurt when you decided to take the job with Marion because I don't like him, and I thought you knew that. But then I realized that maybe I haven't done enough to show you I'm not like my dad—that I'm the kind of person you can depend on, a man who will never break your heart or make you cry."

There's such sincerity in his beautiful eyes. Hot, sweet emotion spills from my heart and spreads throughout my body until I'm dizzy with joy.

"You got under my skin the moment you walked into my office for your interview. You're smart. You're beautiful. The more I get to know you, the more I love you."

My eyes start to heat and prickle.

"So I have a question to ask you—just you. It isn't about the baby or the responsibility I feel for it." He drops to one knee, pulls out a box from his pocket and opens the lid. A gorgeous princess-cut diamond sparkles against navy velvet. "Will you marry me, Amy Sand?"

Tears blur my vision, and my fingers seem to move up of their own accord to cover my lips. "Yes," I whisper. "And I love you too, Emmett."

He gifts me with the most brilliant smile I've ever seen and places the ring on my finger. It fits perfectly. I put a hand over my racing heart, but there's no way to contain the sweet swelling of love I feel for this man.

"When did you buy this?" I ask.

"I just picked it up today. They had to adjust the band."

"How did you know my ring size?"

"I've been watching you closely for almost two years, Amy." He winks playfully. "I know *a lot* about you."

I laugh, look down at the ring and shake my head. "This is perfect."

"Thank you for being brave enough to make the first move." He kisses my forehead, then my cheeks and my mouth. "By the way, can I ask why you're in that trench coat?"

"Oh?" I look down. "It's, ah, something Sasha suggested when I was trying to figure out how to make my case."

He cocks an eyebrow. "Go on..."

"She said I should wear nothing but a trench coat with some sexy lingerie underneath, but I told her it wasn't going to work. I mean, it didn't work when Brenda tried."

"I don't want to belabor the obvious, but Brenda isn't you." A wicked gleam lights his eyes. "We can't have your effort go to waste."

"Oh, we can't...?"

"Nope. I want to see for myself just how good Sasha's suggestion is."

"Do you now?" I stand up, my eyes on his. Then, with a slow smile, I open the coat, projecting all the queen-of-the-world attitude I can muster.

Emmett's lips part, his eyes blazing. "Hot *damn*. Sasha's getting a fat bonus."

I laugh in triumph, but the sound is almost immediately muffled as he claims my mouth.

53

AMY

I roll over, burying my face in the pillows. It's getting bright in the room, but I'm still tired and sleepy. Besides, Emmett's placing lots of light kisses over my neck and shoulders and arms. Why should I give that up?

I hear a phone vibrating.

"Is that mine?" I ask in a small voice.

"Nope. Mine."

"You need to go in." It's practically preordained, but I wish he didn't have to go to work.

There's a pause while he taps his phone. "I scheduled a meeting, but they can handle it themselves."

I lift my head off the pillows and look at him with bleary eyes. "Who are you and what have you done with my former boss?"

He grins. "My name is Emmett Lasker, and I've decided to spend the morning in bed with my super-sexy fiancée. Nice to meet you."

I flush at the possessive way he says *my fiancée*. "Well, if you insist. But I do feel just the tiniest bit guilty. I don't remember you missing work ever."

"First time for everything."

True. And why not? It feels wickedly decadent to be lazy on a Saturday morning. He places a small kiss on the corner of my mouth, then another one on my ear. I start to smile. I shift around for a deeper kiss, but then my stomach growls so thunderously that I can feel the sound vibrating all the way to my head.

Emmett laughs. "Wow."

I put a hand over my belly, my face flushing. "That was...loud."

"Yeah, it was. Did you eat anything yesterday?"

"Uh... The last meal I had was...lunch? I was too nervous for dinner."

"Okay, can't have that. You're eating for one and a half, after all."

"A half?"

"The baby. It's like poppy seed right now. Maybe a little bigger. But it can't be bigger than a gummy bear."

I laugh at how serious he seems. We get out of bed. I borrow one of Emmett's dress shirts, since I can't exactly run around in a trench coat and lingerie. He gives me a long look, digging his teeth lightly into his lower lip.

"That's hot as hell."

"What? This?" I look down at the starched shirt.

"Uh-huh. Something about a woman in her man's shirt..."

I give him a saucy grin. "You got that right."

As we walk down the stairs together, he says, "We should start thinking about the wedding. I want us to have a tasteful and awesome ceremony."

"Let's make it small, and preferably sometime very soon," I say.

"We can do it within two months."

"That fast?" Even Peggy I-Need-an-Appointment-to-See-My-Hubby spent a year on her rather simple ceremony. And she had the help of two wedding planners.

"Money can speed a lot of things up. And we can use our

335

garden as the venue." He gestures at the windows overlooking the meticulous yard.

I love the way he says *our* garden. Just that one word makes me feel like we're really going to be together.

He adds, "It'll look gorgeous with the right flowers."

"That sounds perfect," I say with a smile. "As long as it's not a Vegas Elvis ceremony, I'm all for it."

"Deal. I think we can manage to avoid Elvis." He kisses me, and we enter the kitchen in laughter.

A few glossy real estate brochures lie on the counter.

"You buying a new vacation home?" I pick up one of them. Mostly properties in Malibu, some in Florida.

Emmett runs his fingers through his hair. "More like a retirement home."

"You're going to *retire*? Seems a little extreme just to spend time with the baby... What are you going to do with yourself when the child starts preschool?"

He looks horrified. "No, no. I'd go stir crazy without anything to do. It's for your dad."

I look down at the brochures, then back at Emmett. "I don't understand."

"You said you wanted to buy him a beach cottage in Florida, and I thought, why don't I do it? Your dad sounds like an amazing guy, so..." Emmett shrugs. "Plus, honestly? I figured it'd help me get some Brownie points."

I laugh. It's great that he already likes Dad for the amazing person that he is, and touching that he's spending time and energy on making my dream of getting Dad a retirement home on the beach come true.

"That's *really* sweet, but it's not necessary," I say. "And you have all the points you need, trust me."

"Good to hear. But I'm entitled to do something nice for the man who single-handedly raised the love of my life. Besides, think about it. It'd be difficult for us to move to Florida, right?"

"Well, yeah, with the firm here in L.A. and all."

He nods. "And your dad is probably going to want to hang around and see the baby. Not to mention any other kids that might come along."

Other kids...? I'm still getting used to the idea of this one. "He will definitely want to see the baby."

"*And* he wants to live on a beach. So a home in Malibu seems perfect."

Emmett knows exactly how to make my insides feel like squishy marshmallow. This is so thoughtful—especially since he put in all this effort while envisioning an ideal future he'd like to share with me. "I don't know what to say. This is just...amazing."

"Nothing compared to all the happiness you've given me." He hugs me, takes my hand and kisses the ring. "I'm going to do everything in my power to ensure you're happy."

I cradle his face between my palms. "We're going to be the happiest people in the world."

54

-Sasha: So. How did it go?

    -Me: Perfect! I'm so happy!

    -Sasha: I knew it! I take cash or PayPal.

    -Me: What are you talking about?

    -Sasha: Our bet! Remember?

    -Me: Oh, that. Well, actually, YOU need to hand over the money.

    -Sasha: Did you trip, fall on your face into a mud puddle and bloody your nose? Because that's the only way my method would fail.

    -Me: LOL, no! I never got to do it. It's sort of silly to talk when you're practically naked, you know?

    -Sasha: Poll any red-blooded man, and he'll tell you there's nothing silly about a virtually naked woman.

    -Me: Whatever. Point is, I got him without having to take off the coat.

    -Sasha: You're kidding.

    -Me: Not even a little. Take a look at this!

    -Sasha: Holy shit! Look at that rock!!! LOVE IT!!!!! Tell me what happened after you said yes!

–Me: What do you think happened? We enjoyed a lot of make-up sex.

–Sasha: Aha! So you DID take off the coat!

–Me: Well... OK, let's call it even on the bet.

–Sasha: I feel like I've been ripped off, but okay. *wink* I get to be your maid of honor, right?

–Me: Of course! Can you find the time, though?

–Sasha: Grant will have to let me take some PTO. I have so many hours carried over from last year that HR is after me to use them up. Otherwise they'll have to pay me money for the unused hours, and you know HR would rather cut off its own balls.

–Me: LOL, there's some imagery. Regardless, awesome!

–Sasha: Let me know when you're going to be home so I can drool all over your ring!

–Me: Sunday evening? Emmett and I have some stuff to go over regarding the ceremony and so on.

–Sasha: Okay! I'll be sure to be home. Hey, does this mean you're coming back to GrantEm?

–Me: I think so. I'll have to talk with Emmett about it, but I don't want to work anywhere else.

–Sasha: Awesome. I'm so happy for you, girl!

–Me: Love you!

–Sasha: Love you back! *blowing kisses*

55

—Dad: So where's my grandbaby?

—Me: It hasn't even been a month, Joey. Also stop pretending to be my father. It's really annoying.

—Dad: I speak for him via my fingers.

—Me: The same fingers you use to wipe his ass?

—Dad: Your crudity doesn't deserve a response.

—Me: If he's too lazy to type up his own texts, he doesn't get to bug me.

—Dad: I suggest you be more accommodating. Unless you really want be embarrassed.

—Me: Not really a threat. One, he's an embarrassment just by being who he is. And two, I've become immune.

—Dad: You don't think so? He'll boycott your wedding. Just imagine how that will feel.

—Me: Please tell my father that I wish him the best of luck boycotting a wedding he won't be invited to.

—Dad: WHAT?! You can't do that.

—Me: Watch me.

56

EMMETT

–two weeks later

The entire mansion is spotless, scrubbed and buffed and waxed until you could run your tongue all over the floor. The air smells fresh with flowers, and sunlight comes in through windows so clear it seems like the panes are gone.

I hired a huge cleaning crew. Amy's father is coming to L.A. to see Amy—and meet me for the first time. I plan to make an excellent impression.

And I want to meet him as well. He turned down my offer to send a private jet and opted for driving. Said it would be more comfortable for him that way.

"He should be here any minute," Amy says, checking her phone.

Just then, the intercom buzzes, and I have the security system open the gates immediately.

Here we go. I inhale, readying myself mentally to meet the man who means the world to Amy.

We go out and wait at the main entrance. Amy's beaming, and I have on a patented warm and friendly smile that never fails to charm.

A slightly dusty Camry pulls up, and a tall man of impressive width steps out of the car. A pale blue shirt stretches over thick muscles, and his jeans are worn but clean. Silver streaks his tightly cropped hair, and his eyes are warm as he hugs Amy.

"Sweetie pie!" he says.

"Dad!" She hugs him tightly. "So good to see you! How was the drive?"

"Not bad. Not bad at all." He grins. His gaze cools a few degrees, sharpening and more observant as he turns his attention to me. "I take it you're Emmett?"

"Yes, sir." I extend a hand, disguising my nerves as best I can. No man wants a nervous wreck for a son-in-law. "Nice to meet you."

The man crushes my hand—or tries to. I'm ready for the move, and make sure to get a deep grip and rotate my wrist upward slightly. Then I just smile as he squeezes away.

His eyebrow quirks. "Mac," he says. "Nice to meet you as well. I heard you're my girl's boss, too."

"Was," I say with a that's-been-taken-care-of smile. "Please, this way." I indicate the house. "Do you have any bags?"

"Just this." He takes a small duffel bag from the trunk. "I thought you were still working at the firm," he says to Amy as we walk inside together.

"I am, but not under Emmett. It's better that way."

Amy and I agreed that we should compartmentalize our personal and professional lives, but not so much that she works elsewhere. Mostly I don't want her working for some other asshole in finance. They might not be as nice as I am.

But Amy thought it'd be awkward for her husband to give her professional feedback. So we compromised, and Grant and I swapped—Sasha for Amy.

"She won't think it's weird to get feedback from her brother-in-law?" Grant asked.

"You probably don't feel like a real brother-in-law to her. Just look at me and you. Who's going to believe we're related?" I gave him a superior shrug.

To be honest, I think he got the best of the deal, since Amy does better work. Not that I'm biased.

Mac doesn't look at the soaring ceiling, slick and expensive interior or the contemporary paintings hanging on the walls with the awe of somebody overwhelmed by material opulence. He also doesn't dismiss it like someone who shrugs off anything they don't understand. His attitude is more like somebody sizing the place up for an estate sale. The man probably needs to reassure himself his princess isn't going to be living in a hovel by marrying me.

"Let us show you to your room," Amy says.

Mac gives a frown. "The task isn't so complicated we need two Ivy League-educated people for it. Why don't you just take me there and let Emmett get to whatever he has to do?"

"Sure." He probably just wants a moment alone with her. Maybe examine the ring I gave her more closely, measure my worthiness.

Good thing I bought the biggest non-vulgar rock I could find in SoCal.

As they go upstairs, I check my phone, which keeps pinging.

–Dad: I'm not amused.

–Dad: You can't decline to invite me.

–Dad: Do you know how ridiculous you're going to look?

–Dad: What do Sandra's parents think about this?

I roll my eyes. More of Joey speaking for Dad. Clearly, neither of them can remember Amy's name. I'd bet half my brain cells they believe such a trivial detail isn't important—the name Ted Lasker alone should get him what he wants.

–Dad: They're probably worried about entrusting an asshole with their daughter.

No. Amy's dad is probably happy he doesn't have to endure your bullshit.

Amy and her dad return to the living room, sans his bag.

"How's the room?" I ask him. We prepped the best guest bedroom for his arrival.

"Seems all right," he says.

Not so easy to read. "Well, if you need anything, let us know."

"I'll do that."

"Are you hungry? I'm not sure if you had a chance to grab a bite on the way."

"Yeah, I could eat."

"How about some brunch at Nieve?" Amy says. "You really liked it last time you were here."

She told me how much he enjoyed their weekend champagne brunch, so I reserved one of their nicest tables for two hours, since we weren't sure exactly when Mac would arrive.

"Yeah, that sounds great. They serve the best Belgian waffles I've ever had."

We take my yellow Urus to the Aylster Hotel. Mac looks at the car with interest—but again, not like "Hey, it's an expensive car," but more like "Look at that gorgeous piece of engineering."

I was hoping we could bond over car talk—but nope. He doesn't say anything about it. Even has his lips pressed.

He's determined to not weaken his position. Not giving even a hint of approval until he's sure about me.

When we arrive, the maître d' takes us to our table with cheery alacrity. We order—an egg omelet and bacon for me, French toast and bacon for Amy and a gigantic Belgian waffle for her father.

"I'm getting a sparkling pear and peach cider," Amy says.

"I'll have one too," I say.

"No, you and Dad should enjoy the champagne. I don't mind. We should toast in style."

The drinks come out first. We toast to good health and happiness. Then the food arrives and Amy digs into her French toast with gusto.

Her dad eyes her. "No morning sickness?"

"Not yet. Just constantly hungry," she says.

"Hopefully it'll stay this way," I say. "I read that some women never get it."

I reach for my drink and almost knock it off the table when somebody smacks my shoulder. *Hard.*

"Emmett! You didn't tell me you were going to be here," comes Dad's loud voice.

Fuck!

I swivel around fast. "What are you doing here?"

"Brunch, of course. Like any normal person."

He's not alone. He's with a scantily dressed blonde, who I hope to God is legal. At least he's in a button-down shirt and slacks.

He smiles at Amy. "Hi. Emily, right?"

"It's Amy," she says thinly.

Mac's eyes go flinty, like he's the Terminator eyeing a loud-mouthed punk.

"Right," Dad says. If you asked him again what her name is, he'd say "Amelia" or some such.

"So. When's the baby due?" He sticks his neck out like a lemur scouting for food. "You aren't showing."

"And she won't for a while," I say. "It's just the first trimester."

"I heard from Joey about the ceremony. I'm a busy man, but I'll see what I can do."

It's all *I* can do to not throw my cold water at the smarmy smile. He thinks he's so clever, bringing that up now. Joey probably whined about the difficulty he's having with the invitation, so Dad's going to play dirty.

He then turns to Amy's dad like he's just noticed him. "I'm sorry, I didn't see you. You are...?"

"Mac Sand. Amy's father."

"Oh." Dad's shock is so exaggerated, it's borderline ridiculous. "I'm Ted Lasker. Emmett's dad." He extends his hand.

Mac smiles, half stands and pumps Dad's hand.

Dad winces. "Ow, *ow!* That's some grip."

Thank you, Mac. Can you be my father?

Mac's mouth is smiling, but his eyes aren't.

"I guess we'll see more of each other at the wedding," Dad says.

"If Joey hasn't told you already, you aren't invited," I say.

"What?" Dad lets out a my-son-is-such-a-comedian laugh. "Of course I'm invited. I'm your dad! And granddad to Emmy's baby."

Joey must've told Dad if he wants to make a personal appeal, he should use the other person's name. Too bad it doesn't work if you use the wrong name.

Amy places a soothing hand on her father's forearm and says to my dad, "You are *not* invited. I don't think you'll be good for the baby."

"Ludicrous."

"Dad, you're making a scene," I say. "Somebody's bound to record it and post it all over social media. Imagine going viral for not getting invited to your son's wedding." *Wouldn't that be hilarious.*

Dad's lips purse. "We'll discuss this later, when we're more private."

He and his date go to another table, and we're back to having peace. Sort of. Amy's dad looks like he has a lot to say.

"I didn't realize you had family issues. I want Amy to be with a man who doesn't," he says.

Fuck. Of course he'd be upset about that.

She tugs at him. "*Daaaad.*"

"What? Family is important."

"That man deserves what he got. He's like Mom," she adds.

Mac sits back a little, processing that information.

Giving him a second, I put down my utensils.

"I understand your concern," I say, facing him directly. "I wish I *didn't* have a parent issue, but the fact is I do. There's nothing I can do about that, except minimize the damage he can cause to our relationship and family. And basically, the only way to do that is to cut him out. Not inviting him to the wedding is the first step. He won't be part of our lives, and unless our children want it, he won't be part of theirs, either."

Mac grunts softly. "So you're just going to cut ties with your dad? For her? You aren't going to regret it?"

"Not at all. I love your daughter more than anything, sir. The most important person in my life is Amy. My priority is her happiness."

We lock eyes for a long moment. "You really mean it," he says slowly.

"One hundred percent."

He smiles, this time for real. "Huh. Well, I guess you'll do. A man who can say all that to a girl's father with such conviction passes."

Thank God. "Thank you."

"I'll be watching." He makes a V with his fingers and points them at his eyes, then at me.

"Please do. You'll see nothing but Amy's smile."

57

AMY

"All set! You look perfect!" Sasha says, clasping her hands together.

I check myself in the mirror. The wedding gown is elegant, with little sparkly diamantes sewn along the edge of the skirt. It doesn't have a train, since the wedding is outdoors and I don't want my dress sweeping up detritus like a broom. Diamond chandelier earrings drop from my ears; a rope of diamonds circles my neck. My hair's twisted into a simple updo—Sasha's handiwork.

The makeup is subtle but brings out my eyes and turns my lips a lush shade of apple. I can't quit looking at the mirror in front of me.

"You look gorgeous," Clara, the makeup artist Emmett and I hired, says.

Pleasure flushes my cheeks. "Thank you. You did amazing work. I didn't know I could look this good!"

"It's easy to make a happy bride beautiful," Clara says with a smile.

I realize that I *am* happy. Emmett makes me happy. Working at GrantEm is still demanding—Grant is no slouch, and there are times when Emmett and Grant work on the same portfolio companies. But Emmett always makes sure to do little things to let me know how much he loves me. At first I thought he might do something really crazy and over-the-top to make his feelings known. After all, he's a billionaire, and even though he has cut his father out of our lives, he grew up seeing a level of excess that I find uncomfortable.

But he knows me too well. It's always the little things. A small box of chocolates in my office drawer that draws a surprised smile from me. A handmade lavender-scented candle on my desk when I'm feeling blue. Or just a note tucked between the pages on my desktop calendar that simply says, "I love you."

Sasha and I look out through the window. The sky's blue, not a cloud in sight. Fresh-cut flowers cover the garden—lined up along the aisle where my dad will walk me. They're also set in a giant arch at the altar for us to stand under and exchange our vows.

We have live piano music for the ceremony. Apparently, Huxley is a piano whisperer. Guests have already arrived and are milling around. It's just our family and closest friends. I only want people who will truly wish us the best at our wedding. Emmett's dad's not here—we didn't invite him and he doesn't have a passcode for the gates, although he's been impossibly demanding. I'm fine with that, since I don't understand the point of inviting a man who can't bother to remember my name.

Two rapid knocks.

"Amy, you ready?" Dad calls out from the other side.

"Yes!" I say as Sasha opens the door for him.

He takes one step inside, then stops and goes still.

Finally, he exhales. "Wow."

"Wow to you too, Dad." He definitely looks dashing in his tux.

"Well?" he says, holding out one arm. "Let's go."

"Let's."

Sasha hands me my bouquet, and I lay my hand on Dad's arm. We walk down the stairs and into the garden outside.

Emmett is standing by the arch, impossibly handsome in his black-and-white tux. My heart flutters, my belly doing a cartwheel. I lay a hand over where our baby is growing.

Huxley starts in with "Here Comes the Bride."

And I start walking toward the love of my life.

58

EMMETT

It's been two weeks since our honeymoon in Mexico. My dream of taking Amy to an overwater bungalow in gorgeous French Polynesia has been postponed since she's pregnant, and we don't feel too comfortable being that far from home, just in case.

I look at the big box sitting on the kitchen counter. The housekeeper must've left it there. No huge black Amazon smirk on the outside. Hmm.

The address label says: Mr. and Mrs. Lasker. The sender is Silicone Dream. For some reason, the name sounds familiar, but I can't quite place it.

Whatever. I get a box cutter and run it over the tape. Inside is a riot of pink, green and purple packing peanuts. Very girly. If the label didn't have my name on it, I might've assumed the box was only for Amy.

I push the Styrofoam pieces around until my fingers touch something smooth and flat. I fish it out.

A sparkly purple box. Looks pretty high-end. Gold embossed swirly letters read, *The Ultimate Kit: The Second Edition.*

Huh. I pull the lid off—

Well, well, well.

Individually sealed sex toys gleam inside. Dildos. Vibrators in all shapes and sizes. Butt plugs. Blunt nipple clamps with electro attachments. Fur-lined cuffs. Flavored syrups. A silk blindfold. A scarlet flogger. And lots and lots of soft, slightly stretchy rope.

My blood heats as I think about what we can do with the items in the box. If Amy wants to get adventurous, I am *all* for it.

The door opens, and Amy walks in.

"Honey, I'm home!" she announces as she slips off her shoes.

"Welcome back," I say with a huge grin.

"You look happy to see me." She comes over and kisses me.

Before she can pull away, I wrap my arm around her waist and pull her closer for another kiss. "I'm always happy to see you."

She laughs, slightly breathless. "*Especially* happy."

Her gaze shifts to the kitchen counter. "Oh my *God*. What is all—?" She laughs. "Did you order these?"

"No. I thought you did."

"Nope. Not me." Her face slowly scrunches. "Do you think it's...your dad?"

Ugh. "No. He's still in a snit over the wedding. Plus, if it had come from him, the box wouldn't say Mr. and Mrs. Lasker."

Amy grows thoughtful. "Let's see if there's anything else in the box."

She sticks her hand and moves the peanuts around.

"Ah-ha!" She pulls out a card, then reads out loud.

Dear Mr. And Mrs. Lasker,

I'm sorry I can't personalize this more. I asked Griffin, but he wouldn't tell me anything. Anyway, congratulations on your marriage! I hope these toys help bring additional joy to your life. If you want more, just go to our website and use the promo code GRIFFIN15 to get an additional 15% off on our entire catalogue!

Sierra

P.S. The code has no expiration date!

This has something to do with Griffin? My strait-laced, overly particular brother?

"Who's Sierra?" Amy asks. "Griffin's TA?"

"Doubt it. He's too uptight. Why don't I call him?"

"Great idea."

I call him, putting it on speaker. He picks up.

"Yeah?" he says, sounding slightly harried.

"Hey, we got a box from you," I say.

There's a pause. "I didn't send you anything."

"It came through Sierra," Amy explains.

A beat of deafening silence. "*Are you fucking kidding me?*"

"No," Amy says, giving me an is-he-okay look.

As I shrug, Griffin says, "That should never have gone to you!"

"We don't mind," I say, hoping Amy's interested in trying them out. If she isn't too eager... Well. Maybe I can figure out an angle to convince her. I excel in making my cases.

"They're in beta testing!" Griffin says.

Whaaaat? "How do you beta-test a dildo?" I ask.

"I don't know. I didn't ask. I don't *want* to know. She's crazy!"

"Who?" Amy asks.

"Sierra! The woman never follows a schedule. She never plans for anything. She respects nothing! She thinks life is fun and game! Wears really annoying perfume—"

"What's annoying about her perfume?" I ask. Griffin isn't allergic to any scent.

"It's distracting!"

Amy gives me a look, and we share an ESP moment. *I don't think he hates her as much as he claims.*

"She laughs too much," Griff says. "Smiles all the time, for no reason. And she's so fucking *pink*!"

"What's wrong with pink?" Amy asks. It *is* weird for anybody to hate pink this much.

353

"Everything! It's so...*bright*. It's just wrong!"

"So." I decide to intervene before he starts complaining about something like how pretty she is when she smiles. "What I hear you saying is she's fun. Spontaneous. Laughs a lot. Smiles a lot, too. And smells good."

"*Distracting.*"

"Uh-huh. Sounds terrible."

"Like a little sparkly dollop of evil," Amy says.

"She's everything that's wrong with humanity," Griffin grouses.

"Right. Because humanity needs more grumpiness. Good thing you're around to balance things out," I say.

"What I have is *discipline*, not grumpiness."

"Po-tay-to, po-tah-to. Anyway, the next time you see this pink ray of sunshine, tell her we said thanks for the presents."

"Yes!" Amy says with a bright gleam in her eyes.

"I'm not having this discussion." He hangs up.

"Bet he's calling Sierra now," I say.

"That poor woman... Although it sounds like she can handle him."

"Most definitely. She has the power to neutralize his grumpiness." Then it finally hits me where I'd heard of Silicone Dream before. It's the name of the company Griffin's supposed to do a case on with his class! He said it was in high tech, but I don't know any high-tech firms that beta-test sex toys.

"So." She runs her hands over the toys. "You think we should help with their *testing?*"

I laugh, picking her up. She grabs the box, and we make our way to our bedroom.

59

EMMETT

After ten hours of labor, Amy is exhausted. But she still glows like only a new mom can.

But I know I'm a mess, too, all choked up and emotionally drained. For some reason, the epidural didn't dull her pain much, and watching her agonized struggle cut hard and deep. What good is modern medicine if they can't make the birthing process painless?

But now it's done and our baby girl is gorgeous. Perfect. Her skin is pink and soft, and she smells like all my future hopes and dreams.

Mom flew in from London and has been dabbing her eyes. Amy's dad's eyes are red too, and he's wearing a broad grin. My brothers come by in a complicated rotation and stare at our baby girl like she's so fragile that she'll shatter if they breathe wrong.

My dad *isn't* here because I never told him.

"She's beautiful," I whisper, then kiss Amy on the forehead. "Thank you."

She smiles. "I love you."

"I love you too." I kiss the baby's head. "Have you decided on a name?"

We have a list, but Amy's been waffling, saying they're all too wonderful.

She nods. "Yes. Monique Emma Lasker."

Mom flushes with pleasure, her hands covering her mouth. Amy's dad pats her shoulder.

"That's a perfect name," I say.

"I know, right?" Amy grins.

I put my arms around the two most precious people in my life, thinking of all the ways I can show them how much I love them.

60

AMY

Emmett takes me to an overwater bungalow in the South Pacific for our third anniversary. Says it's been on his bucket list for almost five years now, which is cute—and so like him. The place has glass sections in the floor that let us see the ocean life below. So far I've spotted small sharks, stingrays and sea urchins. Once a turtle swam by.

As much as I love all the thought and planning he's put into our anniversary trip, including having his mom and my dad babysit Monique, I'm not just here to enjoy myself. I'm a woman on a mission.

I want another baby.

Actually, three would be perfect. But I'm settling for two because Emmett refuses to have another. Says that I had to suffer too much. I told him I regret nothing because Monique is worth it, but he says no future baby is worth the pain I'm certain to go through.

"It was just a one-time thing. Besides, there are other options for managing pain during delivery," I've argued countless times.

"One time because it was one baby," he says, then covers his ears.

Right now, Emmett is "out back," swimming in the shallow emerald waters behind our bungalow. I take the opportunity to get into my battle gear, ordered direct from Silicone Dream. Sierra assures me it's so powerful, it could get a dead man interested.

Twenty minutes later, I hear the shower running on our deck outside.

"The water's amazing. Really warm and clear," Emmett says as he slides the deck door open and walks in, a towel around his waist. I see his wet swim trunks on the rack outside. "We should go in later, maybe do some snorkeling."

"That sounds like a plan." I quickly shrug into an ankle-length gown, making sure that he can't see what I have on underneath. No need to tip my hand yet. "But I have a proposal that requires your immediate attention."

"I'm not looking at another PowerPoint presentation on why we should have another baby," he says.

"Ha! Don't worry. I didn't bother, considering you didn't look at the last one I made."

He puts his arms around me. "Babe, we already discussed this."

"No, I *tried* to discuss it. You covered your ears."

"I can still say what needs to be said using my uncovered mouth. I don't need ears to speak."

I put my hand on his bare chest. "Come on. Just one time. We try this once, and if it doesn't happen, I won't ask again."

Emmett starts shaking his head, but I reach up and take hold of his chin.

"Don't say no so fast."

"Do I need to cover my ears again?" he says dryly.

"If you want. Just keep your eyes open."

He sighs, a tad resigned and a tad exasperated. "You know I hate saying no to you."

"I do know that. So why not make things easy on yourself? Say yes."

I undo the sash around my waist and drop the gown.

His lips part, and he stares, his eyes wide and unblinking.

I'm in nothing except my battle outfit. A silver chain loops around my neck, and it drops down, connecting to rechargeable nipplettes, which can not only pinch but also vibrate. We liked playing with them last time, and I decided to get a new set for the occasion. I'm in a sheer black thong, garter belt and fishnet stockings.

He puffs out a breath, his eyes going impossibly dark. "That's playing dirty."

"What are you going to do? Spank me?" I lick my red-tinted lips slowly.

For once, my husband is at a loss for words. *Yes.*

"Like I said—just one time. If it doesn't work, I won't ask again." But I'm pretty sure it's going to work. I've been tracking my cycle very closely over the last three months.

"And, uh, if I say no..."

"Then I guess I'll just have go put on some *other* outfit. Something boring and with *much* more material." I sigh. "And we'll go swimming." I give him a pouty look. *That would be such a shame.*

His Adam's apple bobs once. His eyes look feverish, probably from desire, but also from trying to calculate the possibility of me getting pregnant from just one time. But the deciding body part is none too well hidden by the towel.

"Okay," he says finally.

I smile triumphantly. "Perfect."

I jump on him. His mouth crushes mine as he lifts me and carries me backward to our bed. Gotta make this count.

61

AMY

–Dad: How are you doing, sweetie pie?

I smile as I wait for the elevator in the GrantEm lobby at two. He hasn't changed, not even a little, even though he's retired in style. He moved into the place Emmett bought for him in Malibu, so we see each other more often. But he always acts like it's been ages.

–Me: I'm doing fabulous! Here.

I take a quick selfie and send it to him. And because he's awesome, I also attach a photo of Monique and Emmett playing from this morning.

–Dad: Look at all of you! You look great together!

–Me: Thanks! You're coming over this Saturday, right?

–Dad: Yup. Can't wait.

–Me: Me either. Love you.

–Dad: Back atcha. Have a great day!

I smile and start to put the phone away. The elevator doors open, and I step inside.

My phone buzzes.

–Emmett: Yes or no?

I almost laugh at how blunt he is. He's probably dying right now. For some reason, the two pregnancy tests I bought gave opposite results. I told him we should buy more, in case the ones we bought were defective, but he insisted on consulting a doctor to be sure.

–Me: I'll tell you in person.

–Emmett: You're killing me.

I smother a laugh.

–Me: Relax, I'm already in the elevator.

The elevator doors open with a ping. I put on a serious expression and start toward his office. Emmett, of course, is outside the door. Mr. Impatient.

I bite my lip so I don't start laughing.

He walks over and puts his hand at the small of my back. "So what did the doctor say?"

"Let's talk inside your office." Don't want him to collapse in front of the staff. Or scream.

Lines of concern appear between his eyes. "That bad?"

I finally laugh as we step inside his office and close the door behind us. "No. It's just... You're funny with your reaction."

"It *is* kind of a life-or-death situation, you know."

"No, it's not." I kiss him, holding his warm, strong hands. "Congratulations, Mr. Lasker. We are most definitely pregnant."

"Oh my God," he says shakily. "It was just that one time."

"Yeah, but you know... That's all it takes." I grin. He should know. It only took that one time for me to get pregnant with Monique. "Besides, we're super lucky."

"How come?"

"Because we're having twins!" I wrap my arms around him.

"Twins? Holy... God help us all."

I laugh. "Pretty sure He already did." I look up at Emmett with all the love I have in my heart. "He gave us each other."

Holding me tight, Emmett kisses me.

And all is perfect in my world.

Thanks for reading *Baby for the Bosshole*! I hope you enjoyed it. If you want a special bonus epilogue, join my list at http://www.nadialee.net/vip

If you want more fun billionaire romantic comedy, check out *Marrying My Billionaire Boss*. Nobody told Evie that saving her boss from his mink fur bikini-wearing ex-girlfriend/stalker would involve a bachelor auction, a Vegas wedding they don't remember, and a baby they don't recall making.

TITLES BY NADIA LEE

Standalone Titles

Baby for the Bosshole

Beauty and the Assassin

Oops, I Married a Rock Star

The Billionaire and the Runaway Bride

Flirting with the Rock Star Next Door

Mister Fake Fiancé

Marrying My Billionaire Hookup

Faking It with the Frenemy

Marrying My Billionaire Boss

Stealing the Bride

The Sins Trilogy

Sins

Secrets

Mercy

The Billionaire's Claim Duet

Obsession

Redemption

Sweet Darlings Inc.

That Man Next Door

That Sexy Stranger

That Wild Player

Billionaires' Brides of Convenience

A Hollywood Deal

A Hollywood Bride

An Improper Deal

An Improper Bride

An Improper Ever After

An Unlikely Deal

An Unlikely Bride

A Final Deal

The Pryce Family

The Billionaire's Counterfeit Girlfriend

The Billionaire's Inconvenient Obsession

The Billionaire's Secret Wife

The Billionaire's Forgotten Fiancée

The Billionaire's Forbidden Desire

The Billionaire's Holiday Bride

Seduced by the Billionaire

Taken by Her Unforgiving Billionaire Boss
Pursued by Her Billionaire Hook-Up
Pregnant with Her Billionaire Ex's Baby
Romanced by Her Illicit Millionaire Crush
Wanted by Her Scandalous Billionaire
Loving Her Best Friend's Billionaire Brother

ABOUT NADIA LEE

New York Times and *USA Today* bestselling author Nadia Lee writes sexy contemporary romance. Born with a love for excellent food, travel and adventure, she has lived in four different countries, kissed stingrays, been bitten by a shark, fed an elephant and petted tigers.

Currently, she shares a condo overlooking a small river and sakura trees in Japan with her husband and son. When she's not writing, she can be found reading books by her favorite authors or planning another trip.

To learn more about Nadia and her projects, please visit http://www.nadialee.net. To receive updates about upcoming works, sneak peeks and bonus epilogues featuring some of your favorite couples from Nadia, please visit http://www.nadialee.net/vip to join her VIP List.

Printed in Great Britain
by Amazon